DEBBIE MACOMBER

One of America's favorite storytellers!

Praise for Debbie and her previous novels:

Debbie Macomber "retells the parable of women's age-old concerns with gentle humor and charm."
–Publishers Weekly

"Debbie Macomber is the queen of love and laughter."
–Elizabeth Lowell

This Matter of Marriage is
"so much fun it may keep you up till 2 a.m."
–The Atlanta Journal

"I've never met a Macomber book I didn't love."
–Linda Lael Miller

"Popular romance writer Macomber has a gift
for evoking the emotions that are at the
heart of the genre's popularity."
–Publishers Weekly

"Debbie Macomber's name on a book is a guarantee of
delightful, warmhearted romance."
–Jayne Ann Krentz

Dearest Friends,

I'm so pleased that MIRA is reissuing the ORCHARD VALLEY trilogy— *Valerie, Stephanie* and *Norah*. These three sisters have long been favorites of mine.

The small town of Orchard Valley was based on the two communities I've lived in for most of my life. I was born and raised in Yakima, Washington. I now live in Port Orchard, Washington, where my husband, Wayne, and I raised our own family.

What makes Orchard Valley special is that it could be any small town where there's a sense of family and community, where people help each other. A town where neighbors become friends. I was thrilled with all the letters I received from readers when the trilogy was first published—and I'm delighted so many of you feel I successfully captured that wonderful small-town feeling.

In many ways, the ORCHARD VALLEY trilogy is responsible for the two six-book series I worked on after that. I enjoyed writing about Orchard Valley immensely, and because of the popularity of these books, I was approached by Harlequin to attempt a longer series of connected stories. That's when MIDNIGHT SONS was born. The response to these stories—about a town in Alaska called Hard Luck—spurred me to create the next six-book project, HEARTS OF TEXAS. This series is set in the hill country of central Texas, in a small ranching community I named Promise. And my next novel with MIRA Books, PROMISE, TEXAS—which comes out in October—will take readers back there!

Over the years I've had a lot of inquiries about *Valerie, Stephanie* and *Norah*—from readers who were looking for one or all of the books. Now they're together once more, this time in a single volume! Enjoy them again (or for the first time), and watch how each sister comes to recognize and appreciate what's really important in life: family, love and home.

As always, thank you for your continued support of my books. I love to hear from readers, and can be reached at P.O. Box 1458, Port Orchard, WA 98366.

With my best wishes,

Debbie Macomber

DEBBIE MACOMBER

ORCHARD VALLEY

MIRA

MIRA

ISBN 1-55166-308-2

ORCHARD VALLEY
Copyright © 1999 by MIRA Books.

VALERIE
Copyright © 1992 by Debbie Macomber.

STEPHANIE
Copyright © 1992 by Debbie Macomber.

NORAH
Copyright © 1993 by Debbie Macomber.

Visit us at www.mirabooks.com

Printed in U.S.A.

CONTENTS

VALERIE

To Dr. John T. and Kelly Dykstra—
in grateful appreciation for their continued
support of the American Heart Association

One

"Norah? Is that you?" Valerie Bloomfield's voice rose expectantly. She'd been trying to reach her sister for the past hour with no success.

"Valerie, where are you? You don't sound right."

"That's because I'm somewhere over Nebraska—at least I think it's Nebraska." It was difficult to tell thirty thousand feet above the ground. "How's Dad?"

Norah hesitated and that slight pause sent Valerie's worry escalating into panic. "Norah…" she began.

"He's doing as well as can be expected."

"Did you tell him I'm on my way?" Valerie had been in the middle of a New York business meeting when she received the message. Her youngest sister had called the Houston office first, and they'd passed on the news of her father's heart attack. Valerie had left immediately, catching the first available flight to Oregon.

"Dad knows you're coming."

"Were you able to get hold of Steff?"

Norah's answering sigh signaled her frustration. "Yes, but it took forever and my Italian is nonexistent. She's planning to catch whatever she can out of Rome, but she has to get there first—she's in some little village right now. It might take her a couple of days. The connection was bad and I couldn't understand everything she said. Apparently there's some sort of transportation strike going on. But she's doing her best...."

Valerie's sympathies went out to Stephanie, the middle Bloomfield sister. She must be frantic, stuck halfway across the world and desperate to find a way home.

"When will you arrive?" Norah asked anxiously.

"The plane's scheduled to land at six-ten."

"Do you want me to meet you? I could—"

"No," Valerie interrupted. She didn't think it was a good idea for Norah to leave their father. "I've already ordered a car. It shouldn't take me more than forty minutes once I land, so don't worry about me."

"But the hospital's an hour's drive from the airport. You shouldn't even try to make it in less."

It generally did take a full hour, but Valerie had every intention of getting there a lot sooner. "I should be at the hospital somewhere around seven," she said evasively.

"I'll see you then," Norah said, sounding resigned.

"Don't worry, kid, everything's going to be all right."

"Just be careful, will you?" Norah pleaded. "Having you involved in an accident won't help Dad any."

"I'll be careful," Valerie promised, smiling at her sister's words. Trust Norah to take the practical approach. After a brief farewell, Valerie replaced the telephone in the slot in front of her.

Closing her eyes, she tried to rest, but the effort was useless. Her thoughts seemed to be traveling at the speed of light, zooming through her head, quickening her pulse.

Her father was dying. Her dear, precious father... His hold on life was precarious, and the burning need to get to him as quickly as possible drove her like nothing she'd ever experienced.

Sleep was out of the question. Valerie bent down for her purse, rummaging through it until she found the antacid tablets. She popped one in her mouth and chewed it with a vengeance.

No sooner had she swallowed the chalky tablet than she reached for a roll of the hard candies she always carried with her. Two years earlier she'd given up smoking, and sucking on hard candy had helped her through the worst of the nicotine withdrawal. If she'd ever needed a cigarette, it was now. Her nerves were stretched to the breaking point.

Dear heaven, not her father, too. Valerie was only beginning to come to grips with her mother's death. Grace Bloomfield had died of cancer almost four years ago, and the grief had shaken Valerie's well-ordered life. She'd buried her anguish in her work; the biggest strides in her career with CHIPS, a Texas-based computer software company, had come in the past few years. She'd risen quickly up the corporate ladder, until she was the youngest executive on the management team.

Her father had reacted similarly to Grace's death. Working too many hours, driving himself too hard. Norah had tried to tell her, but Valerie hadn't paid attention. She should have done something, anything, to get their father to slow down, to relax and enjoy life. He should have retired years before; he could be traveling, seeing exotic places, meeting with old friends and making new ones. In the years since her mother's death, Valerie had been able to convince her father to leave Orchard Valley only once and that had been a two-week trip to Italy to visit Steffie.

And now he was fighting for his life in a hospital.

Valerie hadn't said anything to him because... well, because they were so much alike. David Bloomfield was working out his grief the same way she was. Valerie couldn't very well criticize him for something she was doing herself.

Before she knew it, she'd chomped her way through two rolls of candy and another of antacid tablets.

When the plane landed, Valerie was the first one off, scurrying with her carryon bag down the concourse to the rental car agency. Within fifteen minutes, she was on the freeway heading east toward Orchard Valley.

Heading toward home.

Norah was right; it took Valerie longer than forty minutes to reach Orchard Valley Hospital. She was there in forty-five. She claimed the first available parking space, unconcerned about whether the rental car would be towed away. What did concern her was seeing her father.

Norah was standing in the hospital lobby when Valerie walked through the double glass doors. Her sister, looking drawn and pale, was visibly relieved by her presence. "Oh, Valerie," she said, covering her mouth with one hand. "Oh, Valerie... I'm so glad you're here."

"Dad?" Valerie's throat closed up. If her cantankerous father had had the audacity to die before she arrived, she'd never forgive him. The thought made her realize how mentally and physically drained this ordeal had left her.

"He's resting comfortably...for now."

Valerie hugged her sister. Norah looked dreadful, her stylish shoulder-length blond hair brushed away from her face as if her hands had swept it behind her ears countless times. Her blue eyes, normally so clear and bright, were red-rimmed from tears and lack of sleep.

Valerie hadn't had much rest herself, but she was still running on adrenaline. She wouldn't collapse until after she'd had a chance to spend some time with her father.

"What exactly happened?" she asked as they hurried to the elevator. Their shoes made sharp, clicking sounds against the polished linoleum floor, sounds that reminded Valerie of similar visits almost four years ago, when her mother was dying. She remembered similar nighttime walks down these silent corridors. She hadn't been to this hospital since. The memories overwhelmed her now, tearing at the facade of her poise.

"After dinner, Dad went out onto the porch," Norah began, her voice quavering.

As far back as Valerie could remember, after the evening meal her parents had adjourned for coffee to the sweeping front porch of their large colonial home. They'd sat together on the old wicker chairs, sometimes holding hands and whispering like teenagers. Valerie was never sure what they discussed, but she'd learned early on not to interrupt her parents then. In the winters, they'd sat in front of the basalt fireplace in her father's den, but spring, summer and as far into the autumn as possible, it was the porch.

"I should have known something was wrong then," Norah continued. "Dad hasn't sat on the porch much since Mom's been gone. After dinner he generally goes right into his office and works on the bookkeeping."

The guilt Valerie experienced was crushing. Norah had repeatedly told her how hard their father was driving himself. She should have listened, should have demanded he hire an assistant, take a vacation, *something*. She should have stepped in. As the oldest, she felt responsible.

His heart was weak and had been since a bout of rheumatic fever in his early thirties. By all accounts he should have died then, but a young nurse's devotion had pulled him through. The nurse was Grace

Johnson, who became David's wife, and Valerie, Stephanie and Norah's mother.

"I brought him out a cup of coffee," Norah went on, "and he looked up at me and smiled. He...he seemed to think I was Mom."

"Was he in terrible pain?"

Norah bit her lower lip. "Yes, he must have been. He was so pale... Only he was too proud to admit it. I asked him what was wrong, but he wouldn't answer. He just kept saying he was ready."

"Ready for what?"

Norah looked away, pain etched in her eyes. "Ready to die."

"Die," Valerie cried, "that's ridiculous. If there was ever a man who had something to live for, it's Dad. Good grief, he's worked hard all his life! Now, it's time to reap the fruits of his labors, to enjoy his family, to travel, to—"

"You don't need to convince me," Norah said quietly as they reached the third floor and stepped out of the elevator. The Coronary Care nurses' station stood directly in front of them. Norah walked to the counter.

"Betty, would you tell Dr. Winston my sister's arrived?"

"Right away," the plump matron replied. Even if the other woman hadn't been wearing a crisp white uniform, Valerie would have known Betty was a nurse. The signs were all there. She appeared to be gentle, compassionate—and practical. No-nonsense.

Valerie recognized the look because the other woman shared it with Norah. And with their mother…

Valerie had to suppress a sudden smile at the memory of her youngest sister lining up dolls in her bed and sticking thermometers in their mouths. She'd fussed over them like an anxious mother, bandaging their limbs and offering reassurances and comfort.

Norah came by this temperament naturally, Valerie supposed, since their mother had been the same. Although she'd given up her hospital job when she married David Bloomfield, Grace continued to nurture those around her all her life. It had been her gift. It was Norah's gift, too.

"Who's Dr. Winston?" Valerie asked. She'd never heard of him before; he must be a recent addition to the hospital staff. But the last thing their father needed at a time like this was some hayseed family practitioner. He should be in a major hospital with the best heart surgeon available!

"Dr. Winston's been wonderful," Norah returned, her eyes lighting up briefly. "If it hadn't been for Colby, we would've lost Dad in the first twelve hours."

"Colby?" The doctor was named after a cheese? This didn't sound promising.

"I don't know what I would have done without him," Norah said. "I wasn't sure what to do with Dad at first. I guessed he was in a lot of pain, but I knew he'd object if I called for an Aid Car. He'd argue with me and that would have made matters even worse if it was his heart, the way I suspected."

"So you phoned Dr. Winston?"

"Yes. Luckily I was able to reach him, and he drove out, pretending to drop in out of the blue. He knew the minute he saw Dad that it was a heart attack. He sat down on the porch and had a cup of coffee with him."

"He drank coffee while our father was suffering a heart attack?" Valerie wasn't finding this doctor too endearing.

"I believe it was what saved Dad's life," Norah said, her eyes flashing a protest. "Dr. Winston was able to convince Dad to go to the hospital voluntarily. It wasn't until he'd been admitted that he suffered the worst of the attack. If he'd been at home arguing, no one could have done anything to save him."

"Oh." That took some of the heat out of Valerie's argument. She suspected she was looking for someone to blame. It would help ease her guilt for having ignored Norah's concerns about their father.

The door Betty had disappeared behind opened then, and a tall dark-haired man walked toward them, his eyes serious. Valerie couldn't help noticing how attractive he was. In fact, the man had movie-star good looks, but good looks that had nothing insipid or soft about them.

"Hello," he said, his voice deep and resonant. "I'm Dr. Winston." He held out his hand.

"Valerie Bloomfield," she replied briskly, placing her hand in his. She'd always been taught it was impolite to stare, but she couldn't stop herself. Her father's physician didn't look much older than her own twenty-eight years. "Excuse me," she said, not glancing at Norah, who would, she suspected, immediately leap to Dr. Winston's defense. "I don't mean to be rude—but how old are you?"

"Valerie," Norah groaned under her breath.

"I just want to know how long he's been practicing medicine. Good grief, Norah, this is our *father*."

"It's quite all right," Dr. Winston said, with a reassuring smile at Norah. "If David was my father I'd have a few questions myself. I'm thirty-six."

Valerie found it hard to believe, but she couldn't very well insist on seeing his birth certificate. Besides, her thoughts were muddled and she was exhausted. Now wasn't the time to question his qualifications. "How's my father?" she asked instead.

"He's resting."

"When will I be able to see him?"

"I'd rather you didn't go in right away."

"What do you mean?" Valerie snapped. "I've flown all the way across the country to be with my father. He needs me! Certainly I should be able to go to him."

"It wouldn't be a good idea just now. He's sleeping for the first time in nearly twenty hours and I don't want anything to disturb him."

"I think you should wait," Norah seconded, as if she feared Valerie might be on the verge of making a scene.

Valerie sighed; her sister was right. "Of course I'll wait. It's just that I'm anxious."

"I understand," Dr. Winston said. But he spoke without emotion. He led them to a waiting room not far from the nurses' station. Two well-worn couches faced each other, and several outdated magazines littered the coffee table that rested between them. A coffeepot stood in one corner, with powdered creamer and an ample supply of disposable cups.

Norah sat first, covering her mouth in an effort to hide a wide yawn.

"How long have you been here?" Valerie asked, realizing even before she asked that Norah had stayed at the hospital since that first night. Her youngest sister was exhausted, physically and emotionally. "Listen, kid, you go on home and get some rest. I'll hold down the fort for a while."

Norah grinned sheepishly. "I used to hate it when you called me kid, but I don't anymore."

"Why not?" Valerie asked softly, resisting the urge to brush a stray curl from her sister's forehead. She wasn't the maternal type, but she felt protective toward Norah, wanting to ease the weight of her burden.

"You can call me kid anytime you like because that's exactly the way I feel, like a child whose world has been tossed upside down. I'm scared, Val, really scared. We almost lost him—we still could."

"I know," Valerie whispered, briefly hugging her. Norah had suffered through the worst of the nightmare, facing the fear alone, not knowing from one minute to the next if their father was going to live or die.

"Valerie's right," Dr. Winston added. "There's nothing you can do here. Go home and rest. I promise I'll call you if there's any change."

Norah rubbed a hand across her eyes and nodded. "I'll take a shower and try to sleep for a couple of hours. That's all I need. Two, maybe three hours."

Valerie wondered if Norah was too exhausted to drive by herself. But Dr. Winston must have had the same concerns.

"We'll phone for a cab from the nurses' station. I don't want you driving like this." He placed his arm around Norah's shoulders, apparently intending to walk her to the elevator. As they left, he turned to Valerie. "I'll be back in a few minutes."

While he was away, Valerie poured herself a cup of coffee. There was no telling how long the pot had been sitting there. The coffee was black and thick and strong, just the way she needed it.

The urge for a cigarette was nearly overwhelming, so when Dr. Winston returned to the room she looked up at him and automatically asked, "I don't suppose you have any hard candy with you?"

"I beg your pardon?"

"Mints, anything like that." She was pacing the room, holding her coffee cup between both hands.

"I'm afraid not. Would you like me to see if I could get you some?"

Valerie dismissed his offer with a shake of her head. He was polite to a fault. The first thing she'd done had been to insult him, question his competence, and he'd taken it all with a smile.

"Please, tell me about my father."

They sat and for the next fifteen minutes, Dr. Winston explained exactly what had happened to her father's heart. He did his best to outline it in layman's terms, but much of what he said was beyond Valerie's comprehension. She'd never been comfortable with medical matters. Her mother and Norah had always dealt with those. For her part, Valerie hated anything to do with hospitals or doctors. She detested being sick herself, and knew her father felt the same way.

"There's one underlying problem that needs to be dealt with, however."

"Yes?" Valerie asked, hating the way her voice betrayed her concern. Any show of weakness distressed her. If she'd ever needed to be strong, it was now, for everyone's sake, including her own. She was the oldest, and the others would rely on her.

"Your father's lost his will to live."

"But that's ridiculous," she cried, battling the urge to argue with him. "My father's life is brimming over, it's so full. Why he's—"

"Lost without your mother," Dr. Winston finished simply.

Valerie bolted to her feet and resumed pacing. What Dr. Winston said was absolutely true; she had to admit it. Her father had been crushed under the load of grief, and while Valerie and her two sisters struggled to regain their own balance, their father had been slowly destroyed by his loss.

"What can we do?" she asked, trying to swallow her fears and her guilt.

"Support him, give him your love. The only thing keeping him alive now is his desire to see all three of his daughters before he dies."

"But... Okay, then don't let him know I'm here." It was the obvious solution. And if that was what it took to keep him alive, she was willing to play a little game of hide-and-seek. Norah could make up a series of excuses. No, forget Norah, Valerie mused bleakly. Her youngest sister couldn't tell a lie without blushing.

"How well do you lie?" she asked, thinking fast.

Dr. Winston blinked. "I beg your pardon?"

"We can't let my father know I've arrived. And that means lying to him."

"Miss Bloomfield—"

"Ms."

"Whatever," he said, sounding impatient with her for the first time. "We aren't going to be able to fool your father. Norah talked to him shortly after you phoned from...where was it? Nebraska? He knows you caught a flight out of New York. No one's going to make him believe something more important came up that's kept you from him."

"Steffie!" Valerie cried. "When Norah spoke to her, she said something about a transportation strike."

"Yes, but these are only stop-gap measures. Your father feels there's nothing worthwhile left to live for. He talks about your mother constantly, almost as though he's waiting to join her. We need something concrete that'll give him the will to fight, to hold on to life.''

Again Valerie knew the doctor was right, but her confused brain was having trouble assimilating the most basic details, let alone something as complex as this.

"He's all we have,'' she whispered, shaking her head despondently. "Surely he realizes that.''

"Yes, but at the same time, he believes you have one another.''

"We don't get along that well,'' Valerie told him insistently. "And we have nothing in common. Steffie's a crazy woman who flies off to Europe to study the Italian Renaissance, and Norah's main goal in life is to become another Clara Barton. We don't even *look* alike.'' Valerie was grasping at weak excuses, and she knew it. Anything she could think of to enlist Dr. Winston's help in keeping her father alive.

"You don't need to convince me, Valerie,'' he told her gently. "I'll do everything I can to see that your father regains his health and lives to a ripe old age.''

Blinking away tears, Valerie nodded, reminding herself once again that she was the oldest of David Bloomfield's daughters. In a crisis everyone looked to her; she was the one who needed a cool, decisive head, who couldn't let her emotions dictate her reactions.

But it was different this time.

The man in that hospital bed, barely holding on to

life, was her father, the man she idolized and loved beyond reason. Her emotions were so close to the surface that the force of them frightened her.

"I'd—I'd like to see him as soon as possible. Please." She'd grovel if necessary. She *had* to be with her father. "I won't make the least bit of noise, I promise." The last thing she wanted to do was disturb his rest. Somehow, though, she had to reassure herself that he was still alive. She'd never been more frightened.

Dr. Winston hesitated. "Wait here, I'll be right back."

He returned a few moments later. "He's awake and asking for you."

Valerie was so eager that she nearly vaulted out of the room, but Dr. Winston stopped her. "Before you go to your father, let me prepare you for what you're going to see." He spent the next five minutes explaining the different medical devices used to monitor his patient's heart. He explained how the small electrodes on her father's chest detected the electrical impulses that signal the heart's activity. He warned her about the tubes going in and out of his body.

However, nothing he said could have prepared Valerie for what she saw. Her father was connected to so many devices that it hardly seemed possible they could all be flowing into one body. His face was ashen, so pale and bloodless that his skin seemed iridescent. His eyes, which had always seemed to spark with vitality, revealed no emotion, only a weariness that was soul deep.

"Oh, Daddy," Valerie whispered, fighting tears. She locked her fingers around his hand, careful not to disturb the intravenous needle.

"Valerie...so pleased you're here...at last."

"Where else would I be?" she asked, forcing a smile. With the back of her other hand, she brushed a stray tear from her cheek.

"She's beautiful, isn't she?" her father said, apparently talking to Dr. Winston, who hovered in the doorway. "Only what did you do to your hair?"

"Do you like it?" Valerie asked, rallying somewhat, surprised he'd even noticed that she'd changed the style. "I had it cut." The new look was short and frothy.

"She's got the temper to go with that red hair, you know."

Her father was speaking to Colby Winston again.

"My hair isn't even close to being red," she argued, annoyed by the doctor's struggle not to grin. "It's auburn."

"Looks like you haven't combed it in a month," her father mumbled.

"Dad, this is the latest style. I'll have you know I paid good money for this."

"In that case, you should demand a refund." His voice was weak, and speaking had clearly drained him of what little energy he possessed.

"Dad," Valerie whispered, doing her best to disguise her concern. "Instead of complaining about my hair, you should rest."

He seemed too weak to reply. He closed his eyes and sighed audibly.

"I'm going to leave you for a little while," Valerie said. "But I'll be right outside the door, so if you want to tell me how much you like my hair and beg my forgiveness, then all you need to do is signal the nurse." Dr. Winston had explained earlier that she'd be allowed to visit her father five minutes out of every hour, depending on how well he was doing.

His responding smile was barely discernible.

"Rest now, Daddy. I'm here."

Dr. Winston's hand was at her elbow directing her out of the glass-enclosed cubicle.

"Doc?" Her father's voice had a sense of urgency.

"What is it, David?"

"She's the one I was telling you about. You remember what I said, don't you?"

"Yes. Now don't you worry about a thing."

"Her hair doesn't generally look like a rag doll's."

"Daddy!" Valerie hadn't a clue what was taking place between the two men but she wasn't going to idly stand by and let them insult her.

"This way," Colby Winston said, directing her from the Coronary Care Unit.

"What was that all about?" Valerie demanded the instant they were out of earshot.

"I'm not sure I know what you mean," he said without meeting her gaze.

Valerie wasn't fooled. There was definitely something going on, and she wanted to know what. She'd been in business too long to allow questionable remarks to slip past her unchallenged.

"What did Dad mean, I'm 'the one'?"

Dr. Winston's eyes still refused to meet hers. "While we—your father and I—were talking earlier, he voiced a few concerns about his daughters."

"Yes?" Valerie pressed. Making an effort to appear nonchalant and relaxed, she walked over to the coffeepot and lifted it to him in silent invitation.

Dr. Winston shook his head and Valerie refilled her own paper cup. "So, what did Dad have to say about us girls?" she asked softly.

"He's very proud of all three of you."

"Naturally. We're his children. What I'd like to know is what he meant when he said I was 'the one.'"

"Yes, well..." He walked away from her and stood gazing out the window into the night sky.

"Come now, Doctor, I'm a mature woman and this is my father. I'm sure if I pressed him he'd tell me." They both knew that coercing her father was out of the question; nevertheless, it was an effective ploy. Dr. Winston went to the coffeepot and filled a cup, even though he'd refused one moments earlier.

"It seems he's the most worried about you."

"Me?" Valerie cried. Of the three girls, she was by far the most stable. She was not only gainfully employed, but living on her own. For heaven's sake, she was the only one with any investments! "That makes no sense at all."

"Yes, well..."

"Why is he worried about me? Furthermore, why didn't he say something to *me* instead of talking it over with you?"

"There are any number of reasons—"

"Just tell me what he said," Valerie interrupted impatiently.

"Your father seems to think—"

"Yes?" she prompted when he hesitated.

"That you should be married."

Valerie couldn't restrain her laughter. It shot out of her, like bubbles from a champagne bottle.

"In fact," Colby continued grimly, "your father seems to think you should be married to me."

Two

"Married to you?" Valerie echoed, her laughter fading suddenly. Dr. Colby Winston! She'd never heard anything so preposterous in her life. She had no intention of marrying *anyone* within the foreseeable future. There was simply no room for a man in her life. She wasn't much of a romantic; even when she was younger and in college, she hadn't dated much. Her father knew all that, and he'd never seemed particularly worried about it. This latest revelation shocked her nearly as much as Norah's call.

"I don't think there's any reason to be too concerned," Colby said, his voice gentle as though he understood that his announcement had unsettled her. Generally she was better at disguising her emotions.

"This sort of delusion isn't unheard of in heart patients," he continued. "As I said, I certainly don't think you need to concern yourself."

"You mean your patients generally try to marry you off?"

"No." He smoothed his tie as if he needed something to do with his hands. "Your father fully expects to die. It's what he wants, and deep down he'd feel better about leaving the three of you behind if at least one of you was married. Your father and I are friends and it's only natural that he'd attempt to pair me up with one of his daughters.''

''It should have been Norah. She seems more your type.''

His smile was fleeting. ''Perhaps, but it's your name he repeatedly mentions.''

''Then apparently I'm the one,'' Valerie said, not realizing what she was saying until the words had left her mouth. ''I mean—'' She stopped abruptly.

''I know exactly what you mean,'' Colby assured her. ''I don't think we have to take any of this seriously.''

''Oh, I agree. That would be foolish in the extreme.''

''Maybe your father feels you should marry first because you're the oldest,'' Colby ventured.

''Maybe,'' Valerie agreed after a moment. But something inside her suggested that wasn't the sole reason. She tucked her arms around her stomach and inhaled deeply, hoping to breathe in a bit of calm and sense.

''I wouldn't have said anything,'' Colby said, ''but I thought it was best to air this. If he mentions marriage again, my feeling is we should go along with him, at least for now.''

''Go along with him? You've got to be kidding.'' Valerie could barely believe her ears.

Colby shrugged. ''I'm sure you know your father better than I do,'' he muttered. ''He's as stubborn as they come. Don't lie, but whenever he mentions the subject of…marriage, if he does, take the route of least resistance, then try to channel the conversation in a different direction."

"I'm not going to give my father any false hopes. Or for that matter, you." She added the last part coyly and was rewarded when she saw him swallow tightly—as if he were swallowing his irritation. An angry spark momentarily leaped into his dark eyes, but was quickly quelled.

Sitting down, Valerie rummaged through her purse for a spare roll of antacid tablets. Her stomach ached and she was weary to her very bones.

Colby ignored her, although he made no move to go. The preoccupied look on his face suggested that he had something else to say; he seemed to be searching for words.

Valerie considered what Colby had told her. If she ever decided to marry—*if*—she'd settle down with someone who possessed the same drive, the same will to succeed, as she did. A man who knew where he was going, who'd set his sights high. Not some well-meaning small-town doctor.

She'd marry a man like Rowdy Cassidy.

The name sprang into her mind with a suddenness that shocked her.

Until that moment, Valerie didn't realize how deeply she admired her employer. Rowdy had started his computer software business out of a friend's garage fifteen years earlier. He'd built the company into one of the most successful in the country. Although he'd earned more money than he could possibly spend in a lifetime, he continued to work ten-and twelve-hour days, demanding as much of his staff as he did of himself.

"It might, uh, help matters if you were involved with someone," Colby said in a casual voice. Valerie found his nonchalant tone a bit exaggerated, which for some reason made her suspect that he *wasn't* "involved with someone."

"I'm not in a relationship at the moment, but I might be soon," she told him. Valerie and Rowdy— a couple. Odd that she'd never thought of him in romantic terms before. He'd be the perfect husband for her. She liked him and respected him, as a man and a professional. Rowdy had hand-picked her for his management team because he believed in her abilities.

In retrospect, she realized Rowdy had sought out her company on several occasions. Several private meetings, in fact. But she'd been so absorbed in proving herself worthy of his faith that she hadn't guessed he might hold any personal feelings for her.

For months she'd been blind to what was right in front of her. Not that she was entirely to blame, though. Rowdy wasn't exactly a heart-throb kind of guy. Oh, he was handsome enough, with his rugged cowboy looks, but his brusque, outspoken manner didn't encourage romantic aspirations. As far as she knew, he'd never dated anyone seriously, at least not in the years she'd worked for him.

For that matter, Valerie wasn't any expert on falling in love, either. She'd dismissed the possibility of

romance in her own life; it was fine for her sisters
and schoolfriends, but not for her. There'd always
been too much she wanted to do, too much to strive
for. Too much to achieve before settling down in a
permanent relationship.

"I'm afraid I don't understand," Colby said,
breaking into her thoughts. At her blank look, he
elaborated. "You said you weren't involved with
someone *yet,* but you will be soon. I may be over-
stepping my bounds here, but I wouldn't advise you
to invent a phony relationship. Your father would see
through that in a minute."

"I agree. I wouldn't even attempt anything so
foolish. But there's a man I work with, and, well, it
seems natural for the two of us to...get involved."

Dr. Winston looked so relieved that she might
have been offended if she hadn't been warmed by
the newly risen hope of a romance with Rowdy Cassidy.

"I've given your father something to help him
rest," Colby went on. "He should sleep through the
night without a problem, so if you want to drive
home and join your sister—"

"No," Valerie interrupted quickly. "I won't leave
Dad. I realize I can't see him yet, but I want to be
here...in case anything happens. It's important to
me."

"I understand."

Valerie was grateful. "Thank you."

He nodded, then yawned, revealing for the first
time his own fatigue. "I've left orders that I'm to be

contacted the minute there's any change in his condition.''

"I can't thank you enough for everything you've done.''

"No thanks necessary. I'll talk to you in the morning.''

Valerie smiled and sat down to leaf through a six-month-old news magazine. She'd just finished reading the letters to the editor when the nurse appeared, carrying a pillow and a blanket.

"Dr. Winston thought you might need these," she said, setting the bundle down next to Valerie.

It was a thoughtful thing to do, she mused later as she rested her head against the pillow and tucked the thin blanket around her shoulders. She felt a twinge of guilt, especially since she'd already decided to call in the country's top heart surgeon first thing in the morning.

By noon, it was unlikely that her father would still be a patient of Dr. Colby Winston's.

He liked her, Colby realized. He'd been prepared not to. Valerie Bloomfield was everything her father had claimed. Professional, astute and lovely. But when it came to relationships, she was exactly the type of woman Colby made a point of avoiding.

He liked his women soft and feminine. He was looking for a wife, and David Bloomfield had somehow intuited that, or he wouldn't have dragged his eldest daughter into almost every conversation. But Colby didn't have a business executive in mind. He needed a helpmate, a woman who understood the never-ending demands of a doctor's work. A woman who'd understand the long hours, the emotional stress, the intrusions into his private life.

What he didn't need was a career-obsessed executive. Perhaps he was a bit outdated in his thinking. He certainly acknowledged that a woman had every right to pursue her own profession, to choose her own calling in life, but Colby was looking for a woman who'd make that calling *him*.

He had to admit it sounded selfish and egocentric to expect his wife to wrap her life around his. Nevertheless that was exactly what he wanted.

His own career was all-consuming; there weren't enough hours in the day to do everything that needed to be done. When he arrived home at night he wanted someone there to greet him, to offer comfort, serenity.

Sherry Waterman fit the bill perfectly. They'd been dating off and on for almost a year. Lately, it seemed, more off than on. Colby wasn't sure why he'd allowed his relationship with Sherry to taper off. He hadn't talked to her in nearly two weeks now—maybe longer. He didn't remember anymore. But he knew she'd be an ideal wife for him, and for that matter so would Norah Bloomfield. Yet he couldn't picture spending the rest of his life with either of them.

If he was going to analyze his lack of interest in both Sherry and Norah, then he might as well examine what it was he found so attractive about Valerie. Not the briefcase she carried with her like a second purse. Certainly not the way she popped antacid tablets, or the way she dressed in a sexless gray suit that disguised every feminine curve of her slender frame.

What appealed to him most was the contrast he read in her. Outwardly she appeared calm and collected, asking intelligent questions with the composure of someone inquiring about commonplace statistics instead of her father's chances of survival.

Colby hadn't been fooled. He noted how she gnawed on her lower lip even while her gaze steadily met his. Valerie had been badly shaken by the ordeal. There were depths of emotion in this woman, a real capacity for feeling that was—or so he guessed—usually kept hidden.

He also noticed the love in her eyes when he took her to see her father. He'd watched her struggle to keep the emotion at bay. Her fingers had trembled when they reached for her father's hand and her face had grown gentle. There was a strong bond between those two.

It hadn't been necessary to repeat David's comment about their marrying, and Colby wasn't sure why he had.

He suspected he'd been hoping to discover if she was involved with someone. Knowing that she was, or rather that she was about to be, should have reassured him. But it hadn't. If anything, he was more curious than ever.

* * *

Norah's arrival stirred Valerie into wakefulness early the following morning. She hadn't slept much, too exhausted and keyed up to let herself relax. Toward dawn she'd drifted into an uneasy slumber.

"How's Dad?" Norah asked, handing Valerie a white sack that contained breakfast.

"The same. I haven't been in to see him, but I've talked to the CCU staff several times." She'd paced the hospital corridor most of the night and as a result had received intermittent reports.

"He's been like this almost from the first, as though he's balancing on the edge of a cliff. He could fall either way."

"He'll live," Valerie said fervently, as though her determination was enough to keep him alive.

"I hope you're right."

"I am," Valerie returned, forcing her voice to remain confident.

"Oh, before I forget," Norah said, sitting opposite Valerie, "there were two messages on the answering machine when I got home last night. The first was from Mr. Cassidy at CHIPS. He's your boss, isn't he?"

Valerie nodded, opening the bag her sister had brought. She removed a warm croissant and cup of fresh coffee. The last time she could remember eating had been on the plane, and although the meal had looked fairly decent, she'd been too upset to feel very hungry.

"What'd Rowdy have to say?"

"Just that he'd heard about Dad's heart attack. He asked if there was anything he could do."

Valerie smiled to herself, pleased that Rowdy had taken a few moments from his busy schedule to call her. It seemed to confirm her thoughts of the night before; she was increasingly convinced that his interest in her was more than business.

"Who else phoned?" she asked, purposely turning her mind from Rowdy. There'd be plenty of time later to mull over her recent revelation.

"Steff."

"How's she doing?" Valerie asked before biting into the flaky croissant.

"Not very well, I'm afraid." Norah's shoulders slumped forward slightly. "She sounded almost desperate."

"I take it she hasn't left Italy yet?"

"She can't. Apparently the whole country's at a standstill. Like I told you, she's trapped in this tiny village a hundred miles or so outside of Rome. She'd gone there to spend a few days with a friend's family."

"Why doesn't she rent a car?"

"Apparently everyone else thought of the same thing. There's not a car to be had."

"What about her friends?"

"From what I understand, the people she's with don't have a car. She and her friend got a ride there from someone else, and everyone she knows is away on spring break. She sounded dreadful. I called her back, but she was out, so I left a message." Norah shook her head in frustration.

"What did you tell her?"

"That you'd arrived and...Dad's condition was stable." It was a small lie, but necessary, Valerie agreed, for their sister's peace of mind.

"I'll try to give her a call later," Valerie said, sipping the rapidly cooling coffee. She glanced at her watch and calculated the time difference between Oregon and Texas. If she phoned now she might be able to catch Rowdy. If he was in the office, she'd ask him to locate the best heart surgeon in the state.

The pay phone didn't afford Valerie much privacy, but that couldn't be helped. To her relief, she was immediately connected with her boss.

"Valerie," he said, his big voice booming over the wire. "Good to hear from you. How's your father?"

"We don't know yet. It could go either way."

"I'm sorry to hear that." Rowdy sounded genuinely concerned and again her heart warmed toward him. "If there's anything I can do, let me know."

"There is," Valerie said, lowering her voice in an effort not to be overheard. She glanced around to make sure no staff members were within earshot. "I need the name and phone number of the best heart surgeon in this state. No, make it the West Coast. Dad's too ill to be transferred to another hospital just yet, but the one here in Orchard Valley is small. I can't be sure he's getting the best possible care. I want to make other arrangements as soon as I can."

"Of course, I'll get right on it."

Not for the first time, Valerie felt a twinge of conscience. Colby Winston obviously cared about her father. If she hurt his professional pride by going behind his back, then she'd apologize. For now, though, her primary concern had to be her father, and if that meant offending a family friend, well, it couldn't be helped.

"How can I reach you at the hospital?" Rowdy asked.

Valerie gave him the number of the pay phone, which was the best she could do.

"I'll get back to you within the hour."

"I really appreciate this," Valerie told him.

A few moments later, she strolled into the waiting room where she'd left Norah. Colby had joined her and it struck Valerie a second time how perfect Norah would be for him.

Valerie should have been pleased by the idea. Excited, too. But she wasn't and she didn't know why.

Norah smiled at something Colby was saying, and Valerie realized with a small pang that her youngest sister was half in love with him already. If she could see it, then surely her father had, too. He was probably just confusing the two of them in his mind, Valerie reasoned, which was certainly understandable under the circumstances.

"Dad's doing about the same," Norah said when she became aware that Valerie had entered the room. "Colby was just in to see him."

"Good morning," he greeted her, smiling briefly.

"Morning." Feeling guilty, she couldn't meet his eyes.

"You may both take turns visiting your father if you'd like, but you can only stay five minutes, and I'd prefer that you waited an hour between visits."

"Fine," Valerie murmured. "Since I was with him last night, do you want to go first?" she asked Norah.

"All right."

Valerie assumed that Dr. Winston would go with her sister, but he stayed behind, pouring himself a cup of coffee from the freshly brewed pot. His back was to Valerie.

"Your father's going to require open-heart surgery," he said once he'd turned around to face her. "Right now his heart's too weak to withstand the additional stress, but we're fast approaching a crisis point, and you and your sisters need to prepare yourselves."

"Here?" Valerie challenged. "And who'd perform the surgery?"

"I will— I *am* a qualified cardiovascular surgeon. And Orchard Valley has one of the best heart units in the state," Colby offered in a reassuring voice.

"I don't want *one* of the best, I want the *very* best! This is my *father* we're talking about." Valerie knew she sounded unreasonable, even rude, but her concern about David overrode all other considerations, including her embarrassment at misjudging Dr. Winston. Why had Norah never mentioned that the man was a heart surgeon? Still, it didn't matter; her father deserved the best-equipped facility and the best-trained specialist around. She spoke in a calmer voice. "If he needs surgery, then he'll have it, but not here. Not when there's a better hospital and more experienced…"

"Heart surgeons?" Colby finished for her.

She stiffened, wanting to avoid a confrontation and knowing it was impossible. "Exactly."

"You're welcome to a second opinion, Valerie. I'd be happy to review my credentials with you, as well."

Her arms cradled her middle. Her breakfast seemed to lie like a deadweight in her stomach.

Colby had begun to speak again. "Norah—"

"You already mentioned the possibility of open-heart surgery to Norah?" she flared, disliking the fact that he'd talked to her sister first.

He nodded. "Just now. While you were out."

That hurt her pride. She, after all, was the oldest, the decision maker, the strong one.

"If you'd like to talk to another specialist, I'd be happy to recommend several."

"That won't be necessary," Valerie returned stiffly, feeling like a traitor. "I'm having a friend get me the names of the top heart surgeons on the West Coast."

A vacuum of silence followed her words.

"I understand."

She glanced toward him, surprised not to hear any resentment in his voice.

"It isn't that we don't appreciate everything

you've done," she rushed to explain. "Norah's told me several times that if it weren't for you, we'd have lost Dad that first night. I'm grateful, more than you'll ever know, but I want to stack the odds in Dad's favor, and if that means bringing in another surgeon, then I'll do it."

Her impassioned words were met with a cool but not unfriendly smile. "If David were my father I'd do the same. Don't worry, Valerie, you haven't offended me."

She was so relieved that she nearly sagged onto the sofa.

"Let me know who you want to call in and I'll be happy to confer with him."

"Thank you," she whispered. "Dad and Norah are right," she added, almost to herself.

"About what?" Colby asked on his way out the door.

She looked up, realizing he'd heard her. "You really are wonderful."

Their eyes met, all too briefly, but in those few seconds an odd understanding passed between them. It wasn't a look lovers would exchange, she thought, but one close friends would.

Norah returned from the five-minute visit with their father, pale and obviously distressed. Slowly she lowered herself onto the sofa, her hands gripped tightly together.

"Dad's not doing so well this morning?" Valerie ventured.

Norah nodded. "He's so weak...he's talking about

dying and…'' She paused, her light blue eyes glassy with tears.

"He isn't going to die," Valerie said vehemently, clenching her fists at her sides. She *refused* to let him die.

"He'd prefer if you and Steff and I were married, but that can't be helped now, he says. He told me he's sorry he won't be around to enjoy his grandchildren, but—''

"Norah," Valerie admonished briskly, "you didn't honestly listen to that garbage, did you? We can't allow him to talk like that."

"He seems to think you should marry Dr. Winston.''

Valerie frowned. "So I heard. That just goes to show you how illogical he's become. If anyone should marry Colby Winston, it's you."

Norah lowered her eyes and an attractive shade of pink flowed into her cheeks. "Every female employee in the hospital's in love with Dr. Winston. Even the married ones have a crush on him. He's so strong, yet he's gentle and caring. I—I don't know what I would have done the last couple of days without Colby."

"You really care about him, don't you?" Valerie whispered, fighting down an unexpected sense of disappointment.

"I'm not in love with him—not exactly. I admire him the way everyone else does, and if he ever asked me out, I'd accept without thinking twice, but he hasn't."

Valerie was sure she would. She paced the small room. "Damn, I need a cigarette," she blurted, uncertain what prompted the outburst—her father's apparent death wish or Norah's feelings for Colby Winston.

"I've been busy this morning myself," Valerie said, not looking at her sister. "I asked Rowdy Cassidy if he'd get us the name of the best heart surgeon on the West Coast. Dad's going to need the finest medical—"

Norah's head shot up. "You *what?*"

"Listen, if you're concerned about offending Colby, I've already spoken to him and he agrees we should get a second opinion."

"But Colby teaches at Portland University. He's the best there is!"

"For Orchard Valley." Of that Valerie was confident, but there was a whole world Norah knew little or nothing about. Her sister's entire universe rotated around Orchard Valley and their five-hundred-acre apple orchard ten miles outside of town.

"Colby's one of the best cardiovascular surgeons in the state." Norah didn't bother to disguise her irritation. "Don't you realize what you've done?" she demanded. "You've just insulted one of this country's most—"

"I didn't insult him," Valerie insisted, interrupting her sister's tirade. "I made sure of that myself. Furthermore, you never even let me know he was a heart surgeon— I thought he was just a G.P. And even if he's considered good here in Orchard Valley,

Dad needs absolutely the best one available anywhere. Shouldn't you be concerning yourself with his problems and not worrying about offending your doctor boyfriend?''

Norah's eyes widened with shock and hurt. She stood, and without a word walked out of the room, leaving Valerie swamped in immediate remorse. She hadn't meant to snap at her sister, nor had she wanted to sound so overbearing. Referring to Colby as Norah's boyfriend had been childish and petty, which went to prove how badly her nerves were frayed.

The pay phone at the end of the high-ceilinged corridor started to ring and Valerie hurried out of the room, knowing even before she answered that it was Rowdy with the information she'd requested.

"Hello," she said breathlessly, yanking the receiver from the hook.

"Valerie, it's Rowdy. Listen, you're in luck. There's an up-and-coming heart surgeon who's working out of Portland University. Apparently he's developed an innovative surgical technique. I've talked to three of the top heart specialists in the country and they all highly recommend him."

"Great." She groped through her purse until she found a pen and a notebook, which she positioned against the wall. "Ready."

"His name is Dr. Colby Winston."

Valerie dropped her arms and turned to slouch against the wall. "Dr. Colby Winston," she repeated.

"I've got his phone number here."

"Thanks, Rowdy," she said, pride and shame clogging her throat, "but I've already got it."

She hadn't been home for twenty-four hours and she'd already managed to alienate her sister, insult a family friend and at the same time disparage a highly regarded doctor.

"Just great, Valerie," she muttered to herself. "Can things get any worse?"

Three

"Steffie?" David Bloomfield's eyes fluttered open and he gazed up at Valerie.

"She'll be here as soon as she can," Valerie reassured him.

How weak he sounded, she thought, as though death was only hours away. Her heart clamored with dread and fear; she wanted to shout at him to fight, to hang on...

That was impossible, and Valerie knew it. In the past two days she'd learned more about the functions of the heart than she'd ever imagined. In more ways than one. She'd learned that the symbolic heart, the center of human emotion, grew larger with the sorrows as well as the joys of love. And the physical heart was subject to its own stresses and risks.

Colby had strived to make the explanation as uncomplicated as possible. Simply put, her father was experiencing heart failure; his heart was pumping blood less efficiently than it should. The decreased strength of the muscles then resulted in distended blood vessels that leaked fluid into his lungs, which interfered with his breathing. Each hour he was growing weaker and closer to death.

"Can't...hold out much longer."

"Of course you can," Valerie insisted, fighting down defeat and discouragement. "You're going to live long enough to be a problem to your children. Isn't that what you've always said? You've got years and years left. Good years, with a houseful of grandchildren."

Her father's smile was fleeting at best. "Go home, sweetheart," he whispered. "You haven't even been to the house yet."

"There's nothing there for me without you." She rubbed her thumb soothingly across the back of his hand, avoiding the I.V. needle. "Get well, Daddy, please get well. We all need you."

His eyes drifted shut, and the oppressive need to give in to the weakness of tears nearly overcame her. She blinked furiously in an effort not to cry, succeeding despite the enormous lump in her throat.

Valerie was grateful her features were outwardly composed when Colby entered the cubicle a few moments later. He read over the clipboard that outlined her father's progress, then made a brief notation.

"He'll sleep now," he said, guiding her out of the room.

"What's happening?" she asked once they'd left the Coronary Care Unit. "Why is he so much weaker than before? It's like watching his life ebb away. Surely you can do something?" She heard the note of hysteria in her own voice and didn't care. Perhaps she was being selfish for wanting him to live when he so clearly wanted to be released from his life. But she loved him so desperately. She *needed* him, and so did Steffie and Norah.

"We're doing everything we can," Colby assured her.

"I know—but it's not enough."

"Valerie, trust me, I love that crotchety old man myself. I don't want to lose him, either." He led the way to the elevator. "Come on, I'll buy you a cup of coffee."

She was on the verge of pointing out that there was coffee in the waiting room, then hesitated. He was right. She needed a break, even if it was only ten minutes in the hospital cafeteria.

They rode the elevator down to the basement and walked into the large, open room, which was mostly empty now. Colby reached for a serving tray and slid it along the counter, collecting a green dinner salad, a cellophane-wrapped turkey sandwich and coffee. Valerie surveyed the cottage cheese salad with the limp pineapple and instead grabbed a bottle of cranberry juice. She wasn't the least bit hungry, although she'd eaten very little in the past few days.

He withdrew his wallet and paid the cashier, then carried the tray to a table at the back of the room, near the window.

He chose one far removed from any of the occupied tables, and that started Valerie's heart pounding with a renewed sense of anxiety. Colby had brought her here to help her face the inevitable.

"I'm going to lose my father, aren't I?" she asked outright, determined to confront the truth head-on.

Colby looked up, his dark eyes filled with surprise. "Not if I can help it. What makes you ask?"

She slumped against the back of the chair, so relieved that it was all she could do not to weep openly. "I thought that was why you brought me here—what you intended to tell me." With trembling hands, she reached for the container of juice and removed the top.

"We aren't going to lose him." He spoke with such fierce conviction that she realized his will to keep her father alive was as strong as her own.

"How long have you known my father?" she asked, leaning forward and resting her elbows on the table.

"A few years now."

Valerie vaguely recalled hearing Colby's name mentioned once or twice, but she couldn't remember when or for what reason. With her hectic work schedule she'd been home only intermittently. Her last visit had been nearly six months ago, although she phoned weekly.

"We met soon after your mother died," Colby explained. "Your father made a generous donation to the hospital in her name."

Valerie knew that David's contribution had been large enough for the hospital to begin construction of a new wing. The irony of the situation struck her for the first time, and she drew in a deep, painful breath. The new wing housed the Coronary Care Unit.

"Your father and I've played chess once a week or so since then."

"You ever beat him?"

Colby grinned. "Occasionally, but not often."

Valerie was good at chess herself, which was hardly surprising since her father had taught her to play. One day, perhaps, when all this was over, she'd challenge Colby to a game. Odd how easy it was to assume they'd continue to know each other....

"He's very proud of you," Colby stated casually as he unwrapped his sandwich.

Valerie suppressed a sudden urge to giggle. "So— he mentioned me *before* his attack."

"At every opportunity." He frowned as he said it. He was, no doubt, thoroughly sick of the subject.

Valerie settled back and crossed her arms, enjoying herself. "In other words, Dad's preoccupation with matching the two of us up isn't something new."

Colby paused, averting his gaze. "Let's put it this way. He wasn't quite as blatant about it as he's been the past few days."

"You must have been curious about me."

He shrugged. "A bit."

"And?" she prompted. "What do you think?"

Once again Colby lifted his shoulders, as if to say she hadn't impressed him. Or was he saying she hadn't disappointed him? Valerie couldn't tell.

"That doesn't tell me a thing," she complained.

"You're everything your father said and more,"

he muttered, obviously hoping to satisfy her and at the same time put an end to the conversation.

Valerie knew it was sheer vanity to be so pleased. He might have intended his remark as a compliment, but she didn't read any admiration in his eyes. If Dr. Colby Winston was attracted to her, he concealed it well. She hated to admit how much that dented her pride. The truth was, she wanted him to be fascinated with her. She wanted him to feel enthralled, enchanted, impressed—the way she was with him. Because, despite herself, and despite their awkward beginning, and despite the prospect of a relationship with Rowdy Cassidy, she couldn't get Colby out of her mind.

In a strictly objective way, Valerie knew she was slim and attractive. No matter what her father said about her hair, it was styled in an exuberant tangle of russet curls that highlighted her cheekbones and unusual gray-green eyes.

Those eyes were her greatest asset in the looks department, although her mouth tended to be expressive. Being tall, almost five eight, was a plus, too. Norah was barely five three, and it seemed the entire world towered above her sister. When Valerie wore heels, there wasn't a man in her field she couldn't meet at eye level, which she considered a definite advantage.

"You don't like me, do you?" she asked bluntly.

Her question clearly took him aback, and he hesitated, frowning. "I don't dislike you."

"I make you nervous?"

"Not exactly."

"Then what is it?" she prodded. "Don't worry. I'm not planning to fall in love with you. As I said before, there's someone else on the horizon. I'm just…curious."

"About what?"

"How you feel about me."

His mouth tightened, and Valerie could tell he wasn't accustomed to dealing with a woman as direct as she was. Most men weren't. Valerie didn't believe in suggestion or subtlety. The shortest distance between any two points was a straight line. She'd learned that in high-school geometry and it had worked equally well in life.

"I think you're very good at what you do."

He was sidestepping her question and doing a relatively good job of it, but she wasn't fooled. "Which is?" she pressed.

"Functioning in a male-dominated field."

"Are you implying I've sacrificed my femininity?"

His lips tightened again. "You're good at putting words in someone's mouth, too, aren't you?"

"Sometimes," she agreed, "but only when it suits my purposes."

"No doubt."

"You're not sure how you feel about me, are you?"

"On the contrary, I knew the minute we met."

She cocked an eyebrow, waiting for him to finish.

"Well?" she asked when he didn't immediately supply the answer.

"You're bright and attractive."

"Thank you." It wasn't exactly what she'd hoped to hear. He'd revealed no emotion toward her. She'd rarely met a man who was so...she searched for the right word. Staid, she decided. Stoical. He seemed to close himself up whenever he was around her, almost as though he felt he needed protection.

Valerie knew she could be overpowering and opinionated, but she wasn't cold or hard. Just straightforward. They were alike in that way, both sensible, seasoned professionals. It was common ground between them, yet Colby seemed determined to ignore their similarities.

He'd been kind to her, she reminded herself. But she sensed he would have behaved in the same compassionate manner regardless of who she was. Valerie understood that, even applauded it.

So why was she looking for something that wasn't there?

She shook herself mentally. "All right, Dr. Winston," she began in a brisk voice. "Tell me about my father."

Norah was asleep on the sofa when Valerie returned from the cafeteria. She spread the blanket over her sister, wondering why Norah wasn't spending the night at home. Norah stirred, her eyes fluttering open.

"Hello, Sleeping Beauty," Valerie said, smiling softly.

"Where were you?" Norah asked, sitting up. She brushed the hair from her face, and Valerie saw that her soft blue eyes were puffy, as though she'd recently been crying.

"Down in the cafeteria with Colby."

Norah blinked, looking mildly surprised.

"He hadn't had dinner yet and asked me along so we could talk."

"I felt bad about what happened this morning," Norah said. "I was upset about Dad and angry with you for going behind Colby's back. But then I realized I should have explained things better—you know, told you about his qualifications." She sighed. "I was angry that you hadn't talked to me first."

"If I had, I might have saved myself a lot of trouble," Valerie agreed. "Don't worry about it, sis—I would've been upset, too."

"If there was ever a time we need to stick together, it's now. We can't allow a quarrel to come between us."

Valerie nodded. Norah looked small and lost, and Valerie crossed the room to sit down beside her, placing a protective arm around her sister's shoulders.

"I wish Steffie was here," Norah murmured.

Valerie did, too, but in some ways perhaps it was best that their sister hadn't arrived yet. Her absence might well be the only thing keeping their father alive.

"What did you and Colby talk about?" Norah asked, pressing her head against Valerie's shoulder.

"Dad, and what's going to happen."

"Does Colby know?"

Valerie shook her head. "No, but it looks like he may not have the option of waiting until Dad's lungs clear before performing open-heart surgery."

"But his chances of survival would be practically nil if Colby went ahead with it now!"

Valerie had felt the same alarm when Colby described the procedure to her. He'd drawn a detailed outline of the procedure on a napkin and answered a multitude of questions. Although the surgery would be risky, it seemed to be the only alternative available to them. Valerie had understood and accepted Colby's reasoning, even though her father's chances were slim. She prayed it wouldn't come to this, but that was looking less promising every hour.

"The likelihood that he'll survive is a whole lot better with the operation than without," Valerie reminded her sister.

"I know but...oh, Val, it's so scary to think of what our lives would be like without Dad."

"I know." Gently she stroked her sister's hair, offering what reassurance and comfort she could.

"Isn't Colby wonderful?" Norah asked after a while.

Valerie smiled to herself, then nodded. He'd made the surgery, with all its risk, seem the logical thing to do. For the first time since her arrival, she felt hopeful for her father's chances. She held on to that small surge of confidence with both hands. Colby had been patient, answering her questions, giving her reassurance and hope when she'd felt none.

"Now can you understand why everyone likes him so much?" Norah asked, her voice soft.

"Yes." She'd intentionally baited him, determined to find out how he really felt about *her*. She'd looked for some reaction, some sign, but he'd given nothing away.

The more reserved he was, the more challenged she felt. Valerie doubted he'd ever raised his voice or lost his cool, composed air. Even when she'd pressured him, he'd revealed almost no emotion. Yet Valerie couldn't shake the conviction that he was a man of deep feeling—and strong passion.

Colby was smiling; he'd been smiling ever since he'd left the hospital. He wasn't sure what had prompted him to invite Valerie down to the cafeteria. But he suspected it was because…well, because he enjoyed being with her. He'd never known a woman who was so willing to speak her feelings. She was direct and honest and, damn it all, *interesting*. It wasn't that he found Sherry, or for that matter Norah, boring. He enjoyed their company in an entirely different way.

But Valerie kept him on his toes. She didn't take anything at face value, but challenged and confronted until she was satisfied. He admired that. In fact, he admired *her*. But that wasn't the end of it. This was a woman he could grow to love.

He'd gone off the deep end. Worked too many

hours without a real break. He'd listened to David Bloomfield once too often. There could never be anything between him and Valerie. She wasn't what he needed in a woman; not only that, she'd never be satisfied with life in Orchard Valley again.

And they both knew it.

The following morning, with Norah at the hospital, Valerie felt comfortable about leaving for the first time since her arrival from New York. She desperately needed a change of clothes. She was still wearing the business suit she'd had on when she'd received Norah's message two—no, three—days earlier.

She drove to the family home, down the mile-long driveway that led to the colonial house. She took a moment to glance at the hundreds of neat rows of apple trees, all in fragrant blossom. Then she hauled her suitcase up to her old bedroom, showered and changed into a pair of slacks and a soft blue sweater.

By the time Valerie returned to the hospital she felt a thousand times better. Norah was still asleep, curled up on the sofa, her knees tucked under her chin. She was so blond and delicate that for a moment Valerie had an almost overpowering recollection of their mother. She came to an abrupt stop. The words of greeting froze on her lips and she turned into the hallway.

Quietly she fought back the tears. She'd barely managed to compose herself before Colby strolled purposely down the wide corridor, heading straight toward her, his face taut.

"Have you got a few moments?" he asked stiffly.

"Sure," Valerie said, puzzled by his obvious tension. "Is something wrong? Is it Dad?"

"No, this is between you and me." Colby actually seemed angry. Furious, even, although he hadn't raised his voice. This was certainly the most emotion she'd seen in him yet.

He marched toward the elevator, with Valerie following, and then down the narrow passageway to the back entrance of the hospital and the employee parking lot. He was several yards ahead of her.

"Where are we going?" she demanded. His pace was too swift for her to keep stride with him.

"Outside."

"In case you hadn't noticed, we already are."

"I don't want anyone to hear this."

"Hear *what?*" she almost shrieked, losing her patience.

Colby whirled around to confront her. "I want to know exactly what you said to your father."

Valerie was confused. "About what?"

"Us." The simple little word resonated with anger, contempt, disgust.

Well, so much for her assumption that Colby Winston felt any attraction for her, Valerie mused.

"Us?" she repeated. "Don't be ridiculous. There isn't any us."

"My point exactly," he snapped. "Perhaps you can tell me why your father suddenly announced that you were falling in love with me—and that he expected me to *do* something about it.''

''He what?'' she exploded.

''You heard me. What in the name of heaven did you say?''

''Nothing.'' In the three or four times she'd seen him yesterday evening and this morning, her father had been asleep. At least, his eyes had been closed and his breathing was shallow but regular.

''He knew we'd talked in the cafeteria,'' Colby informed her coolly.

''He did?''

''He mentioned it himself.''

''Maybe Norah—''

''Norah nothing. It came straight from the horse's mouth. That and a whole lot more.''

Valerie frowned, staring down at the ground in an effort to think.

''Valerie!''

''I…thought he was asleep.''

''What did you say?'' he demanded a second time.

She was flustered now, which happened so rarely that it unnerved her even more. ''Uh…just that we'd talked the other night and I…''

''Go on,'' he insisted, his jaw muscles tightening.

''I, uh, have this tendency to talk when I'm upset. I don't mind telling you Dad's condition has really scared me. So if he's asleep, like he's been most of today, I sit at his side and tell him the things I've been thinking about.''

''Which included me?''

Reluctantly, she nodded. Rarely could she recall being more embarrassed. Color burned in her cheeks.

"Valerie, what did you say to him?" Colby's voice was quiet but his face had sharpened with tension.

Momentarily she closed her eyes. She didn't remember everything she'd mumbled, but what she did recall made her cringe. She'd rambled on, saying whatever came into her mind, and most of her thoughts seemed to concern Colby. Not for a second had she believed her father was awake enough to understand a word of it.

"I told him how impressed I was with you," she began hesitantly. "Although I don't know you well, I sense a strength in you. I told him how grateful I was to you because I've felt so helpless the last couple of days."

She chanced a look in his direction but his expression was impassive. Not knowing what else to do, she continued. "In any family crisis there's always one person who has to be strong, and everyone else leans on that person for support. I'm the oldest and I feel responsible for the others. But when I saw my father that first time, I just couldn't cope. It's even harder for Norah. I realized that the strong one in this situation is you. I told Dad that...and some other things."

"What other things?"

It didn't get any better. "That I...found myself attracted to you. Not physically," she rushed to explain, conscious that she was lying. "I'm attracted to the emotional stability I sense in you. Only I didn't bother to explain all that to Dad because I didn't think he could hear me anyway.

"Was that so terrible?" she asked, when Colby remained silent.

"No," he finally admitted in a hoarse voice.

"What exactly did Dad say to you?" she asked curiously.

Colby's gaze touched hers, then withdrew. "That you'd fallen head over heels in love with me. And that's a quote."

"What?" Valerie said incredulously. "No wonder you were so upset."

"Upset's not the word for it. I'm worried about how this is going to affect David's recovery, especially since he seems to have all kinds of expectations now—expectations that are going to be disappointed. I didn't know what you'd told him, but he's built hopes on it. Eventually he'll just have to realize that you're not the kind of woman I intend to marry."

"Believe me, Dr. Winston, you have nothing to worry about," she murmured, annoyed now. "If I *was* going to fall in love, it would be with a man who was a little more sensitive to my pride."

"I apologize," he said, shrugging indifferently. "Your father unfortunately read more into your words. I'm afraid you'll have to say something to him."

"Me?"

"You're the one who started this."

"Why can't we just let the whole thing drop? By tomorrow he'll have forgotten I said anything."

Colby shook his head. "That's not likely. He asked me to bring in a preacher so we could be married at his bedside."

Valerie couldn't help it, she burst out laughing. It was as though all the tension, all the waiting and frustration had broken free inside her. She laughed until the tears streaked down her face and her sides ached, and even then she couldn't stop. Clutching her stomach, she wiped the moisture from her cheeks.

"Colby, darling," she said between giggles. "What shall I wear to the ceremony?"

Colby apparently didn't find her antics at all humorous.

"I'll want children, of course," she told him when she'd managed to stop giggling. "Nine or ten, and I'll name the little darlings after you. There'll be little cheeses running around our happy home—Cheddar and—"

"I have absolutely no intention of marrying you."

"Of course you don't right *now,* but that'll all change." She found that she enjoyed teasing him, and the laughter was a welcome release after all the tension of the past few days.

"You're not serious, are you?"

Valerie sighed deeply. "If you want me to say something to Dad, I will."

"I think that would be best."

"I'm really not so bad, you know," she felt obliged to tell him. She was disappointed in his reaction, although she'd never admit it. If she was going to make a fool of herself over a man she didn't need to travel across the country to do so!

"We don't have a thing in common and shouldn't pretend we do."

"Well, but—"

"Let's leave it at that, Valerie."

His attitude hurt. "Fine. I'm not interested in you, either," she muttered. Without another word, she turned around and marched back into the hospital.

The man had his nerve. He made a relationship with her sound about as attractive as one with a...a porcupine! Colby acted as though she'd purposely set a trap for him, and she resented that.

Norah was awake when she returned to the waiting room. Her younger sister looked up, smiling, as Valerie hurried in and began to pace.

"Is something wrong?" Norah asked, pouring herself a cup of coffee. She gestured toward the pot, but Valerie shook her head.

"Have you ever noticed how opinionated and high-handed Colby Winston can be?" she asked, still pacing furiously.

"Dr. Winston?" Norah repeated, amazed. "Not in the least. I've never known him to be rude, not even when someone deserved it."

Valerie impatiently pushed the sleeves of her sweater past her elbows. "I don't think I've ever known a man who irritated me more."

"I thought you liked him."

"I thought I did, too," she answered darkly.

"Steffie phoned," Norah said, cutting off Valerie's irritation as effectively as if she'd flipped a light switch. "She got through to the nurses' station here when she couldn't reach either of us at the house."

"Where is she?" Valerie asked. "Is the transportation strike over?"

"No," Norah said with a shrug. "She's still trapped in whatever the name of that town is. If she was in one of the big cities I don't think she'd be having nearly as much trouble. She asked about Dad, and I told her that everything's about the same. She sounded so worried…I think she was close to tears."

"Poor Steffie."

"She said she'd give everything she owns to find a way home." Norah shook her head. "If something doesn't break soon, I think Steff's going to hike her way over the Alps."

She'd do it, too; Valerie didn't doubt that for a moment.

"I was with Dad earlier," Norah said, changing the subject a second time. "He was a little more alert than he has been."

Valerie frowned, well aware of the reason. Her dear, manipulative father seemed to think he was about to get his wish. Little did he realize she had no intention of marrying Dr. Colby Winston. Or that Colby was no more interested in her than she was in him.

Four

David Bloomfield's condition didn't change throughout the day that followed. Valerie saw Colby intermittently. He was in surgery most of the afternoon and stopped in, still wearing his surgical gown, to check on her father early that evening. Valerie happened to be there at the time, and she read the weariness in Colby's face. Without saying anything to her father, she followed Colby out of the room.

"How about a cup of coffee?" she suggested, and when he hesitated, she added lightly, "I thought you might like to know how I warded off the preacher."

He grinned, then rubbed a hand across his eyes. "All right," he said, checking his watch. "Give me fifteen minutes and I'll meet you in the cafeteria."

Valerie headed downstairs, taking her briefcase with her. Early that afternoon she'd had her secretary fax the contents of several files to her. Even if she had to be out of the office while her father was ill, there were still matters that required her attention. She'd spent the better part of the afternoon calling clients and updating her files. Working out of the hospital waiting room wasn't ideal, but she'd managed.

She was reading over her notes when Colby arrived. As he pulled out a chair, she straightened, tucked the papers inside her briefcase and closed it.

After a somewhat perfunctory greeting, Colby reached for the sugar canister in the middle of the table and methodically poured out a teaspoon, briskly stirring it into the hot coffee. "I wanted to apologize," he began.

His words took her by surprise. "For what?"

"I was out of line, coming down on you the way I did about the marriage business. I should have realized your father was stretching whatever you said out of proportion. I took my irritation out on you."

She dismissed his apology with a shake of her head. "It was understandable—don't worry about it. As far as I'm concerned, the entire matter's forgotten."

His eyes met hers as though he couldn't quite believe her. "You spoke to him?" he asked abruptly.

Valerie nodded, trying to disguise her amusement. "My poor father was devastated, or at least he tried to persuade me he was. But—" she sighed expressively "—he'll get over it just as I will." She fluttered her eyelashes melodramatically, teasing Colby just a little.

His eyes shot to hers, and a slow grin moved across his face, relaxing his features. "Disappointed, were you?"

"Oh, yes. I've always dreamed of a traditional white wedding gown—one that matches the sheets on my father's hospital bed." She smiled and relaxed, too, feeling at ease with him now. She'd been angry, but that was over, and she had to admit she actually liked this man. She certainly admired him.

Colby sipped his coffee, and once again she noted the lines of fatigue that marked his eyes and mouth.

"Rough day?"

He nodded. "I lost a patient. Mrs. Murphy. She died this afternoon in surgery. We knew there was a risk, but..." He shrugged heavily. "No matter how often it happens, I never get used to it."

"I'm so sorry, Colby." Her hand reached for his in a gesture of friendship and understanding.

His fingers gripped hers as if to absorb the comfort and consolation she offered. At the feel of his hand closing over hers, Valerie felt a thrill of happiness, and even more inexplicable, a sense of *rightness*. She didn't know how else to describe it. Yet almost immediately, the doubts and uncertainties flowed into her mind.

They were friends, nothing more, she reminded herself. Neither of them was looking for anything else. Neither of them *wanted* anything else. But if that was really the case, why should she experience this deep ache of longing? For one impulsive moment she yearned to burrow her way into his arms, rest her head against his shoulder and immerse herself in his strength. Lend him hers.

Valerie decided she had to ignore these uncharacteristic sensations. She withdrew her hand, hoping he wouldn't notice the telltale tremble.

"I'd better get back before Norah wonders where

I am," she said firmly. Valerie was a woman who needed to be in control, who looked at a problem from all angles and worked toward the most favorable solution. But Colby Winston wasn't a problem that needed to be solved. He was a man who left her feeling vulnerable and confused.

She was already on her feet, briefcase in hand, when Colby spoke. "Don't go...not yet." His voice was soft, hesitant.

Unsure, Valerie sank back into her chair, helpless to refuse him.

"No, never mind." Colby shook his head, eyes suddenly guarded. "Actually, I should be leaving myself," he said quickly, bounding to his feet. He drank down several gulps of coffee, then strode out of the cafeteria, with Valerie following close behind.

"Colby." She stopped him in front of the elevator. "What is it you don't like about me?" The question was out before she had time to analyze the wisdom of asking.

"I do like you," he answered, frowning.

"But you wouldn't want to marry someone like me?"

"No," he agreed calmly. "I wouldn't want to marry someone like you."

"Because?" Valerie wasn't sure why she continued to probe, why it was necessary for her to understand his reasons. She only knew that she felt a compelling urge to ask.

"You have a brilliant future ahead of you," he said, not meeting her eyes. "Your father's proud of your accomplishments, and rightly so. I admire your drive, your ambition, your ability.''

"But." She said it before he could. There had to be a *but* in there somewhere.

"But," he said with the slightest hint of a smile. "I'm not interested in becoming involved with an up-and-coming female executive. When it comes to committing myself to a woman and a relationship, I want someone who's more...traditional. Someone who'll consider making our home and rearing our children her career."

"I see." He was wise to recognize that she wasn't the type who'd be content to sit quietly by the fireplace and spin her own yarn. No, Valerie would soon figure out how to have that yarn mass-produced, then see about franchising it into a profit-making enterprise. Business was in her blood, the same way medicine was in his.

"I don't mean to offend you," he said.

"You haven't," she assured him, and it was the truth.

The elevator arrived and they stepped inside together. Neither spoke as Colby pushed the appropriate button. The doors silently glided shut.

Valerie wished they weren't alone. It seemed so intimate, so private, just the two of them standing there.

"Valerie, listen..."

"It's all right," she said, smiling up at him. "Really. I asked, didn't I? That's the way I am. You were honest with me, and I appreciate that. It's true I'm attracted to you, but that's probably fairly common in our circumstances. Being attracted doesn't mean I'm in love with you.''

''I know, it's just that—'' He broke off hastily, his eyes probing hers. ''Oh, what the hell,'' he murmured, the words so low that Valerie had to strain to hear him. Then his hands were taking hold of her shoulders and drawing her toward him. His mouth unerringly found hers and without conscious intent, she responded to his kiss, feeling none of the awkwardness she experienced with other men. Delicious tremors were moving down her spine. The kiss was much like the man. Gentle, deliberate, devastating.

She heard a soft moan easing its way from the back of her throat.

His head shifted restlessly before he released her. He dropped his arms, looking completely shocked. Valerie didn't know what had distressed him most— the fact that he'd kissed her or that he'd enjoyed it.

''Valerie, I...'' Her name was a whisper.

Just then the elevator doors opened, and Colby cast an accusing glare at the nurse who entered. Grabbing Valerie's hand, he jerked her onto the floor before the elevator doors closed again.

''This isn't CCU,'' she protested, glancing around. Good grief, they were on the maternity floor. Directly down the hall, a row of newborns was on display behind a glass partition.

But Colby didn't give her a chance to get a closer look. Still holding her hand, he led her to the stairwell. He held open the door for her, then dashed up the steps. He was halfway up the first flight before he seemed to realize she was no longer beside him. He turned back impatiently.

"Colby," she objected. "If you want to run up the stairs, fine, but you're in better physical condition than I am. I sit at a desk most of the day, remember?"

"I didn't mean for that to happen."

"What, racing up the stairs?"

"No, kissing you!"

"It was nice enough, as kisses go," she said, out of breath from the exertion, "but don't worry, you aren't going to have to marry me because of a simple kiss." The only way she could deal with this experience was to deny how strongly it affected her, push aside these unfamiliar, unwelcome feelings. She suspected that was how Colby felt, too.

"Our kiss may have been a lot of things, but simple wasn't one of them," he muttered.

"You're worrying too much about something that really isn't important."

His eyes held such a quizzical expression that Valerie continued talking. "You're tired, and so am I," she said, making excuses for them both. "We're under a lot of stress. You've had a long, discouraging day and your guard slipped a little," she went on. "My being so damn pushy didn't help matters, either. You kissed me, but it isn't the end of the world."

"It won't happen again." He spoke with absolute certainty.

Pride stiffened Valerie's shoulders. "That's probably for the best." Colby was right. Her personality was all wrong for someone like him. A doctor's work was emotionally and physically draining; she couldn't blame him for seeking a wife who'd create a warm cocoon of domesticity for him. A home filled with comfort and love and peace. Valerie couldn't fault his preference. She wished him well and determined to put the kiss out of her mind, once and for all.

The streets of downtown Orchard Valley greeted Valerie like a long-lost friend. Her heart cheered at the sight of the bright, flower-filled baskets that hung from every streetlight.

The clock outside the Wells Fargo Bank was still ten minutes slow, even after thirty years. When Valerie was thirteen, a watchsmith from somewhere out East had arrived to repair the grand old clock. He spent the better part of a day working on it, then declared the problem solved. Two days after he'd left town, the clock was back to running ten minutes late and no one bothered to have it repaired again, although it came up on the town council agenda at least once a year.

The barber shop with its red-and-white striped pole whirling round and round like a fat candy cane was as cheery as ever. Mr. Stein, the barber, sat in one of his leather chairs reading the *Orchard Valley Clarion*, waiting for his next customer. Valerie walked past, and when he glanced over the top of the paper, she smiled and waved. He grinned and returned the gesture.

The sense of homecoming was strong, lifting her spirits. She strolled past the newspaper office, two doors down from the barber shop; looking in the window, she noted the activity inside as the staff prepared the next edition of the *Orchard Valley Clarion.* She hadn't gone more than a few steps when she heard someone call her name.

She turned to find Charles Tomaselli, the paper's editor, directly behind her. "Valerie, hello. I wondered how long it'd take before I ran into you. How's your dad doing?"

"About the same," she answered.

"I'm sorry to hear that." He buried his hands in his pants pockets and matched his pace to hers. "I haven't seen Stephanie around."

"She's still in Italy."

Although he gave no outward indication of his feelings, Valerie sensed his irritation. "She didn't bother to come home even when her father's so ill? I'd have thought she'd want to be with him."

"She's trying as hard as she can," Valerie said, defending her sister. "But she's stuck in a small town a hundred or so miles outside of Rome—because of that transportation strike. But if there's a way out, Steffie'll find it."

Charles nodded, and Valerie had the odd impression that he regretted bringing up the subject of her sister. "If you get the chance, will you tell your father something for me?"

"Of course."

"Let him know Commissioner O'Dell called me following last week's article on the farm labor issue. That'll cheer him up."

"The farm labor issue?" Valerie repeated, wanting to be sure she understood him correctly.

Charles grinned almost boyishly, his dark eyes sparkling with pleasure. "That's right. I don't know if you're aware of this, but your father would make one hell of an investigative reporter. Tell him I said that, too. He'll know what I mean."

"All right," Valerie agreed, wishing she knew more about the article and her father's role in it.

"Nice seeing you again," Charles said, turning to head back to the newspaper office. He hesitated. "When you see Stephanie, tell her I said hello, will you?"

"Of course. I'll be happy to." Thoughtfully, Valerie watched him walk away from her. Charles not only edited the *Clarion,* he wrote a regular column and most of the major features, like the farm labor story he'd just mentioned. Considering his talent and energy, she was surprised that he'd stayed on with a small-town paper; he could have gone to work for one of the big dailies long before now.

She found it interesting that he'd asked about Steffie. Several years ago, Valerie had felt sure there was something romantic developing between them. Steffie had been a college student at the time and Charles had recently moved to Orchard Valley. She remembered Steffie poring over every article, every column, exclaiming over Charles's skill, his style, his wit. To Valerie, it had sounded like romance in the making.

But then, romance was hardly a subject she knew much about. So if there was something between Steffie and Charles, it was their business and she was staying out of it. She knew just enough about relationships to make a real mess of them. A good example of that was how she'd bungled things with Colby.

She experienced a twinge of regret. Since their kiss, he'd been avoiding her. Or at least she assumed he was. Until then, he'd made a point of stopping in and chatting with her when he could. They'd always been brief visits, but their times together had broken up the monotony of the long hours she'd spent at the hospital. She hadn't realized how much those short interludes meant to her until they stopped.

Norah was the one who'd sent Valerie on the errand into town. Some flimsy excuse about picking up a roll of film their father had left for developing. It was a blatant attempt to get her out of the hospital— not that Valerie minded. She was beginning to feel desperate for clean, fresh air and sunshine.

Although most of the orchards were miles out of town, she could have sworn that when she inhaled deeply she caught a whiff of the apple blossoms, which were just beginning to bud.

Spring had always been her favorite time of year. But although she'd been home intermittently over the years, she'd never spent more than a day or two and had never visited during April or May. She wondered now if she'd been unconsciously avoiding Orchard Valley then, knowing the charm and the appeal of her home would be at their strongest during those two months. Perhaps she'd feared she might never want to leave if she came while the white and pink blossoms perfumed the air.

Not wanting to examine her thoughts too closely, Valerie continued down the street, past the feed store and the local café until she arrived at her destination. Al's Pharmacy.

Al's was a typical small-town drugstore, where you could buy anything from cards and gifts to aspirin and strawberry jam. At one end of the pharmacy Al operated a state-run liquor store and in the opposite corner was a small post office. The soda fountain, which specialized in chocolate malts, was situated at the front. Valerie had lost count of the number of times she'd stopped in after school with her friends. She wondered if "going to Al's for a chocolate malt" remained as popular with teenagers these days as it had been when she was growing up. She suspected it did.

"Valerie Bloomfield," the aging pharmacist called to her from behind the counter. "I thought that was you. How's your dad doing?"

"The same."

"Norah phoned and said you were on your way. I put those snapshots aside for you and just wrote it up on the bill. You tell your dad I'm counting on him to go fishing with me come July, and I won't take no for an answer this year."

"I'll tell him," Valerie promised.

She collected the package and wandered outside. Curiosity got the better of her, though, and she paused on the sidewalk to open the envelope. Inside was an array of snapshots her father had taken earlier in the month.

Valerie's heart constricted at the number of photos he had of her mother's grave site. In each, a profusion of flowers adorned the headstone. There were a couple of shots of Norah, as well. The first showed her sitting in the chair by the fireplace, a plaid blanket tucked around her knees and an open book on her lap. The second picture was taken outside, probably in late March. The wind had whipped Norah's blond hair about her face, and she was laughing into the sun. In both photographs her resemblance to their mother was uncanny.

Grief and pity tugged at Valerie's heart as she imagined her father snapping those pictures. He was so lost and lonely without his Grace, and the photographs told her that in an unmistakable and poignant way.

Her thoughts oppressive, Valerie walked aimlessly for some minutes. When she saw that she was near the community park, she strolled in, past the swimming pool, now drained and empty, and followed the stone walkway that meandered through the manicured lawns. As she reached the children's playground, a gentle breeze caught the swings, rocking them back and forth.

Memories of her childhood flooded her mind, and

she sat in one of the old swings, almost wishing she were a little girl again. It would have been easy to close her eyes, pretending she was eight years old. She allowed herself a minute to remember Sunday afternoons spent in this very park, with David pushing her and a tiny Stephanie on these swings, catching them at the bottom of the slide. But she was twenty-eight now and her father, whom she adored, was fighting for each breath he drew in a hospital room.

She refused to even consider the thought of losing him. Was she being selfish and thoughtless? Valerie wondered. She didn't know. Her father was ready to die, ready to relinquish his life.

She dragged the toe of her shoe along the ground, slowing the swing to a halt. When the time came to let go of her father, Valerie prayed it would be with acceptance and strength. When death came to him, she wanted it to be as a friend, not an enemy with a score to settle. *But not yet. Please, not yet.*

As she drove back toward the hospital, past the strip malls that marked the highway, she caught sight of a recent addition. A movie theater, a six-plex. It astonished her that little Orchard Valley would have six movies all playing at once. The downtown theater she remembered so well from her teenage years still operated, but to a limited audience; according to Norah the features were second-run and often second-rate.

Orchard Valley had its share of national fast-food restaurants now, too, many of them situated along the highway. But as far as Valerie was concerned, hamburgers didn't get any better than those at The Burger Shack, a locally owned drive-in.

The summer she was sixteen, Valerie had worked there as a car hop, waiting on customers for minimum wage, thinking she was the luckiest girl in town to have landed such a wonderful job. How times had changed! How much *she'd* changed.

As she neared the hospital, Valerie felt a reluctance take hold of her heart. For nearly a week now, she'd virtually lived on the CCU floor with only brief visits home to shower and change clothes. It had been a strange week, outside ordinary time somehow. Nearly four years ago, when her mother was dying, she'd experienced something similar. But then her father and both her sisters had been there to share it. Now there were only two—she and Norah. And Colby...

She pulled into the parking lot and found a vacant spot, then walked toward the main entrance, sorry to leave the sunshine.

The minute she entered the lobby, Norah sprang up from the sofa she'd been sitting on. "I didn't think you'd ever get back," she said breathlessly. "What took you so long?"

"I stopped off at the park. What's the matter?"

"Steffie called from Rome. She's flying home by way of Tokyo. I know it sounds crazy, but it was the most direct flight she could catch. She's hoping to arrive sometime tomorrow night. She wasn't sure exactly when, but she said she'd let us know as soon as possible.''

"How'd she make it to Rome?"

"I asked her the same thing, but she didn't have time to explain. I told Dad she'd probably be here by tomorrow night.''

Valerie felt herself relax. Until now, she hadn't realized just how tense she'd been over Steffie's situation.

"Colby wants to see you,'' Norah informed her next.

"Did he say why?"

Norah shook her head, frowning a little. "You two didn't have an argument, did you?"

"No. What makes you ask?"

Norah shrugged vaguely. "Just the way he looked when he asked for you.''

"Looked?"

"Oh, I don't know,'' Norah said, clearly regretting that she'd said anything. "It was like he was eager to see you, but then relieved when I told him you'd gone into town. I know that sounds absurd, but I can't think of any better way of describing it.''

"I'll catch him later.'' For some reason, Valerie wasn't quite ready to see him yet.

"I'm sure he'll stop by this evening.''

"How's Dad doing?'' Valerie asked as they headed for the elevator.

"Not so good. His breathing is more labored and the swelling in his extremities isn't any better. That's not a good sign. Colby's doing everything he can to drain his lungs, but nothing seems to work. In the meantime, Dad's growing weaker every hour.''

"He misses Mom even more than we realized,'' Valerie whispered, thinking about the snapshots she'd picked up at Al's Pharmacy. She wondered how often he'd visited their mother's grave without anyone's knowing. How often he turned to speak to the woman he'd spent a lifetime with, remembering too late that she was gone.

"What will we do if anything happens to Dad?'' Norah asked quietly.

A few days earlier, Valerie would have rejected that possibility, adamantly claiming their father wasn't going to die. She'd stubbornly refused to consider it. She wasn't nearly as unyielding now.

"I don't know,'' she admitted, "but we'll manage. We'll have to.''

They were seated in the waiting room when Colby arrived. Valerie glanced up from a business publication she was reading and knew instantly that something was wrong. Terribly wrong. His eyes, dark and troubled, held hers for several seconds. Without being consciously aware of it, she stood, the magazine slipping unnoticed to the floor.

"Colby?'' His name became an urgent plea. "What's happened?''

He sat down on the sofa and reached for Valerie's hands, gripping them tightly with his own. His gaze slid from her to Norah. "Your father's suffered a second heart attack.''

"No,'' Norah breathed.

"And?" Valerie's own heart felt as though it were in danger of failing just then. It pounded wildly, sending bursts of fear through her body.

"We can't delay the surgery any longer."

Norah was on her feet, tears streaking her face. "You can't do the surgery now! His chances of survival are practically nil. We both know that."

"He doesn't have *any* chance if we don't." Although he was speaking to Norah, it was Valerie's gaze he held, Valerie's eyes he looked into—as if to say he'd do anything to have spared her this.

Five

Colby had been with her father in the operating room almost six hours, but to Valerie, it felt like six years.

While she waited, she recalled the happy times with her father and, especially as she grew into adolescence, the not-so-happy ones. Her will had clashed often with his, and they'd engaged in one verbal battle after another. Valerie had found her father stubborn, high-handed and irrational.

Her mother had repeatedly assured Valerie the reason she didn't get along with her father was that the two of them were so much alike. At the time Valerie had considered her mother's remark an insult. Furthermore, it made no sense. If they were alike, then they should be friends instead of adversaries.

It wasn't until her mother became ill that Valerie grew close to her father. In their concern and love for Grace, they'd set aside their own differences; not a cross word had passed between them since.

Valerie couldn't say which of them had changed, but she figured they'd both made progress. All she knew was that she loved her father with a fierceness that left her terrified whenever she thought about losing him.

The passage of time lost all meaning as she paced, back and forth, across the waiting room floor. It wasn't the waiting room she was so familiar with, since Surgery was on the hospital's ground level; a small brick patio, bordered with a waist-high hedge, opened off glass doors. Every now and again, Valerie or Norah would wander outside to breathe in the cool night air, to savor the peace and tranquility of the night.

Somehow word got out about her father's crisis. Pastor Wallen from the Community Church stopped by and prayed with Valerie and Norah. Charles Tomaselli was there for an hour, as well. Al Russell from the pharmacy and several other friends came, too.

At midnight, an exhausted Norah had curled up on the sofa and fallen into a troubled sleep. Valerie envied her sister's ability to rest, but found no such respite for her own fears.

Pacing and sucking on hard candy to relieve her nerves were the only methods she had of dealing with the terrible tension. After her third roll of candy, she'd joked to Norah that she had fabulous lungs from not smoking, but her teeth were in danger of rotting from all the sugar.

Now she stood staring out the window at the bright moon-filled night. She turned suddenly when she heard a soft footfall behind her. Colby stood there, still wearing his surgical greens.

Valerie's eyes flew to his, but she could read nothing.

"He made it."

She nearly slumped to the floor with relief. Tears filled her eyes, but she promptly blinked them back. "Thank God," she whispered, raising both hands to cover her mouth.

"I nearly lost him once," Colby said hoarsely, shaking his head. How exhausted he looked, Valerie noted. "I didn't think there was anything more we could do. It seemed like a miracle when his heart restarted. In some ways, it was. Only so much of what happens on the operating table is in my hands."

"I'm sure it was a miracle," Valerie whispered, hardly able to speak. She walked to the sofa on unsteady legs and bent to wake Norah. Her sister woke instantly—her training as a nurse, no doubt—and Valerie told her, "Dad made it through the operation."

"The danger's not over yet," Colby cautioned. "Not by a long shot. I wish I could tell you otherwise, but I can't. If he survives the night—"

"But he survived the surgery," Norah said, her voice raised with expectant hope. "I didn't think that would be possible. Surely that was his biggest hurdle?"

"Yes," Colby agreed, "but his condition is extremely critical."

"I know," Norah answered, but a faint light began to glow in her eyes. From the little Norah had said, Valerie realized her sister hadn't expected their father to live through the ordeal. Now that he had, she was given the first glimmer of promise.

"I'll be back in a few minutes," Colby said, rubbing his eyes in an oddly vulnerable gesture. He must be running on pure adrenaline, Valerie thought. He'd been in surgery earlier in the day and he'd lost a patient; he'd feared he was about to lose another one. He still could. He didn't need to say it aloud for Valerie to know.

Colby didn't expect her father to live until morning.

"I wish Steffie was here," Norah whispered after Colby had left.

Valerie also yearned for her missing sister. "I do, too."

Colby had been gone only a couple of minutes when a male nurse appeared. He knew Norah and greeted her warmly, then told them they could each see their father, but for only a moment.

Valerie went first. She'd assumed she was emotionally prepared, but the sight of her father destroyed any self-control she might have attained. Seeing him lying there so close to death affected her far more acutely than she'd anticipated.

Hurriedly she turned and left, feeling as though she could barely breathe. She walked past Norah and the others without a word. She stumbled onto the patio, hugging her arms around her middle, dragging in one deep breath after another in a futile effort to compose herself.

The tears, which she'd managed to resist all evening, broke through in a flood of fear and anger. It was *unfair*. It was so unfair. How could she lose her father so soon after her mother?

She didn't often give in to tears, but now they came as a release. Huge sobs shook her shoulders. Slowly, she lowered herself onto a concrete bench, then rocked back and forth as the hot, unstoppable tears continued to fall.

A hand at her back felt warm and gentle. "Go ahead and let it out," Colby whispered.

He sat beside her, his arm around her shoulders, and gradually drew her to him. She had no strength or will to resist. Nestling her face against his jacket, Valerie sobbed loudly, openly. Colby rubbed his cheek along her hair and whispered indistinguishable, soothing words. His arms were strong and safe, and she desperately needed him and he was there.

When there were no more tears left to shed, a deep shudder racked her body. She straightened and used her sleeve to wipe her damp face.

"Feel better?" Colby asked softly, his hand brushing the hair away from her temple.

Valerie nodded, embarrassed now that he'd found her like this. "Norah?"

"She's talking to Mark Collins. One of the nurses who assisted me in surgery."

"I...thought I was prepared...didn't know I'd fall apart like this."

"You've been under a lot of strain."

"We all have." She edged away from him, and

taking the cue, he dropped her arm. She offered him a trembling smile, her gaze avoiding his.

"I'd give anything to be able to assure you your father's going to make it through this," he said, his voice heavy. "But I can't do that, Val."

"I know." Spontaneously, as though he'd silently willed it, she raised her eyes to his. His hands grasped her shoulders, tightening as he urged her closer. His eyes seemed to darken as his mouth made a slow descent toward hers, stopping a mere fraction from her lips.

Valerie closed her eyes, and his warm breath caressed her face. She inhaled the pungent scent of surgical soap and something else, something that was ineffably him.

"We shouldn't be doing this," he whispered.

It certainly wasn't what she'd expected him to say. "I...know," she agreed, but she was beyond listening to common sense. She needed Colby. His warmth, his comfort, his touch. And she wouldn't be denied.

"Please," she whispered.

The driving force of his kiss parted her lips, and Valerie was instantly caught in a whirlwind of sensation. Her hands reached for him, sliding up his solid chest, her fingers locking at the base of his neck.

He moaned, and she did, too. There was no resistance in Valerie, none. Willingly she surrendered herself to his kiss, to his need and her own.

With what seemed like reluctance, he broke away

and slipped his mouth from hers, burning a path down her neck to the hollow of her throat.

She felt instantly cold when he lifted his face. Opening her eyes, she glanced toward the waiting room, grateful to see that it was empty. They were alone in the shadows of the hedge, but a few seconds earlier it wouldn't have mattered if they'd been standing in the middle of the bustling emergency room.

"I shouldn't have let that happen. We both—"

Valerie placed her finger over his lips, silencing him. "Don't say it. Please." Her hands cupped his face and she gazed into his eyes, dark now with desire. "I need you. Right or wrong, I need you. Just hold me."

A faint quiver went through her as he brought her back into his arms. Closing her eyes again, Valerie surrendered to the strength and safety she felt in the circle of his embrace.

He kissed her forehead lightly. His breath was uneven, and she found pleasure in knowing that he was no less affected by their encounter than she was.

As she'd already told him, Valerie didn't want to question the right or wrong of it now. Neither of them was in any real danger of falling in love. Colby had already explained the reasons a relationship was unfeasible for them. And she agreed with him. But their calm, rational words didn't take into account what she was experiencing now. This excitement, this weightless sense of release and longing. She didn't want it to end. Apparently Colby didn't, either, because he made no move to let her go.

"You shouldn't feel so good in my arms," he told her gently.

"I'm sorry." But she wasn't, not really. Soon they'd both regret these moments, but she'd save all the remorse for another time.

While she was in Colby's embrace, she didn't have to think about what the future might hold. She didn't have to worry about facing the world without anyone to guide and support her. For the first time since she'd come home to Orchard Valley, Valerie didn't feel inadequate or alone.

True, Norah was with her and Steffie was due to arrive any time. The three of them had each other, yet Valerie couldn't quite escape the old roles; she was the one they'd always depended on for encouragement, guidance, a sense of strength. Only Valerie didn't feel strong. She felt shaken, knocked off balance. She felt completely helpless...

"Norah's looking for you," Colby whispered close to her ear.

Valerie sighed and grudgingly broke away from him. She glanced into the waiting room and noticed her younger sister. Norah's gaze found her at the same moment. She didn't do a good job of concealing her surprise.

Valerie stood and turned to Colby. "Thank you."

He remained sitting on the concrete bench and sent her a smile full of private meaning.

Norah met her at the door, her eyes shifting from Valerie to Colby. "Is everything all right?"

Valerie nodded. "Dad's doing as well as we can expect."

"I didn't mean Dad. I meant with you."

"Of course," Valerie answered, forcing a light, casual tone. "I...just needed a good cry, and Colby lent me his shoulder."

Norah slipped her arm around Valerie's waist. "His shoulder, you say?" she asked, with more than a hint of a smile in her soft voice. "It looked like more than that to me."

"Dad's been asleep for nearly twenty hours." Valerie voiced her concern to Norah, who was far more knowledgeable about what was and wasn't usual following this kind of surgery. "Isn't that too long? I realize the anesthesia has a lot to do with it, but I can't help worrying."

"He's been awake for brief periods off and on today," Norah assured her. "He's doing very well, all things considered."

Her father wasn't Valerie's only concern. It was now after nine in the evening, and she'd been waiting since morning for some word from Steffie, who was supposed to be arriving sometime that day. But no one had heard from her, and Valerie couldn't help feeling anxious.

"Dad tried to talk the last time I was with him," Norah told her.

"What did he say?"

She shrugged. "It didn't make any sense. He looked up at me and blinked, then grinned as if he'd heard the funniest joke in years and said 'six kids.'"

"Six kids?"

"I don't get it, either," Norah continued. "I'm going to ask Colby about it when I see him, but we keep missing each other."

Valerie sat down and thumbed through the frayed pages of a two-year-old women's magazine. It was a summer issue dedicated to homes and gardens, which only went to prove how desperate she was for reading material that would take her mind off her fears.

She glanced at photographs of bright glossy kitchens and "country" bedrooms, wicker-furnished porches and "southwest-themed" living rooms—all of them attractive, none of them quite real. None of them *home*.

And she knew with sudden certainty that home was here. Here in Orchard Valley, in the upstairs bedroom at the end of the hallway. Home was curling up with a good book by the fireplace in her father's den, and it was eating meals around the big oak table in the dining room her mother had loved.

That was home. She *lived* in her Texas condo in an executive neighborhood. She'd had a decorator choose the color scheme and select the furniture since she didn't have the time for either task. A housekeeper came in twice a week to clean. The condo was a place to sleep. An address where she could pick up her mail. But it wasn't a place of memories and it wasn't home.

She read an article in the same magazine about herb gardens. Gardening had always been her mother's hobby, but every now and then Valerie had helped her weed. The times they'd shared working in the garden were among the fondest memories she had of her mother.

Perhaps in an attempt to recapture some of that simple happiness, Valerie had bought several large plants. But the housekeeper was the one who watered and fertilized them, since Valerie traveled so much.

Neither a home, at least not like the one she'd been raised in, nor a garden seemed to be in her future. Colby had recognized that from the beginning. Just as well, although it hadn't warded off the magnetic attraction between them.

Valerie's mind wandered to their exchange the night before. Their kissing was undoubtedly a mistake, but it was understandable, and certainly forgivable. Both were emotionally drained, their resistance to each other almost nonexistent. Yet Valerie couldn't bring herself to regret the time she'd spent in Colby's arms.

It hurt a bit that he was avoiding her, because it told her he didn't share her feelings. In those moments with Colby, Valerie had experienced something extraordinary. She'd always considered romantic love a highly overrated commodity. Dr. Colby Winston was the first man who'd given her reason to reevaluate that opinion.

Just when she was beginning to think he planned never to seek her out again, Colby surprised her. Norah had gone to talk with the nurse who'd been assigned to care for their father, and Valerie sat alone in the SICU waiting room, shuffling through her thoughts. Colby was on her mind just then—not that he was ever far from her musings.

She happened to glance up as he walked in. He was wearing a dark gray suit; she didn't think she'd ever seen a handsomer man.

Their eyes met and held. "Hello," she said, with a breathless quality to her voice. Over the course of her career, Valerie had made presentations before large audiences. Her voice was strong and carried well, yet when it came to Colby she felt like a first-grader asked to stand before the class and confess a wrong.

"Valerie." He paused and cleared his throat, then began again, sounding stilted and formal. "I've tied up matters here and I'm addressing a seminar this evening at the university. However, I have time for a bite to eat before I leave. Would you join me?"

"I'd be happy to," she answered automatically.

"I thought we might eat someplace other than the cafeteria." His voice was more relaxed now. "There's an Italian restaurant near here that serves excellent food."

"Great." Valerie brightened until she realized he hadn't chosen the restaurant because he had a craving for spaghetti. He wanted to talk to her somewhere away from the hospital. Somewhere he could be assured none of his peers would be listening.

After leaving word for Norah, they left the hospital in his car, a late-model maroon sedan. Sitting beside him, watching his strong, well-shaped hands on the steering wheel, gave Valerie a sense of intimacy, a feeling of familiarity.

The restaurant was elegantly decorated in black and silver. The lighting, low and discreet, created a welcoming impression.

"You didn't need to pay for my dinner to apologize, you know," Valerie said, reading over her menu. She quickly decided on a bowl of minestrone soup and fettuccine with fresh asparagus. No wine, because it would send her to sleep.

"Apologize?" Colby repeated.

Valerie lowered her menu, and crossing her arms, leaned toward him. "Not apologize exactly. You brought me here to tell me you regret what happened last night, didn't you? I mean, it's fairly obvious, since you've been avoiding me all day. But don't worry about it," she said off-handedly, "I understand."

He scowled and set aside his menu. "I sometimes forget how direct you can be."

"I'd rather everything was in the open between us. There's no need to concern yourself with what happened. I—needed you, and you were there for me."

His scowl intensified. "In other words, any man would have suited your purposes?"

"No," she said, surprised he'd ask. "Only you. What we shared was very...sweet. I'll always be grateful to you for letting me cry."

"It's not the crying that concerns me."

"The kissing was very special, too," she said softly.

"Yes, I suppose it was. But it might be best to put that, uh, particular part of last night out of our minds."

The waitress approached with pad and pen in hand. They each placed their orders, then Valerie resumed the conversation. "You're welcome to forget the kissing," she said in a mild tone, "but I don't think it'll be that easy for me."

Colby's gaze left hers. "Personally, I don't think I'll be able to forget it, either," he said.

They both fell silent but a faint smile curved her lips as she savored his words. He'd tried to dismiss the attraction between them and couldn't. Neither could she.

"It doesn't change anything," he told her, his voice calm and resolute.

He'd meant everything he'd said earlier; that much Valerie understood clearly now. She couldn't change who she was. Easy as it would be to fall in love with him, Valerie knew she'd never be truly happy as a homemaker. She had too much ambition, too many dreams. A business career was what she wanted, what she did best, and she couldn't relinquish that any more than Colby could give up his medical practice.

"Your father's doing remarkably well," Colby told her in an obvious attempt to change the subject.

Valerie was delighted. Norah had told her repeatedly what excellent progress their father was making, and it was thrilling to have it confirmed.

"I've got him listed as critical at the moment," Colby went on, "but I have a strong feeling that he's going to surprise us all and live to be a hundred."

Valerie beamed Colby a happy smile, hardly able to speak for the emotion clogging her throat. "We owe you so much, Colby."

He brushed off her words and seemed grateful that the waitress appeared just then to deliver their meal.

The soup was delicious, but after a few spoonfuls and only a taste of her fettuccine Valerie was finished, her appetite gone. Colby glanced over, frowning, when she pushed the plate aside.

"Is something wrong?"

She shook her head. "No."

"You barely touched your meal."

"I know."

"What's wrong?" he pressed.

Valerie lowered her eyes. "I was just trying to decide how I was going to leave you, Colby, and not cry." She hadn't meant to sound quite so serious; she'd meant to sound light and wryly amused.

Her words silenced him. His steady gaze met hers, and when he spoke, his voice revealed his sincerity. "You'd be very easy to love."

"But." She said the dreaded word for him.

"But we both know it wouldn't work."

"You're right," she said, convincingly enough. Only why wouldn't her heart listen?

"Valerie." Her father smiled weakly as she entered the cubicle in SICU. His hand reached for hers, brought it to his lips. "I wondered when I'd see you."

"I...went out for dinner."

"All by yourself?"

"No." But she didn't want to tell him she'd been with Colby.

Besides, there were other matters to discuss. Norah had met Valerie with the most unbelievable story. Apparently while Valerie was out for dinner, their father had told Norah about a vision he'd had. A vision? Valerie didn't know what to make of the story, any more than Norah did.

"What's all this Norah was telling me?" she asked gently.

Once again her father smiled, only this time it was brighter and a sparkle appeared in his tired eyes. "I died, you know. Ask Colby if you don't believe me."

Vaguely Valerie remembered Colby saying something about her father's heart stopping and restarting, and considering it a miracle. "I know we're very fortunate to have you with us."

"More fortunate than you realize. Now, I don't want you getting all excited the way your sister did, but then I don't expect you will. I had what those television reporters call a near-death experience."

"The long dark tunnel with the light at the end?"

Valerie had heard about the phenomenon herself and knew that Norah probably had, as well.

"Nope," he said, shaking his head. "I was in a garden."

"The Garden of Eden?" Valerie asked lightly.

"Might have been. I couldn't say."

He hadn't realized she was joking. "I didn't notice the trees so much, but there might have been an apple. What I did notice was the pretty woman tending the roses."

"Mom?" Valerie breathed the question, hardly knowing where it came from.

David smiled and shut his eyes. "We had a good, long talk, your mother and I. She convinced me it wasn't my time to die, that there was still plenty for me to do on this good earth. I wasn't pleased to hear it because I've been thinking for some time now that I'd rather be with her."

"Daddy, I don't think—"

"Shush now, because I have lots to tell you and I'm getting weaker by the minute."

"All right."

"Your mother loves you and is very proud of everything you've accomplished, but she told me to tell you to take time to enjoy life before it passes you by."

That sounded like something her mother would say.

"She also told me I was an old fool to try and match you up with Colby."

"But—" She snapped her mouth closed, unwilling to say more.

"Grace feels my pushing the two of you to marry was a ridiculous thing to do. Said I should apologize for that."

Valerie remained silent.

"There was more," David continued, "lots more. Grace wanted to be sure she gave me plenty of reasons to come back to this world."

"I'm very glad she succeeded in convincing you."

Her father's eyes drifted shut, but he opened them again with apparent effort. "She talked to me about Stephanie and Norah, too."

"Good, Daddy," she said softly, patting his hand. "You can tell me all about it next time."

"Want to explain now..."

"Shh, sleep."

"You're all going to marry. Your mother assured me all three of you would."

"Of course we will. Eventually."

"Soon. Very...soon."

"I'm glad," she whispered, although she wasn't sure he heard her.

So her father had gone through a near-death experience. Valerie didn't know how much credence to put into what he was saying. Marriage was the farthest thing from her mind at the moment. Obviously, marrying Colby was out of the question. And she'd lost interest in the idea of a relationship with Rowdy Cassidy.

"She gave me twelve reasons to live," her father announced sleepily. "Twelve very good reasons."

Valerie recalled that Norah had said something about the number six. She couldn't imagine why her father was speaking in figures all of a sudden.

"Twelve reasons," Valerie echoed, then leaned forward to kiss his cheek.

Her father's eyes fluttered open and he grinned boyishly. "Yup, my grandchildren. You, my darling Valerie, are going to give me three. All within the next few years."

Six

"When was the last time you spoke to your father?" Colby asked Valerie when she arrived at the hospital the following morning, carrying an armful of apple blossoms for the nurses' station. He seemed to be waiting for her, and none too patiently.

She sighed, realizing what must have happened. "I take it Dad told you about his experience in the Garden of Eden?"

"It was the Garden of Eden?"

"Figuratively, I suppose."

"So you know, then," Colby muttered. A hint of a frown flickered across his expression.

"Look at it this way—at least Dad's given up his matchmaking efforts." Valerie had assumed Colby would be happy about that, so his reaction puzzled her.

His scowl deepened. "He apologized for even making the suggestion."

"See, what'd I tell you?" Valerie said, her mouth quirking with a smile. "We're both in the clear."

Apparently, this wasn't what Colby wanted to hear, either. "He also claimed you'd be married before the end of the summer—and that you'd promptly present him with three grandchildren.''

"In the next few years. It looks like I'm going to be busy, doesn't it?'' Valerie hadn't take her father's announcement too seriously; he'd had some kind of pleasant hallucination, she supposed, and if it made him feel better, if it gave him a reason for living, then that was fine. She'd go along with it, though she wouldn't actively encourage him.

Besides, it was highly unlikely she'd marry anytime soon, and even if she did, she had no intention of leaping into this motherhood business. Marriage would be enough of an adjustment. She enjoyed children, and naturally assumed that if she married she'd eventually want a family, but certainly not in the first year or two following her marriage.

"Did he say *who* you're supposed to marry?''

"No. He wouldn't tell Norah, either, although he seemed to enjoy letting her know that she's going to give him six grandchildren. Three boys and three girls. You don't really believe any of this, do you?''

His mouth twisted into a wry grin. "That would be ridiculous, only... Never mind,'' he finished abruptly.

"No, tell me.''

He shrugged, clearly regretting that he'd said anything. "Another patient of mine, an older woman, had a near-death experience. It was all rather... strange.''

"She came back convinced she knew who her

children would marry and how many grandchildren she was going to have?'' Valerie asked sarcastically.

''No.'' Colby threw her an annoyed glance.

''What happened?'' She was curious now, unable to disguise her interest.

''She seemed to know certain things about the future. She—predicted, I guess is the word—certain political events. She wasn't entirely sure how she knew, she just did.''

''I'm not sure I understand.''

Colby clearly wasn't comfortable outlining the details of his patient's experience. ''She didn't have any more than an eighth-grade education, and she'd never had much interest in history or politics. But following the near-death phenomenon she was suddenly able to discuss complicated world problems with genuine insight and skill. She didn't understand it herself, and I certainly didn't have any medical explanation to offer her. The whole thing was as much a mystery to me as it was to her.''

Until then, Valerie had to admit, she'd found her father's experience somewhat…entertaining. She'd been willing to tolerate it, since whatever had happened had been very real to her father. This ''dreamtime'' with her mother had given his life a new purpose, and she was grateful for that, if nothing else.

''What are you saying?'' she asked Colby.

''I don't actually know.''

Suddenly none of this seemed quite as amusing. ''Dad insists I'll be married before the end of the summer.''

"He told me the same thing," Colby said. "Is it feasible? I mean, is there someone back in Texas you're seeing on a regular basis?" He gripped his hands behind his back and strolled slowly down the corridor. "Someone other than this person you were hoping to date soon?"

She puffed out her cheeks with air, debating how much to tell him about Rowdy Cassidy. "Not really, but..."

"Go on," he urged when she hesitated.

"My boss, Rowdy Cassidy." She shifted the spray of apple blossoms, conscious of their heady aroma in the antiseptic-smelling hospital corridor.

"The owner of CHIPS?"

Valerie nodded. "I've never actually gone out on a formal date with him, although until recently we saw each other nearly every day. We've traveled together, and frequently attend business dinners together. It wasn't until I arrived here and Dad started talking about you and me marrying that—I don't know, but Rowdy seems the natural choice for me. He's as dedicated to his career as I am and...we get along well."

"He's a wealthy man. Prominent in his field."

"Yes."

Colby's jaw clenched as though he disapproved. "Do you know something about Rowdy I don't?"

"I've never met the man. Everything I know about him I've read in the newspapers. But from all outward appearances, the two of you should be an ideal couple." His words were indifferent. Then without saying anything more, he turned and walked away from her.

"Colby," Valerie called, once she'd recovered from her initial surprise. She hurried after him. "What's wrong? You're acting like I've done something to offend you."

"I'm not angry," he said, his voice low. His gaze held hers with a disturbing intensity. "I remember what you said yesterday about wondering how we were going to say goodbye. I was just thinking the same thing. I don't know how I'm going to be able to stand by and watch you marry another man."

To her the solution was simple. He could marry her himself. But they'd both already decided that wouldn't work.

"What about you?" she asked, needing to know. "Is there someone special you've been seeing?"

"Yes."

Her heart felt as if it had done a nosedive, colliding with her stomach. Her face must have revealed her shock because he elaborated.

"Sherry Waterman. I thought Norah might have mentioned her."

"A nurse?"

Colby nodded. "She has her nursing degree and she's also trained as a midwife. That's what she's been doing for the past five years. She's good with children and she enjoys weaving and gardening." His voice was brisk and matter-of-fact as he listed Sherry's qualifications.

"She...sounds exactly right for you." The aching

admission was torn from her throat. Although it was painful to think of Colby with another woman, Valerie knew he'd chosen well in Sherry Waterman. Domestic, talented, perfect in all the ways Valerie wasn't.

"We've been dating for the last year."

"A year," Valerie repeated slowly, surprised he hadn't swept Sherry off her feet long before now. "You shouldn't keep her waiting then."

"I keep telling myself the same thing."

His words hurt, although Valerie pretended otherwise. "I'm delighted for you, Colby."

"Rowdy Cassidy will make you a good husband." His eyes, dark and intense, probed hers.

Valerie smiled and nodded, then they both turned and walked in opposite directions. And although she was tempted, she didn't look back.

"Valerie, it's Rowdy. Thought I'd check and see how everything's going with your father. No one's heard from you in a while."

When had she last reported into CHIPS headquarters? Two days before, she decided. Two whole days! Valerie found that hard to believe. Until recently, her job had been the most important thing in her life, but it wasn't that way now. She'd completely overlooked her responsibilities, forgotten everything that had once been so important. It seemed impossible that she could have allowed so much time to slip past.

"My father had open-heart surgery."

"I understand. How's he doing now?"

"Fabulously well. His recovery in the last twenty-four hours has been remarkable." She didn't tell him that much of the improvement was a result of a change in attitude. Since his "conversation in the garden" with Grace, David Bloomfield's will to live was stronger than ever. If there was something to worry about now, it was the fact that Steffie hadn't arrived yet and no one had heard a word from her. Valerie had spent part of the morning calling the airlines to find out which flight she was on, but to no avail.

"We miss you around here," Rowdy said in that casual way of his. Valerie could picture him sitting in his office, leaning back in his plush leather chair, cowboy boots propped on the mahogany desk. She couldn't remember ever seeing Rowdy without his boots and hat. She always thought of him as the Texan of frontier legend, the man who tackled life with robust energy, who considered no problem insurmountable. He worked hard, played hard and lived hard.

"I miss CHIPS, too."

"Any idea when you'll be back?"

"I'm sorry, no, but if you need me because of the Old West Bank deal—"

"No, no," Rowdy said, breaking in. "We're handling that from our end, so don't you worry about a thing. I just wanted you to know I missed you."

The personal pronoun didn't escape Valerie's notice. Rowdy *was* attracted to her. "My father wanted me to thank you for the flowers," she said. "Th-they got here yesterday morning." She'd hardly noticed at the time, although the nurses had all exclaimed over the lavish bouquets. Now, she felt flustered and nervous with him, something that had never happened before. Their relationship was moving into new territory, and Valerie found the ground unstable and a bit frightening.

"Actually the flowers were for you. I thought you needed something to brighten up your day."

"It was very thoughtful of you."

"It's the least I could do for my favorite executive. You hurry back, you hear?"

"I will. And, Rowdy, thanks for calling." She replaced the phone, and let her breath escape in a deep sigh.

Norah was already in the waiting room when Valerie returned there. "That was Rowdy Cassidy," she explained unnecessarily.

"Are you in love with him?" Norah asked without preamble. "I thought you and Dr. Winston might be hitting it off, but..." She let the rest fade.

"Colby's already involved with Sherry Waterman." Valerie kept her voice steady, making a strenuous effort to feign disinterest.

One glance at Norah told her she hadn't succeeded. "You'll notice I never bothered to mention Sherry. There's a reason."

"Oh?" Valerie shrugged. "I wondered...I mean, even Colby seemed to think you had, or rather that you should have." She'd wanted to ask her sister earlier, but had hesitated, almost preferring not to know.

"Those two have been dating for almost a year. If Colby was serious about Sherry he would have asked her to marry him before now. Even Sherry's given up on them, although Colby doesn't seem to have figured that out yet. The last thing I heard, she was seeing someone else. Not that I blame her," Norah was quick to add. "It must be the most frustrating thing in the world to be crazy about a guy and have him lukewarm toward you."

"I'm sure it must be."

"You still haven't answered me," Norah pressed. "What about Rowdy? Are you in love with him?"

Valerie shrugged again, uncomfortable with the subject of her boss, unsure of her own feelings toward him. "Yes and no."

"You're beginning to sound like Colby. I think he loves everything Sherry represents. She's a nurturing, kind-hearted woman. She fits the image of what Colby wants in a wife."

"Then what's stopping him?"

Norah gnawed on her lower lip for several moments. "My guess is that she bores him. Don't get me wrong, Sherry's not a colorless kind of person. Actually when I think about it, Sherry and I are a lot alike. She's a homebody like me, and little things mean a lot to her. She doesn't need an active social life or fancy clothes. Given the choice between a stay-at-home date with a rented movie or dining in a world-class restaurant, she'd opt for the movie."

"I see."

"You're much better suited to Colby."

"Me?" Valerie asked, her voice rising in astonishment. Hadn't Norah just finished describing the kind of woman Colby wanted—a woman completely unlike Valerie?

"I've seen the looks the two of you exchange," Norah continued, looking thoughtful. "I'm not blind, you know. I feel the electricity whenever I'm with you. It's mutual and it's hot."

"Really," Valerie said, becoming preoccupied with the crease in her wool slacks.

"Yes, really!"

"Yes, well, we've decided differently. We're attracted to each other, but nothing's going to come of it." She glanced at her watch, wanting an excuse to leave. "I'm going to stop in and see Dad."

Norah's smile seemed all-knowing. "Okay."

David Bloomfield's color was better, and he grinned happily when he saw his eldest daughter.

"Hello, Dad," she said in a cheerful voice as she bent over to kiss his cheek.

"Valerie," he whispered, holding out his hand to her. "Listen, sweetheart, you're spending too much time here at the hospital. Take the day and get out in the sunshine. You're beginning to look pale."

"But..."

"It'll do you good. No more sleeping on some dilapidated couch here at the hospital, either."

She'd slept in her own bed in her own room for the first time the night before. In the morning, she'd been amazed at how well rested she felt. And she'd indulged in a long, hot shower, followed by a good breakfast—cooked by Norah, needless to say.

The crews were just beginning to spray the apple trees and she'd heard the familiar sounds of men busy working in the orchards. It brought back memories of years past, of racing down the long, even rows, and climbing onto the low limbs of the trees, sitting there like a princess surveying her magical kingdom. Orchard Valley *was* magical, a town set apart in time.

For Valerie, coming home was like escaping to the past. The people were friendly, the neighbors neighborly, and problems were shared. It was a little piece of heaven.

"I wasn't at the hospital last night," she told him, pulling herself from her musings. She loved Orchard Valley more than any place on earth, but she'd never be content living here. There wasn't enough challenge, enough to tax her mind. No, Texas was her future and she accepted that with only one regret. Colby.

"So I heard," her father answered. "I saw Colby earlier."

Valerie watched his expression, hoping for—what?—some sign, some indication of her father's thoughts. And of Colby's... There was none.

"Well? What did the good doctor have to say?"

"Nothing much."

"Did he mention me?" she couldn't prevent herself from asking.

"Nope, I can't say he did. Does that disappoint you?"

"Of course not."

"Is there any reason he should mention you to me?"

Valerie was sorry she'd brought up the subject. "Not that I know of."

Her answers seemed to make him smile. "So you like my doctor?"

"He's been wonderful to you," Valerie agreed.

"I wasn't talking about me," David answered gruffly. "I'm referring to you. You're attracted to him, aren't you, Valerie? You never were much good at disguising your feelings."

"I've never met a man who appeals to me more," Valerie said truthfully. There was no point in trying to deceive her father. He knew her all too well, and he understood her better than anyone, sometimes better than she understood herself.

"He feels the same way?" The question was gentle, as though he were speaking to a child.

Valerie lowered her eyes before shaking her head. "It'd never work, and we both know it."

She expected an argument from her father, was even looking for one. She wanted him to tell her she was wrong, that love could work when two people were committed to each other. That it wouldn't matter how dissimilar they were, how differently they viewed life. That nothing mattered but the love they shared...

Her father, however, said nothing.

Discouraged, Valerie said a quick goodbye and returned to the waiting room. On her way, she noticed that Norah sat talking to another doctor at the end of the hallway. She was grateful her sister had left, because she needed time alone to think.

If she was looking for evidence that people with very different personalities could fall in love and make the relationship work, she need look no further than her own parents. The story of how they'd met and fallen in love was like a fairy tale, one that, as a child, she'd never tired of hearing.

Her father had fought in the Korean War. Afterward, he'd gone to university on the G.I. Bill and obtained his degree in business administration. Armed with his dreams, he'd built a financial empire and became a millionaire within a matter of years. Then he'd collapsed with rheumatic fever, nearly losing his life. It was while he was in the hospital recuperating that he'd met a young nurse. David knew the moment he met Grace Johnson that he was going to love her. It never occurred to him that she would refuse his marriage proposal.

It took him several months of relentless pursuit to convince Grace to marry him. Despite the fact that she was deeply in love with David, Grace had been afraid. She was a preacher's daughter who'd lived a simple life. David was a business tycoon who'd taken automation technology to new industry heights. Grace's fears about a marriage to David Bloomfield were well warranted. But over the years, love had proven even the most hardened skeptics wrong, and the two had lived and loved together until her mother's death a few years before.

Her own romance wasn't going to have a fairy-tale ending, the way her parents' had. Her father knew it, too, otherwise he would have been the first to encourage her.

Her father, however, had said nothing.

Valerie was working in the den, putting her CHIPS files in order, when she saw the red car hurtle down the driveway. She thought, for one hopeful moment, that it might be Colby, but then remembered he drove a maroon Buick. Still, she hastened to answer the door.

It was Charles Tomaselli, looking tired and frustrated.

"Have you heard anything from Stephanie?" he demanded without so much as a greeting.

Her sister's absence had been weighing on Valerie's mind, too. She'd done everything she could think of; she'd even placed a call to the American Embassy in Rome, with no results.

"I haven't heard a word. I don't know what could have happened to her."

"How late is she?"

Valerie had to think for a moment. In the past week, she'd lost all track of time. "Norah was the last person to speak to Steffie," she explained. "Let me see—that was just before Dad's surgery. Steffie thought she'd be home within twenty-four hours."

"That was forty-eight hours ago."

He didn't need to remind her, Valerie thought irritably. "She's coming by way of Tokyo."

"Tokyo? She's heading for Oregon by way of *Japan?*" Charles snapped.

"I don't believe she had much choice."

"Don't you think you should be making some inquiries?" he asked gruffly.

"I already have. Tell me who else I should call and I'll be happy to do so."

Charles settled down on the top porch step, resting both elbows on his knees. "I don't mind telling you, Valerie, I'm worried. She should have been here before now."

"I know."

"I have some friends, some connections," Charles said absently, "and I've checked with them. But they can't find any trace of her on the scheduled flights out of Rome. If she hasn't arrived by tomorrow afternoon, I don't think you have any alternative but to contact the authorities."

Valerie swallowed tightly, then nodded. She could just slap Steffie silly for putting them through all this worry.

"She's okay, Charles," Valerie said after a moment.

"What makes you so sure?" He turned to look up at her.

"I...don't know, I just am."

Charles stood agilely, his gaze leveled on the long narrow driveway that led in from the road. "I hope you're right, Valerie. I hope you're right."

* * *

Norah came back from the hospital a half hour later, talkative and lively. "I can't get over how much Dad's improved in such a short time."

Valerie took the shrimp salad she'd prepared for their dinner from the refrigerator. Salads were her specialty. That, and folding napkins. She could do both without a hitch.

For the first time since her arrival, Valerie had spent most of the day away from the hospital. When her father had suggested she leave, she'd initially felt a bit piqued. But as she revisited the life that had once been hers in this quiet community, she accepted the wisdom of his words. She *had* needed to get out, to breathe in the serenity she found in Orchard Valley and exhale the fear that had choked her from the moment she'd received Norah's frantic message. Then, after her walk, she'd come back to the house, and because she'd never been idle in her life, she'd set up a communications center in her father's den.

"I'm going back to work, starting tomorrow," Norah announced between bites of lettuce, shrimp and slices of hard-boiled egg. "The hospital's understaffed, but then when isn't it? I'll still be able to see Dad, maybe even more often than before. You don't mind, do you?"

"Of course I don't mind. You do whatever you think best."

"You're not going to leave, are you?" Norah asked, rushing the words together. "I wouldn't do this if the hospital didn't need me so badly."

"I realize that."

Norah sampled another forkful of salad. "You're quiet tonight. Is anything wrong?"

"Not really." She didn't want to worry Norah about Steffie's disappearance.

"Colby asked about you."

She felt her stomach churn with contradictory emotions. Part of her was thrilled that he'd even mentioned her, yet she experienced a growing sense of apprehension, too.

"He wanted to know where you were."

"Did you tell him?"

"Of course," Norah answered blithely. "He said he thought it was a good idea for you to get out of the hospital more. You've practically been living there ever since you arrived." She slowly chewed another bite of her salad. "He asked me what I knew about Rowdy Cassidy," she said casually.

Valerie put down her fork, her appetite having fled. "What did you tell him?"

"The truth. That I've never met the man, but Dad seems to think he's wonderful. You probably weren't aware of this, but Dad's been following CHIPS ever since you started working there. He thinks Rowdy's a genius. Funny, though—I got the impression that wasn't what Colby wanted to hear."

"The shrimp was on sale at Vern's Market," Valerie said, changing the subject abruptly, not wanting to talk about Colby. Not now when she felt so vulnerable, so conscious of the attraction between them. "Vern said he cooked it himself this morning."

"You don't want to talk about Colby?"

Valerie grinned. Her sister hadn't graduated magna cum laude for nothing.

"You're not going any place tonight, are you?" Norah asked next.

"I thought I'd drive in to the hospital and visit Dad, but other than that, no. What did you have in mind? Do you need me to do something?"

Norah shrugged. "I may be wrong, but I think Colby wanted to talk to you. I have a feeling he might call."

Norah was right.

When Valerie returned from her trip to the hospital, her sister had left a note taped to her bedroom door.

COLBY PHONED. SAID HE'D TALK TO YOU IN THE MORNING.

Valerie read the message with mixed feelings. Thrill and dread went at it for round two, again evenly matched. She determined to forget everything—love, Colby, the future—for tonight. The morning would be soon enough to resume her worries. She craved the forgetfulness of sleep, the escape from thought and feeling.

Valerie had assumed she'd fall asleep with the same ease she had the previous night. For a solid hour she beat her pillow, tossed and turned in an effort to find a comfortable position. Finally giving up, she reached for the light on the bed stand and read until her eyes drifted shut and the business journal slipped from her fingers.

But Valerie's exhausted sleep wasn't the restful

oblivion she'd longed for. Colby wandered into her mind like an uninvited guest.

He looked devilishly handsome, dressed in the suit he'd worn the night he'd taken her to the Italian restaurant.

"You're not going to be able to forget me, are you?"

In her dream, Valerie said nothing, but only because she had no argument. She merely stared at him, adoring every feature, every movement.

A noise disturbed her, distracting her from Colby. Irritated, she looked over her shoulder to see what it was and when she looked back, he was gone. She cried out in frustration, the sound of her own voice jerking her awake. She was sitting upright in the bed, heart pounding furiously.

It took her another moment to realize there was some sort of commotion going on downstairs. She climbed out of bed and grabbed her robe.

From the top of the stairs, she saw Norah, laughing and crying at once. A battered-looking suitcase stood on the floor, along with a leather coat and an umbrella.

"Steffie!" Valerie cried excitedly, racing down the stairs.

Her sister was home.

Seven

Colby checked the clipboard at the foot of David Bloomfield's bed and scanned the notations the nursing staff had written through the night. Although his gaze was lowered, he couldn't help being aware of David Bloomfield's cocky grin.

"You must be feeling more like your old self this morning," he observed genially.

David's smile widened. "I'm feeling more chipper each and every day. How much longer do you intend to keep me prisoner? I'm itching to get home."

"Another week," Colby answered, replacing the clipboard. "Perhaps less, depending on how well you do."

"A week!" David protested. "Are you sure you aren't holding me up just so you'll have an excuse to visit with Valerie twice a day?"

Colby's hackles rose, and he was about to defend his medical judgment when he realized the old man was baiting him—and enjoying it.

"I'm going to have you transferred out of the Surgical Intensive Care Unit this morning," Colby continued, "but first I want you up and walking."

"I've been up."

Colby glanced back at the chart, surprised to see no indication of the activity.

"I just didn't let anyone know. I felt a bit dizzy, so I only walked around the bed. Not much of a trip, but it tired me out plenty."

"You're not to get out of this bed again unless there's someone with you, understand?" He used his sternnest voice.

"All right, all right," David agreed. Stroking his chin, he studied Colby. "She's pretty as a picture, that oldest daughter of mine. Isn't she, Doc?"

Colby ignored both the comment and the question. "I'll have one of the nursing staff down in a few minutes and we'll see how well you do with the exercise. I imagine by the end of the day you'll have conquered the hallway."

"From what I hear, that Rowdy Cassidy's been calling her two, three times a day."

Colby stiffened at the mention of the other's man name. He'd tried to tell himself that Valerie would be happier married to Cassidy. They shared the same attitudes, beliefs and ambitions; together they'd take the business world by storm. Rowdy was exactly the type of dynamic personality who'd help Valerie fulfill her goals and dreams. She'd never be content as a physician's wife. He knew it. And she knew it. Nevertheless Colby was having trouble accepting the obvious.

He'd never thought of himself as romantic. His career had consumed his life from the time he was a high-school sophomore. His much-loved grandfather had died of heart disease, and it was then that Colby had decided to become a doctor. Everything else in his life had been subordinated to that goal. Only in the past year or so had he felt the desire to marry and start a family.

He'd acted upon that desire with methodical thoroughness, mentally tabulating a list of his wants and needs. He'd looked around at the single women in Orchard Valley and decided to date Sherry Waterman. If things didn't work out with Sherry, Norah Bloomfield was next on his list, although he was a bit concerned about their age difference.

Things *had* worked out with Sherry, at least in the beginning. He'd found her refreshing and genuine and fun. Problems crept up later, when he realized she was entirely predictable. Involved with a woman who embodied every trait he wanted in his life's partner, he'd been...bored. He wasn't sure anymore that he needed someone quite so even-tempered and domestic.

According to the schedule he'd set for himself, he should have been married by now.

He wasn't.

To irritate him further, the only woman he'd found himself strongly attracted to in the past year was Valerie Bloomfield, and anyone with a lick of sense could see they weren't the least bit compatible.

For months, long before his heart attack, David Bloomfield had found excuses to drag his eldest daughter's name into their conversations. By the time he met Valerie, Colby was thoroughly sick of hearing about her. He hadn't even expected to *like* her. Instead, his heart and his head had been spinning out of control from that first moment.

It was time to put an end to such nonsense, before either of them took this attraction business too seriously.

"Cassidy would be a good match for a woman like Valerie," he said as offhandedly as he could. The last thing he wanted was for Valerie's father to know how attracted he was to her, though he suspected David already knew. The old man seemed to have a sixth sense about such matters.

"Rowdy will, at that," David returned matter-of-factly. "I should know, too." The cocky grin was back in place.

Colby's chest tightened, his anger brewing just beneath the surface. David hadn't mentioned his dream lately, the one he'd termed his near-death experience. But from bits and pieces of conversation, Colby had learned that David was still predicting Valerie's wedding. It made sense that the man he expected her to marry was Rowdy Cassidy.

All the better, damn it. He—

"Stephanie's home," David continued conversationally, cutting into Colby's thoughts. "I saw her briefly this morning. What a lovely sight she was to these tired eyes."

Colby nodded, finding it difficult to dispel the image of Valerie married to her employer. Well, he'd better get used to the idea, because it was likely to happen soon. And because he refused to deliberately ruin his life by marrying the wrong woman.

He'd call Sherry this afternoon, Colby decided with renewed determination, and ask her out to dinner. One thing was certain; he intended to steer clear of Valerie Bloomfield, no matter how hard that was.

So much for the best laid plans, Colby mused as he left the Surgical Intensive Care Unit. Valerie was standing in the corridor waiting for him. As always, when he first saw her, his heart gladdened. An old-fashioned expression, perhaps, but he didn't know how else to describe what came over him when he was with Valerie.

He remembered the time he'd sought her out after losing Joanna Murphy. Just being with her had taken the sharp edge off the pain of that unexpected death, had helped him deal with the frustration, the sense of powerlessness. When she'd suggested coffee, his first inclination had been to refuse, but he'd found he couldn't. Sharing his concerns with her had, in some indefinable way, comforted him.

It seemed to him that their conversation had helped her, too, in coming to terms with her father's illness.

They'd helped each other. In thinking about those moments together, Colby understood why he couldn't simply dismiss his fascination with her as sexual attraction. That was part of it, all right. But more than any woman he'd ever known, Valerie Bloomfield was his equal. In intelligence, in emotional strength, in commitment to those she loved.

Every time Colby had been with her since, he experienced an elation, a small joy that left him feeling bewildered. Left him wanting to be with her more and more. Yet he knew he couldn't afford to pursue a relationship that had no chance of lasting.

"You wanted to see me?" Valerie asked, her gaze meeting his expectantly.

He frowned and shook his head. "No."

"Norah left a note for me last night, saying you'd phoned."

"Oh, that. It was nothing." He wanted to kick himself for that phone call now. He'd been looking for a reason to talk to her. His day had been long and tiring, and his defenses down, so he'd made up an excuse to hear the sound of her voice.

"I just wanted to tell you I'm transferring your father from SICU this morning," he went on quickly. "His progress has been nothing short of remarkable. If it continues like this, he'll be out of the hospital inside a week."

Valerie's eyes sparkled with relief. "That's wonderful news! It seems everything's happening at once. I don't know if you heard, but Steffie got home last night."

"So I understand." Colby watched her closely. Although she said nothing more, he realized that something was troubling Valerie. Her brow had furrowed, ever so briefly, when she mentioned her sister's name. Colby was convinced she wasn't aware of the tiny, telltale action.

"Something happened with your sister?"

Her eyes widened in surprise. "Yes, just now. She

was sitting in the waiting room reading a copy of the *Clarion* when she leaped to her feet, demanding to know if I'd read it. Before I could say anything, she left, taking the newspaper with her. I can't remember ever seeing Steffie so angry. I'm not sure what got into her, but I'm guessing it has something to do with Charles Tomaselli.''

"I'm sure she'll tell you eventually.''

"I'm sure she will, too, though I have a sneaking suspicion this is connected to a news article he wrote with Dad's help. I just don't understand what she found so offensive. Those two can't seem to get along. They never could. It's always surprised me, because she seemed to be so keen on him.''

The temptation to linger, even to suggest they have coffee together, was strong, but Colby resisted. He was doing a lot of that where Valerie was concerned. Resisting. He only hoped his willpower held firm until she went back to Texas—and to Cassidy—where she belonged.

"Valerie,'' Steffie said, standing in the doorway outside Valerie's bedroom. "Have you got a moment?''

"Sure.'' Valerie was sitting up in bed reading, but her mind wasn't on the latest computer technology she'd had every intention of studying. With infuriating frequency, her thoughts drifted away from superresolution monitors and narrowed in on Colby. She welcomed her sister's visit, not least as a distraction.

Steffie crossed the room and sat on the edge of Valerie's bed. "I made a complete fool of myself this morning," she admitted, her eyes downcast.

Valerie waited for her to explain, but further details didn't seem to be forthcoming. Her curiosity was aroused, but she didn't want to pry.

"With Charles," Steffie finally said, drawing her knees up and circling them with her arms. "It isn't the first time, either. He's the one person in the world I swore I never wanted to speak to again and the first few hours I'm home, I make a complete idiot of myself over him."

Valerie set aside her business journal and drew up her own knees. "He's been worried about you."

"You've talked to him? When? What did he say?" Steffie's head came up. Her long dark hair fell to the middle of her back, and her eyes, so dark and earnest, probed Valerie's. Although Steff was twenty-four, she looked closer to sixteen. Especially now, when she felt so embarrassed and unsure.

"I haven't talked to him recently. Charles asked about you shortly after I got home, and later he was concerned because you didn't arrive when we expected you. Apparently he made some inquiries, trying to track you down. Both Norah and I were so caught up in what was happening with Dad that we weren't as concerned about your late appearance as we should have been. Charles, however, seemed terribly anxious."

"He was just hoping I'd get home in time to make an idiot of myself, which I did."

Valerie thought that was unfair of Steffie. "Charles has been wonderful," she protested.

"To you and Norah. I'm the one he can't get along with." Steffie's shoulders rose as she gave a deep, heartfelt sigh. "How do you know when you're in love, really in love?" she asked plaintively.

Their mother should be the one answering that question. Not Valerie. She hadn't figured out her relationships with Colby *or* Rowdy. Bemused, she shook her head. She could outsmart the competition, bring down some of the biggest deals in the industry, but she didn't know how to tell if she was in love.

"I wish I could answer that myself," Valerie said quietly. "I know next to nothing about love. I was sort of hoping you'd be able to enlighten me."

Steffie frowned. "Don't tell me we're going to have to go to Norah about this."

"We can't," Valerie said, then started to laugh.

"What's so funny? Listen, Val, this isn't a time for humor, or pride, for that matter. If Norah knows more than we do, which she probably does, then we should forget she's the youngest and come right out and ask her."

"We can't ask Norah about love, because she isn't here," Valerie explained. "She's out on a date."

Steffie started to laugh, too, not because it was particularly funny, but because it was a rare moment of shared closeness between sisters.

"Reading between the lines of your letters, I assumed you'd fallen in love with your boss," she said next. "You never admitted it, but the two of you seemed to be spending a lot of time together."

"I think I might have been half in love with him until I met Colby."

"Dad's heart doctor?"

Valerie nodded. "When I first arrived home, Dad was fully expecting to die. He actually seemed to be looking forward to it, which annoyed everyone. Although not being able to get home must have been a nightmare for you, it might well be the one thing that kept him hanging on as long as he did."

"You're sidestepping the issue. Tell me about Colby."

"It started with Dad's matchmaking efforts, which I found rather amusing and Colby found utterly frustrating, but then as we got to know each other we realized there was a spark." More of a blowtorch than a spark, really, but she wasn't going to say so.

"If you're in love with Colby, then why do you look like you're going to cry?"

"Because we both know it wouldn't work. He's a small-town doctor, who occasionally lectures at Portland University. Although he could practice anywhere, he wants to stay right here in Orchard Valley."

"And you don't?"

"I don't think I could be happy here," Valerie said miserably. "Not anymore. And there are other problems, too..."

"But if you truly loved each other, you'd be able to find a solution to your differences."

"That's just it. I don't know if this *is* love, and I don't think Colby does, either. Everything would be so much easier if we did.

"I'm attracted to him. I think about him constantly, but is that enough for me to forsake all my ambitions? Give up my career? I don't know, Steffie, and it's got me tied up in knots. How do I decide? And if I *did* quit CHIPS and found some other job around here, how do I know I wouldn't resent him five years down the road? How do I know he wouldn't end up resenting me for not being a more traditional kind of woman—which is what he wants? Besides, even if I do love Colby, how can I be sure he feels the same way about me?"

"I wish Mom was here."

"So do I," Valerie said fervently. "Oh, Steffie, so do I."

Valerie didn't see Colby for several days. Four, to be exact. As her father's health improved, she spent less and less time at the hospital, therefore decreasing her chances of casually bumping into him. She was working out of the house, and that helped. Being in a familiar place, doing familiar tasks, alloyed her fears and tempered her frustrations.

She knew she should think about returning to Texas. The crisis had passed, and by remaining in Orchard Valley she was creating one of a different sort. CHIPS, Inc., needed her. Rowdy Cassidy needed her. She'd already missed one important business trip, and though Rowdy had encouraged her to stay in Orchard Valley as long as necessary, he'd also let her know he was looking forward to her return.

Valerie had almost run out of excuses to remain in Oregon. Her father was scheduled to be discharged in record time and Valerie, with her two sisters, planned a celebration dinner that included Colby.

She was surprised he'd accepted the invitation. Surprised and pleased. She was hungry for the sight of him. He was in her thoughts constantly, and she couldn't help wondering if it was the same for him.

All afternoon, she'd been feeling like a schoolgirl. Excited and nearly giddy at the prospect of her father's return—especially since Colby would be driving him back home.

Norah had been in the kitchen most of the afternoon. Since Valerie's culinary skills were limited to salad preparation and napkin folding, she'd been assigned both jobs, along with setting the table.

"What time is it?" Steffie called from the kitchen.

Valerie, who was carefully arranging their best china on the dining-room table, shot a glance toward the grandfather clock. "Five."

"They're due in less than thirty minutes."

"Do I detect a note of panic?" Valerie teased.

"Dinner isn't even close to being done," Steffie told her.

They'd chosen a menu that included none of their father's favorites. David Bloomfield was a meat-and-potatoes man, but that was all about to change. Colby had been very definite. From here on, David would be a low-cholesterol-and-high-fiber man.

"The dining-room table's set," Valerie informed the others. To the best of her memory, it was the first time they'd brought out the china since their mother's death. But their father's welcome-home dinner warranted using the very best.

Fifteen minutes later, Valerie glanced out the living-room window to see Colby's maroon car coming down the long driveway. "They're here!" she shouted, hurrying to the front porch, barely able to contain her excitement.

This moment seemed like a miracle to her. She'd come to accept that she was going to lose her father, and now he'd been given a second chance at life. Gratitude filled her heart. This was so much more than she'd dared hope.

Steffie and Norah joined her on the porch. Colby climbed out of the car first and came around to assist David. It was all Valerie could do not to rush down the steps and help him herself. Although her father had made phenomenal progress in the eight days since his surgery, he remained terribly pale and thinner than she'd ever seen him. But his eyes glowed with obvious pride and satisfaction as he looked on his three daughters.

He turned to Colby and said something Valerie couldn't hear. Whatever it was made Colby's eyes dart toward Valerie. She met his gaze, all too briefly, then they looked hurriedly away from each other, as though embarrassed to be caught staring.

"I'm afraid dinner's not quite ready," Norah said as Colby eased David into his recliner by the fireplace.

"I've been waiting two weeks for a decent meal," David grumbled. "Hospital food never did sit well with me. I hope you've outdone yourself."

"I have," Norah promised, smiling at Valerie. Their father wasn't expecting poached salmon and dill sauce with salad and rice, but he'd adjust to healthier eating habits soon enough.

"Can I get you anything, Dad?" Valerie asked, expecting him to request the evening paper or a cup of coffee.

"Walk down and see if the Howard boy is still in the orchard, would you, Val?"

"Of course, but I don't think you should be worried about the orchard now."

"I'm not worried. I just want to know what's been going on while I was laid up. I promise I'm not going to overdo it. Colby wouldn't let me. I tried to die three times, but he was right there making sure I didn't. Don't think I'd want to ruin all that effort now, do you?"

Valerie grinned. "All right, I'll check and see if the foreman's still around."

"Colby," David said, raising his index finger imperiously, "you go with her. I don't want her walking in the orchard alone."

The request was a shamefully blatant excuse to throw them together, but neither complained.

Colby followed her out the front door and down

the porch steps. "You don't need to come," she said, looking up at him. "I've been walking through these same orchards since I was a toddler. I won't get lost."

"I know that."

"Dad was just inventing a way for us to be alone."

"I know that, too. He told me what he intended when we arrived."

"But why?"

"Isn't it obvious?"

"Yes, but..." Her father had all but announced that he anticipated a prompt wedding between her and Rowdy Cassidy. He seemed downright delighted at the prospect, too, talking about her marriage as if it were a foregone conclusion.

"How have you been?" Colby asked. They strolled in the late-afternoon sunshine toward the west side of the orchard, where the equipment was kept. There was a small office in the storage building, as well, and if Dale Howard was still in the orchard that was the most likely place to find him.

"I've been fine. And you?" Valerie could tell him the truth about her feelings, or a half-truth. She chose the truth. "I've missed you."

Colby clasped his hands behind his back. It might have been wishful thinking on her part, but Valerie thought he did so in an effort to keep from touching her.

"I understand your boss is calling you every day," he said stiffly.

"I understand you took Sherry Waterman out to dinner this week," she returned.

"It didn't help any," he muttered. "The whole time we were together I kept thinking how I'd rather be with you. Is that what you were hoping to hear?"

Valerie dropped her gaze to the soft dirt beneath her feet. "No, but I'll admit I'm glad."

"This isn't going to work."

How rigid his words sounded, as though he was holding himself in check and finding it more and more difficult. "What isn't?"

"You—being here."

"Here? You didn't have to come with me. I've already explained that I'm perfectly capable of finding my way—"

"CHIPS stock went up two dollars a share last week."

Colby was leaping from one subject to the next. "That's wonderful," she said cautiously. "I'm sure Rowdy's thrilled."

"You should be, too."

"As a stockholder myself, I am, but what has that got to do with anything?"

"Houston is where you belong, with Rowdy Cassidy and all his millions."

Rowdy had been telling her the same thing. Not in quite the same words, but he wanted her in Texas. With him. Not a day passed that he didn't let her know how much he missed her. Rowdy wasn't a romantic kind of man; fancy words weren't his forte. He was as straightforward as Valerie herself. He

missed her, he said, missed the time they spent together and the discussions they'd shared. He hadn't
realized how much until she'd left.

"When are you going back?" Colby demanded.

Valerie realized this was the whole purpose of
their being alone together. This was the reason he'd
fallen in with her father's schemes and had walked
in the orchard with her. He wanted her out of Orchard Valley and out of his life.

"Soon," she promised and her voice cracked with
pain. Damn, but it hurt. The intensity of it took her
by surprise; embarrassed, she increased her pace to
a half trot, wanting to escape.

"Valerie." His voice came from behind her.

"No, please, I understand…you're right. I'll—"
She wasn't allowed to finish her thought. Colby
caught her by the upper arm and turned her to face
him, bringing her into his warm embrace.

He drew her wrists up and placed them around his
neck as though she were a rag doll, then circled her
waist with his arms and brought her tight against
him. Before she had a chance to catch her breath, his
mouth was on hers.

Valerie felt as though she'd drown in the sheer
ecstasy of being in his arms again. It wasn't supposed
to be like this. It wasn't supposed to feel so right, so
good. His mouth was hungry and eager and she
opened to him as naturally as a flower to the sun.

She clung to him, and then he suddenly jerked his
head away. Valerie pressed her face into his shoulder
and shuddered. She might have been able to forget

him, forget these feelings, if he hadn't kissed her again, if he hadn't taken her into his arms.

"Valerie, can't you see what's happening?"

She nodded. "I'm falling in love with you."

"We can't allow this to continue."

"But—"

"Are you willing to risk everything we've both worked all our lives to achieve? Are you going to change, or do you expect me to? The fact is, you know damn well that *neither* of us wants to give anything up. So we've got to put an end to this. Because, Valerie, we have nothing in common."

Offhand, Valerie could think of several things they had in common, but she didn't mention them. There was no point. She understood what Colby was saying. If they continued as they were, in each other's arms, it would lead to the inevitable, and they'd be so deeply in love that they'd forget what was keeping them apart. They'd choose to forget that Valerie had a wonderful career waiting for her back in Houston. They'd choose to forget that Colby wanted a woman who'd be a dedicated homemaker. They'd overlook even the most obvious differences. For a while, their love would be enough, but that wouldn't last, not for long. Not long enough.

"It's time to go back," Colby said, releasing her completely.

"Dad won't be worried."

"I'm not talking about your father. I'm talking about you, Valerie. Go back to Texas," he said, his dark eyes holding hers, "before it's too late." He turned and walked away from her then. It was the second time he'd pleaded with her to leave, and this time it hurt even more than it had the first.

Eight

"Colby's taken Sherry Waterman out three nights in a row," Norah said casually over a cup of coffee early Saturday morning. "They've gone out every night since Dad's been home." She nibbled her toast, but her gaze just managed to avoid Valerie's, as though she felt guilty about relaying the information.

"I take it there's a reason you want me to know this."

"Yes," Norah murmured. "Sherry was at the hospital, and we had a chance to talk. She says she can't understand why Colby keeps asking her out. The spark just isn't there. They enjoy each other's company, but they're never going to be more than friends. It almost seems as if Colby wants to make it into something it's not."

"Perhaps Sherry's reading more into the situation than there is." Valerie didn't actually believe that, but she felt compelled to suggest it. She knew exactly what Colby was doing—escaping her, fighting everything he felt for her.

"Sherry realizes Colby's in love with someone else, and she also knows he's fighting it." Norah's words were an eerie echo of her own thoughts. "It's you, isn't it, Val? Colby's in love with you."

"I can't speak for him," Valerie insisted, munching furiously on her toast.

"Do you love him?"

She gave a tolerant shrug and answered the question with one of her own, always a good business move. "What do I know about love?"

"You know enough," Norah argued. "Please, do everyone a favor and put the poor guy out of his misery."

"How am I supposed to do that?" Valerie asked, genuinely curious. She was miserable, too, but no one seemed to take *that* into consideration. In other circumstances, she would have talked to Steffie, but her younger sister was having relationship problems of her own.

"For the love of heaven," Norah cried, "just marry him. He's crazy about you. Any fool can see that, and you're in love with him, too."

"Sometimes love isn't enough."

"Yes, it is," Norah argued.

Perhaps to Norah, who was young and idealistic, love would be enough, but there were too many complications Valerie couldn't afford to ignore in her relationship with Colby. Besides, he'd been pretty explicit about wanting her to leave.

"I think you should quit your job, move back home and marry Dr. Winston," Norah said decisively.

"And do what?" Valerie asked. "Take up politics? Learn to knit? If I was *really* lucky, I might find some job in town that was about a tenth as interesting as the job I have. Listen, I've been an active businesswoman for the last six years. Do you honestly think I'd be happy sitting at home knitting sweaters for the rest of my life?''

"You would be in time. It'll take a little adjusting, that's all."

"Oh, Norah." Valerie sighed and gave her starry-eyed sister a pitying smile. "You make everything sound so simple. It just isn't. Colby isn't exactly pining away for me, not if he's spending all that time with Sherry. If he wants me to stay, he'll ask."

"What if he doesn't? Are you willing to throw away a chance for happiness because you've got too much pride? You should tell him you're willing to stay, don't you think?" Norah returned heatedly. "Why does everything have to come from Colby?"

"It doesn't, believe me. But it's too late."

"What's too late?" their father asked from the kitchen doorway. He was dressed in his plaid housecoat, the belt cinched tightly at the waist. He ran a hand down his disheveled hair, looking as though he'd only recently awakened.

Norah automatically stood and guided him to a chair.

"What are you two arguing about?" he asked. "I could hear you all the way to the back bedroom."

Their father was sleeping downstairs because Colby didn't want him climbing stairs yet. Although he hadn't complained, Valerie knew her father was anxious to return to his own room.

"We weren't arguing, Dad," Valerie said, ignoring Norah's angry look.

"I heard you," David countered, smiling up at Norah as she brought him a cup of coffee. "It seems to me I heard Norah suggest you should marry Colby. It's the same thing I've been saying for weeks. So has everyone else who's got a nickel's worth of sense."

Valerie's throat seemed to close up on her. "He has to ask me first. And...and I thought you—Rowdy and I—"

"Phooey. Rowdy Cassidy's a good man, but he's not for you. That was just to get you—and that stubborn doctor—thinking. And as for Colby not asking you, ask him yourself."

"Dad..." The list of objections was too long to enumerate. The best thing to do was ignore the suggestion, Valerie decided.

"You've never been shy about going after what you want. I've always admired that about you. You love him, don't you? So ask him to marry you. You might be pleasantly surprised by what he says," Norah suggested.

"It wouldn't work," Valerie said sadly. "Colby's as traditional as they come. When he's found the woman he wants to marry, he'll propose himself."

Neither Norah nor her father offered a rebuttal, which suited Valerie. A few minutes later she left the kitchen and wandered up to her room to dress, but she didn't get far. Sitting on the end of her bed, she closed her eyes and tried to think. Was she being unnecessarily stubborn? Was Norah right? Was she allowing pride to stand in the way of happiness? Questions came at her from all directions, and she felt at a loss to answer them.

There seemed to be only one way of finding out what she needed to know and that meant confronting Colby. For years she'd been working at finding solutions in unlikely situations. It was her greatest strength in business, but when it came to her own life, she drew a blank. There had to be an answer that suited them both, but for now it escaped her.

She was obviously the last person Colby expected to see when he answered his front door. Valerie saw the astonishment in his eyes and felt encouraged. She'd hoped to catch him off guard and had succeeded.

"Hello, Colby," she said softly.

"Valerie...hello."

She'd dressed carefully, taking time to choose the perfect outfit for her purposes. Something that would remind him she was a woman—but not a pushover. She found the solution in a lovely soft pink sweater dress Steffie had brought with her from Italy.

"Would it be all right if I came in for a few moments?" she asked when he didn't immediately invite her inside.

"Of course. I didn't mean to be rude. I was writing."

"Writing?" She followed him into his living room and when he gestured toward the sofa, she sat there, hoping she appeared serene and cool. As though this was nothing more than a social call, when in fact the direction of her whole life rested on this meeting with Colby. She had too much experience in negotiating to allow her feelings to show, but she was more nervous about this visit than about any business deal she'd ever accomplished.

"I've been working on an article for the *American Journal of Medicine*," he elaborated. "The editor asked me six months ago if I'd be willing to contribute a piece and I'm only getting around to it now."

Valerie felt a surge of pride. Colby had a wonderful future ahead of him. The world would be a better place because of his dedication and caring. Their eyes held for several moments. Valerie wanted to tell him how much she admired him, how proud she was of him, but she couldn't. She didn't want anything she said now to sway his decision later.

"I have something to ask you," she said, standing abruptly. She glanced around, then slowly sat back down again.

"Yes?" His gaze fell to her hands and she realized she was rubbing her palms together. She instantly stopped, embarrassed by this small display of nervousness.

"The last time I saw you," she began in a voice that was more hesitant than she'd intended, "when we last talked, you asked me to leave Orchard Valley.''

''Yes,'' he admitted harshly.

''Why?''

''You know the answer to that as well as I do. Your father's recovery has amazed everyone. Eventually you're going back, so I can't see any reason to prolong this…interlude. Texas is where you belong.''

''In other words, if a man's going to hold me and kiss me, it should be Rowdy Cassidy.''

A brief flash of anger showed in his eyes, but was almost immediately quelled. ''That's exactly what I mean,'' he returned smoothly.

''I can't help asking myself something,'' she said, her voice growing smaller despite her best efforts. ''Is my leaving what you really want?''

''What do you mean?''

''I could stay in Orchard Valley.'' Her gaze clung to his, hopefully, eagerly. ''This is my home. It's where I was born and raised, where I attended school. Some of my friends still live here and I know just about everyone in town.'' The words were rushed, crowding one another.

Colby breathed in deeply and seemed to hold his breath. His hands tightened into fists. ''Why would you do that?''

Valerie had wondered how Colby would respond. She knew what she wanted him to say—that he longed for her to stay, that he needed her in his life.

Instead, he'd responded with a cruelly flippant question.

"Why would I stay?" she repeated slowly, her gaze never wavering from his. "Because, Colby, you're here."

Her words were met with a brief, tension-wrought silence as though her frankness had shocked him. He looked away.

"Are you saying you love me?" he demanded in a voice that suggested this wasn't what he wanted to hear.

"Yes." The lone word was husky with something close to regret. "All morning I've been wishing I'd dated more in high school and college, because then I'd know what to say. I've always been too... forward. I can't help it. It's just part of my nature."

Colby said nothing, which made her hurry to fill the silence.

"This is when you're supposed to admit you love me too," she prompted anxiously. "That is, if you do... I may not have been a Homecoming Queen, but I'm woman enough to know you care for me, Colby Winston. The least you can do is admit it and let me salvage what little pride I have left."

"Loving you has never been the problem."

"Thank you for that," she whispered.

"It isn't enough."

"But how do we know that? We haven't even tried. It seems to me no one would have gotten anywhere in this world if they'd decided to quit before even trying.''

"You make it so damn tempting."

"I do? I really do?" His words thrilled her. They gave her the first sign of encouragement since her arrival. "I was thinking…there are other companies around Oregon that I could work for…that would be glad to have me."

Colby stood and walked away from her. Not knowing what else to do, Valerie followed him.

"I think you should kiss me," she said hoarsely.

"Valerie." He turned as he said her name. He wasn't expecting her to be so close behind him because he nearly collided with her. His hands reached for her shoulders in an effort to steady her.

It was exactly what Valerie had hoped would happen. She moved automatically into his embrace, wrapping her arms around his middle, hugging him close. She raised her mouth expectantly to his and wasn't disappointed.

With a groan, Colby claimed her lips. His hands were in her hair as he tilted her head back and kissed her with a hunger that left her breathless and weak.

"Valerie…no." Reluctantly he eased away from her, bracing his hands against her shoulders.

"But why?" she pleaded.

Deftly Colby stepped back, putting as much distance between them as possible. "What's wrong with you?" he asked angrily.

"Wrong?" she repeated, still trapped in the excitement his kiss had aroused.

"Did you think coming here and seducing me would mean an offer of marriage? It's not very original, Valerie. I would have thought better of you."

"Seduce you?" Hot color instantly sprang into her cheeks. "I wasn't…I had no intention—"

"Well, that's the way it looked to me."

If he was trying to rile her, he was certainly doing an effective job. She forced herself to take several deep, calming breaths. "I didn't come here to seduce you, Colby, nor am I going to allow you to annoy me into an argument. Believe what you want. I came because I had to know. I had to find out for myself if there was a chance for us. If not, tell me so right now and I'll leave. I'll walk out that door and we'll both forget I was ever here."

He frowned, his expression fierce, but he didn't answer.

"Say it," she demanded. "Tell me you don't want me. Tell me to get out of your life and I'll go, Colby. I won't even look back."

She remained on the far side of the room, frozen in misery.

Still Colby said nothing. Nothing.

"You don't need to worry about any unpleasant scenes. I'll pack up my belongings, drive myself to the airport, and you'll never hear from me again." Her voice remained steady despite the hoarseness of pain.

He remained silent.

"Just say it," she cried. "Tell me to go…if that's what you want. But if you had an ounce of sense, you'd ask me to stay right here and marry you. You don't have any sense, though, do you? I know—because you're going to do what you think is the noble thing and send me away. Well, I won't make it easy for you, Colby, not this time. If you want me out of your life, you're going to have to say it."

"I might if I could get a word in edgewise."

Valerie choked on a sob and swallowed the laughter. "I love you! Doesn't that mean anything to you?"

His hands clenched into tight fists again, and his eyes, his beautiful eyes, didn't stray from her.

"Say it!" she shouted. "Tell me you don't want me. Better yet, tell me you're crazy in love with me and that you're willing to find a way to make everything right for us. Tell me that instead."

He closed his eyes.

"This is it, Colby. If I walk out that door, whatever was between us is over. I'll go about my business and you'll go about yours. I refuse to waste the rest of my life waiting for you." She dashed the tears from her cheeks with the back of her hand.

"You'll always be someone very special in my life." The words were so that she barely heard them.

"That's not good enough," she sobbed. "Tell me to get out of your life. Make it strong enough so I'll know you mean it, so I won't question it later. So *you* won't question it later."

"You don't belong here."

"That's better," she gulped. "But still not good enough. Haven't you ever heard of being cruel in order to be kind? Just make sure you mean what you say, because this is the only chance you'll have." Her voice broke. "You don't even have to promise to marry me. Just ask me to stay."

"No!" It was shouted at her, as though something had snapped inside him. "You want me to be cruel, is that what it takes? Does it need to come to this? You're an intelligent woman, or so I assumed, but this...this performance is ridiculous. I owe you nothing. You want me to tell you to go? Then go. You don't need my permission." He stormed to the other side of the room and held open the door for her. "Go back to Texas, Valerie. Marry your cowboy."

Stunned, she was afraid to move, afraid her legs would no longer support her. She nodded. Trembling, she moved past him.

"Goodbye," she whispered and then, unable to resist, brushed her fingertips down the side of his face. When she looked back to this moment, there would be no regrets. She'd offered him everything she had to give, and he was turning her away. There was nothing more she could do.

Colby glanced at his hands, the very hands he used to save lives, and saw they were trembling with the force of an emotion so strong that it was all he could do not to smash them into a concrete wall.

When Valerie had first left, he'd been furious. He would have preferred it if she'd packed her bags and quietly disappeared. That was what he'd envisioned.

Not this dreadful scene. Not dragging out their emotions like this.

He wanted to shake her for forcing him to send her away. But he was the one left trembling. It shouldn't have been so difficult. This wasn't a new decision, but one he'd made long before he'd ever kissed her, long before he'd held her in his arms and comforted her.

The phone rang and he reached for it, grateful for the reprieve from his thoughts. "Hello," he snapped, not meaning to sound so impatient.

"Colby, is this a bad time?"

"Sherry...of course not. I was just thinking..." He let the rest fade.

"I'm sorry, but I won't be able to make our dinner date tonight, after all."

How sweet she sounded, Colby mused. Sweet and gentle. Oh, Lord, why couldn't he feel for her the things he felt for Valerie Bloomfield? Heaven knew he'd tried in the past few days. He'd done whatever he could think of to spark their interest in each other, but to no avail.

"My Aunt Janice arrived and my parents thought it would be a good idea if I took her over to my brother's place," Sherry explained. "I hope this isn't inconvenient for you."

"No problem." He heard something else in her voice, a hesitancy, a disappointment, but he chose not to question it.

"Colby."

"Yes?" The irritation was back, but it wasn't

Sherry who'd angered him. It was his own lack of feeling for her. This past week, he'd spent four evenings with her. He'd held her and kissed her, and each time her kisses had left him cold and untouched.

"I don't mean to be tactless, but I don't think we should date each other anymore."

Her words shocked him. "Why not?" he demanded, although he knew the reasons and didn't blame her.

"It's not me you're interested in, it's Norah's sister. I like you, Colby, don't get me wrong, but this just isn't working. We've been seeing each other for over a year now, and if we were going to fall in love it would have happened before now."

"We haven't given it a real chance." Colby didn't understand why he was arguing with her when he was in full agreement. Sherry would make some man a wonderful wife. Some *other* man.

"You're using me, Colby."

He had nothing to say in his own defense. He hadn't realized until she'd said it, but Sherry was right. He *had* been using her. Not to make Valerie jealous, or in any devious, underhanded way, but in an effort to prove to himself that he could happily live the rest of his life without Valerie.

But the experiment had backfired. And now he was alone, wondering how he could have allowed the only woman he'd ever loved to walk out of his life.

"What's this I hear about you going back to Texas?" David Bloomfield asked when Valerie joined him on the front porch following the evening meal. She sat on the top step, her back pressed against the white column while her father rocked gently in his old chair. Her gaze wandered over the blooming apple orchard, the soft scent of pink and white blossoms perfuming the air. The setting sun cast a golden glow across the sky and over the land.

Valerie hadn't said anything at dinner about returning to Texas, and was surprised that her father was aware of her intention. She'd sat quietly in her place at the table, pushing the food around her plate and hoping no one would notice she wasn't eating.

"It's time for me to go back, Daddy."

"It hurts, doesn't it?" he asked, his voice tender.

"A little." *A lot,* her heart cried, but it was a cry she'd been ignoring from the moment she left Colby's home. "You're better now," she said with forced cheerfulness. "You don't need me around here any longer."

"Ah, but I do," her father countered smoothly, continuing to rock in his chair. "Colby needs you, too."

His name went through her like the blade of a sharp sword, and her breath caught at the unexpected pain. Her father was the reason she'd come home, but Colby was the reason she was leaving.

"Love is funny, isn't it?" she mused, wrapping her arms around her knees the way she had as a young girl.

"You and I are so much alike," her father said.

"Your mother saw it before I did, which I suppose is only natural. I'm proud of you, Valerie, proud of what you've managed to accomplish in so short a time, your professionalism. Cassidy's lucky to have you on his team, and he knows it, otherwise he wouldn't have promoted you."

"I've got a wonderful future with CHIPS." She said it to remind herself that her life did have purpose. There was somewhere to focus all her energy. Something that would help her forget, give her a reason to go on.

"Your mother's and my romance wasn't so easy, either, you know," her father continued, rocking slowly. "She was this pretty young nurse, and I was head over heels in love with her. To my mind, she was lucky to have me. Problem was, she didn't seem to think so. I was a millionaire. In the years since the war I'd amassed a fortune. But none of that impressed your mother." His smile was wryly nostalgic, his eyes gazing at a long ago world. "Convincing Grace to marry me was by far the most difficult task I'd faced in years."

"She didn't love you?" That seemed impossible for Valerie to comprehend.

"She loved me, all right, she just didn't think she'd make me the right kind of wife. I was wealthy, socially prominent, and your mother was a preacher's daughter. Before I contracted rheumatic fever I was one of the most sought-after bachelors in California, if I do say so myself. But I hadn't met the woman I wanted to marry until your mother became my nurse.''

How achingly familiar this sounded to Valerie. She'd been content with her own life until she met Colby. Falling in love was the last thing she'd expected when she returned home.

''There were other problems, too,'' David went on. ''Your mother seemed to think my work habits would kill me, and she wasn't willing to marry me only to watch me work myself to death.''

''But you solved everything.''

''Eventually.'' A wistful look stole over him. ''I loved your mother from the first moment I opened my eyes and saw her standing beside the hospital bed. I remember thinking she was an angel, and in some ways she was.'' His face shone with the strength of unending love. ''I knew if she'd ever agree to marry me, I was going to have to give up everything I'd worked so hard to achieve. That meant selling my business and finding something new to occupy my time.''

''You did it, though.''

''Not without a lot of deliberation. I'd already made more money than I knew how to spend, but I realized I wasn't going to be happy retiring before the age of forty. I had to have something to do. It took a couple of years—and Grace's help—to figure out what that should be.''

Valerie nodded. ''I feel the same way. I'd never be content just sitting at home— I'm too much like you.'' The extent of his sacrifice shook her. ''How could you have given up everything you'd worked all those years to build?''

''My life without your mother would have been empty. My work didn't matter anymore. Grace was important, and the life we were going to build together was important. I gave up one life, but gained another, one that I found far more fulfilling.''

''But didn't you ever get bored or restless?''

''Some, but not nearly as much as I expected. When we'd been married a year or two, your mother realized I had too much time on my hands and we looked around for something to occupy me, some interest. That was when we bought the orchard and moved here.'' He grinned. ''My own Garden of Eden.''

''I don't think I ever realized how much you'd altered your life to marry Mom.''

''It was a sacrifice, and at the time it seemed like a huge one, but as the years passed, I realized she'd been right. I would have killed myself had I continued in business. Your mother brought balance into my life, the same way Colby will bring balance into yours.''

She allowed a moment to pass before she spoke. ''I'm not marrying Colby, Dad. I wish I could tell you I was, and that we were going to seek the same happiness you found with Mom, but it isn't going to happen.''

It was as if she hadn't said a word. ''You're going to be so good for him, Valerie. He loves you now, and you love him, but what you feel for each other doesn't even begin to approach the love you'll experience over the years, especially after the children arrive.''

"Dad, you're not listening to me." He seemed to be in a dream world that shut out reality. She had to make him stop, had to pull him out of the fantasy.

"He needs you, too, you know, even more than you need him. Colby's lived alone too many years. It's only been recently that he's recognized how much he wants a woman in his life.''

"He doesn't want me."

Her father closed his eyes and smiled. "You don't honestly believe that, do you? He wants you so much it's eating him alive.''

She hadn't the strength to argue with her father, not after her confrontation with Colby earlier in the day. Nor did she have the energy to explain what had passed between them. In her mind, it was finished, over. She'd told him she wouldn't look back and she meant it. She'd swallowed her pride and gone to him and he'd cast her out of his life.

She didn't hate him for being cruel; she'd asked for that. Nor had she made it easy for him to reject her. But he'd done it.

David sipped his coffee, and his smile grew even more serene. "You have such happiness awaiting you, Valerie. This business with my heart is a good example of good coming out of bad. My attack was what brought you racing home. Heaven only knows how long it would have been before you met Colby if it weren't for this bum heart of mine.''

Valerie reached for her own mug of coffee and took a sip. "You want anything more before I head in?"

"So soon? It's not even dark."

"I have a lot to do."

"Are you going to think about what I said?"

She hated to disappoint him, hated to disillusion a romantic old man whose judgment was clouded by thirty years of loving one woman.

"I'll think about it," Valerie promised, but it was a lie. She fully intended to push every thought, every memory of Colby completely from her mind. It was the only way she'd be able to function. She got slowly to her feet.

"Good." He nodded, still smiling. "Stay with me, then. There's no need for you to hurry inside."

Valerie hesitated. This conversation was becoming decidedly uncomfortable. She didn't want to disillusion her father, but she had to face what had happened between her and Colby, accept it as truth and get on with her life. Pining away for him would solve nothing. And listening to her father only added to the pain.

"I need to do a few things before I leave." The excuse was weak, but it was all she could think to say.

"There's plenty of time. Sit with me a spell. Relax."

"Dad...please."

"I want to tell you something **important**."

"What is it, Dad?" she asked, her voice barely a whisper.

"I know for a fact that you're going to marry Colby," he said, smiling up at her, his eyes bright and clear. "Your mother promised me."

Nine

"Dad," Valerie said, suppressing the urge to argue with him. "If it's about your dream, I don't think—"

"It was more than a dream! I was dead. I told you—ask Colby if you don't believe me. I crossed over into the valley of shadows. Your mother was waiting for me there and she wasn't pleased. No, sir. She was downright irritated with me. Said it wasn't my time to die yet, and I was coming home much too early."

"I'm sure this seemed very real to you—"

"It *was* real." His voice was strong. "Now you sit down and listen, because what I'm about to tell you happened as surely as I live and breathe."

Trapped, Valerie did as her father asked, lowering herself to the top porch step. "All right, Dad, I'll listen."

"Good." He smiled briefly down at her, apparently appeased. "I've missed your mother, and I didn't want to continue living in this world without her. She told me my thinking was all wrong. She promised me the years I have left will be full and happy ones, with nothing like the loneliness I've endured since she's been gone.''

"Of course they will be.'' Valerie didn't put much stock in this near-death experience of her father's, but he believed it and that was the important thing.

"Problem was, I didn't much care about my life back here,'' he continued, almost as if he hadn't heard Valerie. "I was with Grace and that was where I wanted to be. As far as I was concerned I wasn't going back.''

Valerie was completely familiar with her father's stubbornness; she'd inherited a streak of it herself.

"Your mother told me there was a reason for me to return. To tell you the truth, I'd already decided I wasn't going to let her talk me into it. She was darn good at that, you know. She'd drag me into the most outlandish things and make me think it was all my idea.''

Her father was grinning as he spoke, his eyes twinkling with a rare joy.

"That was when she told me about you girls. Your mother and I were standing by a small lake.'' He frowned, apparently trying to remember each detail of his experience. "She asked me to look into the water. I thought it an unusual request, considering the seriousness of the discussion we were having.''

"What did you see?'' Valerie was thinking of trout and maybe some bass, knowing how much her father enjoyed lazing away a summer's afternoon fishing.

"I saw the future.''

"The future?'' This sounded like something out of a science-fiction novel.

"You heard me," he said irritably. "The water was like a window and I was able to look into years ahead. I saw you and your sisters, and you know what? It was the most beautiful scene I could ever have imagined. So much joy, so much laughter and love. I couldn't stop looking, couldn't stop smiling. There were my precious daughters, all so happy, all so blessed with love, the same way your mother and I had been."

"It sounds lovely, Dad." Her father had undergone traumatic surgery and just barely survived. If he believed in this dream, if he maintained he'd actually spoken to her mother, then Valerie couldn't bring herself to disillusion him with reality. Nor did she want to argue with him. Especially not now, when her own heart had taken such a beating.

"I remember every single moment of that meeting with your mother. You know, I didn't see a single angel. I don't mind telling you, that was a bit of a disappointment. Nor did I hear anyone playing the harp."

Valerie suppressed a smile.

"You understand what I'm saying, don't you?"

"About angels?"

"No," he returned impatiently. "About you and Colby. He's the one I saw you with, Val. You had three beautiful children."

"Dad, why now?" At his quizzical gaze, she elaborated. "Why are you trying so hard to convince me to marry Colby? After the surgery, you seemed to have given up the idea. What happened to change your mind?"

"You did."

"Me?"

"You're both so darned stubborn. I hadn't counted on that."

"But you apologized for the matchmaking, remember?"

"Of course I remember. I did give it up on Grace's advice, but only because I felt you two wouldn't need any help from me. But I quickly found out you need my help more than ever. That's why I talked about Cassidy so much. To get you thinking about what you really wanted. And to make Colby a little jealous. Face it, Val. Eventually you're going to marry him—there's no doubt of it."

"Dad, please, I know you want to believe this, but it just isn't going to happen." Without realizing what he was doing, her own father was making everything so much more painful.

"Don't you understand, child? Colby loves you, and you love him, and you're going to have a wonderful life together. Naturally there'll be ups and downs, but there are in any marriage."

"I'm not marrying Colby," she said between gritted teeth.

"You think I'm an old man whose elevator doesn't go all the way to the top, but you're wrong." He gave her a lazy smile. "I know what I saw. All I'm asking is that you be patient with Colby and patient with yourself. Just don't do anything foolish."

"Like what?"

"Returning to Texas. You belong here in Orchard Valley now. It's where you're going to raise your children and where Colby's going to continue his practice.''

"It's too late.''

"For what?''

Valerie stood, her chest aching with the effort to breathe normally. She felt so empty, so alone. More than anything, she wanted to believe her father's dream, but she couldn't. She just couldn't.

"I've already booked my flight. I leave in the morning.'' She didn't wait for her father to argue with her, to tell her what a terrible mistake she was making. Instead she hurried into the house and up the stairs, not stopping until she was inside her room, with the door firmly closed.

She hauled her suitcase from the closet. There wasn't much to pack, and the entire process took her all of five minutes. She didn't weep. Her tears had already been spent.

When she returned to Texas, she'd be more mindful of love. It had touched her life once; perhaps it would again. In time. When her heart had healed. When she was ready.

With that thought in mind, she reached for the phone on the nightstand and held it in her lap, staring sightlessly at the numbers. After an endless moment, she tapped out the long-distance number.

"Hello.'' The deep male voice sounded hurried and impatient.

"Hello, Rowdy,'' she said quietly.

"Valerie.'' He seemed delighted to be hearing from her. "I'm glad you phoned. I tried to reach you earlier in the day, but your sister told me you were out. I don't suppose she happened to mention my call?''

"No. Was it something important?" It could only have been Norah, since Steffie was out most of the day. Romantic Norah, who wanted so badly for Valerie to marry Colby and live happily ever after.

"It wasn't urgent. I just wanted to see how soon CHIPS could have you back. There's been a big hole here since you left."

"I realize my being gone has been an inconvenience—"

"Don't be silly. I wasn't referring to the workload, I was talking about *you.* Like I told you before, I sort of got used to having you around," he said gruffly, as though he was uncomfortable saying such things. "It doesn't seem right with you not here. You're an important part of my team. That's how come I'm giving you a ten percent raise—just so you'll know how much you're appreciated."

Valerie gasped. "That isn't necessary."

"Sure it is. Now, when are you flying home?"

Home. It wasn't in Texas, it never really had been, but Rowdy wouldn't understand that.

"Valerie?"

"Oh, sorry. That was actually the reason for my call. I've booked my flight for tomorrow morning. I'll arrive early in the evening and be at the office bright and early Monday morning." She forced some enthusiasm into her words.

"That's great news. It's just what I was hoping to hear. We'll celebrate. How about if I pick you up at the airport and take you to dinner?"

The invitation took her by surprise, although she

supposed it shouldn't have. "Ah..." She didn't know what to say. She'd already promised herself she wasn't going to pine away the rest of her life for Colby Winston. Yet when the opportunity arose to place the past firmly behind her and begin a new life, she hesitated.

"I don't think so," she told him regretfully. "Not just yet. I'm going to need some time to readjust after being away for so long." It had been less than three weeks, but it felt like a whole lifetime.

"You've been gone too long," Rowdy said, his voice low and resonant. "I've missed you, Valerie. I haven't made a secret of it, either. When you get back, I'd like it if the two of us could sit down and talk."

Sudden dread attacked her stomach, her nerves. This wasn't what she wanted to hear. "I—I don't know if that'd be a good idea, Rowdy. I don't mean to be—"

"I know what you're thinking," Rowdy cut in. "And I have to admit, I share your concern. An office romance can lead to problems. That's why I want us to talk. Clear the air before we get involved."

It didn't seem to occur to Rowdy that she might be unwilling to date him. But not so long ago, the prospect of a relationship with him would have filled her with excitement.

Rarely had Colby spent a more uncomfortable night. He hadn't been able to sleep and, finally giving up, had gone downstairs to read. Another hour ticked slowly by, and still his mind refused to relax. Feeling even more disgruntled, he set the novel aside.

It would have helped if Sherry had kept her dinner date, but she'd cancelled. Not only that, but she'd let him know she didn't want to see him again. She was right to have done it, too—a fact that didn't improve his disposition.

When it came to his relationships with women, Colby just wasn't getting anywhere. Okay, so he was behind schedule. He'd underestimated the difficulty in finding the type of wife he wanted. That was understandable.

His requirements were very specific, which was why he'd intended to conduct his search in a methodical, orderly manner. It wasn't as though he'd discovered any shortage of "old-fashioned" girls, either. It just so happened that most of them didn't appeal to him.

This realization only served to confuse him further. Obviously there was some kind of flaw in his plan. Of one thing he was certain—Sherry was out of the picture. For that matter, so was Valerie.

Valerie.

Her name burned his mind, and by sheer force of will, he turned his thoughts in another direction. He got up and moved into his den for the printout of the article he'd been working on earlier that day. Although he'd shrugged off the importance of this article when he spoke to Valerie, he was well aware that the invitation to submit it was a real honor. He'd done exhaustive research, and every word he'd written had been carefully considered.

But right then and there, Colby realized it meant nothing. Nothing. With an angry burst of energy, he crumpled the sheets and tossed them into his waste-basket.

Colby rarely acted in anger. Rarely did he allow himself to display any emotion. He'd schooled himself well; he'd needed to. He dealt with death so often, with fear, with grief. It became crucial, a matter of emotional survival, to keep his own feelings strictly private. Over the years, it had become second nature. For the first time in recent memory, he regretted his inexperience at expressing emotion.

He had no trouble recognizing that his inability to sleep, his lack of interest in a good novel, his discontent with the article he was writing, were all wrapped up in what had happened between him and Valerie that morning.

He'd done what he had to do. It hadn't been easy—for either of them—but it was necessary. She'd made him angry, he realized, with her demand that he be cruel. She wouldn't accept anything less. By the time she left, he'd been furious. She'd prodded and pushed and shoved until, backed into a corner, he'd had no choice.

Every harsh word he'd spoken had boomeranged back to hit him. She'd insisted repeatedly that he tell her to get out of his life. And he'd done it....

It was over, which was exactly what he wanted. Valerie would go back to Texas and he'd continue living here in Orchard Valley.

Her eyes would haunt him, he decided next, rubbing his face with a weary hand. They'd been gray and sad, and it had taken the better part of the afternoon to forget the feel of her fingertips as they grazed his face.

His intention had been to send her away, hurt her if he had to, so the break would be final. What took him by surprise was how much it had cost him.

Twenty hours later, and he was still angry. He still hurt.

Walking back into his living room, Colby sank into the recliner and reached for the television remote control. It was early morning; surely there'd be some movie playing that would hold his attention for an hour or two.

He was wrong. The only show he could find was a 1950s love story, filmed in nostalgic black and white. The last thing Colby was in the mood to watch was a sentimental romance with a happy ending. He turned off the television and stood up.

It had been three days since he'd been out to the Bloomfields'. Although David was home and they'd scheduled an appointment at the office early in the week, it wouldn't be a bad idea to stop in and see how the older man was recovering. They were friends, and it was the least Colby could do—for the sake of a longstanding friendship.

With that decision made, he found himself yawning loudly. Fatigue greeted him like an old comrade, and in that moment Colby knew he'd be able to sleep.

Valerie was dressed, her suitcase packed. She'd lingered in her room far longer than necessary. Her flight wasn't scheduled until 1:00 p.m.—not for another four hours—so she had plenty of time, yet she felt a burning need to be on her way. But there was another feeling that ran even deeper, even stronger: she dreaded leaving.

"Valerie?"

She turned to find Steffie standing in her bedroom doorway, frowning as her gaze fell on the suitcase. "Are you sure you're doing the right thing?"

Valerie gave her a wide and completely artificial smile. "I'm positive."

"How can you smile?"

"It's such a beautiful morning, how could I possibly be sad? Dad's home and thriving, you're here, and Norah's in seventh heaven because she's got someone to cook for."

Steffie grinned. "Yeah, I know. But I can't help feeling you shouldn't go."

"My life's in Texas now."

Steffie strolled into the room and sat on the end of the bed. "If you're running away, it's a mistake. I made the same one myself three years ago. I made an idiot of myself over Charles Tomaselli, and then because I was so embarrassed and because I couldn't bear to face him again, I decided to study in Europe."

"You had a wonderful opportunity to travel. Do you honestly regret it?"

"Yes. Oh, not the travel and the experience. But my leaving was wrong. I didn't realize it then, but I do now. I went into hiding. I know that sounds melodramatic, but it's the truth. At the time it seemed like the only thing to do, but I realize now I should have swallowed my pride instead of walking away from everything I loved."

"Sometimes we don't have any choice."

"And sometimes we do," Steffie countered softly. "Don't make the same mistake I did. Don't run away, because at some point down the road, you're going to regret it, just like I did."

Her sister's eyes were intent, silently pleading with Valerie to reconsider. If she hadn't gone to Colby the day before, Valerie might have hesitated, but there was no reason now for her to stay. There was no reason to hope Colby would change his mind.

"Someone's coming," Steffie said, wandering over to look out Valerie's bedroom window.

Valerie moved aside the white curtains and glanced outside. Steffie was right. A maroon car was making its way down the long driveway.

Colby.

A surge of excitement shot through her. He'd come to tell her he'd changed his mind, to ask her not to leave. Only seconds before, she'd been so certain there was no hope and now it flowed through her like current into an electrical wire. Try as she might, she couldn't squelch it.

"It—it's Colby," Valerie said, when she found her voice.

Steffie let out a cry of sheer joy. "I knew it. I knew he wasn't going to be able to let you go. It didn't make sense. Everyone knows the way he feels about you, the way you feel about him. He'd be a fool if he let you go back to Texas."

"He didn't know I was leaving this morning," Valerie said calmly, though he must have figured it out for himself. She wouldn't stay in Orchard Valley any longer than necessary, and they both recognized that.

"I'll find out what he wants," Steffie said, her voice high and excited. "Let's play this cool, okay? You stay up here and when he asks to see you, I'll casually come get you."

"Steffie..."

"Valerie, for heaven's sake, be romantic for once in your life."

"There could be plenty of other reasons Colby's here."

"Are you going to make him suffer, or are you going to forgive him right away? Personally, I think he should suffer...but only a little."

The doorbell chimed and Steffie hurried downstairs without another word.

Valerie couldn't keep her heart from racing, but she refused to play this silly game of wait-and-see. She reached for her suitcase and started resolutely down the stairs, the way she'd originally intended.

She was on the top step when she heard Colby ask to see her father. *Her father—not her.* If it hadn't hurt so much, Valerie would have laughed at Steffie, who looked completely stunned. Her sister stared at Colby, her mouth dangling open, hand frozen on the door, blocking his entrance.

"My father," Steffie repeated after a shocked moment. "You're here to see Dad?"

"He is my patient."

"I know, but..."

Some slight, telltale sound must have alerted Colby that Valerie was standing at the top of the stairs. His gaze rose and linked with hers before slowly lowering to the suitcase in her hand. Valerie detected a slight frown, as though he'd been caught by surprise.

"Valerie's leaving this morning," Steffie announced in a loud, urgent voice as though Colby had better do something fast.

What Steffie hadn't grasped was that Colby didn't intend to do anything—other than bid her a relieved farewell.

"You might want to tell Dad Dr. Winston's here," Valerie said mildly. "He's probably in the kitchen."

Steffie left, and Valerie gradually descended the stairs.

"Looks like you're packed up and ready to go," he said in a conversational tone.

She nodded. "My flight leaves at one."

"So soon?"

"Not soon enough, though, is it, Colby?"

He ignored the question, and Valerie regretted the pettiness that had prompted her to ask. He stood before her, his expression unreadable. She was grateful when her father appeared. Grateful because she wasn't nearly as expert at hiding her feelings as Colby. She feared he could read much more of her emotional turmoil than she wanted him to.

"Colby, my boy, it's good to see you. You've been making yourself scarce the last few days." David steered Colby into the kitchen, then glanced back at Valerie, scowling at the suitcase in her hand. "You've got plenty of time, Val. Come and have a cup of coffee before you leave."

For her father's sake, she resisted the temptation to argue. Shrugging, she set her luggage aside and dutifully followed Colby and David into the large family kitchen.

The two men sat at the table while Norah served them coffee. Valerie didn't sit with the others, but pulled out a stool in front of the counter and perched on that.

"I thought I'd check in and see how you were feeling," Colby was saying.

"Never felt better," her father replied.

Valerie noticed how Colby avoided glancing in her direction. He was uncomfortable with her; his back was stiff, his shoulders rigid with tension. Perhaps he'd expected her to have left by now.

Valerie sipped her coffee and briefly closed her eyes, wanting to savor these last few moments with her family. Norah, an apron tied around her waist, was busily pulling hot cinnamon rolls from the oven. Homemade ones, from the recipe their mother had used through the years. The scent of yeast and spice filled the kitchen, and it was like stepping back in time. Their kitchen had always been where everyone gathered, a place of warmth and laughter and confidences shared.

Steffie couldn't seem to stand still. She paced to one side of the room, then crossed to the other, as though debating her next course of action.

Valerie found it endearing that her sister cared so much about what happened between her and Colby, especially when Steffie's own romance continued to be so trying. Valerie sensed that things weren't going well between her sister and Charles Tomaselli, but she wasn't in any position to be offering advice.

Steffie paused, her eyes pleading with Valerie. She

seemed to be begging her to reconsider. To stay in Orchard Valley, to listen to her heart...

After a moment Valerie couldn't meet her sister's gaze and purposely looked away.

Conversation floated past her, but she wasn't aware of what was being said or who was saying it. The sudden need to leave was too strong to ignore. If she didn't do it soon, she might never be able to go. Slipping down from the stool, she deposited her mug, still half full of coffee, in the sink.

"The rolls will be ready to eat any moment," Norah said, looking at her anxiously. She, too, seemed to want Valerie to linger.

"Don't worry, I'll pick up something to eat at the airport later."

"Are you leaving?" her father asked, as if this was a surprise to him. "You've still got lots of time."

Valerie offered the first excuse that came to mind. "I've got to get the rental car back to the agency."

"You're *sure* you want to go?" Steffie asked forlornly, moving toward her sister.

"I'm sure," Valerie answered in a soft voice, giving Steffie an affectionate hug. "It isn't like I'll never be back, you know?"

"Don't let it take you three years, the way it did me," Steffie whispered close to Valerie's ear. "I just can't help thinking you're making a mistake."

"It's for the best," Valerie said.

Norah stood behind Steffie, waiting her turn to be hugged, her pretty blue eyes as sad as Steffie's. "I can't believe you're really going. It's been so good having you home."

"It's been fun, hasn't it, Dad?" Valerie said, trying to lighten the atmosphere. "I'd like to suggest another family reunion, only next time let's plan things a bit differently. If I'm going to take another three weeks away from CHIPS, I'd prefer to see more than a hospital waiting room."

David Bloomfield stood, his gaze holding Valerie's. He seemed to be asking her to remain a few minutes longer, but she firmly shook her head. Every moment was torture.

She dared not look in Colby's direction. That made it easier to pretend he wasn't there.

"I have a great idea for a family reunion," Steffie suggested eagerly. "Why don't we all take a trip to Egypt? I've always wanted to ride a camel and tour the pyramids."

"Egypt?" Norah echoed. "What's wrong with a camping trip? We used to do that years ago, and it was always fun. I can remember us sitting around the camp fire singing and toasting marshmallows."

"Camping!" Steffie cried. "You can't be serious. I remember mosquitoes the size of Alabama."

"But we had fun," Norah reminded them.

"Maybe you did, but count me out," Valerie said, laughing quickly. "My idea of roughing it is going without room service." She glanced from one sister to the other, loving them both so much that her heart felt it would burst. She stepped forward and threw her arms around her father's neck.

"Take care of yourself," she whispered.

"The dream," he returned, his eyes bright and intense. "I was so sure."

Valerie didn't need to be reminded of her father's

dream. "Maybe someday it'll happen." But she didn't believe it, any more than she believed the dead could come back to life.

"You're going to say goodbye to Colby, aren't you?" her father urged.

She'd been hoping to avoid it. But she recognized that it would be impossible to leave without saying something to Colby, who was her father's doctor, her father's guest. David released her and she saw that Colby was on his feet and moving toward her. It would have salvaged her pride just a little if he'd revealed at least a hint of regret. But from all outward appearances it was as if she was nothing more to him than a passing acquaintance. As if he'd never held her in his arms, never kissed her.

"Goodbye, Colby," she said as cheerfully as she could manage. "Thank you for everything you did for Dad—for all of us. You were…wonderful." She extended her hand, which he took in his own. His fingers tightened on hers, his grip almost painful.

"Goodbye, Valerie," he said after a moment. As before, it was impossible to read his expression. "Have a safe trip."

She nodded and turned away, afraid that if she didn't leave soon, she'd do something utterly stupid, like break down and weep.

Everyone followed her to the front porch. Eager to get away now, Valerie hurried down the stairs. Not bothering to open the trunk, she set her lone suitcase on the back seat.

"Phone once in a while, won't you?" Steffie called.

Valerie nodded. "Take care of Dad, you two."

"Bye, Val." Norah pressed her fingers to her lips.

Rather than endure another round of farewells, Valerie slid into the driver's seat and closed the door. She didn't look toward the porch for fear her eyes would meet Colby's.

Escaping was what mattered. Fleeing before she made a fool of herself a second time over a man who didn't want her.

She started the car, raised her hand in a brisk wave and pulled away. The tightness in her chest was so painful it was almost unbearable. For a moment she didn't know if she'd be able to continue. The thought that she needed a doctor was what dispersed the horrible pain. It escaped on a bubble of hysterical laughter.

She needed a doctor, all right, *a heart doctor*. With the sound of her amusement still echoing in her ears, Valerie looked back one last time, her gaze seeking out Colby's.

It cost her everything, but she managed a slow smile, a smile of gratitude for what they'd shared.

She drove away then, and she didn't glance back. Not even once.

Ten

For long minutes, no one said a word. Colby remained frozen on the Bloomfield porch, his gaze following Valerie's rental car as it sped down the driveway. His hands knotted into tight fists at his sides, and his chest throbbed with suppressed emotion.

The timing of this visit couldn't have been worse. He'd had no idea Valerie was leaving that morning, and like a fool he'd stumbled upon the scene. He cursed himself now for not calling first.

He didn't know what he'd been thinking when he'd decided to come here. Visiting David had been an excuse. He'd come to see Valerie. He'd hoped, perhaps, to find a free moment to talk to her. But for the life of him, he didn't know what he'd intended to say. He certainly hadn't changed his mind, hadn't decided to sweep everything under the proverbial rug and pretend that love would conquer all. He'd save that kind of idealism for the world's romantics. He wasn't one of them; he was a physician and he dealt with the real world. He had no intention of deluding himself into believing they had a chance together, even if she did entertain such thoughts herself.

"I can't believe this," Stephanie cried, glaring at

Colby. Tears had misted her eyes, he noted with surprise. He'd always considered weeping females cause for alarm. He never knew what to say to them.

But there'd been that time with Valerie, the night of David's surgery, Colby reminded himself. She'd been sobbing out her grief and fear. With anyone else he would have sought another family member to offer the needed consolation. But he hadn't looked for Norah that night. Instead he'd gone to Valerie himself. At first, he felt a terrible loss. He couldn't hold out hope for her father's recovery, not when everything indicated that David probably wouldn't survive the night. And so he'd sat on the concrete bench beside her and placed his arm around her shoulders.

Valerie had turned to him then, and buried her face against him. The surge of love he'd experienced in that moment was unlike anything he'd ever felt. Stroking her hair, he'd savored the feel of her in his arms.

"She'll be back," David said, interrupting Colby's memories.

"No," Stephanie argued in a trembling voice. "She won't. Not for a very long time."

"Valerie's not like that," Norah said. "She'll visit again. Soon."

"Why should she, when everything she equates with home means pain? It's too easy to stay away, too easy to make excuses and be satisfied with a phone call now and again." It sounded as though Stephanie was speaking from experience, and Colby studied David Bloomfield's second daughter.

She must have felt his scrutiny because she turned suddenly, undisguised anger flashing from her deep brown eyes.

"You might be a wonderful surgeon," she said, her gaze as hard as flint, "but you're one of the biggest fools I've ever met."

Colby blinked in surprise, but before he had a chance to respond, Stephanie ran back inside the house. Amazed at the verbal attack, he looked at Norah. They'd worked together for a number of months and he'd always been fond of her.

"I couldn't agree with my sister more," Norah said with an uncharacteristic display of temper. "You're an idiot." Having said that, she stormed into the house as well.

David chuckled, and Colby relaxed. At least one member of this family could appreciate the wisdom of his sacrifice. Stephanie and Norah acted as if he should be arrested. Both seemed to think it'd been easy for him to let Valerie drive away when nothing was further from the truth. Even now he needed to grip hold of the railing to keep from racing after her.

If only she hadn't turned at the last moment and looked straight at him. And smiled. The sweetest, most beautiful smile he'd ever seen in his life. A smile that would haunt him to his grave.

"I love her," Colby whispered, his eyes never leaving the driveway, although Valerie's car was long out of view. By now she was probably two miles down the road.

"I know," David assured him.

Something in the older man's tone caused Colby to glance at him. The inflection seemed to suggest that Colby might love Valerie but he didn't love her enough. Heaven help him, he did! He loved her so much that he'd sent her out of his life. No one, not even David Bloomfield, could fully appreciate the extent of his sacrifice.

"Rowdy Cassidy will be a much better husband for her than I ever would," Colby said, steeling himself against the pain his own words produced.

"Maybe, but I doubt it," David stated, walking over to his wicker rocking chair and easing himself into it. "I don't suppose you've noticed, but Valerie and I are a lot alike."

Colby grinned. The similarity hadn't exactly escaped him. Here were two people who each possessed a streak of stubbornness that was wider than the Mississippi. Both were intelligent, intuitive and ambitious. Hardworking. Single-minded.

"She'd never be happy living here in Orchard Valley," Colby said, his gaze returning to the driveway. He couldn't seem to make himself look away. It was as if that long narrow road was his only remaining connection with Valerie.

"You're right, of course. Valerie would never be content in a small town again. Not after living in Houston."

The reassurance should have eased the ache in his heart, but it didn't. He told himself there was no reason to linger. Carrying on a polite conversation was beyond him yet he didn't seem to have the energy to leave.

"Did I ever tell you how I met Grace?"

"I believe you did." Valerie must be three or four miles down the road by now, Colby estimated.

"Our courtship was a bit unusual. It isn't every day a man woos a woman from a hospital bed."

Colby nodded. Before long, Valerie would be close to the interstate, and then it would be impossible to catch her. *Not* that he intended to chase after her.

"Grace wasn't keen on marrying me, for a number of reasons. All good ones, I might add. She loved me, that much I knew, but to her mind love wasn't enough."

David's words diverted Colby's attention from the road. He swiveled his gaze to the older man, who was rocking contentedly as though they were discussing something as mundane as the best bait for local trout. He didn't understand.

"Grace was right. Sometimes love isn't enough," David added.

"In your case she was wrong," Colby mumbled, displeased. For the first time he understood where this discussion was leading. Valerie's father was going to force him to admit that he was as big a fool as Stephanie and Norah had claimed. Though he might be more subtle about it.

"Not really. I knew I'd need to make some real changes before Grace would agree to marry me, but

I was willing to make them because I knew something she didn't.''

"What was that?"

A wistful look came over David, and his eyes grew hazy. "Deep in my soul, I knew I'd never love another woman the way I loved Grace. Deep in my soul, I recognized that she was the one chance I had in this life for real happiness. I could have done the noble thing and left her to marry some nice young man. There were plenty who would have thanked me for the opportunity."

"I see."

"I have to tell you, though, it was the most difficult decision of my life. Marrying Grace was the biggest risk I ever took, but I never regretted it. Not once."

Colby nodded. David was telling him exactly what he wanted to hear. He, too, had made his decision, and had set Valerie free to find what happiness she could. Rowdy Cassidy was waiting in the wings, eager to fill his place. Eager to help her forget.

Colby's mind flashed to Sherry Waterman. He liked her and enjoyed her company. He felt the same about Norah. But it was Valerie who set his heart on fire. Valerie who challenged him. Valerie whom he needed. Not anyone else, only Valerie.

"Don't you worry about her," David continued. "She'll be fine. In time, she'll regroup and be a better person for having experienced love. As for her marrying Rowdy Cassidy, I don't think you need concern yourself with that, either."

"Why not?"

"Because I know my daughter. I know exactly what I would have done had Grace decided against marrying me. I'd have gone back to my world, worked hard and made a decent life for myself. But I would never have fallen in love again. I wouldn't have allowed it to happen."

Colby said nothing. By now, Valerie was on the interstate. It was too late. Even if he did go after her, they wouldn't be able to stop. Not on the freeway with cars screaming past. It would be reckless and dangerous and beyond all stupidity to chase her now. Besides, what could he possibly have to say that hadn't already been said?

David stood. "You want another cup of coffee?"

"No, thanks. I should be on my way."

"I'll be in your office bright and early Tuesday morning, then."

Colby nodded. It was time to get back to his life, the life he'd had before he met Valerie Bloomfield.

Valerie refused to cry. She'd never been prone to tears. Even as a child, she'd hated crying, hated the way the salty tears had felt against her face.

What surprised her was how much it hurt to hold everything inside. It felt as though someone had crammed a fist down her throat and asked her to breathe normally.

In an effort to push aside the pain of leaving Colby, she focused her thoughts on all the good he'd brought into her life. Without him, she would have lost her father. Norah had admitted as much that first evening. It had been Colby who'd convinced her father to go to the hospital. It had been Colby who'd performed the life-saving surgery.

If for nothing else than her father's life, she owed him more than anyone could possibly repay.

But that wasn't all he'd given her. Dr. Colby Winston had taught her about herself, about love, about sacrifice.

She would always love him for that. Now she had to teach herself to release him, to let him go. Finding love and then freely relinquishing it might well prove to be a tricky business. She'd never given her heart to a man before. Loving Colby was the easy part. It felt as though she'd always known and loved him, as if he'd always been a part of her life. It seemed impossible that they'd met only a few weeks ago.

Leaving him was the hardest thing she'd ever done.

The self-doubts, the what-ifs and might-have-beens rolled in like giant waves, swamping her with grief and dread.

Dragging in a deep breath, she fought the urge to turn the car around and head back. Back to Orchard Valley. Back home.

Back to Colby.

Instead, she exhaled, tried to relax, tried to convince herself that everything would feel much better once she was back in Texas. She'd be able to submerge the pain in her job. When she resumed her position with CHIPS, she could begin to forget Colby and at the same time treasure the memories she had of him.

Valerie didn't realize there were tears in her eyes until she noticed how blurry the road in front of her had become. Hoping to distract herself, she turned on the radio and started humming along with a country-western singer lamenting her lost love.

"You idiot," Valerie muttered, weeping harder than ever. Irritably, she snapped off the radio. "Damn." She swiped at the tears with the back of one hand, telling herself she was too strong, too independent, for such weak emotional behavior.

It wasn't until she was changing lanes on the freeway that she noticed the Buick behind her. A maroon Buick. It was traveling at high speed, passing cars, going well above the limit.

Colby? It couldn't be.

More than likely it was just a car that looked like his. It couldn't be him. He'd never come after her. It wasn't his style. No, if he ever had a change of heart, something she didn't count on, it wouldn't be for weeks, months. Colby wasn't impulsive.

The Buick slowed down and moved directly behind Valerie's car and followed her for a moment before putting on the turn signal. If it hadn't been for the tears in her eyes she would have been able to make out the driver's features.

The car honked irritably. It *had* to be Colby. He didn't honestly expect her to stop on the freeway, did he? It wouldn't be safe. There was an exit ramp only a few miles down the road and she drove toward that, turned off when she could and parked. Luckily traffic was light, and the shoulders on both sides of the road were wide enough for her to park safely. When she eased to a stop, Colby pulled in behind her.

She'd barely had time to unfasten her seat belt before he jerked open her door.

"What are you doing here?" she demanded.

"What does it look like? I'm chasing after you."

Legs trembling, she climbed out of her car, and stood leaning against it, her hands on her hips. "This better be good, Winston. I've got a plane to catch."

"You've been crying."

"There's something in my eye."

"Both eyes apparently."

"All right, both eyes." She didn't know what silly game he thought he was playing, but she didn't have the patience for it. "Why are you here? Surely there's a reason you came racing after me."

"There's a reason."

"Good." She crossed her arms and shifted her position. Whatever Colby wanted to say was obviously causing him trouble, because he started pacing in front of her, hands clenched.

"This is even harder than I expected," he finally admitted.

Not daring to hope, Valerie said nothing.

"I can't believe what a mess I've made of this. Listen," he said, turning to face her, his expression as closed as always. "I want you to come back to Orchard Valley."

"Why?"

"Because I love you and because I'd like us to talk this through. You love me, too, Valerie. I don't think I appreciated how much until just now. It must have been so hard to come to me, to lay your heart out like that and then have me send you away. I—"

"You don't need to apologize," she broke in.

"I do."

Valerie had no idea, not the slightest, where all this was leading. She took a deep breath. "All right, you've apologized."

"Will you come back?"

"If you want to talk, we can do it at the airport." It seemed like a fair suggestion.

"I want to do more than talk," he said from between gritted teeth. "I want you to show me how we're going to make this marriage work, because damned if I know. We haven't got one thing working in our favor. Not one thing."

"Then why try?"

"Because if you leave now I'm going to regret it for the rest of my life. Sure as anything, I'm going to think back to this moment for the next fifty years and wish I'd never let you go. The problem is, I'm not sure what to do now—you've got me so tied up in knots I can't even think clearly anymore."

"You don't look happy about it."

"You're right, I'm not happy. I'm downright furious."

Valerie grinned. "Love *is* rather frightening, isn't it?"

Colby grinned, too, for the first time. "But you know something? It's living without your love that frightens me."

"Oh, Colby..."

"Let's say we did get married," he said, the gravel under his feet crunching as he paced in front of her.

"All right, let's say we did."

"Are you going to want a job outside the home?"

"Yes, Colby, I will."

"What about children?"

"Oh, yes, at least two." She found it astonishing that they should be discussing something so personal, standing at the side of a road.

"How do you propose to be both a mother and an executive?"

"How do you intend to be both a father and a surgeon? Not to mention a husband? You have a career, too, Colby."

"You can't have it all, Valerie."

"Neither can you! Besides, it doesn't have to be either or. Half the women in America maintain a career *and* a family, but there have to be compromises along the way. You're right, I won't be able to do everything alone. I couldn't even begin to try."

"I don't like the idea of farming our children out to strangers."

"Frankly, I don't, either, but there are ways of working around that, too. Ways of making the situation acceptable to both of us. For one thing, I could set up an office at home. It's not unheard of, especially these days with computers and faxes and everything. Rowdy might be willing to start a branch of the company on the West Coast, and I think he might be persuaded to pick Oregon—especially if a hard-working executive chooses to live there.''

Colby nodded and thrust his hands into his pockets.

''I know I'm not what you want in a wife, Colby. You'd rather I was the kind of woman who'd be content to stay home and do needlepoint, and put up preserves. But that isn't who I am, and I can't change. I'd give anything to be the woman you want, but if I'm not true to myself, the marriage would be doomed before we even said our vows.''

''I don't think we should be concerning ourselves with some unrealistic image I've invented. What about the man *you* want?''

She smiled, and looked away. ''You're the only man I've ever wanted.''

He reached for her then, wrapping his arms tightly around her, dropping a gentle kiss on the side of her neck. A deep shudder went through him as he exhaled.

''I'm never going to be able to stop loving you.''

''Is that so terrible?'' she asked in a whisper, her throat raw.

''No, it's the most wonderful blessing of my life.'' His eyes were warm and possessive as he brought his hands up to clasp her shoulders. ''I've been arrogant and selfish. I nearly destroyed both our lives because I refused to accept the gift you offered me.''

''Oh, Colby.''

"There won't be any guarantees."

"If I wanted guarantees, I'd buy myself a new car. Everything in life is a risk, but I've never been more willing to take one than with you."

"I'd say we're in for an adventure."

"Yes, but it'll be the grandest adventure of our lives." Her arms went around his neck as he lowered his mouth to hers. One kiss wiped out the pain and the torment of these past few days. Colby must have felt it, too, because he kissed her again and again, their need for one another insatiable, their joy boundless.

A car driving past honked noisily, disturbing them.

Valerie reluctantly broke off their kiss. "You might have chosen someplace a bit more private to propose, Dr. Winston."

"Shall we try this again later with champagne and a diamond ring?"

Valerie nodded because speaking when her heart was so full would have been difficult.

Her father was sitting on the porch when Valerie and Colby pulled up in front of the house late that afternoon.

"Did you tell Dad you were coming after me?"

"I didn't know it myself until I left here. Before I realized what I was doing, I was on the freeway, racing after you like a bat out of hell. I hadn't a clue what I was going to say when I found you."

Valerie tucked her hand in his and pressed her

cheek to his shoulder. "You looked like you wanted to bite my head off."

"I looked like a man who was calling himself every kind of fool in existence."

"For coming after me?"

"No," he said quietly. "For letting you go."

Valerie rewarded him with an appreciative kiss on the corner of his mouth.

Colby groaned softly. "I'm not going to want a long engagement. The sooner we can arrange this wedding, the better."

"I couldn't agree more."

Colby kissed her lightly on the lips. "I have the sneaking suspicion your father hasn't moved since you left for the airport."

They'd been gone for hours, returning the rental car to Portland, and then stopping for an elegant lunch in an equally elegant restaurant. Before leaving the city, they'd visited a well-known jewelry store where Valerie chose a beautiful solitaire diamond engagement ring. That very ring was on her finger now. It felt as if it had always been there.

"About time you two were getting back," her father said as Colby helped her out of his car. "I was beginning to worry."

"How'd you know we were coming?" Colby asked.

"I knew before you left here that you'd be back with Valerie before the end of the day."

"Dad, you couldn't possibly have known." She

waited for a protest, but none came. Her father sat back down in his rocker and grinned knowingly.

"Oh, I know more than that about what's going to happen to you two."

"He's going to start talking about that dream again," Valerie murmured, slipping her arm around Colby's waist and smiling up at him. He brought her close to his side.

"Love's shocked you both," David said, wagging a finger at them. "But there are a few more shocks in store for you. Just you wait and see what happens when my twin grandsons are born."

"Twins?" Colby echoed incredulously.

"You're going to name them after their two grandfathers. The blond one will be David, and he'll be the spitting image of me."

"Twins," Colby said again.

"I don't know," Valerie said with a soft laugh. "I could get used to a few surprises now and again, especially if it means I can be with you."

Colby gazed down at her and Valerie realized her father was right. Love had caught them unawares, but it was the best surprise of their lives.

STEPHANIE

One

Home.

Stephanie Bloomfield lugged her heavy suitcase up the porch steps of the large white-pillared house. She moved quietly, careful not to wake her two sisters, though it occurred to her that they might be at the hospital.

She herself had spent the best part—no, the worst part, she amended tiredly—of the past two days either in a plane or standing at the counter in a foreign airport. Or was that three days? She couldn't tell anymore.

Norah, her younger sister, had managed to call her in Italy nearly a week ago about their father's heart attack. The connection had been bad and she'd had difficulty hearing Norah, but the sense of urgency had come clearly over the wire. Their father was gravely ill, and Steffie needed to hurry home—something that turned out to be much easier said than done.

Steffie had been living just outside Rome, attending classes at the university. She'd been participating in a special program, learning Italian and studying Renaissance history and culture. For three years she'd traveled effortlessly from one end of the country to the other. Now, just when she desperately needed to fly home, the airports were closed down by a transportation strike that paralyzed Italy. It didn't help that, at the time, she was staying in a small, relatively isolated village hundreds of miles from Rome. She'd been on a brief holiday, visiting a friend's family.

It had taken her several days and what felt like three lifetimes to arrange passage home. *Days,* when it should have been only a matter of hours. This past week had been the most stressful of her life. She'd been in touch with her sisters as often as possible, and at last report heard from Norah that their father was resting comfortably. It wasn't difficult to read between the lines and hear the dread in Norah's voice. Her youngest sister, bless her heart, had never been much good at hiding the truth. Although Norah had tried to sound reassuring, Steffie was well aware that her father's condition had worsened. That was when she'd undertaken the most daring move of her life. She'd made contact with some men of questionable scruples, sold every personal possession of value and, at a hugely inflated price, obtained a means out of the country, by way of Japan, with layovers in places she'd never expected to visit. It was decidedly an indirect route to Oregon, but she was home now. Heaven only knew how much longer it would have taken if she hadn't resorted to such drastic measures.

After a whole day of waiting at the Tokyo airport, fighting for a space aboard any available flight to the

States, and then the long flight itself, Steffie was frantic for news of her father. Frantic and fearful. In some ways, not knowing was almost better than knowing....

She opened the front door and stepped silently inside the sleeping house. She'd adjusted her watch to Pacific time, but her mind was caught somewhere between Italy and Tokyo. She was too exhausted to be tired. Too worried to be hungry, although she couldn't remember the last meal she'd eaten.

Setting down her impossibly heavy suitcase, she stood in the foyer and breathed in the scent of polished wood and welcome.

She was home.

Her father's den was to her right, and she immediately felt drawn there. Pausing in the doorway, she flipped on the light switch and stood gazing at the room that was so much her father's. A massive stone fireplace commanded one entire wall, while two other walls were lined with floor-to-ceiling bookcases.

She looked at his wingback chair, the soft leather creased from years of use. Closing her eyes, Steffie breathed in deeply, savoring the scent of old leather and books and the sweet pungency of pipe tobacco. This was her father's room, and she'd never missed him more than she did at that moment.

His presence seemed to fill the den. His robust laugh echoed silently against the walls. Steffie could easily visualize him sitting behind the cherrywood desk, the accounting ledgers spread open and his pipe

propped in the ugly ceramic ashtray—the one she'd
made for him the summer she'd turned eleven.

The photograph of her mother caught her eye. David Bloomfield could leave his daughters no finer
legacy than the love he'd shared with their mother.
He'd changed following Grace's death. Steffie had
noticed it even before she left Orchard Valley. She'd
guessed it from his letters in the years since. And
she'd been especially aware of the changes when he
came to visit her in Italy last spring. The spark was
gone. The relentless passion for life that had always
been so much a part of him was missing now. Each
month his letters were more painful to read, more
lifeless and subdued. Without his wife at his side,
David Bloomfield was as empty as…as that chair
there, his old reading chair, standing in front of the
fireplace.

Steffie's gaze slipped to the newspaper spread
across the ottoman. It felt as though, any minute, her
father would walk through the door, settle back in
his chair and resume reading.

Only he wouldn't.

He might never sit in this room again, Steffie realized, her heart constricting with pain. He might
never reach for one of his favorite books and lovingly leaf through its pages until he found the passage he wanted. He might never sit by the fireplace,
pipe in hand. He might never look up when she entered the room and smile when he saw it was Steffie—his "princess."

The pain in her chest grew more intense and the

need to release her emotions burned in her, but Steffie ignored it, as she had a thousand times before. She wasn't a weeper. She'd guarded her emotions vigilantly for three long years. Ever since that night with Charles Tomaselli when he'd—

She brushed the thought from her mind with the efficiency of long practice. Charles was a painful figure from her past. One best forgotten, or at least ignored. She hadn't thought of him in months and refused to do so now. Sooner or later she'd be forced to exchange pleasantries with him, but when she did, she'd pretend she had trouble remembering who he was, as though he were merely a casual acquaintance and not the man who'd broken her heart. That seemed the best way to handle the situation—to pretend she'd completely forgotten their last humiliating encounter.

If he did insist on renewing their acquaintance, which wasn't likely, she'd show him how mature she was, how sophisticated and cosmopolitan she'd become. Then he'd regret the careless, cruel way he'd treated her.

There was a sound in the hallway, and Steffie moved out of the den just as Norah reached the bottom of the stairs.

"Steffie? My goodness, you're home!" Norah exclaimed, rushing to embrace her.

And then, with a small cry of welcome, Valerie, the oldest of the three girls, bounded down the stairs, her long cotton gown dancing about her feet.

"Steff, I'm so glad you're home," Valerie cried,

wrapping her arms around both her sisters. "When did you get in? Why didn't you let us know so we could meet you at the airport?"

"I flew standby most of the way, so I wasn't sure when I'd land. I caught the Air Porter and then a cab." She took a deep breath. "I'm just glad I'm here."

"I am, too," Valerie said with an uncharacteristic display of emotion, wiping the tears from her cheeks. Normally Valerie was a model of restraint. Seeing her this shaken revealed, more plainly than anything she could have said, how desperately ill their father was.

By tacit agreement, they moved into the kitchen. Valerie set about preparing a pot of tea. According to the digital clock on the microwave, it was a little past three. Steffie hadn't realized it was quite that late. She could hardly recall the last time she'd slept in a bed. Four days ago, perhaps.

"How's Dad?" It was the question she'd been yearning to ask from the moment she'd walked in the door. The question she was afraid to ask.

"He's doing just great," Norah said, her soft voice rising with delight. "We came really close to losing him, Steffie. Valerie and I were in a panic because things looked bad and Dr. Winston couldn't delay the surgery. And Dad pulled through! But..."

"But he..." Valerie began when Norah hesitated.

"He what?" Steffie prompted. Although she was thrilled with the news that her father had survived the crisis, she couldn't help wondering why both her sisters seemed reluctant to continue. "Tell me," she insisted. She didn't want to be protected from the truth.

"Apparently Dad had a near-death experience," Norah finally supplied.

"But isn't that fairly common? Especially during that kind of surgery? I've been reading for years about people who travel through a dark tunnel into the light."

"I wouldn't know how normal it is to talk to someone in the spirit world, would you?" Valerie snapped.

"Dad claims he talked to Mom." Once again it was Norah who supplied the information.

"To Mom?" Steffie felt numb, unsure of how to react.

"Which we all know is impossible." Valerie hurried barefoot across the kitchen floor to pour boiling water into the teapot. She placed three mugs, three spoons and the sugar bowl on a tray; when the tea had steeped, she filled the cups, obviously preoccupied with her task. Carrying the tray to the table, she served her sisters, then leaped up to get a plate of Norah's home-baked cookies. "I think Dad needs to talk to a counselor," she said abruptly.

"Valerie," Norah sighed as though this were a well-worn argument. "You're overreacting."

"You would, too, if Dad was saying to you the things he says to me." Valerie stirred her tea without looking up.

Norah sighed again. "Dad honestly believes he

spoke to Mom and if it makes him feel better, then I don't think we should try to discount his experience."

"What was Mom supposed to have said to him?" Steffie asked, intrigued by the interplay between her two sisters. She helped herself to a couple of oatmeal cookies as she spoke.

"That's what worries me the most." Valerie raised her voice, clearly unsettled. "He's got some fool notion that we're all going to marry."

"Now, that's profound." Steffie couldn't hide her amusement. The three of them were of marriageable age; it made sense that they'd eventually find husbands.

"But he claims to know *who* we're going to marry," Norah said, grinning sheepishly, as though she found the whole thing amusing.

"He's been wearing this silly smile for two days." Valerie groaned, dropping her forehead onto her arms. "He's been talking about a houseful of grandchildren, too. The ones *we're* supposed to present him with—and all in the next few years. If it wasn't so ridiculous, I'd cry."

"Has he said who I'm supposed to marry?" Steffie asked, curiosity getting the better of her.

Valerie lifted her head to glare at Stephanie, and Norah chuckled. "That's something else that's irritating Valerie," she explained. "Dad hasn't told any of us, at least not directly. Not yet."

"He's acting like he knows this wonderful secret

and he's keeping it all to himself, dropping hints every now and then. I swear it's driving me crazy."

"I don't mind it," Norah said. To someone else, she might have sounded self-righteous, but Steffie recognized her younger sister's compassion and knew that it edged out any hint of righteousness. "Dad's smiling again. He's excited about the future and even if he's becoming a bit...presumptuous about the three of us, I honestly can't say I mind. I'm just so glad to have him alive."

Valerie nodded, her argument apparently gone. "I guess I can put up with a few remarks, too."

"This is the first time one of us hasn't stayed all night at the hospital," Norah explained, her mouth curving into a gentle smile. "Dr. Winston insisted there wasn't any need. Not anymore."

"Don't be fooled by that guy," Valerie muttered under her breath. "He may look like your average, laid-back country doctor, but he's got a backbone of steel."

He must have, if Valerie was reacting like this, Stephanie thought with sudden interest. From the sounds of it, her sister had finally encountered a will as strong as her own. So, either Valerie had changed her ways or she had—could it be?—a soft spot for Dr. Winston.

"In other words," Steffie said quickly, "I missed the worst of it. Dad's out of danger now and will eventually recover?"

"Yes," Norah said cheerfully. "Everything'll be back to normal."

"Not exactly," Valerie countered. "Within a few weeks Dad will be the picture of health, but the three of us will be pulling out our hair after listening to all his talk about marriage, husbands and grandchildren!"

Bright sunlight poured through the open window of Steffie's bedroom when she woke. The house was quiet, but the sounds of the day drifted in from outside. Birds chirped merrily in the distance and a spring breeze set the chimes on the back porch tinkling and rustled the curtains lightly. She could hear work crews in the orchard—spraying the apple trees, Steffie guessed.

After those long days of struggling to get home, Steffie exulted in the sensation of familiarity. She wrapped the feel of it around her like a warm quilt. The crisis had passed. Her father would survive, and all the world seemed brighter, sweeter, happier.

Reluctantly she slid out of bed and dressed, pulling a pair of slacks and a light sweater from her suitcase.

She found a note on the kitchen table explaining that both Valerie and Norah were at the hospital. They were going to leave her arrival as a surprise, so she could come any time she was ready. There was no need to rush. Not anymore.

Selecting a banana from the fruit bowl on the kitchen counter, she ate that while reheating a cup of coffee in the microwave. As the timer was counting down the seconds, she walked into her father's den and reached for the newspaper, intending to take it with her to the hospital.

She would read it, Steffie decided, to catch up on the local news. But even as she formed this thought, she knew she was lying to herself.

There was only one reason she was taking the local newspaper with her. Only one reason she'd even picked it up. *Charles Tomaselli.* She turned to the front page. The *Orchard Valley Clarion.* She allowed her eyes to skim the headlines for several moments.

Emotion came at her in waves. First apprehension. She'd give anything to avoid seeing Charles again. Then anger. He'd humiliated her. Laughed at her. She'd never forgive him for that. Never. The agony of his humiliation smoldered even now, years later. Yet, much as she wanted to hate Charles, she found she couldn't. She didn't love him any longer. That was over, finished. He'd cured her of love in the most effective way possible. No, she reassured herself, she didn't love him, but she couldn't make herself hate him, either.

She could handle this. She had to. Besides, he was probably as eager to avoid any encounters between them as she was.

Determined now, she tucked the paper under her arm and grabbed the car keys Norah had thoughtfully left on the kitchen table. With the steaming coffee mug in her hand, she headed out the door.

When she arrived at Orchard Valley General, Steffie paused, taken aback by a sudden rush of grief. The last time she'd gone through those doors had been the day her mother died. Steffie's heart stilled at the nearly overwhelming sadness she felt. She hadn't expected that. It took her a couple of minutes to compose herself. Then she continued toward the elevator.

When she arrived at the waiting room, she found Norah speaking to one of the nurses, while Valerie sat reading. It was so unusual to find her older sister doing anything sedentary that Steffie nearly did a double take.

"Steffie!" Norah said, her face lighting when she saw her sister. "Did you get enough sleep?"

"I'm fine." It would take more than one night's rest to recuperate from the past week.

"Did you fix yourself some breakfast?"

"Yes, little mother, I did. Can I see Dad now or is there anything else you'd like to ask me?" She slipped her arm around her sister's trim waist, feeling elated. It was wonderful to be home, wonderful to be with her family.

"You're here," Valerie said, joining them. "Dad asked me earlier when was the last time we'd heard from you. I told him this morning."

"He's going to be moved out of the Surgical Intensive Care Unit some time tomorrow," Norah said happily. "Then we'll all be able to see him at once. As it is now, only one of us can visit at a time."

"Norah, would you like me to take your sister in to see your father?" A plump, matronly nurse had bustled up to them.

"Please," Steffie answered eagerly before Norah

could speak. The nurse led her through a hallway with glass-walled cubicles. Every imaginable sort of medical equipment seemed to be in use here, but Steffie barely noticed. She was far too excited about seeing her father. The nurse stopped at one of the cubicles and gestured Stephanie inside.

He was sitting up in bed. He smiled and held out his arms to her. "Steffie," he said faintly, "come here, Princess." He was connected to several monitoring devices, she noticed.

She walked into his hold, careful to stay clear of the wires and tubes, astonished at his weak embrace after the bone-crushing hugs she was accustomed to receiving from him. Her sisters had claimed the spark was back in his eyes. They'd talked about how well he looked.

Steffie disagreed.

She was shocked by his paleness, by the gauntness of his appearance. If he was so much better *now*, she hated to think what he must have looked like a week earlier.

"It's so good to see you," her father said, his voice cracking with emotion. "I've missed you, Princess."

"I've missed you, too," Steffie said, wiping a tear from the corner of her eye as she straightened.

"You're home to stay?"

Steffie wasn't sure how to answer. Home represented so much to her, much more than she'd realized, but she loved Italy, too. Still, just gazing out on the orchards this morning had reminded her how much she'd missed her life in Orchard Valley.

She'd left bruised and vulnerable; she'd returned strong and sure of herself. Being in Italy had helped her heal. But there was no longer any reason to stay away. She was ready to come home.

She'd been trying to decide what to do next when she'd received word of her father's heart attack. Her courses were completed, but remaining in Italy had a strong appeal. She could travel for a while, continue her studies, perhaps do some teaching herself. She could move to some place like Boston or New York. Or she could return to Orchard Valley. Steffie hadn't known what she wanted.

"I'm home for as long as you need me."

"You'll stay," her father insisted with unshakable confidence. "Oh, yes."

"What makes you so sure?"

He smiled mysteriously and his voice dropped to a whisper. "Your mother told me."

"Mom?" Steffie was beginning to appreciate Valerie's concerns.

"Yup. I suppose you're going to act like your sister and suggest I see some fancy doctor with a couch in his office. I did talk to your mother. She sends her love, by the way."

Steffie didn't know what to say. Was she supposed to ask him to convey a message for her? "What did Mom...tell you?" she ventured instead.

"Quite a bit, but mainly she said I had quite a few more years left in me. She promised they'd be good ones, too." He paused, chuckling softly. "Your mother always did know I had a soft spot in my heart for babies. And there's going to be a passel of them born in this family within the next few years."

"Babies?"

"An even dozen." The first sign of color crept into his cheeks. "Can you believe it? My little girls are going to make me a grandfather twelve times over."

"Uh..."

"I know it sounds like I've got a screw loose, but..."

"Daddy, you think whatever you like as long as it makes you happy."

"It's more than thinking, Princess. It's a fact, sure as I'm lying here. But never mind that now. Let me get a good look at you. My goodness," he said, grinning proudly, "you're even lovelier than I remembered."

Steffie beamed with pleasure. She knew very well that she was no raving beauty, but her looks were nothing to be ashamed of, either. Her dark hair was straight as a clothespin, reaching to the middle of her back. She wore it pulled away from her face, using combs, a style that accentuated her prominent cheekbones and the strong lines of her face. Her eyes were deep brown.

Steffie had just started to regale her father with the adventures of the past week when the same nurse who'd escorted her in to see him reappeared, ready to lead her back to the waiting area.

Steffie wanted to argue. They'd barely had five minutes together! But she forced back her objections; she wouldn't do anything that might upset her father. She kissed his leathery cheek and promised to return soon.

Valerie was waiting for her, but Norah was nowhere in sight.

"Well?" Valerie asked, glancing up from her magazine. "Did he say anything to you about talking to Mom?"

Steffie nodded, secretly a little amused. "He seems downright excited about the prospect of grandchildren. I hate to see him disappointed, don't you?"

"Hmm?" Valerie muttered.

"Since you're the oldest, it makes sense you should be the first," she teased, taking delight in her sister's blank look.

"For what?" Valerie asked.

"To produce a grandchild for Dad. The last time you wrote, I seem to remember you had quite a lot to say about Rowdy Cassidy. Might as well aim high—marry a multimillionaire—even if he is your boss."

"Rowdy," Valerie repeated as though she'd never heard the name before. "Oh...Rowdy. Of course there's always Rowdy. Why didn't I think of him?" With that, Valerie returned to her magazine.

Baffled, Steffie shook her head.

She wandered over to the coffeemaker, poured herself a fresh cup and sat down near her sister. She reached for the newspaper she'd brought with her and opened it to the front page, reading each article in turn. She was relieved to recognize several names; obviously not much had changed while she was away.

Folding back the second page of the weekly paper, she found that her eyes were automatically drawn to the small black-and-white photograph of Charles Tomaselli. For a wild second her heart seemed to stop.

He looked the same. Still as attractive as sin. No man had the right to be that good-looking. Dark hair, gleaming dark eyes. But what bothered her the most was the impact his picture had on her. It wasn't supposed to be like this. She should be free of any emotional entanglement. She should be able to stare at that photograph and feel nothing. Instead she was swamped by so many confused, uncomfortable emotions that she could hardly breathe.

Determined to focus her attention elsewhere, she started on an article with Charles's byline. He'd written an investigative feature, clearly one of a series, about the unhealthy and often unsafe conditions under which many of the migrant workers lived and worked in the community's surrounding apple orchards.

Two paragraphs into the piece, Steffie had to stop reading. She'd come to her father's name, along with the name of their orchard. Obviously Charles hadn't done his research! Steffie knew how hard her parents had worked to ease the plight of the migrant workers. Her mother had set up a medical clinic. And unlike certain other orchard owners, her father had built them decent housing and seen to it that they were properly fed and fairly paid.

Steffie tried to continue reading, but the red haze of anger made it impossible. Her stomach twisted in painful knots as she rose to her feet.

"Valerie," she demanded. "What was Dad doing when he suffered his heart attack?"

"I think Norah said he was sitting on the porch. What makes you ask?"

"He'd been reading the newspaper, hadn't he?"

"I wouldn't know for sure, but I don't think so."

"He must have been!" Steffie declared, walking toward the elevator. She stabbed the button with her thumb, seething at the sense of betrayal she felt. All the evidence pointed to one thing. She'd found the newspaper spread open in his den. Her father had picked up the *Orchard Valley Clarion,* read the article, and then in shock and dismay had wandered onto the porch.

"Steffie, what is it?"

"Have you *read* this?" she asked, thrusting the newspaper in front of her sister. "Did you see what Charles Tomaselli wrote about our father?"

"No, I haven't, but—"

"Look at the date," she said, folding back front page.

"Yes?" Valerie asked, still sounding confused.

"Isn't that the day of Dad's heart attack?"

"Yes, but—"

"You'd be upset, too, if you'd worked half your life improving the conditions of migrant workers only to have your efforts ridiculed before the entire community!''

"Steffie," Valerie said, gently pressing Steffie's arm. "I can't believe this. Charles is Dad's friend. He's called several times to ask about him. Why, he was even here the night of Dad's surgery.''

"He was probably suffering from a large dose of guilt." It seemed perfectly obvious that Charles knew what he'd done. Her father's heart attack had happened the same day the article was published. So Charles *must* have known, must have figured it out himself. And that was why he'd come calling—she was sure of it.

But it was going to take a whole lot more than a few words of concern to smooth over what he'd done. Once Steffie had confronted Charles, she intended to stop off at Joan Lind's office. Joan might be as old as a sand dune, but she was a damn good attorney and Steffie meant to sue Tomaselli for everything he ever hoped to have.

The elevator arrived and she stepped briskly inside.

"Where are you going?" Valerie wanted to know as the doors started to close.

"To give Tomaselli a piece of my mind.''

The doors blocked Valerie from view, but her sister's words came through loud and clear. "A piece of your mind? Are you sure you have any to spare?''

By the time Steffie reached Main Street and located a parking spot, the anger and hurt actually made her feel ill. Her cheeks were feverishly hot. Her stomach churned.

Charles disliked her, and he was taking it out on her father. Well, she couldn't allow him to do it.

She entered the newspaper office, then hesitated. There was a reception desk and a polished wooden railing; it separated the public area from the work space, with its computer terminals, Teletype machine and ringing phones. Beyond it two rows of desks occupied by reporters and other staff lined each side of the room, creating a wide center aisle that led directly to the editor's desk.

She noticed Charles immediately. As the *Clarion*'s editor, he had a work area that took up the entire end of the room. He was on the phone, but his eyes locked immediately with hers. There'd been a time when she would have swooned to have him look at her like this—with admiration, with surprise, with a hint of pleasure. But that time was long past.

Undaunted, she opened the low gate and walked purposefully down the center aisle until she'd reached his desk. She could hear the gate swinging back and forth behind her, keeping time with her steps. By now, Charles clearly understood that this wasn't a social call.

"Brent, let me get back to you." He abruptly replaced the receiver. "Well, well, if it isn't Stephanie Bloomfield. To what do I owe the pleasure of this visit?"

His casual insouciance infuriated her. Steffie slapped the newspaper down on his desk. "Did you honestly think you'd get away with this?'' she asked, amazed at the calmness of her own voice.

Charles's eyes steadily held hers. "I don't know what you're talking about."

"You published this piece, didn't you?"

"What article do you mean? I publish lots of pieces."

His attitude didn't fool her. "The one about living conditions among migrant orchard workers. Now, I ask you, who owns the largest apple orchard in three counties? The first paragraph is filled with innuendo, but then you get right down to brass tacks, don't you—by naming my father!"

"Stephanie—"

"I'm not finished yet!" she shouted. In fact, she was just warming up to her subject. "You didn't think any of us would notice, did you?"

"Notice what?" He crossed his arms over his chest as though he'd grown bored with her tirade.

"The date of the article," she said, gaining momentum. "It's the same day as my father's heart attack. The very same day—"

"Stephanie—"

"Don't call me that!" Tears rolled down her face, surprising her. "Everyone calls me Steffie." Roughly, she wiped them away, hating this display of weakness, especially in front of Charles. "I—don't know how you can live with yourself."

"If you want the truth, I don't have much of a problem."

"I didn't think your sort would," she muttered

contemptuously. "Well, you'll be hearing from Joan Lind."

"Joan Lind retired last year."

"Then I'll hire someone else," she said, turning on her heel. She marched through the office, slamming the low gate, which had only recently recovered from her entrance.

To her surprise, confronting Charles hadn't eased her pain.

When she pulled out of the parking space, the tires spun and squealed. She felt suddenly embarrassed. She hadn't meant to make such a dramatic exit. Nor was she pleased when she glanced in her rearview mirror to find that Charles had followed her outside.

Two

With the hurt propelling her, Steffie raced home. In her present frame of mind, she didn't dare return to the hospital. Now wasn't the time to make polite conversation with her sisters, or to meet her father's doctor. Not when she desperately needed to vent this terrible sense of frustration and betrayal.

Charles's treachery cut deep. They'd had their differences, but Steffie had never once believed he would purposely set out to hurt her or her family. She'd been wrong. Charles was both vindictive and unforgiving, and that was more painful than the things he'd said to her that last day they'd been together. That horrible day when he'd laughed at her.

She was shocked that Charles still had the power to make her feel this way, but apparently his grip on her heart was as strong now as it had been three years earlier. The time she'd spent away from home, the time she'd given herself to heal, might never have existed. She was no less vulnerable to him now.

From the first time Steffie met Charles, she'd been fascinated with him. Infatuated. In the beginning, she hoped he returned her feelings. She'd been attending the University of Portland, making the fifty-mile commute into the city each day. Her mother had died a few months earlier, so Steffie had decided against moving into a dorm, as she'd originally planned.

In her sorrow, she'd craved the comfort of familiar people and places. She was worried, too, about her father, who seemed to be walking around in a fog of grief.

Valerie was already living in Texas at that point, and although she'd come home often while their mother was ill, her work schedule had kept her from visiting much since.

Norah, who was in the university's nursing program, used to drive to Portland with her. But Steffie would have made the hour's drive twice a day by herself if she'd had to, simply so she could see Charles more often.

It mortified her now, looking back. Her excuses to see him had been embarrassingly transparent. She'd been so wide-eyed with adoration that she'd repeatedly made a fool of herself.

Her cheeks flamed as she recalled the times she'd followed him around like a lost puppy. The way she'd studied every word, every line, he'd written. The way she'd worshiped him from afar, until her love had burned fiercely within her, impossible to contain or control....

It hurt to remember those times and as she so often had in the past, she blocked the memories from her mind rather than relive the humiliation she'd suffered because of him.

Her anger had cooled by the time she'd finished

the ten-mile drive out of Orchard Valley to the family home. Once she arrived, the thought of going inside held no appeal. She needed to do something physically demanding to work off her frustration.

The stables were located behind the house. Valerie and Norah had never really taken to riding, but Steffie, who was the family daredevil, had loved it. The sense of freedom and power had been addictive to a young girl struggling to discover her own identity. Some of the happiest memories she had of her childhood were the times she'd gone horseback riding with her father.

She knew from Norah's letters that he hadn't ridden much lately and had left exercising the horses to the hired help.

The stable held six stalls, four of them empty, and a tack room at the rear. Both Fury and Princess raised their sleek heads when she entered the barn. Princess was the gentle mare her father had purchased and named for her several years earlier; Fury was her father's gelding, large and black, notoriously temperamental. He pawed the ground vigorously as she approached.

"How're you doing, big boy?" she asked, rubbing his soft muzzle. "I'm not ignoring you, Princess," she told the mare across the aisle. "It's just that I'm in the mood for a really hard workout."

After allowing Fury to refamiliarize himself with her, Steffie collected saddle and bridle from the tack room. She slipped on Fury's bridle, then opened the stall gate and led him out. The gelding seemed to be just as eager to run as she was to ride, and he shifted his weight impatiently as she tightened the girth and adjusted the stirrups.

Leading him out of the stable, she'd set her foot in the stirrup, ready to mount, when she noticed a small red sports car racing down the driveway. It didn't take her two seconds to recognize Charles.

Steffie had no intention of speaking to a man she considered a traitor. In fact, she didn't want to ever see him again. She planned to talk to her sisters, then seek legal counsel. Charles would pay for what he'd done to her father, and she'd make sure he paid dearly. Even if he retained bitter feelings about her, that was no reason to take vengeance on her family.

Reaching for the saddle horn, she hoisted herself onto Fury's back. She hadn't used a Western saddle since she'd left home and needed a few moments to get used to it again. Fury scampered in a side trot as Steffie changed her position, leaning slightly forward.

"It's all right, boy," she assured him in a calm, quiet voice that belied her eagerness to escape—and leave Charles behind.

She ignored his honk and although it was childish, she derived a certain amount of pleasure from turning her back on him. She nudged Fury's side and with her chin at a haughty angle, trotted away.

She'd only gone a short distance when she became aware that Charles was following her. Fury didn't need any encouragement to increase his steady trot to a full gallop. Although she was an experienced horsewoman, Steffie wasn't prepared for the sudden burst of speed. Fury raced as though fire was licking at his heels.

Holding on to the reins, Steffie adjusted herself as well as she could, bouncing and jolting uncomfortably, unable to adapt herself to Fury's rhythm. She'd ridden in Italy, but not nearly as often as she would have liked and always with an English-style saddle. Not only was she out of practice, she hadn't the strength to control a horse of Fury's size and power—especially one who hadn't been exercised much lately. She should have thought of that, she groaned. Thank goodness he was familiar with the terrain. He galloped first along the dirt road, bordered on both sides by apple trees. He kicked up a cloud of dust in his wake, which made it impossible for Steffie to tell whether Charles had continued after her. She prayed he hadn't.

Only when Fury took a sharp turn to the left, through a rough patch of ground, did Steffie see that Charles was indeed behind her. She tried to pull in the reins, to slow Fury down to a more comfortable trot, but the gelding had a mind of his own. Next she tried to talk to him but her hair flew about her face, the long ends slapping her cheeks, blinding her. Between her bouncing in the saddle and the hair flapping in her face, she didn't manage a single intelligible word.

By now she had a lot more than Charles to worry about. She was about to lose what little control she had of the horse. And on this rough ground, she feared for the animal's safety, not to mention her own.

Steffie remembered the land well enough to realize they were headed for a bluff that overlooked the valley. It was at the farthest reach of her family's property, and a place Steffie had often gone when she needed to be alone. She approved of Fury's choice, if not his means of getting there.

Her one consolation was that it would be virtually impossible for Charles to follow her any farther. His vehicle would never make it over the rock-strewn landscape. With no other option, he'd be forced to turn back. Or wait. And if he chose to wait by the side of the dirt road, he'd be out of luck—she'd simply take another route home, connecting with the road at a different point.

Once they reached their destination, Fury slowed to a canter. Steffie pulled back on the reins, slid out of the saddle and commanded her trembling legs to keep her upright. She wiped the sweat from his neck and rubbed him down with a handful of long dry grass, then led him to a gentle stream. She was loosely holding the reins, allowing him to drink the clear, cool water, when she noticed a whirl of dust. Thinking at first that it might be a dust devil, she only glanced in that direction. Her heart sank all the way to her knees when she made out the form of a red sports car.

It wasn't possible. The terrain was far too uneven and rocky. Charles must be out of his mind to risk the undercarriage of his car by racing after her.

Squaring her shoulders, she turned to face him, refusing to give one quarter. Charles bounded out of the small car like a spring being released. She nearly flinched at the hard, angry set of his face.

"What the bloody hell do you think you're doing?" he demanded—as though he had a right to ask.

Steffie didn't acknowledge him but resumed her rubdown of the horse.

"You might have been killed, you idiot. And you might have killed that damn horse, too."

It was in her mind to tell him that she was no idiot, but she refused to become involved in a shouting match. And she *did* feel guilty about taking out a horse she couldn't control—her father's horse, yet. But Charles was a traitor, and worse. The next time she spoke to him, Steffie thought angrily, it would be through an attorney.

It looked for a moment as though he intended to grip her by the shoulders; in fact, what she heard him mutter sounded like a threat to "shake some sense" into her. He raised his hands, then briefly closed his eyes and spun away from her.

"You haven't changed a bit, have you?" he cried, jerking one hand through his hair as he stalked toward his car.

Still Steffie remained silent, although she had to bite her tongue in an effort not to lash back at him. He'd purposely hurt her family, hurt her. There was nothing left to be said.

Abruptly he yanked his car door open. Steffie blinked at the unexpectedness of his withdrawal. She wasn't sure what he'd planned to do, but this swift capitulation came as a surprise.

Not wanting him to assume she cared about his actions one way or the other, she tried to ignore him. She looped Fury's reins around a low branch and walked away, too. Her legs were trembling so badly that she decided to climb onto a boulder. Perched there, she gazed out at the sweeping view of the valley below, jewel-like in its green lushness.

Charles's footsteps behind her announced that he hadn't left, after all.

"Read it!" he shouted, slapping the very newspaper she'd given him against her thigh. "*This* time finish the article."

Steffie gasped, then pressed her lips together, tilting her head to avoid looking at him.

"Fine, be stubborn. That's nothing new. But if you won't read the article, I'll do it for you." He grabbed the newspaper.

Steffie wanted to blot out every word, but she refused to resort to anything quite as juvenile as plugging her ears. She cringed inwardly as his strong voice read the opening paragraph. On hearing it a second time, she felt the piece sounded even more hostile to her father than she'd believed earlier. It was as though Charles had taken the very heart of David Bloomfield's accomplishments and crushed it with falsehoods and accusations.

By the time he reached the spot where Steffie had stopped reading, where her father's name was actually mentioned, the anger inside her had rekindled.

She closed her eyes to the wave of pain that threatened to swallow her.

He read on, and she waited with foreboding for the attack she knew was coming. But it didn't happen. As Charles continued, she suddenly realized how wrong she'd been. How *terribly* wrong. Her heart in her throat, she turned toward him. Charles went on, reading a direct quote from David Bloomfield in which he told of the changes he'd made over the years to aid migrant workers.

At first Steffie was convinced she'd misunderstood. Nor was she entirely sure she could believe Charles. He might be making it up as he went along, she thought wildly, instead of actually reading the article. She reached for the newspaper and snatched it away from him.

It only took her a moment to locate the paragraph he'd just read. He hadn't made it up! There, bold as could be, was the quote from her father, followed by two long paragraphs that reported the progressive measures the Bloomfield Orchards had implemented over the years.

Her stomach plummeted, and she began to feel as though she were sitting in a deck chair on the *Titanic*. That feeling intensified as she finished reading the article. Because she soon discovered that not only was her father quoted—approvingly—several times, but their family orchard was used as a model for other local orchards to follow.

Steffie drew in a deep, stabilizing breath before she looked up at Charles. Once again, she'd made a fool of herself in front of him. She cringed in acute embarrassment and self-contempt. Oh, Lord, what a jerk she'd been. What a total jerk.

She'd known that meeting Charles again was inevitable. She'd hoped that on her return he'd view her—from afar, of course—as mature and sophisticated. She'd wanted him to see her as cosmopolitan and cultured, unlike the lovesick twenty-one-year-old who'd left Orchard Valley three years before.

She'd imagined their first meeting. She would step forward, a gentle smile on her face, and hold out her hand politely. She'd murmur ever so sweetly that it was lovely to see him again, but unfortunately she couldn't recall his name. Charles Something-or-other, wasn't it?

"It looks like I owe you an apology," she said instead, her voice quavering a bit despite her efforts to keep it even.

"You're damn right you owe me an apology!" he flared back. "I'd assumed you might have changed in three years. Instead you're an even bigger...nuisance."

His words felt like a slap across the face, and she flinched involuntarily. There wasn't a thing she could say in her own defense, nothing that would take away the shame of what she'd done. No words would erase the way she'd come into his office and created a scene in front of his entire staff.

"So it seems," she said as steadily as her crumbling poise would allow.

"You scared the hell out of me, taking off like that," he raged. "You might have killed yourself."

Again, there was nothing she could say. Had she been in any other frame of mind, she would have recognized that with a horse like Fury, she was heading for trouble.

"You're a crazy woman!" he shouted, his anger fully ignited now. "How do you think I would have felt if you'd been hurt? What about your father? You accuse *me* of causing his heart attack! What do you think would've happened to him if you'd killed yourself?"

"I—I..." Hating the telltale action, she bit her lip to stop its trembling.

"Damn it all," he shouted and to Steffie's dismay, he reached down and pulled her to her feet. His hands clasped her shoulders and he drew her into his arms.

Before she had time to react, she was completely caught in his embrace, her hands trapped against his heaving chest.

One hand left her shoulder and slid into her long, tangled hair.

"Do you even have a clue what I was thinking?" he whispered. "Do you have any idea what was going through my mind?"

Her heart thundered. She should fight her way out of his embrace. She should demand that he release her, tell him he had no right to take her in his arms. But Steffie couldn't make herself move, couldn't make herself speak.

She didn't try to stop him even when it became obvious that he was going to kiss her. Mentally she braced herself, knowing he was angry, suspecting that he intended to punish her with a savage kiss.

As so often of late, Steffie was wrong. When his mouth found hers, it was a gentle brushing of lips. Her eyes opened in wonder and surprise.

Charles kissed her again, longer this time, his mouth gliding over hers, and staying there. Before she realized what she was doing, she moved her arms upward and timidly locked them behind his neck. Her lips parted to his and he pressed her closer.

But only for a moment. "No, Steffie," he said in a raw whisper, gripping both wrists and breaking her hold. He stepped back as though he'd been scorched. Their gazes held for several seconds before he turned and hurried away.

He left as abruptly as he'd arrived, his sports car spitting dirt and small stones as he roared off. She sighed and prepared to mount Fury for the long journey home.

Steffie took a long nap that afternoon, waking sometime in the early evening. The sun was setting, dousing the orchards in a lovely shade of soft pink. Not knowing what time it was, she came downstairs to find Norah humming softly in the kitchen.

"Hi," Norah greeted her, smiling brightly when she saw Steffie. "I was beginning to wonder if you'd ever wake up. You must have been exhausted."

Steffie nodded.

"There's a plate for you in the oven. I bet you're famished."

The last thing she'd eaten had been that banana at breakfast. Murmuring her thanks, she walked across the room and removed the plate from the oven. Her sister had always been a good cook and Steffie gazed longingly at the broiled chicken breast, new red potatoes and fresh green beans.

"Where'd you go this morning?" Norah asked cheerfully, continuing to wash dishes. "Valerie said you seemed upset over something to do with Charles Tomaselli?"

Steffie pulled out a stool at the counter and sat down to eat. "I needed to ask him something."

"Did you get everything settled?"

Steffie lowered her gaze. "Everything's clear now."

"Good. He really has been wonderful through all this. Dad's pleased with how well the article on migrant workers was received. You read it, didn't you? The two of them spent weeks collecting facts, and Dad actually did a bit of undercover work. It was the first time since Mom died that he revealed much interest in anything. I don't think even Charles knows how much Dad put into that piece. He must have gone over every detail a dozen times."

Steffie, who was just about to begin her meal, promptly lost her appetite. "I—I didn't realize that."

"I was planning to mail you the article, but then Dad had the heart attack and everything else fell by the wayside,'' Norah explained conversationally, leaning against the counter as she dried her hands.

''Where's Val?''

''In the den. She's working. You know Val—she's as dedicated a businesswoman as anyone's likely to meet. Within a few days of arriving home, she'd ordered a fax machine so she could get files and stuff from the office. Although I have to admit her mind hasn't been on the job lately.''

''Oh?'' Steffie made an effort to taste her meal. The chicken was tender and delicious. She took a second bite.

Norah wiggled her eyebrows playfully. ''In case you hadn't noticed, there's a romance brewing between Val and Dr. Winston.''

''There is?'' Steffie asked, fork poised in midair. ''What about Valerie's boss? Every time I got a letter from her it was Rowdy this and Rowdy that.''

''I don't know about Rowdy, but I do know what I saw the night of Dad's surgery.''

''Which was?'' Steffie asked anxiously.

''Valerie came apart after we were allowed to go in and see Dad. She didn't realize I knew how upset she was, but I figured she needed a few minutes alone. I hadn't seen Dad yet myself, and when I did, I could understand Valerie's concern. He was very close to death. I don't know how much anyone's told you about Dad's condition, but it's a miracle he survived the open-heart surgery. Anyway,'' she said with a sigh, ''when I went in to see Dad I wondered if he'd last the night. I know Colby didn't think he would. Neither did any of the others who were on the surgical team. Naturally, they didn't say as much, but I could tell what they were thinking. I've worked in surgery often enough myself to know who's likely to survive and who isn't. One look told me we'd be lucky if Dad lasted another few hours, although I was encouraged that he'd survived the surgery itself. There were plenty of complications, with fluid in his lungs and all.''

"Tell me about Valerie," Steffie urged.

"Oh, yeah, Valerie. Well, after she'd been with Dad she went out onto the patio outside the surgical waiting room. She was crying, which we both know is rare for Val. I could tell she needed someone. When I got back from seeing Dad, I started to go out to her, thinking we'd be able to comfort each other, but I stopped when I saw that Colby was with her.''

Steffie had heard wonderful things about Dr. Winston already, but his compassion for her sister confirmed everything she'd come to know of him. She said so to Norah, who nodded.

"They were sitting together and he was holding her in his arms. I don't know how to explain it, but he had this...look. As though he would've done anything within his power to take away her pain. I thought right then that he had the look of a man who's just discovered he's fallen in love.''

"And Valerie?''

"I think she might have realized they were in love with each other before Colby did. You know how strong Valerie is, how she never wants to let anyone do anything for her. Well, for the first time since I can remember, she needed someone and Colby's the person she turned to."

"Valerie and Dr. Winston," Steffie said slowly. She'd often wondered what it would be like when her oldest sister fell in love. Valerie had always been so pragmatic, much too sensible to become involved in a relationship while she was in college. She was there to be educated, not to find a husband, she'd told Steffie.

"Then Dad took a turn for the better," Norah went on, "and he started all this talk about us marrying and having kids. I'm afraid Valerie's taking it much too seriously, worrying about it too much. But then, she's in love for the first time in her life and she's frightened half to death that Colby's the wrong man for her. Or more to the point, that she's the wrong woman for him."

"Love is love, and if they both feel so strongly, then what's the problem?"

Norah's smile was sad and a bit hesitant. "Colby's as traditional as they come. He's looking for more than a wife—I think he wants a woman straight out of the 1950s."

"Valerie knows this?"

"Of course she does. Colby's well aware of the kind of woman Valerie is, too. Her calling isn't the kitchen, it's the boardroom."

"I say more power to her." In Steffie's opinion, Colby Winston should appreciate her sister's God-given talents.

"Exactly!" Norah agreed, "but if Valerie marries Colby she'd probably have to quit her job. For one thing, CHIPS doesn't have a branch in this part of the country. And she's worked too hard and too long to let go of her career."

"In other words, they'd both have to compromise—and they can't?"

"Exactly. No one ever told me love could be so complicated. I feel sorry for them both. They couldn't be more miserable."

Steffie finished off the last of the small red potatoes, not wanting her sister to guess how curious she was about her father's "chat" with her mother. "What do you think of all this talk about Dad's... experience?"

Norah pulled up a stool and sat across from Steffie. "I don't know. *He* believes he actually talked with Mom and that's what's important, don't you think?"

Steffie wasn't sure of anything anymore. She'd once been confident that she knew what she wanted in life. Then everything had fallen apart. But the time she'd spent in Italy had helped her regain a perspective on her own life...hadn't it?

It suddenly occurred to Steffie with a sense of horror that she'd spent three years studying and traveling in Europe, and her primary purpose had been *to impress Charles Tomaselli* when she returned.

She'd impressed him, all right, by making an even bigger fool of herself than before.

"Dad's been talking about his grandchildren all afternoon," Norah continued, breaking into Steffie's thoughts. Actually Steffie was grateful for the intrusion.

"Grandchildren," she repeated softly. "From you, naturally?" She couldn't imagine Valerie as a mother, and she herself had no intention of marrying. When her father was well enough to come home, Steffie intended to find herself an apartment in Portland and to apply for a fellowship and begin her doctorate. She'd completed her master's in Italy after an intensive language program, and in her last year there, she'd taken several advanced courses. It was hard to believe someone so well educated could be so dismally unaware of her own motives, she mused unhappily.

"Dad claims I'm going to present him with six grandchildren," Norah said, barely restraining a smile. "Can you imagine me with six children?"

"Which means Valerie's going to be responsible for another six."

"No, three. According to Dad's rumblings, you're going to have three of the little darlings yourself."

Steffie grinned, despite her depression. The picture of herself married and with a brood of children was somewhat amusing. She'd only loved one man in her life and the experience had been so painful that she was determined never to repeat the mistake.

"I guess we'll see," Steffie said, sliding off her stool to carry her now-empty plate to the sink.

"I guess we will," Norah concurred.

Although she'd slept for a good part of the afternoon, two hours later Steffie was yawning. Making her excuses, she returned to her bedroom, showered and got into bed, savoring the crisp, clean sheets.

Sitting up, her knees tucked under her chin, she pondered her conversation with Norah. In the years since she'd moved away, a number of her friends had married. She'd gotten wedding invitations, passed on by Norah, every few months. And several of her high school and college friends were already mothers, some two times over.

While she was in Italy, Steffie hadn't allowed herself to think about anything more pressing than her studies, which had occupied most of her time. She'd traveled and studied and worked hard. But at odd moments, when she received a wedding invitation or a birth announcement, she'd occasionally taken a moment to wonder if her life was missing something. Or when she was with Mario, the adorable young son of her landlady in Rome, she'd imagined, more than once, how it would feel to have a family of her own…. She'd usually managed to suppress the yearning quickly.

And now she was experiencing it again, and more sharply than ever before. All this talk of weddings and children troubled her. She felt excluded, somehow. In the end, Valerie would probably marry her Dr. Winston, and there'd be a wonderful man for Norah, she was sure of it.

But for her? She found she couldn't believe in the same kind of happy ending.

Three

Although she was exhausted, Steffie couldn't sleep. After tossing about restlessly and tangling her sheets, she sat on the edge of the bed and pushed the long hair away from her face.

She'd prefer to think the nap she'd taken that afternoon was responsible for this inability to sleep.

But she knew better.

She couldn't sleep because her thoughts wouldn't leave her alone. The memory of what a fool she'd made of herself with Charles hounded her until she wanted to scream.

With graphic clarity she recalled the first time she'd heard of Charles Tomaselli. She'd read his introductory column in the *Clarion* and had loved his wit and style. No matter what she thought of him now, she could never fault his talent as a writer. Charles had a way of turning a phrase that gave a reader pause. He chose his words carefully, writing in a clear, economical manner that managed to be both clever and precise. And he had a wide range of subjects, covering everything from social trends to the local political scene.

When she'd read his first few columns, she'd assumed he was much older, because the confidence of his observations and his style suggested a man of considerable experience. It wasn't until several weeks later that she actually met him. At the time she'd been so dumbstruck she could barely put two words together.

She'd tried to tell him how much she enjoyed his editor's column, but the words had twisted on the end of her tongue and came out sounding jerky and odd, like something a preschooler might say.

She'd been terribly embarrassed, but Charles had responded graciously, thanking her for the compliment.

It wasn't just the fact that he was in his late twenties—and not his fifties—that had taken Steffie by surprise. Nor was it the fact that he was strikingly handsome, although he was certainly easy on the eyes, with his dark Italian looks. What struck Steffie like a fist to the stomach was the instant and powerful attraction she felt for him.

Unlike Valerie, who'd gone out on only a handful of dates through high school and college, Steffie had had an active social calendar. She'd always been well liked by both sexes—popular enough to be voted Prom Queen her senior year of high school. But although she had lots of friends who happened to be boys, Steffie had never been in love. She'd thought, more than once, that she was, but she'd been wise enough to realize she was only infatuated, or in love with the idea of being in love.

Although she was twenty-one, she'd never been

involved in a serious relationship. She hadn't considered herself ready for one—until she met the newly appointed editor of the *Orchard Valley Clarion.*

When she met Charles, she knew immediately that she was going to love this man. How she could be so certain was unclear, even to her, but to the very depths of her young heart, she was absolutely convinced of it.

Following that initial meeting, Steffie had driven home in a daze. She didn't tell anyone, including her sisters, what she felt. She didn't know how she could possibly explain her feelings without sounding silly. Love at first sight was something reserved for movies and romance novels.

She'd been filled with questions, wondering if Charles had felt it, too; she soon persuaded herself that he had.

He was older, twenty-seven she discovered, amazingly mature and sophisticated, while she was an inexperienced third-year college student.

Steffie lived for the next edition of the *Clarion,* ripping open the newspaper until she found his column, and devoured each word Charles had written. Occasionally he wrote a feature article, and she read those just as avidly. She soon discovered that others were equally taken with his work. He'd been in town for less than two months and had already become a source of pride and pleasure to the entire community.

Steffie straightened and reached over to turn on her bedside lamp. Obviously she wouldn't be able to sleep, and sitting in her room, dredging up memories of Charles, wasn't helping.

The house was dark and silent, which meant Valerie and Norah were both asleep. Not wanting to wake either of her sisters, Steffie slipped quietly down the dimly lit stairs.

She thought about making herself a cup of tea, then decided against it. Instead, she tiptoed into her father's den. She turned on a soft light and reached for *Sonnets from the Portuguese*—an especially lovely edition her father had given her mother years ago, before they were married. Steffie cuddled up in his reading chair, already comforted.

The leather felt cool against her skin. An afghan her mother had knitted when the girls were still young lay neatly folded on the ottoman. Valerie must have brought it in with her, since it hadn't been there the night before.

Steffie reached for the rose-colored afghan and tucked it around her, then turned to one of her favorite poems.

She might have made it through two pages, maybe even three, before her mind drifted back to Charles. Back to that first year...

He hadn't noticed her. Hadn't shared the instant attraction. In fact, he hadn't even remembered her name. Steffie was stunned. She'd dreamed of him every night since the day they met. Wonderful dreams of laughing and loving, of strolling hand in hand through the apple orchard, sharing secrets and planning the rest of their lives. Her heart was so full of love that it was all she could do not to tell him outright.

Getting a man to notice her was a new challenge to Steffie. Until then, it had always been the other way around. The men—no, *boys*—had been the ones to seek her out. For the first time in her life, Steffie found herself at a disadvantage in a relationship. Clearly the only option open to her was to let Charles know as subtly as possible that she was interested. It shouldn't be such a difficult task for a former Prom Queen.

Except that it was...

The first thing Steffie did was to write him a letter commending his writing ability and his opinions. She'd agonized over every word, then waited for nearly two weeks for a reply.

There hadn't been one.

Charles hadn't printed her letter and didn't respond, either. Steffie had been crushed. Never one to quit, though, she'd visited the newspaper office with suggestions for a wide variety of stories. As she recalled, she'd managed to come up with 150 such ideas. Admittedly some were better than others.

Charles had been polite, but had made it plain that although he appreciated her suggestions, he already had an enthusiastic staff whose job it was to come up with regional stories.

Her plan had been for Charles to be so awed by her concern about local issues and her invaluable ideas that he'd invite her to dinner to discuss her interest. Although, in retrospect, it sounded terribly naive, she'd actually believed this would happen.

Apparently, she spent more time than she realized hanging around the newspaper office and making a nuisance of herself because Charles unexpectedly asked her out for coffee one morning.

Steffie had been so excited that she could barely sit still. She was further encouraged when Charles chose a booth in the farthest, most private corner of the local coffee shop.

Even now, three years afterward, Steffie could recall how thrilled she'd been. She'd slid into the red vinyl seat across from him, sure he could read all the love and adoration in her eyes.

The encounter, however, proved to be a bitter disappointment for Steffie. Charles had been kind, but firm. He couldn't help noticing, he'd said, how much time she spent at the newspaper office, and was sure her studies must have been suffering. He'd also gotten her letter and the other notes she'd sent him, and although he was flattered by her attention, he was much too busy with the paper to become involved in a relationship.

When Steffie had pressed him for more of an explanation, he'd told her without a second's pause that he considered her too young to date. Furthermore, he felt she was…too innocent.

Having recently turned twenty-one, Steffie was aghast at his lack of foresight. She was a mature woman, and six years' difference in their ages was unimportant. If she didn't object, then he shouldn't, either.

As an active member of her high school debating team, Steffie had learned how to argue, and now she'd used every skill at her disposal.

It didn't work.

He'd finally told her she was a nice *kid* but he simply wasn't interested. That he was a busy man and didn't have the time or the patience to be a baby-sitter. A baby-sitter! He wasn't exactly impolite, but it was clear he had no intention of asking her out. Ever.

Their coffee had just been served, and Charles hadn't taken more than a sip of it before he tossed some money on the table and left.

Steffie had remained there, too hurt to breathe, too numb to feel anything more than a painful kind of disappointment. She couldn't remember how long she'd sat in the booth. Long after her coffee had cooled, she knew.

Obviously she'd sat there much too long because she had decided with a sigh of relief that Charles Tomaselli was obviously lying.

"Steff."

The gentle voice was followed by a warm hand on her shoulder.

"What are you doing sleeping down here?"

Steffie raised her head and blinked. Valerie, dressed in a long housecoat, stood beside her.

"What time is it?"

"Morning," Valerie said with a smile. "How long have you been here?"

Moving her legs, Steffie winced at the unexpected discomfort. She wasn't sure how long she'd been asleep, but her legs were stiff and sore and the book still lay open on her lap.

"I was going to fix myself a cup of coffee and some toast before heading to the hospital. Do you want some?"

"Please." She worked one shoulder and then the other and rotated her neck, hoping to ease the crick. Her thoughts had been so full of what had happened between her and Charles in those early days that she couldn't remember falling asleep. It surprised her that she had. She wondered if her musings had followed her into her dreams, then decided it would be better if they hadn't.

"I can't tell you how good Dad looks compared to a week ago," Valerie said when Steffie joined her in the kitchen. "It's like a miracle."

"It was so crazy being stuck in Italy like that."

"You know—" Valerie paused, clutching a large earthenware mug "—in a way I'm grateful you couldn't get home for a while. It might be the one thing that kept Dad alive. He was determined to see you before he died."

Steffie wasn't sure she followed her sister's thoughts. "Do you mean to say Dad had a means of controlling the timing of his...demise?"

"Sort of. Death was what he wanted. If I've

learned anything through all this, it's that the human will is an amazing thing.''

Steffie began making toast, bringing the butter and Norah's homemade strawberry jam out of the refrigerator. ''I'm not sure I understand what you mean about the human will.''

''I don't know if I can explain it,'' Valerie said after a moment, her look distant and thoughtful. ''All I know is that Dad was on the brink of death for days. When I first arrived, Colby explained that Dad would require open-heart surgery. He wanted to perform the operation immediately but couldn't because of a variety of complications Dad was experiencing. If you want the medical terms for all this you can ask Norah or Colby, but basically it boiled down to one thing. Dad had lost the will to fight for his life. He's been miserable without Mom. We both know that, but I don't think anyone fully appreciated exactly how *lonely* he's been.''

''I shouldn't have left him.'' Despite Valerie's immediate reassurances, Steffie partially blamed herself for her father's failing health. She'd known when he came to visit her in Italy last year that something was wrong. He'd taken the trip to Europe not out of any desire to travel but because Valerie and Norah had thought it would help revive his spirits. The fact that Steffie was living in Italy had been a convenient excuse.

Steffie had enjoyed the time with her father, and had been excited about showing him the country she'd come to love and introducing him to her new friends. She'd carefully avoided any conversation having to do with Orchard Valley or her mother. Her father had urged her to come home, but she'd already registered for new courses and paid her rent in advance and planned another trip. All excuses. Because it really came down to one thing: she'd been afraid to go home.

Steffie Bloomfield afraid! The family daredevil. Dauntless, reckless Steffie Bloomfield was afraid of a mere man. More precisely, she was terrified of having to speak to Charles again, of looking him in the eye and pretending it didn't hurt any longer. Pretending she didn't love him. Pretending she didn't feel humiliated.

She was incapable of shrugging off the past, especially when it was much simpler just to stay in Europe. She loved her history courses, she enjoyed traveling throughout Italy, she was fond of her landlady's family, she had lots of friends and acquaintances. She'd discovered, too, that she had a real aptitude for languages; besides being proficient in Italian, she'd picked up some French and German and hoped to continue learning them. No, she had decided, there were far too many good reasons to remain in Europe. And so she'd stayed.

"Do you want to ride into the hospital with me?" Valerie asked, apparently deep in her own thoughts.

"Sure."

"I might need to do a few errands later, but you might be able to get a ride home from Norah if I'm not back."

"I'm not worried. I haven't been able to spend much time with Dad yet." Steffie felt guilty about rushing out of the hospital the day before without returning to see him.

As it turned out, Steffie couldn't have chosen a better morning to be with her father. It was the day he was being transferred out of the Surgical Intensive Care Unit and onto the surgical ward. His time in the SICU was a short four days, his recovery nothing short of remarkable. Even Dr. Winston seemed to think so.

"I can't get over how beautiful you've become," her father said when he woke from a short nap. Steffie was sitting at his bedside, doing the *New York Times* crossword puzzle and feeling downright self-satisfied that she'd managed to fill in a good half of the answers.

"I'll tell you what I've become," Steffie said with a laugh, "and that's Italian. The first day after I left Rome I slipped from English to Italian and then back again without noticing. I think I spent twice as long clearing customs as anyone else, simply because the agent didn't know what to make of me."

"So can you cook me some real Italian spaghetti?" her father asked.

"I certainly can, and I promise it'll be so good you'll dream about it the rest of your life."

"With plenty of garlic?"

Steffie raised the tips of her fingers to her lips and made a loud smacking sound. "With enough garlic to ward off vampires for the next hundred years. Besides, I hear garlic's good for your heart.''

"But lousy for your love life.''

"I don't think either of us needs to worry about that,'' she teased.

"Ah.'' David Bloomfield shook his head. "That's where you're wrong, Princess. You, my darling Stephanie, are about to discover what it means to be in love.''

Steffie didn't have the heart to say she already knew all she cared to on that subject. *Thanks, Dad—but no thanks,* she told him silently. Falling in love wasn't an experience she wanted to repeat.

"You aren't going to argue with me the way Valerie did, are you?''

"Would it do any good?''

"No,'' he said, smiling broadly.

"I didn't think so.''

"You don't believe I actually talked to your mother, do you?''

"Uh…'' It wasn't that she disbelieved him exactly. *He* was convinced that something had happened, so her opinion was irrelevant. He claimed to have enjoyed a lengthy conversation with her mother while strolling around some celestial lake. Valerie had mentioned it almost immediately after Steffie's arrival home. Norah had talked about it, too. Steffie found their accounts fascinating. Did she believe it had really happened? She didn't know. She was inclined to think he'd experienced some kind of revelation, all right—but whether it was spiritual, as he thought, or a dream, or a fantasy of his own making, she had no idea. And it didn't matter.

"You won't be the only one who doesn't believe my talk with your mother was real."

"It isn't that, Dad."

"Don't you worry about it. Time will prove me right."

"Prove you right about what?" a distinctive male voice asked from behind her. Steffie froze and the dread washed over her like a huge wave.

Charles Tomaselli.

He was the last person she'd expected to meet here. The last person she wanted to see again.

"How're you feeling, David?" he asked.

"I've been better."

"I'll bet you have," Charles said wryly.

Steffie was on her feet immediately. "I'll leave you two to chat," she said with a cheery lilt, anxious to leave the room.

"There's no reason for you to go," her father countered, holding out his hand to her. "Your smile is the brightest sunshine I've seen in days. Isn't that so, Charles?"

Steffie cringed inwardly, and not giving Charles time to comment, quickly squeezed her father's hand. "I don't think it's a good idea for you to have too much company all at once."

"She might be right," Charles agreed. "Besides, I've got some business to discuss with you. I thought you'd be interested in hearing what happened as a result of that article we did on the migrant-worker situation.''

Steffie's breath caught in her throat until she realized Charles wasn't referring to the stunt she'd pulled in his office the day before. She went weak with relief when she heard him mention something about Commissioner O'Dell initiating an inspection program.

Steffie still hadn't looked at Charles, still hadn't turned to face him. She delayed it as long as possible, leaning forward to gently kiss her father's cheek. ''I'll get a ride back to the house with Valerie or Norah, but I'll be in again this evening and we can finish our...discussion.''

''I'll see you then, Princess.''

Steffie nodded and mentally braced herself as she turned away from her father's bed. She looked shyly at Charles. It amazed her how their eyes instantly met, how they were drawn to gaze at each other, as though neither could resist the pull of mutual attraction. Her own heart gave a small burst of joy and she wondered if, deep within, his did, too.

''Hello, Steffie.''

''Charles.'' Her voice was low and wispy. ''I'll see you later, Dad.''

''Bye, Princess.''

Her gaze skidded past Charles as she hurried from the room, eager now to make her escape. By the time she was at the end of the corridor, her heart was roaring and she was breathless—all because of a casual encounter with Charles. Obviously she'd need to prepare herself mentally for even such minor confrontations.

She hadn't been nearly as shy with him that summer three years earlier, she remembered with chagrin. It mortified her now to think of her brazen behavior...

If Charles considered her a *kid* when he'd invited her for coffee, then Steffie decided she owed it to herself to prove him wrong. Without difficulty, she'd been able to discover where Charles lived. Crime had never been much of a problem in Orchard Valley, and Charles had been kind enough to leave his front door unlocked.

By the time he appeared several hours later, there were scented candles lit throughout the living room and a bottle of champagne chilling in the kitchen.

"Is that you, darling?" Steffie had called out from the bathroom. She'd been sitting in a bubble-filled tub for the better part of an hour, and her skin had started to shrivel. She was also worried about the candles dripping and the champagne getting warm, but she dared not leave, fearing she'd never be able to adjust the bubbles again. It was important that he think she was completely nude, though in reality she wore a skimpy bikini.

Charles didn't answer. He stalked into the room, stopping abruptly in the doorway as his shocked gaze fell on her.

"What the hell are you doing here?" he'd demanded.

"I thought it was important for you to know I'm not a child."

"Then what are you—a mermaid?"

She forced a soft laugh and said in what she hoped was a sultry, adult voice. "No, silly man, I'm a *woman* and if you'll come here, I'll prove it to you."

"Get out."

"Out? But...but I was hoping you'd join me."

"No way, sweetheart. Now either you remove yourself from my home or I'm calling the police."

She pushed her big toe under the water tap. "I think my toe might be stuck."

"Fine, I'll call the plumber."

"But Charles, darling..."

"Charles, nothing," he snapped, marching into the bathroom and gripping her by the upper arm. The force of his strength lifted her halfway out of the tub. She screeched, stumbling to find her balance. As soon as she was upright, Charles tossed a towel at her and told her she had five minutes to leave before he called the police.

Steffie had fled, but she'd seen the gleam of male admiration in Charles's eyes, seen the way he'd looked at her for a second or two. And, fool that she was, she hadn't been the least bit discouraged. Instead, she'd devised yet another plan.

Steffie wandered into the waiting area searching for Valerie. One of the orderlies mentioned that her sister had gone to pick up office supplies. Steffie remembered hearing something about an errand, but she hadn't been paying enough attention to recall whether Valerie was returning to the hospital or going straight home.

Oh, well, there was always Norah.

Tracking down her youngest sister didn't take long. Within five minutes, Steffie found her in the emergency room—preparing to go on duty. The hospital was understaffed, and now that their father was beginning to recover, Norah had returned to work. Steffie didn't bother to ask for a ride.

Hoping Charles would be gone, she returned to the surgical ward. Her luck hadn't improved, and they met at the elevator.

"I thought you were headed home?"

"I'll have to wait for Valerie," she said, preparing to edge past him. "Or try to get a cab."

His arm blocked her escape. "There's no need to do that. I'll drop you off at the house."

"No, thanks," she returned stiffly.

"I want to talk to you, anyway," he said, none too gently guiding her into the elevator. "And as they say, there's no time like the present."

"This really isn't necessary, Charles."

"Oh, but it is."

She noticed, when he led her out of the hospital to the parking lot, that he was driving the same red sports car she'd seen the day before. It eased her conscience a bit that it hadn't been damaged during his free-for-all race across the countryside.

He opened the door for her, and Steffie climbed inside. She was adjusting the seat belt when Charles joined her. The space seemed to shrink like silk pressed against a hot iron. Their shoulders touched, their thighs, their arms. For a moment, Steffie held her breath.

"You said you wanted to talk to me?" she said after he'd pulled out of the hospital parking lot. She was leaning as close to the passenger door as she could.

"I thought we'd discuss it over a glass of iced tea. You did plan on inviting me inside, didn't you?" He turned and grinned at her, that boyish, slightly skewed grin she'd always found so appealing.

She'd planned to tell him she had no intention of letting him in; instead she cleared her throat and said, "If you'd like."

"I would."

The ten-mile drive to the house generally took fifteen minutes. Steffie could have sworn Charles was purposely dragging out the time, driving well below the speed limit. They were so close in the small cramped car that she couldn't avoid brushing against him, even though she tried not to. She was trying to forget that he'd kissed her the day before, and this didn't make it any easier! She was trying not to wonder what it would be like to experience his kiss a second time....

Steffie closed her eyes. It was all she could do not to shout at him to hurry. Why was he prolonging these moments alone? The least he could do was make polite conversation.

"My father seems downright cheerful, doesn't

he?'' If Charles wasn't going to say something, then she would. Anything to ease this terrible awareness.

"He certainly does.''

"He's got a reason to live now, and that's made all the difference in the world. I'm not sure what to think about his dream, but—''

"What dream?''

"Uh...nothing...it's not important.'' Steffie couldn't believe what she'd done. In her nervousness, in her eagerness to fill the silence, she'd blurted out what should never have been shared.

She relaxed when Charles turned off the road onto the mile-long family driveway. He parked in front of the house.

Steffie didn't wait for him, but threw open her door and jumped out, her keys already in her hand. She had the front door open by the time he caught up with her, and tossing her purse onto the hall table, led him briskly into the kitchen.

Norah had made some iced tea that morning. Steffie silently thanked her sister for her thoughtfulness as she took out the cold pitcher. It didn't take more than a couple of minutes to find two tall glasses, add ice and slice a fresh lemon. Another minute, and the drinks were ready.

"What was it you wanted to say?'' Steffie finally asked, leaning against the counter. She hadn't realized how warm she was and she held the glass between both hands, enjoying the coolness against her palms.

"It's about what happened yesterday,'' Charles

said, walking away from her. He paused at the bay window that overlooked the backyard. Just beyond his view was the stable. "Or more appropriately, what shouldn't have happened."

Four

"**I**'d rather not discuss it," Steffie said adamantly. She didn't want to hear any more about her irresponsible accusations and rash actions. Nor did she wish to hear how much Charles regretted kissing her.

"If anyone needs to apologize, it's me," she said quickly. "Why don't we just leave it at that? I was wrong."

Charles's back was to her as he stared outside toward the stables. "I don't think anyone's ever infuriated me this much," he said quietly. He turned, set his glass of iced tea aside and thrust his hands into his pockets. "I've never met a woman who manages to irritate me the way you do."

Steffie stiffened. "I've already apologized for leaping to conclusions. I admitted I was wrong." She shrugged elaborately. "My only excuse is that I spent a hellish week trying to get home and I haven't slept properly in days and I—"

"This isn't necessary," he said, interrupting her. "I'm not looking for an apology... Actually I'm here to make my own. I want you to know I'm sorry about chasing after you. It was a dangerous thing to do. I might have spooked Fury into throwing you."

"Not to mention damaging your car."

"True enough."

"Let's put it behind us," Steffie suggested with a weak smile. "I was wrong to run away. It was... childish."

"You were angry, too."

"I've never met a *man* who manages to irritate me the way you do," she said, consciously echoing his words.

"We always seem to get on each other's nerves, don't we?" His grin was warm and gentle, just as his kiss had been. Strangely, Steffie found his smile just as devastating.

"We certainly have a history of annoying one another." It took her more courage than he'd ever know to mention the past. But suddenly she hoped they could put that behind them, too.

"I'd never be able to forgive myself if anything had happened to you."

"I wasn't really in any danger of Fury throwing me." Okay, so that was a slight exaggeration, but she *had* remained in the saddle.

"It was a hell of a way for us to meet again." Charles's voice was husky. He moved closer to her and she lowered her gaze, but not before she noticed how his attention seemed to center on her mouth. "There's one thing I'm not sorry about." He took another step toward her and raised his hand to touch her cheek. His fingers brushed aside a stray lock of hair. Steffie found she couldn't move. She couldn't think coherently. She could barely breathe.

"I don't regret kissing you," Charles whispered.

Then Steffie did move. Trembling, she stepped backward and bolted to the other side of the room.

"Stephanie?"

"Call—call me Steffie," she stuttered. Her hands were shaking so badly that she jerked them behind her.

"I prefer to call you Stephanie. You're not a little girl anymore."

She smiled brightly. Now was the perfect time to convince him how sophisticated she'd become after three years in Europe, sophisticated and *experienced*. She was sure that was the type of woman he expected, the type of woman he wanted.

"As kisses go, it certainly was nice," she agreed in an offhand manner. Was she overdoing it? she wondered. "Yours had a gentleness, and that surprised me. Most men aren't like that, you know? When they kiss a woman it's hot and sweaty; they leave a girl breathless."

"I see," Charles said, raising one eyebrow.

She placed her hands on her hips, fashion-model style, and tilted back her head, letting her long brown hair swing lightly. "I'm not the same person I was three years ago. You're right about that. I'm all grown up now."

"So it seems."

"I appreciate the ride home," she said, walking out of the kitchen. She hoped Charles would follow her because she wasn't sure how much longer she could maintain this performance.

"Is there anything else these…hot, sweaty men taught you?" he asked in a dispassionate voice. He reached for his iced tea, apparently disinclined to leave quite so soon.

She turned around and smiled serenely. "You'd be surprised." Deciding to give him the answer he deserved, she rashly went on. "As you know, I met men of all nationalities—students from all over Europe—and I sampled my fair share of kisses." Mostly chaste kisses of greeting or farewell, but he didn't have to know that. And then there were Mario's exuberant hugs… Mario was only four years old, but Charles didn't have to know that, either.

Charles scowled then, and set his glass down on the counter hard enough to slosh liquid over the edges. He stalked past her. "Goodbye, *Steffie*," he said coldly, throwing the words over his shoulder.

It wasn't until he'd slammed the front door that she understood that his words had been meant as an insult. He was telling her he'd changed his mind, reconsidered. He'd seen through her little dramatization and decided he'd been wrong, she wasn't an adult. She remained a foolish, immature girl.

Steffie wandered between two rows of budding apple trees, contemplating her latest disaster with Charles. The setting sun cast a rosy splendor over the orchard. As a girl, Steffie had often walked out here when she needed to think. This was where she found peace, and a tranquillity that eased her burdens. Since her last meeting with Charles, there'd been plenty of those. And regrets. She hadn't seen him in several days and that helped. But it also hurt. There were so many unanswered questions between them, so many unspoken words.

Hearing footsteps behind her, Steffie turned to find Norah walking toward her.

"You've got to do something!" Norah moaned.

"About what?" she asked when Norah moved three agitated paces ahead of her.

"You've got to help Valerie. You're older than I am. You've had more experience with men."

Steffie suppressed the urge to laugh at the irony of this statement, considering her ludicrous performance in front of Charles. She reached up to run her fingers along the smooth bark of a branch. "What's wrong with her?"

"She's making the biggest mistake of her life," Norah said dramatically. It wasn't often that her little sister sounded so distraught. Unfortunately Steffie was hardly the ideal person to advise Valerie on romance.

"I told you before that Valerie and Dr. Winston are in love," Norah continued. "Everyone around them can see it. And whenever Valerie and Colby are together, they can't keep their eyes off each other."

"Then what's the problem?"

"They aren't seeing each other anymore."

"What do you mean?"

"They're avoiding each other. I don't think they've talked in days."

Norah's words struck a chord in Steffie. She knew exactly what Valerie was doing, because she was guilty of the same thing herself. She hadn't seen Charles since the day he'd driven her home from the hospital. They were obviously taking pains to avoid each other—just like Valerie and Dr. Winston.

"I don't see what I can do," Steffie muttered.

"Talk to Val," Norah argued. "She might listen to you."

"What am I supposed to say?"

Norah hesitated, frowning. "I don't know, but you'll think of something. I've given it my best shot and nothing seems to influence her, but you know Valerie... I just wasn't getting through to her. Maybe you can."

"I'm glad you have so much faith in my abilities," Steffie said lightly.

"I do have faith in you," Norah said, her blue eyes serious. "You're different now than before you left."

"Three years in Italy will do that to a girl." As she had with Charles, Steffie strived to sound flippant and worldly.

"I don't mean that. You're more thoughtful. More—I don't know—mature, I guess. Before you left Orchard Valley it seemed that you had to prove yourself to the world, but it isn't like that now. I can't see you doing some of the crazy things you used to do."

Just as well that Norah didn't know about some of her "mature" behavior these past few days. And thank heaven no one in the family had any idea of the embarrassing stunts she'd pulled trying to attract Charles's attention three years ago.

"I remember the time you stood on Princess bareback and rode around the yard. You were lucky you didn't break your neck."

Steffie remembered the incident well. It had been shortly before their mother died. She'd been grieving so terribly and doing something utterly dangerous had helped vent some of her pain and grief. But Norah was completely right. It had been a foolish thing to do.

"Okay, I'll talk to Valerie," Steffie promised, "but I don't know how much good it'll do."

Steffie tried. But the conversation with her sister hadn't gone as planned. One look at Valerie told her how much her sister was suffering. Valerie tried to hide it, but Steffie knew the signs from her own limited experience with love.

They'd become involved in a lengthy discussion about love, then decided neither one of them was qualified to advise the other. They'd thought of bringing Norah in on the conversation but that suggestion had resulted in a bout of unexpected giggles. They couldn't ask Norah about falling in love because she was too busy dating.

One interesting detail that emerged from their talk was something Valerie mentioned almost casually. While Steffie was struggling to find a way home, Charles had seemed very concerned about her. He'd even pulled a few strings in an effort to find her when she didn't arrive on schedule.

Although they'd never openly discussed her relationship with Charles, Valerie seemed to know how Steffie felt. It wasn't that Steffie had tried to conceal it; with one breath, she admitted how she'd made a fool of herself over the newspaper article and with the next, she'd asked her sister about falling in love. Valerie was certainly astute enough to figure out Steffie's feelings for Charles.

David Bloomfield was now recuperating at home and doing well. Steffie still hadn't seen Charles. She'd thought maybe he'd be stopping by the house to visit her father, whose release from the hospital had been a festive event.

Steffie was pleased to see that Valerie and Colby were able to steal a few moments alone that afternoon, but she didn't think their time together had gone well. They'd gone for a walk in the orchard; Valerie had looked pale and sad when they returned, and Colby had remained silent throughout the celebration dinner that followed.

Knowing it was inevitable that she'd see Charles again, Steffie tried to mentally prepare herself for their next meeting.

She couldn't have guessed that it would be at the local gas station.

"Why, Steffie Bloomfield," Del of Del's Gas-and-Go greeted her when she went inside to pay for her fill-up and buy a bottle of soda. "I swear you're a sight for sore eyes."

She laughed. Del was pot-bellied and close to sixty, but he had to be the biggest flirt in town. "It's good to see you again, too. What do I owe you for the gas?"

"If I were a rich man, I'd say the gas was free. Looking at your pretty face is payment enough. Right, Charles?"

It always happened when she was least prepared, when seeing him was the last thing she expected.

"Yeah, right," Charles answered from behind her with a decided lack of enthusiasm.

"Hello, Charles," she said, turning around to greet him, trying to sound casual and slightly aloof. She pasted a smile on her face, determined not to let him fluster her as he had every single time they'd encountered each other.

"Stephanie."

"I don't know if you heard, but Dad's home now."

"I got word of that the other day." Charles took his wallet out of his hip pocket and paid for his gas.

Steffie twisted the top off her soda and took a deep swallow. It tasted cool and sweet, bringing welcome relief to her suddenly parched throat. "I was thinking you might stop by and visit." *Hoping* more aptly described her thoughts, but she couldn't admit that.

He didn't answer as he followed her outside. The service-station attendant was washing her windshield and Steffie lingered, wanting to say something, anything, to make a fresh start with Charles.

"As I recall, you wrote one of your first columns about Del's, didn't you?"

"You've got a good memory," Charles said, his words a bit less stiff.

The boy had finished with her windows and there was no further excuse to dawdle. Reluctantly she opened her car door. "It was good seeing you. Oh, by the way, Valerie told me you made several efforts to find me when I was trying to get home from Italy. I appreciate all the help you gave my family."

He shrugged. She set one foot inside the car, then paused and glanced back at Charles. She *had* to say something. "Charles." He turned around again, a surprised expression on his face. "There's something you should know."

"What is it?"

"I'm very grateful for your friendship to my family—and to me." With that she ducked inside her car, heart racing, and drove off without looking back.

Unfortunately dinner that evening was a strained affair. Norah had come to Steffie an hour before with the news that Colby had dated another nurse, a friend of Norah's, three nights running. Norah didn't know whether to tell Valerie, and had asked Steffie's advice.

Steffie thought it best not to say anything to their sister until Norah had slept on the matter.

But Steffie suspected that Valerie was already

aware of it, suspected that Valerie knew it in her heart. Although her sister hadn't said anything to the family, Steffie believed she'd quietly made arrangements to return to Texas and her job as vice president of CHIPS, a software company based in Houston.

Everyone could feel something was wrong, but no one said a word during dinner. Everyone was terribly polite—as though the others were strangers—which only heightened the tension.

Their father had made his excuses, claiming to be especially tired, and with Norah's help retired to his room almost immediately after dinner.

Apparently Valerie wasn't in the mood for company either, because she excused herself and retreated to her bedroom, leaving Steffie and Norah to their own devices.

After they'd finished with the dinner dishes, Norah left to attend a wedding shower for a friend.

Feeling at loose ends, Steffie inspected the kitchen. On impulse, she decided to make the spaghetti sauce she'd promised her father. She dragged out the largest pot she could find and began to assemble ingredients. Fresh tomatoes, onions, tomato paste, garlic. No fresh herbs, so dried would have to do. Oh, good, a bottle of nice California red...

Humming to herself, she slipped a tape of Verdi's *Aida* in the cassette player and turned up the volume until the music echoed against the kitchen walls. The emotional intensity and dramatic characterizations of the Italian composer suited her mood.

She found an old white apron her father had used

years before whenever he barbecued. Wrapping it around her waist, she drew the long strings around to the front and tied them.

Half an hour later, she was stirring the last of the tomato paste into the pot. She added a generous amount of red wine, all the while singing at the top of her lungs. The sound of someone pounding at the back door jolted her back to reality.

Running barefoot across the kitchen, she pulled open the door and saw Charles standing there, holding a pot of purple azaleas.

"Charles! What are you doing here?"

"No one answered the front door," he remarked dryly.

"Oh. Sorry." She walked to the counter to turn off her cassette player. "Come in." The silence was nearly deafening.

"I thought you said your father was home from the hospital?" As though self-conscious about holding a flowerpot, he handed it to Steffie.

"He is," she said, setting the plant aside. "How thoughtful. I'm sure Dad will love this."

"It isn't for David."

"It isn't?"

"No, I was...we just got a full-page ad from How Green Is My Thumb Nursery and I felt it might be a gesture of good faith to buy something. I thought you'd appreciate an azalea more than your father would."

Steffie wasn't quite sure what to say other than a soft "Thank you."

He shrugged, apparently eager to leave. He stepped toward the door and she desperately tried to think of something to keep him there, with her.

"Have you eaten?" she asked quickly, even though the sauce was only just starting to simmer and wouldn't be properly ready until the following day.

"What makes you ask?"

"I was just putting together a pot of spaghetti sauce. Dad asked me to cook him something Italian and...well, if you wouldn't mind waiting a bit, I'll be happy to fix you a plate. It really needs to simmer longer, but I know from experience that it's perfectly edible after an hour." She sounded breathless by the time she'd finished.

"I've already had dinner, but thanks, anyway," Charles told her. "I could do with a cup of coffee, though." He nodded toward the half-full pot sitting beside the stove.

"Sure...great. Me too. I'd get Dad but he's sleeping," she explained as she poured him a cup, then one for herself.

"Through that?" Charles motioned toward the cassette player.

"Sure. He loves listening to the same music as I do. Besides he's way over on the other side of the house. I doubt he could even hear it." She didn't mention that a tragic love story was sure to suit Valerie's mood, though. And since her sister's bedroom was directly above the kitchen she was most likely to have been the one serenaded.

Charles cradled the mug in both hands and walked over to examine her efforts. "So you learned to cook while you were away?"

"A little," she admitted.

"I wouldn't have guessed you were the domestic sort." He stirred the sauce with a wooden spoon, lifted it out of the pot and tasted it, using one finger. His brows rose. "This is good."

"Don't sound so surprised."

"There must have been some Italian man you were hoping to impress."

The only man she'd ever wanted to impress was the one standing in the kitchen with her right that moment.

"I was too busy with my studies to date much," she admitted, dumping the empty tomato-paste cans in the garbage.

"That isn't the impression you gave me the other day."

She hesitated, her back to him. "I know. I certainly seem to make a habit of playing the fool when I'm with you."

Charles's voice was rueful. "I've occasionally suffered from the same problem."

The unexpectedness of his admission caught her off balance, and she twisted around to face him. For a long, unguarded moment she soaked in the sight of him.

"There wasn't anyone I dated more than a few times," she told him in a raw whisper.

"Surely there was someone?"

She shook her head. They gazed silently into each other's eyes, and Steffie seemed to lose all sense of time.

Charles was the one who broke the trance. "Uh, your pot seems to be boiling."

"Oh, darn, I forgot to turn down the burner." She raced across the kitchen, flipped the knob on the stove and stirred the sauce briskly, praying it hadn't burned.

While she stood at the stove, Steffie basked in a glow of unfamiliar contentment. It felt so wonderful to be with Charles—not fighting or defensive, not acting like a love-struck adolescent. For the first time, she was truly comfortable with him.

"I'm sure the sauce will be fine," she murmured, picking up her coffee mug.

He pulled out the chair and sat.

As she was getting cream, sugar and teaspoons, she thought she heard some noise from upstairs. Glancing at the ceiling, she frowned.

"Is something wrong?"

Steffie joined him at the table, adding only cream to her own coffee and pushing the sugar bowl toward Charles. "I'm worried about Valerie," she said frankly. "So is Norah. Everyone is, except Dad, which is for the best—I mean, he's got enough on his mind healing from the surgery. He shouldn't be worrying about any of us."

Charles added a level teaspoon of sugar to his coffee, then paused, the spoon held above his cup. "How'd you know I use sugar?"

Her gaze skirted away from his. "We had coffee together once before, remember?"

"No" came his automatic response.

Steffie preferred not to dredge up the unhappy memory again, especially since *he* didn't even seem to recall it. She stared down at the table. "It was the first time you asked me to—you know, leave you alone."

He scowled. "The first time," he repeated, then shook his head in apparent confusion. Just as well, Steffie thought to herself, astounded that he had absolutely no recollection of an incident she remembered in such complete and painful detail.

She decided to change the subject. "Norah baked some cookies the other day, if you'd like some."

Charles declined with a shake of his head. "Tell me what's going on with your sister." His eyes darted to the ceiling.

Steffie wasn't sure how much of Valerie's dilemma she should confide in him, but then remembered Norah's telling her that Charles had been with them the night of her father's surgery. More than likely he knew how Colby and Valerie felt toward each other.

"She's in love," she said after a moment.

"It's Doc Winston, isn't it?"

Steffie nodded. "They seem to have fallen hard."

"So what's wrong?"

Steffie wasn't sure she could explain, when she didn't entirely understand it herself. So she shrugged and said, "I think Colby wants her to be something she can't. Valerie's an incredibly gifted business-woman. But I gather he wants a woman who'd be happy to stay home and be a housewife—there's nothing wrong with that, of course, but it just isn't right for Valerie. It doesn't look like either one of them is going to compromise."

"If she loves him, maybe she should be willing to compromise first," Charles said, then sipped his coffee. "Take the first step."

"What about Colby? Why does it always have to be the woman who compromises? Don't answer that, I already know. Women have been forced to adapt to men's fickle natures for so many generations that it comes to us naturally. Right?"

Charles was silent for a moment. "I didn't come here to argue about your sister."

"I know, it's just that I found your statement so—" She stopped in midsentence because she didn't want to fight with him, either. They'd done so much of that. And she didn't want this encounter to end the way all the others had.

"I'm sorry," she said. "I'm concerned about her, and I can't help feeling a bit defensive. I'm pretty sure she's making arrangements now to return to Texas—and I wish she wouldn't."

"You haven't had much time with her, have you?"

Steffie tapped the mug with her spoon, staring into the dregs of her coffee. "That's not the whole reason I wish she'd stay." She was silent a moment. "Leaving your problems behind simply doesn't work. Not unless you've exhausted every possibility of reaching a compromise. In fact, I think leaving can make everything much worse. The problem is, I can't tell Valerie that. It's one of those painful realities we each need to discover on our own, I guess. I'm going to talk to her, but I doubt it'll do any good.''

Charles's dark eyes were sympathetic. ''I hope she listens.''

Steffie thanked him with a smile. ''I hope she does, too, but the three of us seem to share a wide streak of stubbornness.''

Charles rubbed his eyes, and she realized for the first time that he must be exhausted. ''You won't get an argument out of me,'' he said with a tired grin.

''Are you still working as many hours?''

He nodded. ''Fifty to sixty a week. We're published twice weekly now and eventually we're looking to go daily. Some days I feel like I'm married to that paper.''

The word ''married'' seemed to hang in the air. At one time Steffie had been convinced beyond any doubt that they'd be married, she and Charles. It was this unshakable resolve that had created so many difficulties in her relationship with Charles. Naively, she'd assumed that all she had to do was *show* him they were meant to love each other and after a few short object lessons, he'd be sure to agree. Now she knew that life—and love—didn't work that way.

''Are you still a jack-of-all-trades with the paper?'' she asked, remembering that his job meant he had his hand in every aspect of publishing the weekly newspaper—from writing, editing and layout to distribution.

"Some. We're on a computer system now, which makes everything a lot easier. No more of that cutting and pasting."

"Do you still have an intern?"

Charles relaxed against the back of his chair and nodded. "Wendy. She's a junior at the University of Portland."

A red light went on in front of Steffie's eyes. "What happened to Larry? I thought you were working with him?" The thought of Charles spending long hours with an attractive college student filled her with a sense of dread.

Then it came to her. She didn't need to worry about competing for Charles any longer.

She was out of the running.

Five

"Is someone here?" Steffie heard her father even before he entered the kitchen. He was wearing his plaid housecoat, cinched at the waist, which emphasized the weight he'd recently lost. His white hair was rumpled from sleep.

"David, hello," Charles said, standing to shake hands with him. Her father slowly made his way to the table, declining Charles's gesture of assistance.

"I thought you were still asleep," Steffie said with a loving smile. She'd missed the worst of the crisis, but her sisters had repeatedly told her how close they'd come to losing their father. Now, every time she was with him, she experienced a sense of renewed love and gratitude that his life had been spared.

"How do you expect a man to sleep with such delicious smells coming from the kitchen?" David grumbled good-naturedly. "I swear it's driving me to distraction."

"It's my Italian spaghetti sauce."

Her father squinted. "But we already ate dinner."

"I know. The sauce needs to simmer for several

hours and it's even better if you let it sit overnight. I was hoping to surprise you tomorrow night."

Her father nodded approvingly. "Sounds great, Princess." Then he grinned at Charles. "Good to see you, boy."

"You too, old man."

It was apparent that they'd often bantered like this. The atmosphere was relaxed, one of shared affection and camaraderie.

"You were in the neighborhood and decided to stop by?" David inquired. It wasn't likely Charles would come this way except to visit the Bloomfields, and they all knew it.

"I stopped in to check up on you," Charles said, but his gaze drifted involuntarily toward Steffie. Their eyes met briefly before she looked away.

"That's the only reason?" her father pressed.

"I, uh, brought that for Stephanie," he said and pointed in the direction of the potted azalea.

"You wouldn't by any chance happen to be sweet on my little girl, would you?"

"Dad," Steffie broke in urgently, "how about something to drink? Coffee, tea, a glass of water?"

"Nothing, thanks. I just came to see if I was dreaming about garlic and basil or if this was the real thing. I'll leave the two of you to yourselves now." He stood awkwardly, as though he wasn't quite steady on his feet. Steffie's instincts were to help him, but she knew it was important that he do as much as possible on his own. She stepped back, ready to assist him if it became necessary.

Charles was apparently thinking the same thing because he stood beside her, a concerned look on his face.

"I'll see you to your room," she said. The effort of rising from his chair and walking a few paces seemed to deplete her father's strength.

"Nonsense," he objected. "You've got company. Charles isn't here to visit me. I heard him say so himself. That was just an excuse so he could bring you that pretty flower."

"Don't argue with me, Daddy."

Her father grumbled, but allowed her to wrap her arm around his waist to support him. She looked over her shoulder at Charles. "I'll only be a minute."

"Take your time."

No sooner were they out of the kitchen than her father came to a halt, wearing the most delighted grin Steffie had ever seen. "What's so amusing?" she asked.

"Nothing," he said. Then he started chuckling softly. "It's just that your mother was right about this, too. Surprises me, but it shouldn't."

"What? Right about what?"

"You and Charles."

"Daddy, there's nothing between us! We're barely friends."

"Perhaps, but all that's about to change. Soon, too. Very soon."

Her father continued to mutter under his breath, as pleased as ever. Steffie closed her ears to his remarks, knowing that he had to be referring to his dream—

the time he'd supposedly spent tiptoeing around the afterlife, gathering information. It hadn't bothered her nearly as much when he was going on about Valerie and Colby, but now that it was her turn, she was decidedly uneasy.

"Charles isn't here to see me," she insisted. "Bringing me the azalea didn't mean anything. He got a new advertising account, that's all. I'm sure he intended to give it to you, but you were sleeping."

"Whatever you say, Princess."

Arguing wouldn't do either of them any good, and besides, she didn't want to keep Charles waiting. She suspected he'd be leaving soon, anyway. Her father sat on the edge of his bed, his eyes frankly curious as he gazed up at her. "I might have guessed. I wasn't sure what to think when your mother mentioned you and Charles. She told me you've been in love with him for quite some time. She's right, isn't she?"

Steffie kissed his brow and ignored his question. "Do you want me to tuck you in?"

"Good heavens, no. You hurry back to your young man. He's waiting for you. Has been for years."

"Good night, Dad."

Her father's grin broadened. "By golly, your mother was right," she heard him mutter as she left the room. "I should have known. Forgive me, Grace, for doubting."

Outside the bedroom door, Steffie started to tremble. Without directly saying so, her father was telling her what she'd most dreaded hearing, and at the same time what she desired above all.

Whether it was the result of fantasy, intuition or, as he believed, spiritual intervention, he'd become convinced that she'd be marrying Charles. The same way he was so certain about what would happen between Valerie and Colby Winston. And Steffie wasn't any more confident about her older sister's relationship than she was of her own with Charles.

"You look like you've seen a ghost," Charles told her when she rejoined him in the kitchen.

She raised her eyes to his, dismayed that he'd noticed. She needed to sit down. He was right, it *had* been a scare, listening to her father talk like that about the two of them, making marriage sound imminent.

"What is it? Is your father all right?"

She nodded. "Oh, he's fine, growing stronger every day..."

"It's good to see him smile again."

Steffie nodded and glanced at the simmering pot of sauce. Anything to keep her gaze away from Charles.

"What's really wrong?" he asked her softly. His concern was gentle and undemanding, and it touched her heart. This was the man she'd always known him to be. The man she'd fallen in love with three years ago—the man she'd never been able to forget.

Had it been anyone else, she would have laughed off her father's words. She would have told her "destined'' husband-to-be in a humorous fashion how her father was bent on playing matchmaker.

She couldn't do that with Charles, not when she'd so blatantly played the role herself. He'd assume, and not entirely without justification, that she was up to her old tricks.

"It's nothing," she said, forcing herself to smile brightly. "I can't help thinking how lucky we are to have him with us again."

Charles studied her intently. "You're sure there's nothing wrong?"

"Of course." She looked at him in what she hoped was a reassuring manner.

"If there's anything I can do..."

"There isn't." She smiled, to take the bite from her words. "You've already done so much. We're all indebted to you...you've been wonderful."

"You make me sound like some saint. Trust me, Stephanie, no one's going to canonize me—especially with the things I'm thinking this minute." He was behind her before she even realized he'd moved. His hands were on her shoulders and he gently drew her back and wrapped his arms about her waist. His mouth nuzzled her neck and he breathed in deeply, as though to drink in her scent.

Deluged with warm sensation, Steffie closed her eyes and savored the moment. She'd never believed this could happen. She dared not believe it even now.

It would be so easy to turn into his arms, to bury herself in the comfort he offered. She'd dreamed of this for so long. But now that it was here, she was afraid.

Her hands folded over his, which were joined at her middle. "I—the flowers are..."

"A gesture of good faith."

His words confused her. He must have sensed the uncertainty in her because he spoke again in a low voice, his words reassuring. "Let's start all over again, shall we? From the beginning."

"I—I'm not sure I know what you mean."

He softly kissed the side of her neck, then released her and turned her around so they were face-to-face. "Hello there, my name's Charles Tomaselli. I understand you're Stephanie Bloomfield. It's a real pleasure to meet you." He held out his hand to her, which she took. If his eyes hadn't been so serious, she would have burst into peals of laughter.

"Charles, you say? Anyone ever call you Charlie?"

"Hardly ever. Anyone ever call you Steffie?"

"Only when I was much younger," she teased. "A mere kid."

"I understand you're only recently back in town. I don't suppose you've had time to notice, but there've been a few changes in Orchard Valley. How about if I drive you around, show you the place?"

She hesitated. "When?"

"No time like the present."

"But we've only just met."

"I'm hoping that won't stand in your way. It shouldn't. I'm completely trustworthy."

"Then I'll accept your kind invitation."

"Do you want to bring a sweater?" he asked.

She shook her head.

He reached for her hand, his fingers entwined with hers as he led her toward the front door. It felt like the most natural thing in the world for them to be together.

They bounded down the stairs, carefree and laughing. Charles opened the car door for her, helped her inside and without warning leaned forward to kiss her. Their lips met briefly, then lingered. When he broke away, Charles seemed surprised himself. Steffie glanced up at him, thinking she might read some sign of regret in his eyes, but there was none. Only a free-flowing happiness that reflected her own feelings exactly.

"Where were you last night?" Norah asked late the following morning. "I came home from Julie's wedding shower and you were nowhere to be found."

Steffie spread a thin layer of her sister's strawberry jam across her English muffin. "I went out for a while." She didn't add any details because her father was sitting at the table, lingering over his cup of coffee and the morning newspaper. He might make all the wrong assumptions if he knew she'd been with Charles.

They'd spent nearly two hours driving around the area. Charles had taken her past several new businesses, including fast-food restaurants and some specialty boutiques. He'd shown her the recently constructed six-plex movie theater, a new housing complex and a brand-new mall on the outskirts of town. The drive had been highlighted by an ongoing commentary that included the latest gossip.

Steffie hadn't enjoyed herself so much in a long time. Charles had been entertaining and fun, and he seemed to take pains never to refer to their past differences.

It was late when they'd gotten back to the house, but they sat in the car for another thirty minutes, talking, before Steffie went inside.

She'd fully expected to lie awake half the night savoring the time she'd spent with him, but to her astonishment, she'd fallen asleep almost immediately.

"Steffie was out with Charles," their father announced without looking up from his paper. "She didn't get home until late."

Steffie feverishly worked the knife back and forth across the muffin, spreading the already thin layer of jam even thinner.

"Charles Tomaselli?" Norah repeated as though she wasn't sure she'd heard correctly.

"Two girls and a boy," David returned cheerfully.

"I beg your pardon?" Steffie asked.

"You and Charles," he answered. "You're going to be married and within the next few years have your own sweet family."

Rather than argue with her father or listen to more of this, Steffie glanced at her sister. "I need to do a few errands around town, but then I'm driving to Portland. Does anyone need anything?''

"Portland?" her father echoed. "Whatever for?"

"I thought it was time I applied for my doctorate and a part-time teaching position at the university. I *am* qualified, Dad, as well you know since you paid dearly for my education."

"But you can't worry about finding work now."

"I realize the country's in a recession, but—"

"I'm not talking about the economy," he muttered. "You're going to be married before the end of the summer, so don't go complicating everything with a job."

Steffie could feel the heat leap into her face. He seemed so sure of a marriage between her and Charles, and that exasperated her no end. "Dad, please listen—"

"It doesn't make sense for you to be starting a job or a course and then immediately taking time off for a honeymoon."

Steffie wasn't sure if it was a good idea to humor him any more. This had gone on long enough, but she didn't know what to say to him. Steffie was aware that her father claimed everything would work out between Valerie and Colby, too. After seeing her older sister's pale, drawn features that morning, Steffie had no faith in her father's words. Not that she'd really ever believed him...

"I don't actually expect to make a lot of contacts, since most of the offices won't be open on a Saturday, but I'm hoping to look around, check out the library, get a few names. Obtaining a teaching position now might be difficult, anyway, especially for the fall session. But I'd like to get started on a thesis soon."

"In other words you're going to Portland, no matter what I say?"

"Exactly."

"Shop when you're finished, then," her father suggested. "Try on a few wedding dresses. Both you and your sister are going to need one. Soon."

Norah was watching Steffie closely and spoke the moment their father had left the kitchen.

"What are we going to do?" Norah pleaded.

"I don't have a clue," Steffie said, fully agreeing with her sister's concern. "If Dad insists on believing—"

"Not Dad," Norah blurted out impatiently. "I'm talking about Valerie."

Steffie's exasperation with her father was quelled by her compassion for Valerie. "What can we do?"

Norah's face was pinched with worry. "That's the entire problem. I don't know, but we can't let her leave town like this. She came down early this morning.... I decided I had to tell her about Colby dating Sherry Waterman."

"How'd Valerie take it?"

"I don't know. She's so hard to read sometimes. It was as if she already knew, which I know is impossible." Norah frowned. "I wish you'd talk to her. She's in her room now and, Steffie, I'm really worried about her. She's in love with Colby—she admitted it—but she seems resigned to losing him.''

Steffie thought she understood her older sister's feelings.

"To complicate matters," Norah continued, "Valerie and I started talking and…arguing, and Dad heard us. He wanted to know what we were fighting about."

"What did you say to him?"

"I didn't get a chance to say anything. Dad did all the talking. At least he and I agree. Dad believes Valerie should go talk this out with Colby, too. But I don't think she will."

"Where's Valerie now?" Steffie asked.

Norah looked away. "She's upstairs."

"Doing what?" Her sister had been spending a lot of time alone in her room lately.

"I don't know, but I think you should go to her. Someone's got to. Valerie needs us, only she's so independent she doesn't know how to ask."

Steffie disagreed. Her sister was getting—and apparently ignoring—advice from just about everyone, when what she needed to do was listen to her own heart.

"What's all this about you and Charles?" Norah asked with open curiosity. "I didn't know you even liked him."

In light of their recent confrontation over the newspaper article, it was natural for her sister to assume that.

"We're just friends."

"Which is definitely an improvement," Norah muttered.

Eager to leave before Norah asked more questions, Steffie went upstairs to her room. She toyed with the idea of talking to her sister, of telling her that seeking a long-distance cure for a broken heart didn't work.

But Valerie was intelligent enough to make her own decisions, and Steffie didn't feel qualified to say or do any more than she already had.

She dressed in a bright blue suit for her trip to Portland, one Valerie would have approved of had she been home. Her sister had mysteriously disappeared without saying where she was headed.

Steffie was on her way out the door when her father stopped her. "Sit on the porch with me a while, will you, Princess?"

"Of course." The wicker chair beside her father had belonged to her mother. Steffie sat next to him and gazed out over the sun-bright orchard she loved so dearly.

"Are you serious about this—getting a teaching position and all?"

"Yes. I can't stay home and do nothing. It'd be a terrible waste of my education."

"Wait, Princess."

All his talk of marriage was beginning to annoy her. "But, Dad—"

"Just for a couple of weeks. You've been home so short a while— I don't want you to move away just yet. All I ask is that you delay a bit longer."

"I won't be moving out right away..." She hesitated. She couldn't deny her father anything, and he knew it. "Two weeks," she promised reluctantly. "We'll visit, catch up, make some plans. Then I'll start looking for an apartment."

"Is Charles coming for dinner tonight?"

"No." She'd invited him, but he had a late-afternoon meeting and doubted he'd be back in time.

"He's going to miss out on your Italian dinner."

"There'll be others."

"You should fix a plate and take it into town for him. A bachelor like Charles doesn't often get the opportunity to enjoy a home-cooked dinner."

"He seems to be doing just fine on his own," Steffie said, hiding a smile. Her father wasn't even trying to be subtle.

"He's a fine young man."

"Yes, I know. I think he's probably one of the most talented newsmen I've ever read. To be honest, I'm surprised he's still in Orchard Valley. I thought one of the big-city newspapers would have lured him away long before now."

"They've tried, but Charles likes living here. He's turned down a number of job offers."

"How do you know?" That he'd received other offers didn't surprise Steffie, but that her father was privy to the information did. Then she remembered he and Charles had worked together on the farmworker article.

"I know Charles quite well," her father answered. "We've become good friends the past few years."

Steffie crossed her legs. "I'd forgotten the two of you wrote that article."

Her father shook his head. "Charles wrote nearly every word of that story. All I did was get a few of the details for him and add a comment now and again, but that was it."

"He credits you with doing a lot more."

Her father was silent for a few moments, reflective. Steffie wondered if he was worrying about Valerie the way Norah had been. She was about to say something when her father spoke.

"Charles is going to make me a fine son-in-law."

Steffie closed her eyes, trying to control the burst of impatience his words produced.

"Daddy, don't, please," she murmured.

"Don't what?"

"Talk about Charles marrying me."

"Whyever not?" he asked, sounding almost offended. "Why, Princess, he's loved you for years, only I was too blind to notice. I guess I had my head in the clouds, because it's as clear as rainwater to me now. Soon after you left for Italy, he started coming around, asking about you. Only...that little devil...he was so subtle about it I didn't realize what he was doing until I saw the two of you together last night."

"I know, but—"

"You don't have a clue, do you?" her father said, chuckling and shaking his head. "Can't say I blame you since I didn't guess it myself."

The way her father made it sound, Charles had spent the past three years pining away for her. Steffie knew that couldn't be true. He was the reason she'd left. He'd humiliated her, laughed at her.

"When your mother mentioned you'd be marrying Charles—"

"Dad, *please.*" Steffie felt close to tears. "I'm not marrying Charles."

He studied her, eyes narrowed in concern. "What's wrong, Princess? You love him, don't you?"

"I did...but that was a long time ago when I was young and very foolish." Her father had no way of knowing just *how* foolish she'd been.

Even after the incident in Charles's home, when she'd soaked in his tub until her skin resembled that of a raisin, she hadn't stopped. Some odd quirk of her nature refused to let her believe he didn't want her, not when she loved him so desperately.

Oh, no, she hadn't been willing to leave well enough alone. So she'd plotted and planned his downfall.

Literally.

Leaving a message at the newspaper office that her father needed to see him right away, Steffie had waited in the stable for Charles's arrival. She'd spread fresh hay in the first stall.

No one was home and she tacked a note on the front door directing Charles to the stable.

He'd arrived right on time. She had to say that for him—he was punctual to a fault. He hesitated when he saw she was there alone, then asked to talk to her

father. He kept his distance—which might have had
something to do with the pitchfork in her hand.

Steffie had planned this meeting right down to the
minutest detail. She'd worn tight jeans and a check-
ered shirt, half unbuttoned and tied at her waist.

She remembered Charles's repeating that he was
anxious to talk to her father. Among other things,
he'd told her, he wanted to clear the air about what
was happening between him and Steffie.

At the time she'd nearly laughed out loud. Nothing
was happening, despite her best efforts.

Steffie remembered again how perfect her timing
had been. As she was chatting with him, explaining
that she wasn't sure where her father had gone, she
set aside the pitchfork and started up the ladder that
led to the loft. At precisely the right moment, she
lost her balance, just as she'd planned. After teetering
for a second, she dropped into Charles's arms.

He broke her fall, but the impact of her weight
slamming against him had taken them both to the
floor, and into the fresh hay. For a moment, neither
said a word.

"Are you all right?" He spoke first, his voice low
and angry.

Steffie had never been more "all right" in her life.
For the first time she was in Charles's arms and he
held on to her as though he never intended to let her
go, as though this was exactly where he'd always
wanted her to be.

Steffie had gazed down on him and slowly shaken
her head. His gaze had gone to her softly parted lips

and then his hands were in her hair and with a groan he'd guided her mouth to his. The kiss was wild, crazily intense. No man had ever kissed her with such hunger or need. Steffie didn't understand what she was feeling; all she knew was that she wanted Charles more than she'd ever wanted anything.

While his kisses had been frenzied, his touch was gentle. His hands had cupped her breasts and she must have gasped with surprise and delight because he abruptly jerked away.

She had protested, wanting him to touch her, begging him. The sheer excitement of what she'd experienced had taken her by force. Not knowing how to tell him, she'd done what came instinctively. She'd kissed him back with the same searing hunger, until it seemed neither of them would be able to endure the intensity of their lovemaking any longer.

Steffie would never forget the way he'd rolled away from her, bounding effortlessly to his feet, breathing hard.

At first he'd said nothing. Steffie knew she'd have to speak first. So she'd looked up at him and said what had been on her heart from the moment they first met. She'd told him simply, honestly, how much she loved him.

Steffie would forever remember what happened next.

Charles had stared down at her in silence for several heart-stopping seconds, and then he'd begun to laugh. Deep belly laughs, as though she'd said the funniest thing he'd ever heard.

She was exactly what he needed, he'd said with a twist of sarcasm, a lovesick teenager following him around like a motherless calf. How many times did he have to tell her he wasn't interested? When he was ready for a woman in his life, he wanted exactly that, a *woman*, not a child. Especially not one as immature as she was.

He'd said more, but by then Steffie was running toward the house, tears streaking her face. The sound of his laughter had followed her, taunting her, ridiculing her.

"Charles has loved you all these years," her father said now. He spoke confidently, crashing into her memories and dragging her back to the present. The past was so painful that Steffie was content to leave it behind.

"He's never loved me," she whispered through a haze of remembered pain.

"Ah, my sweet Princess," her father countered. "That's where you're wrong."

Six

"Dad, listen to me." Steffie stood abruptly and thrust her head away for fear her father would see the tears glistening in her eyes. "Whatever you do, please don't say anything to Charles about—you know?"

"Being in love with you?"

"That, too," she pleaded, "but I'm particularly concerned about this marriage thing."

"That troubles you?"

"Yes, Dad, it troubles me a great deal."

"You don't understand, do you?" he asked softly.

"Oh, Dad, you're the one who doesn't understand."

"Steffie, my Princess, don't limit yourself to the things you understand," her father said in the gentlest voice imaginable, "otherwise you'll miss half of what life has to offer."

She had to leave, had to escape before she dissolved into an emotional storm of tears. Not until she was in the car, heading she didn't know where, did she realize her father hadn't promised one way or the other. He might well blurt out everything to Charles.

By the time Steffie had reached Orchard Valley,

she'd composed herself. She'd do her errands—pick up dry cleaning, visit the small local library, mail a birthday card to little Mario in Italy—before she drove to Portland. Because it was Saturday, Main Street was busy and she was fortunate to find a parking spot. Not so fortunate as she would have liked, however, since the only available space was directly in front of the newspaper office.

For at least ten minutes, Steffie sat in the family station wagon, considering whether to talk to Charles herself. *Should* she warn him about her father's crazy dream, his matchmaking hopes?

She was still debating the issue when she saw him, talking to the girl at the front desk. Her heart gladdened at the mere sight of him. He'd removed his suit jacket and the sleeves of his white shirt were rolled halfway up his arms. He was so attractive, so compelling. For several moments she watched him, mesmerized, and her heart beat faster.

At first glance, Steffie thought Charles might have been talking to Norah, but she quickly realized that was impossible. The resemblance was there, though. This girl was blond and exceptionally pretty. Even from inside her car, Steffie could see how she gazed up at Charles with wide, adoring eyes.

The dread that went through her was immediate and unstoppable. She was jealous, and she hated it. The blonde was probably Wendy, the apprentice Charles had mentioned, and Steffie didn't doubt for an instant that she was in love with him. Not that Steffie blamed her; she'd once played the role of doting female herself. Was playing it even now, despite her most strenuous efforts.

Charles was still talking to his apprentice, his hand resting against the back of her chair. He leaned forward as the two of them reviewed something, their heads close together. The blonde laughed at some remark of his and smiled up at him, her heart in her eyes.

Steffie couldn't watch any more. It was like looking back three years and seeing what a fool she'd made of herself. Hurriedly she got out of the car and swung her purse over her shoulder. Forcing her eyes away from the newspaper office, she locked the car door. She was about to move away when Charles stepped onto the sidewalk.

"Stephanie, hello." He sounded surprised to see her. More than that, he sounded pleased.

"Hi," she returned awkwardly, feeling guilty, though she wasn't sure why. It wasn't as if she'd actually been spying on him.

"Where are you headed?" he asked, giving her business suit an appreciative glance.

"I—I was thinking about driving into Portland and visiting the university, after I do some errands here. I plan eventually to rent an apartment of my own in the city, but Dad..." She hesitated.

Charles grinned knowingly. "But your father wasn't delighted with the idea."

"Exactly. I promised him I'd wait another couple of weeks."

"Why two weeks?"

"Uh..." For a few seconds, she panicked, wondering if Charles had guessed, wondering if her father had mentioned his dream, praying he hadn't. "You'll have to ask him."

"Have you got a moment? I'd like you to meet Wendy. She's the apprentice I was telling you about. Bart's here, as well. You remember Bart, don't you?"

Steffie bit her lip, feeling reluctant. The last time she'd been to the newspaper office she'd come bent on vengeance, with threats of a lawsuit burning in her eyes.

"I'll tell you what, I'll throw in lunch. I've got an appointment at one, but we have plenty of time."

She was still caught in the throes of indecision, when Charles took her firmly by the elbow and escorted her inside. She felt a wave of relief; after all, the opportunity to spend time with him, even a few minutes squeezed in between appointments, was too precious to decline.

It might have been Steffie's imagination, but the people in the newspaper office seemed delighted to see her. She wondered what Charles could possibly have said to salvage her reputation.

A couple of the reporters, one of whom she remembered from high school, welcomed her back to Orchard Valley. Bart, the pressman, inquired about her father's health. Even Wendy seemed inclined to like her, which raised Steffie's guilt by several uncomfortable notches.

"I'll be back at one," Charles said as he guided Steffie out the front door.

"But—" Bart stopped abruptly when Charles cut him off with a glare.

"I'll be here in plenty of time," he promised. "What's your pleasure?" he asked, smiling down at her.

"Whatever's most convenient for you."

"The Half Moon's serving sandwiches now. How does that sound?"

"Great." When Steffie left for Italy, the Half Moon, just down the street from the *Clarion*, had been a small coffee shop.

Now she saw that it had been expanded and modernized. While Charles placed their order, Steffie found them a table. Several customers, old acquaintances, greeted her and asked about her father, and before she realized it, she was completely at ease, laughing and joking with the people around her.

When Charles returned with their turkey-and-tomato sandwiches and coffee, she smiled at him happily, content to shed the troubled thoughts she'd carried into town with her. At least for the moment...

"How's your father this morning?" Charles asked, holding his sandwich with both hands to keep bits of tomato and lettuce from escaping.

"Cantankerous as ever." Opinionated, too, and occasionally illogical, but she didn't mention any of that. Even if she decided to warn Charles, now didn't seem to be the time. Not when they were sitting across from each other, relaxed and light-hearted, and all the world felt right.

The hour passed quickly. This kind of pure, simple happiness never lasted, she told herself. But, oh, how she wished it could. Charles seemed equally reluctant for their time to end.

Steffie walked back to work with him. "Thanks for lunch," she said, standing on the sidewalk in front of the office.

"I'll call you," Charles promised as Bart came out of the office, glancing anxiously at his watch. "All right, all right," Charles told him impatiently. He turned back to Steffie. "Sometime tomorrow?"

"Sure." She nodded eagerly.

Sometime tomorrow. A few, short hours and yet it felt like a lifetime away.

Valerie was leaving.

Steffie did try talking to her. She'd tried to explain that running away from love wouldn't help; it would just follow her wherever she went. Her sister had listened, then quietly packed her bags.

Sunday morning, when Valerie was about to depart, Colby showed up unexpectedly. Steffie didn't think she'd ever been more excited. It was as if everything she'd read about the power of love, everything she'd always secretly believed, was true. Colby would prove it. He'd come to declare his love and sweep Valerie off her feet.

It soon became clear, however, that Colby wasn't there because of Valerie. He hadn't realized she was catching a flight that afternoon, and when he was told, he seemed to accept it as inevitable. Furthermore, he had no intention of stopping her. No intention of asking her to stay. If anything, he seemed almost relieved at her imminent departure.

When the moment came for Valerie to go, Steffie thought she might burst into tears herself. She'd so desperately wanted to believe in the power of love, in its ability to knock down barriers and leap over obstacles.

Valerie had hugged them all farewell, and with shoulders held stiff and straight, walked from the porch to her rental car. Then, just before she left, she'd turned and looked at Colby.

Steffie would always remember the tenderness she saw in her sister's eyes. It was as though she'd reached back, one last time, to say goodbye...and to thank him. At least, that was how it seemed to Steffie. She'd never been so affected by a mere glance. That look of Valerie's was full of love, but it also expressed dignity and a gracious acceptance.

Steffie was left to sort out her mingled emotions of anger and pain as Valerie drove away. She turned to Colby, who still stared after her sister's car. It took every ounce of self-control she possessed not to scream at him. Only the anguish in his eyes prevented her from lashing out, and when she recognized the intensity of his pain, her own anger was replaced by a bleak hopelessness.

"She's gone," he whispered.

"She'll be back," her father said with the same

unquestioning confidence that had driven Steffie nearly mad with frustration.

"No," she answered, her voice quavering. "She won't. Not for a very long time."

She couldn't refrain from voicing a few other hard truths. Then, unable to face either Colby or her father any longer, she dashed back into the house. Norah followed soon afterward, and Steffie realized that her younger sister was crying.

"She's going to marry Rowdy Cassidy," Norah wailed. "What's so terrible is that she doesn't even *love* him."

"Then what makes you think Valerie would do anything so foolish?" Steffie asked calmly. Valerie might be unhappy about losing Colby Winston, but she was too sensible to enter into a loveless marriage.

"You don't understand," Norah said as she continued to sob. "*He's* in love with her. He's called nearly every day and sent flowers and...and Valerie's so vulnerable right now. I just know she's going to make a terrible mistake."

"Val's not going to do anything stupid," Steffie reassured her sister. Valerie wouldn't marry her boss on the rebound—Steffie was confident of that. Deep down, she knew exactly what her sister would be doing for the next three years—if not longer. She knew because she'd done it herself. Valerie would try to escape into her work, to the exclusion of everything else. Because then she wouldn't have time to hurt, time to deal with regrets and might-have-beens. She wouldn't have time to look back or relive the memories.

An hour later, Steffie took a glass of iced tea out to her father, who stubbornly refused to leave the porch. He sat in his rocking chair, anxiously studying the road. "They'll both be back," he said again.

Steffie didn't try to disillusion him. By nightfall he'd be forced to accept the truth without her prompting.

Within ten minutes of Valerie's departure, Colby had left, too. He hadn't raced down the driveway in hot pursuit or given the slightest indication that he was going anywhere but back to town.

"Mark my words," her father said confidently. "Valerie and Colby will be married before the end of June."

"Dad…"

"And you and Charles will follow a few weeks later. All three of my daughters are going to marry this summer. I know it in my heart, as surely as I know my name."

Although she nearly choked on it, Steffie swallowed her words of argument.

Needing some physical activity to vent her frustrations, she saddled Princess. She knew better than to try her luck with Fury again. But the mare, who was generally docile, seemed to sense Steffie's mood and galloped like the wind down the long pasture road and then across the rocky field until they reached the bluff. The same place Fury had taken her.

Holding the reins, Steffie slid off the mare's back and sat on the very rock she had before. She lost track of time as she sat looking out on the valley, thinking about Valerie. And Colby. Remembering her own disastrous relationship with Charles, and how her willful behavior had destroyed any chance they'd had three years ago. Now there seemed to be a fresh beginning for her and Charles, however fragile it might be. Not for Valerie, though... Life wasn't fair, she thought, and love doesn't make everything perfect.

She rode slowly back and had just finished rubbing down Princess and leading her into her stall when Charles appeared. "I thought I heard someone back here." He stood by the stable door, hands on his hips, smiling.

"Charles." She shouldn't have been so surprised to see him. After all, he'd made a point of telling her that he'd be in touch.

"Your dad thought you'd gone out riding, but seemed to think you'd be home soon."

"Have you been waiting long?"

"Not really. Your father's kept me entertained."

"Is he still on the front porch?"

"He hasn't moved since I got here."

Dispirited, Steffie looked away. "That's what I was afraid of. Valerie's gone, and he seems to believe she'll come back if he sits there long enough."

Charles frowned heavily. "Is something going on? A problem?"

"No," she answered quickly, perhaps too quickly

because Charles's eyes narrowed suspiciously. "I mean, nothing you need to worry about. Dad desperately wants to believe Colby and Val will kiss and make up—that's the reason he's being so stubborn. By dinnertime he'll be forced to recognize that it simply isn't going to happen."

It might have been because she was nervous and flustered, or maybe she just wasn't watching where she was going, but Steffie tripped over a bale of hay.

Although she threw out her arms in an effort to right herself, it was too late. She fell forward, but before she completely lost her balance, Charles caught her around the waist. He twisted his body so that when they went down, he took the brunt of the fall.

It was as though three years had evaporated. They'd been in virtually the same position then, with Steffie sprawled over him, her heart pounding. Only this time she hadn't manipulated the circumstances. This time she wasn't in control.

They were both breathing hard. A tumult of confused emotions raged within her, and she braced her arms against him, ready to get up quickly and move away. Instead, his arms, which were around her waist, held her firmly in place.

"It seems we've been here before," he said, his eyes gazing into hers.

"I—" She stopped abruptly and nodded.

"Do you remember what happened that day?"

Incapable of speaking, she nodded again.

"Do you remember the way we kissed?"

She couldn't look at him, couldn't allow him to read the answer in her eyes. "Let me go," she pleaded, her voice weak, her eyes tightly shut.

"Not yet."

She struggled, but he held her fast for another long moment before he gradually eased his hold. "Let's talk about that time."

"No," she cried. The instant she was free, she rushed to her feet, not realizing she must have sprained her ankle. But when she placed her weight on her left foot she experienced a sharp stabbing pain. She couldn't suppress a whimper as she leaned against the stall door for support.

"You're hurt," Charles said, immediately getting to his feet. He slipped his arm around her waist.

"I'm sure it's nothing. I've just twisted my ankle—it hardly hurts at all," she lied.

Without another word, Charles effortlessly scooped her up into his arms.

"Charles, please," she said, growing angry. "I'm perfectly fine. It's a minor sprain, nothing more. There's no need for this."

He didn't reply but began to carry her out of the stable.

"Where are you taking me?" she demanded.

"The kitchen. You should put ice on it right away."

"I want you to know I don't appreciate these caveman tactics."

"That's too bad." He was short of breath by the time he reached the back door, which infuriated Steffie even more. "Put me down this instant," she snapped.

"In a minute." He managed, after some difficulty, to open the door, then deposited her unceremoniously in a chair—like a sack of flour, she thought with irritation. He was pulling open the freezer section of the refrigerator and removing the ice-cube tray.

She rested her sore foot on her opposite knee and was about to remove her shoe when he stopped her. "I'll do that."

"Charles, you're being ridiculous."

He didn't answer, but carefully drew off her shoe and sock. His fingers were tender as he examined her ankle, and it felt strangely intimate to have him touch her like this.

"I told you already—it doesn't hurt anymore," she argued. "I might have gotten up too fast or put my foot down wrong. I don't feel a thing now."

"Try standing up."

Cautiously, she did. His arm circled her waist as she gingerly placed her weight on the foot. "See," she said, feeling both triumphant and foolish. "There doesn't seem to be any damage."

"I wouldn't be so sure. Try walking."

The floor felt cool against her bare foot. She took a guarded first step, biting her lower lip. There was hardly a twinge. She tried again. Same result. "See?" she said. "I'm fine." And she proceeded to prove it by marching around the kitchen.

"Good." Charles replaced the ice-cube tray in the freezer, but he was frowning.

"Don't look so disappointed," she teased as she pulled on her sock and shoe.

He glanced at her, then smiled slowly, sensually. "I've heard of some inventive ways to avoiding kissing a man, but…" He let the rest fade as he sat down beside her, then pulled her chair toward him until they sat face-to-face, so close that their knees touched.

Steffie closed her eyes as his hands came to rest on her shoulders. His breathing grew ragged and he whispered her name. "Stephanie," he called her, leaning forward to touch her lips with his own.

Steffie was afraid—of his kiss and of her own response. But she felt a thrill of excitement, too. He must have sensed that, because the quality of his kiss changed from gentle caress to fierce possession.

Charles groaned, and she trembled at the sound of his desire for her. She slid her hands up his chest, delighting in the feel of hard, smooth muscles as she gave herself fully to his kiss.

Abruptly he broke away, his shoulders heaving with the effort. Caught by surprise, Steffie let her eyes flutter open and for a long silent moment they stared at each other, her breath wheezing through lips that were moist and swollen.

His hand reached out to touch her hair, a small, intimate gesture that moved her unbearably.

Then he stretched out his arms, gripping her by the waist and lifting her from the chair to set her securely in his lap. She wasn't given the opportunity to protest before his mouth claimed hers once more.

This time his kiss was slow and gentle, as tender as the earlier kiss had been hungry and demanding. She felt herself melting in his arms, surrendering the last of her resistance.

"I want to talk about what happened," he whispered.

She knew what he meant, and she wanted none of it. The scene in the stable was much too painful to examine even now. "That was in the past."

"It has to be settled between us."

"No," she argued, trying to change his mind with a deep, hungry kiss.

His voice was whiskey-rough when she finished. "Steff, we have to clear the past before we can talk about the future."

"We only just met, remember?" He was the one who'd suggested they start over again. He couldn't bury the past and then ask that they exhume it.

"Just listen to me…"

"Not yet," she pleaded. Maybe never, her heart insisted, balking at the idea of reliving a time that had been so painful for her.

"Soon." He tangled his fingers in her hair and spread kisses across her face.

"Maybe," she agreed reluctantly.

The sound of laughter broke into the haze of her pleasure. At least Steffie assumed it was laughter. It took her a wild moment to realize the sound was coming from the porch, and that it must be her father.

Not knowing what to think, she slowly broke away from Charles.

"Is that David laughing?" he asked.

Steffie shrugged. "I'd better find out if something's wrong."

He nodded, and they walked hand in hand to the porch.

"Dad?" she asked softly when she reached her father, rocking contentedly on the porch. His smile broadened when he saw her and Charles. His gaze fell to their hands, which were still clasped tightly together, and his eyes fairly twinkled. "Check the freezer, will you? By heaven, I wish I'd thought of this sooner."

"The freezer?" she repeated, glancing at Charles, wondering if her father had lost his wits. "Why do you want me to check it?"

"We need something special to fix for dinner tonight. We're going to have a celebration!"

Steffie frowned in puzzlement. "What kind of celebration?"

"There's going to be a wedding in the family."

Steffie groaned inwardly. "Dad..."

"Don't argue with me, Princess, there isn't time."

"But, Dad..."

"See there?" he said, pointing toward the long stretch of driveway. "What did I tell you?"

Steffie looked, but she couldn't see anything except a small puff of dust, barely discernible against the skyline.

"I was about to give up on those two," he said

with a wry chuckle. "They're both too stubborn for their own good. I have to admit they gave me pause, but your mother was right. Guess I should have known better than to doubt her."

"Dad, what in heaven's name are you talking about?"

"Your sister and Colby. They're on their way back to the house now."

Steffie glanced up again, and this time the make and color of the car was unmistakable. Colby was returning to the house. And although she couldn't clearly tell who the passenger was, she almost knew it had to be her sister.

Seven

"Even now I can't believe it," Valerie said wistfully, sitting cross-legged on her bed. Steffie and Norah lounged on the opposite end, listening.

"Colby actually chased you down on the freeway?" Norah wanted to know.

Valerie's smile lit up her whole face as she nodded. "It really was romantic to have him race after me. He told me he didn't realize he was planning to do it until he was on the interstate."

"You've got everything worked out?" Steffie asked. From what Norah had told her, and from remarks Valerie herself had made, she knew there were a lot of obstacles standing in the way of this marriage.

"We've talked things out the best we can. It's been a struggle to find the right compromises. I've got a call in to Rowdy Cassidy at CHIPS. I think I can talk him into letting me open a branch of the company in Oregon. He's already done a feasibility study for the Pacific Northwest. He was just waiting until he could find the right person to head it up. He didn't originally have me in mind, but I don't think he'll have a problem giving it to me. Then again—"

she paused thoughtfully "—it may be better to discuss this in person."

"Colby doesn't mind if you continue working?" Norah's voice was tinged with disbelief.

"No. Because it's what I need. Naturally he'd rather I was there to pamper him when he gets home from the hospital every night, but this way we'll learn to pamper each other."

"I'm so happy for you." Steffie leaned forward to hug her sister. Valerie's eyes reflected an inner joy that Steffie had never seen in her before. This was what love—real love—did for a person. When two people cared this deeply for each other, it couldn't help but show.

"Now that we've decided to go ahead with the wedding, Colby wants to arrange it as soon as possible," Valerie went on to say. "I hope everyone's willing to work fast and hard because we've got a wedding to plan for next month."

"Next month!" Norah's blue eyes rounded incredulously.

"I was lucky to get him to wait that long. Colby would rather we flew to Vegas tonight and were done with it."

"No way" was Norah and Steffie's automatic response.

"I never thought I'd be the sentimental sort," Valerie admitted sheepishly, "but I realized I want a large fancy wedding. Colby loves me enough to agree to one, as long as I organize it quickly. Once that man makes a decision, there's no holding him back.''

Steffie smiled to herself. Dr. Colby Winston was in for a real surprise. Valerie was talented enough in the organizational department to manage the United Nations. If he gave her a month to arrange their wedding, she'd do a beautiful job of it with time to spare.

A wedding so soon meant the family was about to be caught up in a whirlwind of activity, but that suited Steffie. It was time for them to celebrate. The grieving, the anxiety, were over.

''You've been seeing a lot of Charles lately, haven't you?'' Norah asked, looking expectantly at Steffie. ''Do you think we could make this a double wedding?''

Valerie smiled broadly at Steffie, as though she'd be in favor of the idea, too.

''I haven't been seeing *that* much of Charles,'' Steffie answered, thrusting out her chin. She realized she sounded defensive. ''Well, I—I suppose we have been together quite a bit lately, but there's certainly never been any talk of marriage.''

''I've always liked Charles,'' Norah said, studying Steffie closely. ''I mean, I could go for this guy, given the least bit of encouragement. First Valerie falls in love and now you. You know, it's a little unfair. I'm the one who lives at home and you two fly in and within a couple of weeks nab the two most eligible men in town.''

''Me?'' Steffie argued. ''You make it sound like a done deal. Trust me, it isn't.''

"You're in love with him," Valerie said quietly.

Steffie didn't reply. She was unwilling to openly admit her feelings for Charles. It would be so easy to fool herself into believing he did hold some tenderness for her. But he'd never said so, and other than a few shared kisses he hadn't given her any indication he cared.

But he had, something inside her said.

Steffie refused to listen. She couldn't, wouldn't, forget that she'd made a fool of herself over him, not once but three times. Because she'd cared, and he hadn't.

"I don't know how Charles feels about me," Steffie said in a soft steady voice.

"You're joking!" Norah exclaimed.

And Valerie added, "Steffie, it's obvious how he feels."

Steffie discounted their assurances with a shrug. "For all I know, he could be hanging around me in order to get close to Norah."

"Charles? No way." Both Valerie and Norah burst into loud peals of laughter.

"Are you saying you wouldn't mind me dating him?" Norah teased, winking at Valerie.

"Feel free." In fact, Steffie would throttle Norah if she went within ten feet of Charles, though she could hardly say so.

"I hope you're joking," Norah said, shaking her head. "I should have realized what was going on a long time ago. I don't know how I could've been so dense. Charles and Dad became friends shortly after you left—good friends.''

''That doesn't prove a thing,'' Steffie insisted. She didn't need anyone else building up her hopes, and although her sisters meant well, their encouragement would only make her disappointment harder to bear.

''It wouldn't mean much if Charles hadn't made a point of asking about you every time he stopped by,'' Norah was saying. ''I have to hand it to the guy, though—he was always subtle about his questions.''

''Now that you mention it, whenever I talked to Charles, Steffie's name cropped up in the conversation,'' Valerie reported thoughtfully. ''I should have guessed myself.''

''You were too involved with Colby to see anything else,'' Norah teased and then sighed. She crossed her arms and rested them atop her bent knees. ''Don't get me wrong, I'm happy for you two, but I wish I'd fall in love. Don't you think it's my turn?''

''Aren't you leaping to conclusions here?'' Steffie asked. She wasn't exactly sporting an engagement ring the way Valerie was. She and Charles hadn't arrived at that stage of commitment—and probably never would. Besides, her mistakes with him three years ago had been the result of leaping to certain incorrect conclusions about his feelings, and she wasn't ready for a repeat performance.

Steffie didn't see Charles again until Tuesday afternoon. She wasn't surprised not to hear from him, knowing how involved he was with the production of the newspaper during the first part of every week.

Valerie and Steffie had driven into town to visit The Petal Pusher, the local flower shop. Valerie had decided on a spring color theme for her wedding and had already chosen material for Steffie's and Norah's gowns in a pale shade of green and a delicate rose.

Valerie angled the car into the slot closest to the flower shop. Since the newspaper office was almost directly across the street, it was natural for her to glance curiously in that direction.

"You haven't talked to Charles in a couple of days, have you?"

"He's busy with the paper."

"There's time to stop in now and say hello if you want. I'll be talking to the florist, so you might as well."

Steffie was tempted, but felt uncomfortable about interrupting Charles at work. "Some other time," she said with a feigned lack of interest, though in actuality she was starving for the sight of him. Helping Valerie plan her wedding had forced some long-buried emotions to the surface. Steffie hadn't admitted until these past few weeks how deeply she longed for marriage herself. A family of her own. A husband to love and live with her whole life.

A husband.

Her mind stumbled over the word. There'd only ever been one man she could imagine as her husband, and that was Charles. Even though Steffie knew it was unwise, she'd started dreaming again. She found herself fantasizing what her life would be like if she was married...to Charles. She wanted to blame her sisters for putting such thoughts in her head, but she couldn't. Those dreams and fantasies had been there for years now. The problem was that she couldn't suppress them anymore.

An hour later at the same moment as Steffie and Valerie were leaving the flower shop, Charles happened to walk out of the *Clarion* office.

Steffie instinctively looked across the street, where he was walking with Wendy, deeply involved in conversation. Something must have told him she was there because he glanced in her direction. He grinned warmly.

Steffie relaxed and waved. He returned the gesture, then spoke to Wendy before jogging across the street to join Steffie and her sister.

"Hello," he said, but his gaze lingered on Steffie. He barely seemed to notice Valerie's presence.

"Hi." It was ridiculous to feel so shy with him. "I'd have stopped in to say hello, but I knew you'd be busy."

"I'm never too busy for you." His eyes were affectionate and welcoming.

"See," Valerie hissed close to Steffie's ear. Then, more loudly, "I've got a couple of errands to run, if you two would like a chance to talk."

Charles checked his watch. "Come back to the office with me?"

"Sure." If he'd suggested they stand on their

heads in the middle of Main Street, Steffie would have willingly agreed. Fool that she was!

Valerie cast a quick glance at the clock tower. "How about if I meet you back at the car in—"

"Half an hour," Charles supplied, reaching for Steffie's hand. "There's something I'd like to show you," he told her.

"Fine, I'll see you then, Steff," Valerie returned cheerfully. She set off at a brisk walk, without looking back.

Their fingers entwined, Charles led Steffie across the street to the newspaper office. "I was going to save this for later, but now's as good a time as any." He ushered her in and guided her down the center aisle, past the obviously busy staff, to his desk.

Steffie wasn't sure what to expect, but a mock-up of the *Clarion*'s second page wasn't it. As far as she could see, it was the same as any other inside page that she'd read over the years.

"Clearly I'm missing something," she said after a moment. "Is the type different?"

"Nope, we've used the same printing fonts as always." He crossed his arms and leaned against the desk, looking exceptionally pleased with himself.

"How about a hint?" she asked, a bit puzzled.

"I might suggest you read the masthead," he said next, his dark eyes gleaming.

"The masthead," she repeated thoughtfully as she scanned the listings of the newspaper's personnel and the duties they performed.

"All right, I will. Charles Tomaselli, editor and publisher. Roger Simons…"

"Stop right there," he said, holding up his hand.

"Publisher," she said again. "That's new. What exactly does it mean?"

His smile could have lit up a Christmas tree. "It means, my beautiful Stephanie, that I now own the *Orchard Valley Clarion.*"

"Charles, that's wonderful!" She resisted the urge to throw her arms around him, but it was difficult.

"My dream's got a mortgage attached," he told her wryly. "A lot of folks think I'm a fool to risk so much of my future on an informational medium that's said to be dying. Newspapers are folding all over the country."

"The *Clarion* won't."

"Not as long as I can help it."

Her heart seemed to be spilling over with joy. She knew how much Charles loved his work, how committed he was to the community. "I'm so excited about this."

"Me too," he admitted, his smile boyishly proud. "I'd say this calls for a celebration, wouldn't you?"

"Most definitely."

"Dinner?"

She nodded eagerly and they set the date for Thursday evening, deciding on a restaurant that overlooked the Columbia River Gorge, about an hour's drive north.

Steffie felt as if her feet didn't touch the pavement as she hurried across the street thirty minutes later to meet her sister. Never, in all the time she'd known Charles, had she seen him happier. And she was happy with him, and for him. That was what loving someone meant. It was a truth she hadn't really understood before, not until today. This intense new feeling had taught her that real love wasn't prideful or selfish. Real love meant sharing the happiness— and the sorrows—of the person you loved. She understood that now. She realized that her past obsession with Charles had focused more on her own desires than on his. Her love had matured.

Charles had wakened within her emotions she hadn't known it was possible to experience. Emotions, and sensations. When she was with him, especially when he kissed her, she felt vibrant and alive.

"You look like you're about to cry, you're so happy," Valerie said when Steffie joined her in the car. "I don't suppose Charles popped the question."

"No," she said with a sigh. "But he asked me to dinner to help him celebrate. Guess what? Charles is the new owner of the *Clarion*."

Valerie didn't seem nearly as excited as Steffie. "He's going to be working a lot of extra hours then, isn't he?"

"He didn't say." If he spent as much time at the newspaper as he had three years earlier, there wouldn't be any extra hours left.

"I suppose his eating habits are atrocious."

Steffie suspected they were, but she shrugged. "I wouldn't know."

"I bet he enjoys a home-cooked meal every now and again, though, don't you?"

Steffie eyed her sister suspiciously. "Is there a point to this conversation?"

"Of course," she answered with a sly grin. "I think you should heat up some of that fabulous spaghetti sauce and take it to him later. You know what they say about the way to a man's heart, don't you?"

"Funny, that sounds exactly like a suggestion of Dad's. What's your interest in this?"

"Well," Valerie admitted coyly, "that way I wouldn't feel guilty about asking you if I could take some with me to Colby's. If he tasted your spaghetti sauce and happened to assume, through no error of mine, that I'd cooked up this fabulous dinner—" she paused to inhale deeply "—he'd be so overcome by the idea of marrying such a fabulous cook that he'd go over the wedding list with me and not put it off for the third time."

"There's method in your madness, Valerie Bloomfield."

"Naturally. Colby doesn't know that I can't tell one side of a cookie sheet from the other. I don't want to disillusion him quite so soon. He suggested I cook dinner tonight and, well, you get the picture."

"I do indeed. I'll be happy to share the spaghetti sauce with you."

"I'll hang around the kitchen to be sure some of the aroma sticks to me."

"I'll give you the recipe if you want."

"I want, but if I have trouble cooking with a microwave, heaven only knows what I'll do once I'm around a stove. One with burners and a real oven.''

Steffie chuckled. She certainly had no objection to helping her sister prepare dinner for Colby, but she wasn't sure taking a plate over to Charles's house was such a good plan.

Valerie and Norah convinced her otherwise.

''Charles never did get to sample your cooking,'' Norah reminded her. ''He stopped by and you offered him dinner, but he'd already eaten. Remember?''

''How'd you know that?''

Norah looked mildly surprised, as though everyone must be aware of what went on between Steffie and Charles. ''Dad told me.''

Her dear, matchmaking father. Steffie should have known.

''It isn't going to hurt anything,'' Valerie reminded her. ''If you want, you can ride into town with me. I'll go over to Charles's house with you and we can drop off the meal.''

Steffie still wasn't sure, but Norah and Valerie believed it was a romantic thing to do. They both seemed to think Charles was serious about their relationship.

As for Steffie, she didn't know what to think anymore. In fact she preferred not to think about their relationship at all. And yet...

She remained hesitant about this project of delivering him a surprise dinner but Valerie and Norah were so certain it would be a success that she went ahead with it.

They were apparently right.

Steffie was propped up in her bed reading a new mystery novel at ten-thirty that night. Her bedroom window was open and a breeze whispered softly through the orchard. The house was quiet; her father had gone to bed an hour earlier, and her sisters were both out for the evening.

When the phone chimed, she answered on the first ring, not wanting it to wake her father.

"How'd you do it?" Charles asked, sounding thoroughly delighted. "I came home exhausted and hungry, thinking I was going to have to throw something in the microwave for dinner. The minute I walked into the house, I smelled this heavenly scent of basil and garlic. I followed my nose to the table and found your note."

"You should thank Valerie and Norah. The whole thing was their idea." Had he been furious, Steffie would gladly have shifted the blame, so she figured it was only fair to share the credit.

"I haven't tasted spaghetti that good since my grandmother died. I'd forgotten how delicious home-made sauce can be."

Steffie was warmed by the compliment. "I'm glad you enjoyed it."

"Enjoyed it! You have no idea. It was like stepping back into my childhood to spend the evening with my grandmother. She was a fabulous cook, and so are you."

Steffie leaned against the heap of pillows and closed her eyes, savoring these precious moments.

"The bottle of wine and the small loaf of French bread were a nice touch," he told her, sounding pleased and more than a little tired.

"I'm glad," she said again. A dozen unnamed emotions whirled inside her.

"I wish you didn't live so far out of town," Charles said next. "Otherwise I'd come over right now—to thank you."

"I wish I didn't live so far out, too."

"Since we're both tossing out wishes, there are a few other things I'd like, as well," he added in tones as smooth as velvet.

"You're limited to three." How raspy her own voice sounded.

Charles chuckled softly. "Only three? What happens if I want four?"

"I'm not sure, but I seem to remember reading once about a handsome young newsman who was turned into a frog because he got greedy over wishes."

"How many have I got left?"

"Two."

"All right, I'll choose carefully. I wish we were together in your father's stable right now."

"You're wasting one of your wishes on the stable?"

"That's what I said. It seems as though every time I'm there, you end up in my arms. In fact, I'm looking forward to visiting your father's horses again soon.''

"That can be easily arranged. Fury and Princess will be thrilled.''

"I'm glad to hear it,'' he murmured. Steffie could picture him sprawled comfortably on his sofa, talking to her, a glass of wine in one hand.

"Be warned, you have only one wish left.''

"Give me a moment—I want to make this one good. I've had two glasses of wine and in case you haven't noticed, I'm feeling kind of mellow.''

"I noticed.'' She smiled to herself.

"Know what I'd like?''

"You tell me,'' she teased.

"With my last wish, I'd like to wipe out the past.''

Steffie realized immediately that he was referring to their encounters three years ago. "That one's easy,'' she said, and even though he couldn't see her, she made a sweeping motion with her hand. "There. It's gone, forgotten, never to be discussed again.''

"Uh-oh. I think I made a mistake.''

"Why's that?''

"We can't sweep it away.''

"Why not?'' she asked, striving for a flippant air. "It was one of your wishes, and it's in my power to grant it and so I have.''

"But I don't want it wiped out completely. Let's talk about it now, Stephanie, get it over with once and for all.''

Steffie's heart jolted. "Sorry, it's gone, vanished. I haven't a clue what you're talking about.'' Willfully she lowered her voice, half pleading with him, not wanting anything to ruin these moments.

The silence stretched between them. "You're right, this isn't something we can discuss over the phone. Certainly not when I'm half drunk and you're so far away."

"You're tired."

"It's funny," Charles told her, and she could hear the satisfaction in his voice. "I'm so exhausted I'm dead on my feet, and at the same time I feel so elated I want to take you in my arms and whirl you around the room."

"You never once mentioned buying the paper." She didn't mean it as a criticism. But he'd managed to keep it a secret not only from her, but from just about everyone in town. When Steffie mentioned Charles's news to her father, he'd been as pleasantly surprised as she.

"I couldn't, but believe me, I was dying to tell you. Negotiations can be tricky. I was prohibited from saying anything until we'd reached an agreement with Dalton Publishing and the financing had been arranged."

Steffie snuggled down against her pillows. "So much is happening in our lives. First there was Dad's heart attack, and now Valerie's wedding. Oh, Charles, I wish you were here to see Valerie. I didn't know anything in the world could fluster my sister, but I was wrong. Being in love flusters her.

"I was with her Monday when she tried on wedding dresses. My practical, levelheaded older sister would stand in front of a mirror with huge tears running down her cheeks.''

''She was crying?''

Steffie smiled at the memory. ''Yes, but these were tears of joy. She never allowed herself to believe that Colby loved her enough to work through the things that stood between them. They're so different, and that's been the problem all along. But neither of them seems to understand, even now, that it was those very differences that attracted them to each other.''

''We're different.''

His words gave Steffie pause. ''I know but—''

''And I'm attracted to you, Stephanie. Very attracted.''

It was ironic that she'd told him how love had completely unsettled her sister, only to be sitting on her own bed a few minutes later with the phone pressed against her ear and the tears sliding down her cheeks.

''Aren't you going to say anything?''

''Yes,'' she whispered in a trembling voice.

''Stephanie? What's wrong? You sound like you're crying.''

''That's the silliest thing I ever heard,'' she rallied, rubbing her eyes with one hand.

''Damn, but I wish I was there.''

''Sorry,'' she said laughing and crying at once, ''you're flat out of wishes.''

Eight

"More wine?" Charles asked, reaching for the bottle of Chablis in its silver bucket.

"No, thanks," Steffie said, smiling her appreciation. Their dinner had been delectable. It was one meal she wouldn't soon forget, although it was Charles's company that would linger in her mind more than the excellent halibut topped with bay shrimp.

"How about dessert?"

Steffie pressed her hands to her stomach and slowly shook her head. "I couldn't."

"Me neither." He leaned against the back of his chair and gazed out the window to the Columbia River below. The gorge stretched through one of the most scenic parts of Oregon. Steffie had always loved this view of the mighty river coursing through a rock-bound corridor.

"I've looked forward to this evening for a long time," Charles said, looking back at her.

"I have, too." Until tonight, Steffie had only dreamed of spending time like this with Charles. As his equal, an adult...a woman in love.

"I don't think I've ever seen you look more beautiful, Stephanie."

His words brought a flush of color to her cheeks. Steffie had dressed carefully, choosing a soft Italian knit dress in a subdued shade of turquoise. Small rhinestones drizzled over the shoulders and spilled down the front. Valerie had lent Steffie her pearl necklace and earrings, and Norah had contributed a splash of her most expensive perfume.

It seemed her sisters and her father, too, had put a good deal of stock into this evening's dinner date. Steffie wasn't entirely sure what her family was expecting would happen. No doubt some miracle. For herself, she was content just to spend the evening with Charles

"You look wonderful yourself." She wasn't echoing his compliment, but was stating a fact. He'd worn a dark, double-breasted suit with a silk tie of swirling colors against a pale blue shirt.

"Then we must make an attractive couple tonight," Charles commented, rotating the wine goblet between his fingers.

"We must," Steffie agreed.

Charles finished off the last of his wine and set the glass aside. "You were generous enough to grant me three wishes the other night, remember?"

Steffie wasn't likely to forget. She felt warm and shivery inside whenever she thought about their late-night telephone conversation.

"Being the honorable gentleman I am, not to mention talented and handsome, as you so aptly pointed out, it seems only fair that I return the favor. You, my lady, are hereby granted three wishes.''

''Anything I want?'' Steffie cocked her head.

''Within reason. I'd be willing to drive you to Multnomah Falls to watch the water by moonlight, but I might have a bit of trouble if you decide you want world peace.''

''The Falls by moonlight?''

''I was hoping you'd ask for that one.''

She blinked at the way he'd turned her question into a pre-approved wish. ''Charles,'' she said surprised, ''you're a romantic.''

''Don't sound so shocked.''

''But I am. I'd never have guessed it.''

She was teasing him, and enjoying it and was surprised when he frowned briefly. ''That's because we've never discussed what happened three—''

''Not tonight,'' she said, holding a finger to his lips. ''It's one of my wishes. We'll discuss nothing unpleasant.''

His frown deepened. ''I think we should. There's a lot we—''

''You're the one who granted me three wishes,'' she reminded him solemnly.

He nodded, looking somewhat disgruntled. ''You're right, I did, and if you want to squander one of your wishes, then far be it from me to stop you.''

''It's too lovely a night to dredge up the past, especially when it's so embarrassing. Let's just look forward...''

"Fine," Charles agreed and turned to thank their waiter when he brought two cups of steaming coffee to the table. "We'll just look ahead. Now, remember you have one remaining wish."

Steffie hesitated. "Do I have to claim it now?"

"No, but the wishes expire at midnight."

Steffie laughed softly. "You make me feel like Cinderella."

"Perhaps that's because I'd like to be your prince."

His gaze was dark and unguarded. Steffie lowered her eyes, for fear he would read all the love that was stored in her heart.

"Do I frighten you?" he asked after a moment.

Steffie's gaze flew back to his. "No. I thought I frightened you!"

He laughed outright at that. "Not likely."

They drank their coffee in silence, as though afraid words would destroy the mood. After Charles had paid the bill, he drove toward Multnomah Falls, managing the twisting narrow highway with ease. Steffie had visited Multnomah Falls many times, but had always been a bit frightened by the drive. However, Charles took the sharp turns in slow, easy moves, and she relaxed, enjoying the trip.

The rock walls along the road were built of local basalt more than fifty years earlier, during the Depression.

"I love this place," Charles said as they reached the parking area across the roadway from the waterfall. Because it was a week night, there were only a few cars parked in the lot.

Dusk was settling, and the tall, stately firs bordering the falls were silhouetted against the backdrop of a cloud-dappled sky. The forested slopes were already dark as Steffie and Charles began the gradual, winding ascent to the visitors' viewpoint.

A chill raced down her arms and Steffie was grateful she'd brought a thin coat with her. Multnomah Falls was Oregon's highest waterfall, plummeting more than six hundred feet into a swirling pool, then slipping downward in a second, shorter descent. The force of the falling water misted the night.

With his hand at her elbow, Charles guided them to the walkway that wove its way up the trail. When they reached the footbridge that spanned the falls, Steffie stopped to gaze at the magnificence around her. The sound of falling water roared in her ears.

"If we wait a few moments, the moon will hit the water," Charles told her. He stood behind her, shielding her from the wind that whipped across the water's churning surface.

Steffie closed her eyes. Not to the beauty of the scene before her, but to the sensation she experienced in Charles's protective embrace.

"I've dreamed of holding you like this," he whispered. "Of wrapping my arms around you and feeling you next to me. I love the way your hair smells. It reminds me of wildflowers and sunshine."

Steffie couldn't speak. She couldn't force even one word past the knot in her throat. She swallowed and slowed her breathing, hoping that might help, for there was so much she longed to say, so many things she yearned to tell him.

"I don't ever want to be separated from you again," Charles told her, his voice raw and painful.

She didn't understand. Charles had all but sent her away. He'd all but cast her out of his life. She turned in his arms until they faced each other and raised her hands to his face.

Charles smiled then and gently gripped her wrists. He moved his head until his mouth met the sensitive skin of her palm, and he kissed her there.

"You know, three years ago there was so much I couldn't tell you," he began.

"I have one wish left," she reminded him softly. "I want you to kiss me. Now."

"With pleasure." She could hear the smile in his voice.

They'd kissed before, but they'd never shared what they did in those few moments. Charles's lips found hers in the sweetest, most loving exchange she'd ever experienced, and Steffie's emotions exploded to life.

Steffie wanted this, wanted it more than anything she'd ever known, yet at the same time she felt swamped by confusion. Charles had ordered her out of his life, laughed at her declaration of love, humiliated her until she couldn't bear to live in the same town. Now, he seemed to be suggesting that he *hadn't* wanted her to go, and that he never wanted her to leave again.

Steffie wasn't sure what to believe. With all her heart she longed to lose herself in Charles's kiss, to savor all the sensations that flooded her. And yet the uncertainty remained. Did he merely desire her, or did he, too, feel a forever kind of love?

But his kiss wiped out all thought, as the joy rushed through her, replacing fear and doubt.

"Someone's coming," Charles whispered suddenly. He broke away, still holding her shoulders, and gently brushed his mouth against her forehead. Then he released her.

Steffie's father was sitting by the fireplace in his den when she let herself into the house later that night. She saw the lamplight spilling into the entryway and decided to check on him.

"Dad?" David was sitting in the wingback leather chair beside the fireplace, her mother's afghan tucked around his legs. His head drooped and his lips were slightly parted.

Steffie had spoken before she realized he was asleep. But just as she turned to tiptoe from the room, he stirred.

"Steffie?"

"I didn't mean to wake you," she told him softly.

"Good thing you did. I was waiting for you." He ran one hand through his hair and sat up straighter. "How was your dinner with Charles?"

Steffie sank onto the ottoman, angling her legs to one side. She knew her eyes had a dreamy look, but she didn't care. "Wonderful."

"Did Charles ask you anything?"

"Ask me anything?" she repeated, feigning ignorance. "What could he possibly have to ask me?"

David Bloomfield frowned. "Plenty. I thought—I hoped he was going to mention a wedding. Yours."

"Oh, that!" she said with a light disinterested laugh. If the evening hadn't been so wonderful, she would have felt irritated with his pressure tactics. But she found it impossible to complain when she was this happy.

"He did, you mean? And what did you tell him? Don't keep me in suspense, Princess."

Steffie splayed her fingers and studied the even, smoothly polished nails before sighing. "I told him we'll see about it on Sunday."

"Sunday? You're going to keep that dear boy in agony until Sunday?"

She nodded, affecting a complete lack of concern. "He wanted to know if we could go horseback riding, and I said we could probably do it on Sunday. That's the question you're referring to, isn't it?"

"No," came his disappointed reply. "And well you know it. I expected that boy to ask you to marry him."

"Well, he didn't and even if he had—"

"Even if he had, what?" The frown slid back into place. "I tell you, Stephanie, you're as stubborn as your mother when it comes to this sort of thing. You can't fool me—you've been in love with Charles for years. If he asked you to marry him—"

"But he hasn't and from what I could see, he doesn't have any intention of doing so."

"I don't agree."

"You're free to think what you want, Dad, but keep in mind that this is *my* life and I won't take kindly to your interfering in it. And remember that Charles values his privacy, too."

"He didn't ask you to marry him," her father muttered under his breath. "You don't think he intends to, either?" he demanded, louder now.

"Not to the best of my knowledge."

A look of righteous indignation came over her father's face. "Then I'd best have a talk with that boy. I won't allow him to trifle with your affections."

"Dad!" Steffie had trouble not laughing over the old-fashioned terms he used. She was sure Charles would find it humorous, too, if she suggested he was trifling with her heart.

"I mean it, Steffie. I refuse to allow that young man to hurt you again."

"He only has that power if I give it to him—which I won't. You're looking at a woman of the nineties, Dad, and we're too smart to let a man *trifle* with us."

"Nevertheless, I'd better have a talk with him."

Her expression might have been outwardly serene, but Steffie's insides were dancing a wild jig. "You'll do no such thing," she insisted.

"Apparently Charles Tomaselli doesn't know what's good for him."

"Dad! We talked about this before, remember?" Her good mood was quickly evaporating. "Now I want you to promise you're not going to interfere with Charles and me.''

Her father stubbornly refused to answer.

"I'd be mortified if you even bring up the subject of marriage to him.''

"But—''

"I'm trusting you, Dad. Now good night.'' She stood and kissed his brow before heading up the stairs to her own bedroom.

"I appreciate the ride to the airport,'' Valerie said as they drove out of town early Saturday afternoon. Her sister's flight was scheduled to leave at five, which gave them plenty of time for a leisurely trip into Portland. Valerie was going to meet with Rowdy Cassidy to tell him about her engagement and request a job transfer.

"I'm glad to do it,'' Steffie assured her older sister. Now that Valerie had set the preparations for her wedding in motion, she was free to return to Texas. There were several tasks, besides the discussion with Cassidy, that she needed to take care of. She had to pack her personal things, deal with her furniture and put her condo on the market.

"Colby wanted to come with me, but his schedule's full,'' she explained wistfully. "That's something we're both going to have to adjust to.''

"Heavy schedules?''

Valerie nodded. "I'll need to talk to Rowdy about that while I'm in Houston.''

"Do you think he'll agree to let you head up the West Coast branch of CHIPS?"

"It's hard to say.... I don't think he's going to be pleased about my wanting to leave Houston, but he hasn't got a choice." Steffie noticed a hesitancy in her sister that she hadn't seen earlier. "Rowdy can be hard to predict," Valerie added. "He might be absolutely delighted for me and Colby. But there's also a chance that he'll be angry I took an extended leave of absence to plan my wedding." She sighed. "I didn't tell him the whole truth about why I didn't return the day I said I would."

"Why not?" Steffie prodded, briefly taking her eyes from the road when Valerie didn't immediately offer the information.

"I know I should have, but it just didn't seem the thing to do over the phone. Besides, I'm afraid Rowdy might be...have been interested in me himself. At one point, I even thought I was interested in him! Good heavens, I didn't know a thing about love until I met Colby. I don't mean to hurt Rowdy's feelings but I can't give him any hope."

"Do you want me to fly back with you?"

"Oh, no. Rowdy's really a gentleman beneath that rough-and-tough cowboy exterior."

Steffie's suspicions were raised. "Does the good doctor know how Rowdy feels about you?"

"I think he might. Then again we've never really discussed Rowdy, and why should we? If you want the truth, I think Colby would rather forget about him."

"Maybe he should take his head out of the sand."

"Now don't you go saying anything to him," Valerie said vehemently. "I mean it, Steff. What happens between Rowdy and me is between Rowdy and me."

"Is Colby the jealous type?" Steffie remembered how she'd felt the day she found Charles standing next to Wendy, the apprentice at the *Clarion*. Until that moment, she'd never thought of herself as jealous. Even now the blood simmered in her veins when she recalled how the little blonde had gazed up at Charles, her blue eyes wide with open admiration.

"I don't know if Colby is or not. I only know how I'd feel if the situation was reversed." Valerie seemed to consider her next words. "Before Colby and I became engaged he was dating a nurse. I believe she's a friend of Norah's. Apparently he'd been going out with her for quite a while. Everyone was expecting them to announce their engagement. Norah seemed to feel otherwise, but that's another story."

"I swear Norah's got a sixth sense about these things."

Valerie nodded. "I think she does, too. At any rate, Colby and I decided that although we were attracted to each other, a long-term relationship was out of the question. Colby...asked me to hurry up and leave because my staying made everything so much more painful for us both."

"He didn't!" Steffie was outraged. "It's a good thing he didn't say that around me."

Valerie laughed. "He didn't really mean it. Oh,

maybe he did at the time, but I didn't make falling in love easy for either of us.''

Valerie's stubbornness was a trait the three Bloomfield sisters shared, Steffie thought with a small, rueful grin.

"After we talked, Colby started dating Sherry again. I think they went out four or five nights in a row. I didn't know about it, but in a way, I guess I did. I certainly wasn't surprised when I heard.

"Poor Norah felt she had to let me know what was happening. I think it was harder on her than on me.''

"Were you jealous?''

"That's the funny part,'' Valerie said pensively. "At first I was so jealous I wanted to scratch out Sherry's eyes. I fantasized about hunting down Colby Winston and making him suffer.''

"You should have asked me to help you. I'd have gladly volunteered.''

Valerie smiled and patted Steffie's forearm. "Spoken like a true sister, but as I said that was my *first* reaction. What I found interesting was that it didn't last.

"I sat down and thought about it and realized how selfish and unfair I was being to Colby. If I truly loved him, I should want him to have whatever made him happy. If that meant marriage to Sherry Waterman, then so be it.''

"In other words you were willing to let him go.''

"Yes. And that was a turning point for me. Don't misunderstand me, it hurt more than anything I've ever done. Remember the day I was scheduled to fly back to Houston?''

Steffie wasn't likely to forget it. "Of course."

"When I first got ready to leave, I really had to work at controlling myself. I wasn't sure I could make it down the front steps without bursting into tears."

"I knew you were upset..."

"Naturally, Colby would have to choose right then to stop in for a visit. That man's sense of timing is going to be a big problem." Valerie shook her head in mock exasperation.

Steffie laughed. Give Valerie a week and she'd have Colby's life completely reorganized.

"Somehow I managed to pull it off," Valerie continued. "I remember sitting in the car and—this is odd—I felt such a sense of peace. I don't know if I can explain it. I felt this incredible...nobility. Don't you dare laugh, Steffie, I'm serious. I didn't stop loving Colby—if anything, I found I loved him more. Here I was, willingly walking away from the first man I'd ever loved."

"I wanted to throttle Colby about then."

Valerie grinned. "I remember learning about the tragic hero in my college literature courses. In some ways, I felt like I qualified for the tragic heroine."

"You weren't sorry you'd fallen in love with him, were you?"

"No, I was grateful. I was leaving him and at the same time I was giving him permission to find his own joy. And like I said, that somehow...ennobled me."

Steffie recalled the farewell scene on her front porch when she'd been so angry with Colby. "I...don't know if I could be so noble when it came to Charles."

"What's happening with the two of you?"

"I don't know." Steffie was being entirely honest. "We had a wonderful evening on Thursday, then we drove to Multnomah Falls and watched the moonlight on the water."

"That sounds so romantic."

"It was. We walked up to the footbridge and... talked."

"I'll bet!" Valerie laughed.

"We did—only we did more kissing than talking." Steffie knew that Charles had wanted to talk, wanted to discuss the past with her. She hated the thought of reliving all that pain. But more than anything she dreaded examining her utterly ridiculous behavior. Every time she recalled the scene in his bathroom, with her playing the role of enchantress, she burned with humiliation. Someday they'd talk about it, but not now. It was too soon.

"Dad seems to think you two will get married."

This discussion was a repeat of the one she'd had with her father every day for the past two weeks. "You know Dad when he's got a bee in his bonnet. I've had to make him promise he wouldn't say a word about marriage to Charles."

"Do you honestly believe he listened to you?" Valerie wanted to know.

"He'd better have."

Valerie frowned as she turned to stare out the car window. Steffie's hands closed tightly on the steering wheel and she glanced around her. Wild rhododendrons blossomed along the side of the roadway, their bright pink flowers a colorful contrast to the lush green foliage.

"I'm worried about Dad."

Valerie's words surprised Steffie. "Why? He's getting stronger every day. His recovery is nothing short of miraculous. I've heard you say so yourself, at least a dozen times."

"All right, I'll rephrase that. I'm worried for you."

"Me? Whatever for?" As far as Steffie was concerned, her life had rarely been better. She'd applied for late admission to the Ph.D. program and planned to begin researching thesis topics soon; she'd temporarily put her career plans on hold. And as for Charles…well, things were wonderful. Yes, she still had a lot of murky ground to cover with him, but there'd be time for that later.

"Dad's riding high on success," Valerie reminded her. "He seems to think that because everything fell into place with Colby and me, it should for you and Charles, as well. Remember he's supposed to have dreamed all this."

"I know. We've had our go-arounds on that issue. He's told me at least twice a day for the past two weeks that I'm going to marry Charles by the end of the summer. It's gotten to where I just smile and nod and let him think what he wants."

"It doesn't bother you?"

"It drives me nuts." Possibly because she wanted to believe it so badly.

"Aren't you nervous that Dad's going to get impatient and say something to Charles?"

"No," Steffie answered automatically. "Dad and I've been over this. He knows better than to say anything to Charles."

Valerie nodded. "I wish I shared your confidence."

Steffie put on a good front for the remainder of the trip, but she was growing more and more concerned. She knew one thing; she didn't have the personality to play the role of tragic heroine. She'd leave that to her older, wiser sister.

The flight was on time, and as soon as Valerie boarded the plane for Texas, Steffie headed back to Orchard Valley. As the minutes ticked away, she became increasingly anxious to get home.

It was just like Valerie to plant the seeds of doubt and then fly off, leaving Steffie to deal with the result—a garden full of weeds!

When she pulled into the driveway, Steffie experienced an immediate sense of relief. Her world was in order; her fears shrank to nothing. All was well. Her father was rocking on the front porch, the way he did every evening. He smiled and waved when he saw her.

"Hello, good lookin'," she said as she climbed out of the car. "How was your day?"

"I had a great afternoon. Every day's wonderful now that I've got all these reasons to live. Oh, before I forget, Charles stopped by to see you. Guess he must've been in the neighborhood again." A smile twinkled from her father's eyes. "You might give him a call. I suspect he's waiting to hear from you."

Steffie froze. Doubt sprang to new life. "You didn't say anything to him about...what we discussed, did you?"

"Princess, I didn't say a word you wouldn't want me to."

"You're sure?"

"As positive as I'm sitting here."

Steffie went inside the house, reassured by her father's words. Norah was busy in the kitchen, kneading bread dough on a lightly floured countertop.

"Did you happen to see Charles?" Steffie asked in passing. She opened the refrigerator and removed a cold soda.

"He stopped by earlier and sat on the porch with Dad for a while. I don't think he was here more than fifteen minutes."

Steffie swallowed a long cool drink. "I'll give him a call."

"Sounds like a good idea."

She waited until she was in her room, then sat on her bed and reached for the phone. Although it had been several years since she'd called Charles, she still remembered his number. The same way she remembered everything else about him.

He must have been sitting by the phone, because he answered even before the first ring was finished.

"Charles, hello," she said happily. "Dad said you stopped by."

"Yes, I did."

His voice was cool, and Steffie paused as the dread took hold inside her. "Is something wrong?"

"Not wrong, exactly. I guess you could say I'm disappointed. I thought you'd changed, Steffie. I thought you'd grown up and stopped your naive tricks. But I was wrong, wasn't I?"

Nine

"Dad!" Steffie struggled to keep the anger and distress out of her voice. She hurried to the front porch, her fists clenched against her sides. "You told me...you promised..." She hesitated. "What *exactly* did you say to Charles?"

Her father glanced upward momentarily, clearly puzzled. "Nothing drastic, I assure you. Is it important?"

"Yes, it's important! I need to know." It required every ounce of self-control she possessed not to shout at him and demand an explanation. She longed to chastise him for doing the very thing she'd begged him not to.

"You look upset, Princess."

"I am upset and I'm sure you know why... Just tell me what you said to Charles."

"Sit down a bit and we'll talk."

Steffie did as her father requested, sitting on the top porch step near his chair and leaning back against the white pillar. "Charles stopped in this afternoon, right?"

"Yes, and we had a nice chat. He tried to let me think he was here to visit me, but I saw through that soon enough.'' Her father's smile told Steffie all she needed to know. For one angry second, she thought he resembled a spider, patiently waiting for someone to step into his web.

''Obviously I was the subject under discussion, right?'' She forced herself not to yell, not to rant and rave at a man so recently released from the hospital.

Her father rocked back and forth a few times, then nodded. ''We talked about you.''

Steffie closed her eyes, her frustration mounting. ''I see. And what did the two of you come up with?''

''Let me tell you what Charles said first.''

She balled her hands into fists again, praying for patience. *''What did he say?''*

''Well, Charles stopped by, as I said, pretending it was me he was here to visit, when we both knew he was coming to see you. I went along with him for a while, then asked him flat-out what his intentions were toward you. I fully expected you to be wearing an engagement ring by now, and I let him know it.''

''Dad!'' Without meaning to, Steffie sprang to her feet. ''You breached a trust! I trusted you to keep your word, not to talk to Charles about this. And now you pass it off as…as nothing. Don't you realize what you've done?''

For the first time he looked chagrined. ''I did it because I love you, Princess.''

''Oh, Dad…you've made everything so much more difficult.''

''Aren't you interested in what he had to say?''

His smile was bright and cocky again. "Well, aren't you? Now sit back down and I'll tell you."

"Oh, all right," she muttered, lowering herself onto the porch step, her legs barely able to support her. Already she was shaking with trepidation.

"Charles seemed more concerned with the fact that I'd asked than with answering the question. To be perfectly honest, Princess, he wasn't overly pleased with me."

"I can't believe he even answered you."

"Of course he did. He said if the subject of marriage did come up, then it was between the two of you, and not the three of us. It was a good response."

"You should never have said anything about us marrying."

"Well, Princess, the way I figured it, he was going to pop the question, anyway. Besides, I don't want Charles leading you on, or hurting you again."

"Dad, you've made it nearly impossible for me and—"

"Let me finish, because there's more to tell you." But after silencing her, he went strangely quiet himself.

"Go on," she urged, clenching her jaw.

"I'm just trying to think of a way to tell you this without annoying you even more. I told Charles something you didn't want me to tell him."

"The dream?" The question came out a whisper. "But you said you hadn't told Charles anything I wouldn't want you to. And before—you *promised* you wouldn't mention marriage!"

"No, Princess, I never did promise. I took it under consideration, but not once did I actually say I wouldn't discuss this with Charles. Now don't look so worried. I didn't tell him a thing about talking to your mother, or about the three precious children the two of you will be having someday."

"What did Charles say? No," she amended quickly, "tell me *exactly* what you said first."

"Well, as I said, we were chatting—"

"Get to the part where you mentioned marriage."

"All right, all right. But I want you to know I didn't tell him about the dream. Not because you didn't want me to, but because when it came right down to it, I didn't think he'd believe me. You three girls are having trouble enough, so I can hardly expect someone outside the family to listen."

"You told Colby about it."

"Of course I did. He's my doctor. He had a right to know."

"Great. In other words you blurted out that you expected Charles to marry me—because you didn't want him trifling with my heart?" Spoken aloud, it sounded so ludicrous. Not to mention insulting. No wonder Charles was cool toward her.

"Not exactly. I asked his intentions. He said that was between the two of you. As I already told you."

"Good." Steffie relaxed somewhat. "And that was the end of it?" she murmured hopefully.

"Not entirely."

"What else is there?"

"I told him you were anticipating a proposal of marriage, and for that matter so was I."

Steffie ground her teeth to keep from screaming out her irritation. It was worse than she'd feared. Sagging against the pillar, she covered her face with both hands. It would have been far better had he told Charles about the dream. That way, Charles might have understood that she'd had nothing to do with this. Instead, her father had made everything ten times worse by *not* mentioning it.

Charles was angry with her; that was obvious from their telephone conversation. He'd refused to discuss it in any detail, just repeating that he was "disappointed." He seemed to believe she'd manipulated her father into approaching him with this marriage business. He wasn't likely to change his mind unless she could convince him of the truth.

"Where are you going?" her father asked when she left him and returned a moment later with her purse and a sweater.

"To talk to Charles—to explain things, if I can."

"Good." David's grin was full. "All that boy needs is a bit of prompting. You wait and see. Once you get back, you'll thank me for taking matters into my own hands. There's something about making a commitment to the right woman that fixes everything."

Steffie was drained from the emotion. She found she couldn't remain angry with her father. He'd talked to Charles with the best motives, the best intentions. And he didn't know what had gone on between her and Charles in the past—the tricks she'd played. So he couldn't possibly understand why Charles would react with such anger to being pressed on the issue of marriage.

"I'll wait up for you and when you get home we'll celebrate together," he suggested.

Steffie grinned weakly and nodded, but she doubted there'd be anything to celebrate.

She took her time driving into town, using those minutes to organize her thoughts. She hoped Charles would be open-minded enough to accept her explanation. Mostly, she wanted to reassure him that she hadn't talked her father into interrogating him about marriage. They'd come so far in the past few weeks, she and Charles, and Steffie didn't want anything to spoil that.

Charles was waiting for her, or he seemed to be. She'd barely rung his doorbell when he answered.

"Hello." His immediate appearance took her by surprise. "I—I thought it might be a good idea if the two of us sat down and talked."

"Fine." He didn't smile, didn't show any sign of pleasure at seeing her.

"Dad told me he talked to you about...the two of us marrying." The words felt awkward on her tongue.

"He did mention something along those lines," Charles returned stiffly.

He hadn't asked her to make herself comfortable or motioned her to sit down. It didn't matter, though, since she couldn't stand still, anyway. She paced from one side of his living room to the other. She felt strangely chilled, despite the warm spring weather.

"You think I put Dad up to it, don't you?"

"Yes," he said frankly.

He stood rooted to the same spot while she drifted, apparently aimlessly, around the room. His look, everything about him, wasn't encouraging. Perhaps she should have delayed this, let them both sleep on it, instead of forcing the issue. Perhaps she should have dropped the entire thing, and let this misunderstanding sort itself out. Perhaps she should go home now before everything got much worse.

"I didn't ask Dad to say anything to you," she told him simply.

"I wish I could believe that."

"Why can't you? This is ridiculous. If you intend to drag the past into every disagreement, punish me for something that happened three years ago, then—"

"I'm not talking about three years ago. I'm talking about here and now."

"What do you mean?"

"I'll say this for you, Steffie, you've gotten far more subtle."

"How…do you mean?"

"First, you park in front of the newspaper office just as I happen to be—"

"When?"

"Last week. I was talking to Wendy, and when I

looked up, I saw you sitting in your car, staring at us. Just how long had you been there?''

''I...don't know.''

''Now that I think about it, I realize what a fool I've been. You've been spying on me for weeks, haven't you?''

The idea was so outlandish that Steffie found herself laughing incredulously. Nothing she said would matter anymore, not if he believed what he was saying now. Because if he did, there was nothing of their relationship left to salvage.

''There's no fooling you, is there?'' she threw out sarcastically. ''You're much too smart for me, Charles. I've been hiding around town for days, following you with binoculars, charting your activities. It's amazing you didn't catch on sooner.''

He ignored her scornful remarks. ''It was convenient the way you twisted your ankle the other day, too, wasn't it? Somehow you managed to fall directly into my arms.''

''The timing was perfect, wasn't it?'' she said with a short, humorless laugh. ''You're right, I couldn't have planned that any better.''

He frowned. ''Then there was the dinner waiting for me at the house the other night. Italian, too, just the way my grandmother used to make it.''

''Amazing how I knew that, isn't it?''

''All this adds up to one thing.''

''And what might that be?'' she asked scathingly, folding her arms and cocking her head. She'd assumed far too much in this relationship. She'd lowered her guard and actually believed Charles loved her, because she loved him so deeply. Now she realized how wrong she'd been.

"It adds up to the fact that you're playing games again."

"Don't forget the moonlight the night we were at Multnomah Falls. I arranged that, too, along with everything else. I have to admit it took some doing, but I'm a clever soul."

"There's no need to be sarcastic."

"I don't agree," she returned defiantly.

Charles frowned and muttered something she couldn't understand.

"I must say I'm surprised you caught on so quickly, what with me being so subtle and all."

"Let's clear the air once and—"

"But the air *is* clear," she said, waving her arms wildly. She knew she was going too far with this, but the momentum was building and she couldn't seem to stop. "I've been found out, and now it's all over."

"Over?"

"Of course. There's no need to pretend any longer."

"What are you talking about?"

"Revenge. It's supposed to be sweet, and it would have been if you hadn't caught on when you did."

"Just what did you intend to do?" he demanded.

"You mean you don't have that figured out, as well?"

"Tell me, Stephanie." His voice was hard as ice and just as cold.

"All right, if you must know. Once I got you to the point of proposing—" she paused dramatically "—I was going to laugh and reject you. It seems only fair after the way you humiliated me. You laughed at me, Charles, and it was going to be my turn to laugh at you. Only you found me out first...."

His frown deepened into a scowl. "Your father—"

"Oh, don't worry, he didn't know anything about that part. Getting him to shame you into a marriage proposal was tricky, but I managed it by telling him I was afraid you were trifling with my affections." She gave a deep exaggerated sigh, astonished that he seemed to believe all this.

"I see."

"Oh, you're too clever for me, Charles. What can I possibly say? There's no need to pretend any more."

"Perhaps it would be best if you left now."

"I think you're right. Well, at least you know what it feels like to have someone laugh at you."

Charles walked to his front door and held it open for her. With a jaunty step, Steffie walked out of his house. "Well, I'll see you around, but you don't need to worry—I won't be spying on you anymore."

His jaw was tightly clamped, and Steffie realized she'd succeeded beyond all her expectations. Charles was disgusted with her. And furious. So furious that he couldn't get her out of his home fast enough.

"You can't blame a girl for trying," she said with a shrug once she'd slipped past him.

In response, Charles slammed his door shut.

By the time Steffie was inside the car, she was shaking so badly that she could barely insert the key into the ignition. Her breath seemed to be caught in her chest, creating a painful need to exhale.

Like Charles, she was angry, more angry than she'd ever been in her life. In one rational corner of her mind, she knew—had known all along—that it was a mistake to goad him with all those ridiculous lies.

But the amazing thing, the sad thing, was that he'd believed them. To his way of thinking, apparently, it all fit. And as far as Steffie was concerned, there was nothing more to say.

In time, she'd regret her outburst, but she didn't then. At that moment, she was far too infuriated to care. In time, she'd regret the lies, the squandered hopes—but it wouldn't be anytime soon.

"Well?" her father asked, his expression pleased and expectant as she let herself into the house an hour later. "Are you two going to look for an engagement ring in the next few days?"

"Not exactly," Steffie said, moving into his den. As he'd promised earlier, her father was waiting up for her, reading in his favorite chair.

His face fell with disappointment. "But you did talk about getting married, didn't you?"

"Not really. We, uh, got sidetracked."

"You didn't argue, did you?"

"Not really." Steffie was unsure how much to tell her father. She worried that if he realized the extent of the rift between her and Charles, he'd feel obliged to do something to patch things up.

David set aside his reading glasses and gazed up at her. "You'll be seeing him again soon, won't you?"

Living in Orchard Valley made that highly likely. It was the very reason she'd chosen to study in Europe three years earlier. "Naturally I'll be seeing him."

David nodded, appeased. "Good."

"I think I'll go up to my room and read. Good night, Dad."

"Night, Princess."

As it happened, Steffie met Norah at the top of the stairs. Her younger sister glanced her way and did an automatic double-take. "What's wrong?"

"What makes you think something's wrong?"

"You mean other than the fact that you look like you're waiting to get to your room before you cry?"

Her sister knew her too well. Steffie felt terrible—discouraged, disheartened, depressed. But in her present mood, she didn't have the patience to explain what had happened between her and Charles.

"What could possibly be wrong?" Steffie asked instead, feigning a lightness she didn't feel.

"Funny you should say that," Norah said, tucking her arm through Steffie's and leading the way to her bedroom. "Valerie asked me nearly the same thing not so long ago. What could possibly be wrong? Well, I'd have to say it was probably trouble with a man."

"That's very astute of you."

"Obviously it's Charles, then." Norah didn't react to Steffie's mild sarcasm.

"Obviously." She was tired, weary all the way to her bones and desperately craving a long, hot soak in the tub. Some of her best thinking was accomplished while lazing in a bathtub filled with scented water. She'd avoided bubble baths since the time she'd spent hours in one waiting for Charles.

"Did you two have a spat?"

"Not exactly. Listen, Norah, I appreciate your concern—really, I do... I don't mean to sound ungrateful, but I'm tired and I want to go to bed."

"Bed? Good grief, it's barely seven."

"It's been a long day."

Norah eyed her suspiciously. "It must have been."

"Besides I have a busy day scheduled for Monday."

Norah's interest was piqued. "What's happening then?"

"I'm going to Portland to see about my application at the university and to find an apartment."

For a moment Norah said nothing. Her mouth fell open and she wore a stunned look. "But I thought you told Dad you were going to wait on that."

"I was..."

"But you aren't any longer? Even after you promised Dad?"

Steffie glanced away, not wanting her sister to realize how deeply hurt she was. How betrayed she felt that Charles would believe she was so deceitful as to trick him into marriage. It seemed that whenever Charles Tomaselli was involved, she invariably ended up in pain.

"I feel better than I have in years." David greeted Steffie cheerfully early the next morning. He was sitting at the kitchen table, drinking a cup of coffee and going over the Portland edition of the Sunday paper. He welcomed her with a warm smile, apparently not noticing his daughter's lackluster mood. "It's a beautiful morning," David added.

"Beautiful," Steffie mumbled as she poured herself a cup of coffee and staggered to the table. Her eyes burned from lack of sleep, and she felt as though she were walking around in a nightmare.

She'd spent the entire night arguing with herself about the lies she'd told Charles. In the end, she'd managed to convince herself that she'd done the right thing. Charles *wanted* to believe every word. He'd seized every one of her sarcastic remarks, all too ready to consider them truth.

"What time will Charles be by?" her father asked conversationally.

"Charles?" She repeated his name as though she'd never heard it before.

"I thought the two of you were going horseback riding sometime this afternoon."

"Uh...I'm not sure Charles will be able to come, after all." The date had probably slipped his mind, the way it had hers. Even if he did remember, Steffie sincerely doubted he'd show up. As far as she was concerned, whatever had been between them was over now. In fact, the more she reviewed their last discussion, the angrier she became. If he honestly believed the things she'd suggested—and he certainly seemed to—then there was no hope for them. None.

"I'd better get dressed for church," Steffie said bleakly.

"You've got plenty of time yet."

"Norah has to get there early." Her sister sang in the choir. Generally Norah left the house before the others, but Steffie thought she'd ride with Norah this morning, if for no better reason than to escape her father's questions. From the looks David was giving her, he was sure to subject her to a full-scale inquisition if she stayed in the kitchen much longer.

Attending church was an uplifting experience for Steffie. During that hour, she was able to forget her troubles and absorb the atmosphere of peace and serenity. Whatever solace she found, however, vanished the minute she and Norah drove into the yard shortly after noon.

Charles's car was parked out front.

Steffie tensed and released a long, slow sigh.

"Problems?" Norah asked.

"I don't know."

"Do you want to talk to him?"

It didn't take Steffie more than a moment to decide. "No, I don't." But at the same time, she wasn't about to back down, either. She wouldn't allow Charles to chase her from her own home. He was on her turf now, and she didn't run easily.

Steffie parked behind Charles's sports car and willed herself to remain calm and collected. Her father must have heard them because he stepped outside the house, his welcoming smile in place. He still moved slowly but with increasing confidence. It was sometimes hard to remember that he was recovering from major surgery.

"Steffie, Charles is here."

"So I see," she said with a decided lack of enthusiasm.

"He's in the stable, waiting for you."

She nodded and, with her heart racing wildly, walked up the steps and past her father.

"Aren't you going to talk to him?"

"I need to change my clothes first."

"To talk? But..." He hesitated, then reluctantly nodded.

By the time Steffie was in her bedroom, she was trembling. Her emotions were so confused that she wasn't sure if she was shaking with anger or with nervousness. But she did know she wasn't ready to face him, wasn't ready to deal with his accusations or his reproach. For several minutes she sat on her bed, trying to decide what to do.

"Steffie." Norah stood in the doorway, watching her, looking concerned. "Are you all right?"

"Of course I—no, I'm not," she said. "I'm not ready to talk to Charles yet."

"Nothing says you have to talk to him if you don't want to. I'll make up some excuse and send him packing."

"No." For pride's sake, she didn't want him to know how badly she'd been hurt by their latest confrontation.

"You look like you're about to dissolve into tears."

Steffie squared her shoulders and met her sister's worried gaze. "I'm not going to give him the satisfaction."

"Atta girl," Norah said approvingly.

Changing into jeans and a sweatshirt, Steffie went down the back stairs into the kitchen. She didn't expect to find Charles sitting at the table chatting with her father. The sight took her by surprise. What unsettled her most was that he gave no outward sign of their quarrel. Steffie slowed her pace as she entered the room.

Charles stopped talking and his eyes narrowed briefly. "Hello, Stephanie."

"I'll leave you two alone," her father said before Steffie could answer Charles's greeting. He rose, a bit stiffly, and made his way to the door. "I guess you've got plenty to discuss."

Steffie wanted to argue, but realized it wouldn't do any good. She merely shrugged and remained where she was, standing just a few steps from the back stairs. She didn't look at Charles. The silence between them lengthened, until she couldn't endure it any longer.

"I didn't expect you to come," she said in a harsh voice. "It certainly wasn't necessary."

"I'm aware of that."

"I'm not in the mood to go riding and I don't imagine you are, either." It went without saying that she wasn't in the mood to go riding with *him*.

"I'm not here to ride."

"Then why are you here?"

Apparently Charles didn't have the answer because he got to his feet and walked over to the window. Whatever he saw must have fascinated him because he stood there for several moments without saying a word.

"Why are you here?" she asked a second time, ready to request that he leave.

He finally turned around to face her. "I don't know about you, but I couldn't sleep last night."

Steffie refused to admit that she'd fared no better, so she made no response.

"I kept going over the things your father said and the things you told me," Charles went on.

"Did you come to any conclusions?" Pride demanded that she not meet his glance, or reveal how much his answer meant to her.

"One."

Steffie tensed. "What was that?" She had to look at him now.

His eyes burned into hers. Although nearly the entire kitchen separated them, Steffie felt as though he was close enough to touch.

"It seems to me," he began, "that since your father's so anxious to marry you off, and you seem to be just as eager, then fine."

"Fine?" she repeated as though this was some joke and she'd missed the punch line.

"In other words," Charles returned shortly, "I'm willing to take you off his hands."

Ten

"**W**hat?"

"Take me off Dad's hands?" Steffie echoed. Surely he wasn't serious. No woman in her right mind would accept such an insulting marriage proposal.

"You heard me."

"Tell me you're kidding."

Charles shook his head. "I've never been more serious in my life. You want to marry me, then so be it. I'm willing to go along with this, provided we understand each other…"

"In that case I withdraw the offer—not that I ever *made* an offer."

"You can't do that," Charles argued, looking surprised. "Your father thinks we should get married and, after giving the matter some thought, I agree with him."

"That's too bad, since I'm not interested."

Charles laughed softly. "We both know that's not true. You've been crazy about me for years."

Steffie whirled around and folded her arms in front of her as though to ward off his words. "I can't marry you, Charles."

"Why not? I know you love me. You said so yourself before you left for Italy, and I know that hasn't changed."

"Don't be so sure."

"Ah, but I am. And recently you let me know it again."

"When?" she demanded, trying to recall the conversations they'd had since her return to Orchard Valley.

"It was the afternoon we met at Del's."

Steffie cast her mind back to that time. They'd met by accident as they'd gone in to pay for their gas. Steffie remembered how glad she'd been to see him, how eager to set things straight. But she couldn't remember saying one thing that would lead Charles to believe she still loved him.

"I didn't say anything."

"Not in so many words, true, but with everything you did. The same holds true for the night I dropped off the azalea and you asked me to dinner, remember?"

"Yes, but what's that got to do with anything?"

"A whole lot, as a matter of fact. You were continually making excuses for us to be together."

Steffie's face flooded with color. "What has that got to do with anything?" she demanded again.

He ignored her question. "We had a good time that night, touring Orchard Valley. Didn't we?"

Steffie nodded. She wasn't likely to forget that evening. For the first time in her relationship with Charles, she'd felt a stirring of real promise. Not the kind of hope she'd fabricated three years earlier, but one based on genuine companionship. Charles had enjoyed her company and they'd laughed and talked as though they'd been friends for years.

"You told me that when you lived in Italy you were too busy with your studies to date much," Charles reminded her.

"So?"

"So that led me to conclude that you hadn't fallen in love with anyone else while you were away."

"I hadn't."

"Your father came right out and told me on several occasions that he was concerned about you because you didn't seem to be dating anyone seriously."

Steffie glared at him, feeling trapped. "I still don't know what this has to do with anything."

"Plenty. You loved me then, and you love me now."

"You've got some nerve, Charles Tomaselli." She glowered fiercely, hoping he'd back off. "What makes you so sure I'm in love with you now?"

"I know you better than you realize."

"What nonsense!" She forced a light laugh. "You don't know me at all, otherwise you—" She stopped abruptly.

"Otherwise what?"

"Nothing." *Otherwise he wouldn't have believed the things she'd told him.*

"Don't you think it's time we stopped playing games with each other?" he suggested softly.

"What games?" she snapped. "I gave those up years ago."

Charles frowned as though he wasn't sure he should believe her.

Hurt and angry, Steffie raised her hand and pointed at him. "*That's* the reason I refuse to marry you," she cried. Restraining the emotion was next to impossible and her voice quavered with the force of it. "I suppose I should be flattered that you're willing to take me off Dad's hands," she said sarcastically. "Every woman dreams of hearing such romantic words. But I want far more in a husband, Charles Tomaselli, than you'd ever be capable of giving me!"

"What do you mean by that?" He didn't give her a chance to reply before he muttered, "Oh, I get it. You're afraid I'm going to be financially strapped with the newspaper, aren't you? You think I won't be able to afford you."

Steffie was stunned by his words. Stunned and insulted. "You know me so well, don't you?" she asked him, her voice heavy with scorn. "There's just no pulling the wool over your eyes, is there?" She drew in a deep breath. "I think it would be best if you left." She walked across the kitchen and held open the back door for him. "Right now."

Charles frowned at her and shook his head. "Sorry," he said. "I don't want to leave." He pulled out a chair and threw himself down. "We're going to talk this out, once and for all," he told her.

"Dammit, but you're stubborn."

"So are you."

"We'd make a terrible couple."

"We make a good team."

Steffie didn't know why she was fighting him so hard—especially when he was saying all the things she'd always dreamed of hearing.

"I realize I've made one or two mistakes with this," he said slowly. "It sounded a bit callous, offering to marry you the way I did."

"I'll admit that *taking me off Dad's hands* does lack a certain romantic flair," she agreed wryly. She crossed over to the counter for a coffee mug, filling it from the pot next to the stove. If they were going to talk seriously, without hurling accusations at one another, she was going to need it.

"I was angry."

"Then why'd you come here?" she demanded, claiming the chair across from him.

"Because," he answered in a tight, angry voice, "I was afraid I was going to lose you again."

"Lose me?" That made no sense to Steffie.

"You heard me," he growled. "I was afraid you'd return to Italy or take off on a safari, or go someplace else equally inaccessible."

"Portland. I'm moving to Portland, but it isn't because of what happened with you. I intended to do this from the moment I arrived home." She folded her hands around the hot mug. "Why should you care where I go?"

"Because I didn't want you leaving again."

"Why do you want me to stay, especially if you believe the things I told you yesterday?"

His eyes held hers. "I don't believe them."

"You gave a good impression of it earlier," she reminded him. A fresh wave of pain assaulted her and she looked away.

"That's because I was furious."

"That hasn't changed."

"No, it hasn't," he agreed, "but the simple fact is I don't want you to leave again."

"Unfortunately you don't have any say in what I do."

Charles frowned. "Now you're angry."

"You're damn right I am! Did you honestly think I was so desperate for a husband I'd accept your insulting offer? Is that what you think of me, Charles?"

"No!" he shouted. "I'm in love with you, dammit. I have been for years. I had to do something to keep you here. I don't want to wait another three years for you to come to your senses."

His words were followed by a stunned, disbelieving silence. Steffie stared down into her coffee, and to her chagrin felt tears well up in her eyes. "I'm afraid I don't believe you."

Charles stood abruptly and walked to the window, as he had earlier. Hands clasped behind his back, he gazed outside. "It's true."

"It couldn't be." She wiped the tears from her face. "You were so...so..."

"Cruel," he supplied. "You'll never understand

how hard it was not to make love to you that day in the stable. I've never been more tempted by any woman."

"I...tempted you?" Her voice was low and incredulous.

He turned around and smiled, but it was a sad smile, one full of doubts and regrets. "I remember when you first started hanging around the newspaper office. I was flattered by the attention. Soon I found myself looking forward to the times you came by. You were witty and generous and you always had an intelligent comment about something the paper had printed. I quickly discovered you were much more than a pretty face."

"I never worked harder in my life to impress anyone," she murmured with self-deprecating humor.

It didn't take Steffie long to get back to the point in question. "If that was how you felt, then why did you ask me not to come around any longer?"

"I had to say something before I gave in and threw caution to the wind. You'd recently lost your mother and you were young, naive and terribly vulnerable. I struggled with my conscience for weeks, trying to decide what I was going to do about you. In case you haven't noticed, I'm six years older than you. At the time that made a big difference."

"The gap in our ages hasn't narrowed."

"True enough, but you're not a girl anymore."

"I was twenty-one," she argued.

"Perhaps, but you were a sheltered twenty-one. And you were still dealing with your grief. Your entire life had been jolted, and I couldn't be sure if what you felt for me was love or adolescent infatuation.''

Steffie closed her eyes and let the warmth of his words revive her. ''It was love,'' she told him softly. A love that had matured, grown more intense, in the years that separated them.

''I realize it probably doesn't mean much to you now, but I want you to know how hard it was for me the night I came home and found you in my bathtub.''

''But you were so angry.''

''It was either that or drag you into my room and make love to you.''

Steffie remained confused. ''You laughed at me when I told you how I felt that day in the stable....''

''I know,'' he said simply. Steffie heard the pain and remorse in his voice. ''I've never had to do anything that's cost me more. But I never dreamed you'd leave Orchard Valley.''

''What did you expect me to do? I couldn't stay— that would have been impossible. So I did the only thing I could. I left.''

Charles's hand reached for hers, twining their fingers together. ''I'll never forget the day I learned you'd gone to Europe. I felt as if I'd been hit by a bulldozer.''

''I had to go,'' she repeated unnecessarily. ''It was too painful to stay.''

His fingers tightened around hers. ''I know.'' Slowly he raised her hand to his lips. ''I've waited three long years to tell you how sorry I was to hurt you. Three years to tell you I was in love with you, too.''

Steffie attempted with little success to blink back the tears.

"If it had been at any other time in your life, if I could have been sure you weren't just trying to re-place your mother's love with mine—then everything would've been different. But you were so terribly young, so innocent. I couldn't trust myself around you, feeling the way I did.''

"And you couldn't trust me.''

He nodded his agreement. "I'm sorry, Stephanie, for rejecting you. Just realize that it was as painful for me as it was for you. Perhaps more so, because I knew the whole truth.''

"You never wrote—not once in all that time. Not so much as a postcard.''

"I couldn't. Believe me, I wanted to, but I didn't dare give in to the impulse. I wasn't sure even then if what you felt for me was genuine love or infatuation.''

"So you waited.''

"Not patiently. I expected you to come home at least once in three years, you know.''

"I dreaded seeing you again. I was thousands of miles away from you and yet I still loved you, I still dreamed about you. It didn't seem to get any better. Even after three years.''

"You'd finished your classes and you were in the

process of deciding if you were going to stay on in Italy.''

"How'd you know that?"

"Your father. He was the only way I had of getting information about you, and I used him shamelessly."

"He told me you started stopping in for visits shortly after I left."

"It's a wonder he didn't figure out how I felt about you. I don't think I could have been any more obvious if I'd tried."

"Dad didn't have a clue until recently and then only because of the—" She stopped when she realized what she was about to tell him.

"Of what?" Charles prodded.

"I...it would be best if you let Dad explain that part."

"All right, I will." He looked away from her momentarily. "Although you never seriously dated anyone, there *was* someone in Italy, wasn't there? A man you cared about?"

"Who?" Steffie frowned in bewilderment.

"A man named Mario?"

"Mario...a man?" He was four now, and the delight of her heart all the while she'd lived in Italy.

"He gave me several restless nights' worry. Your father only mentioned him once. Said you 'adored' him. I went through the agonies of the damned, trying to be subtle about getting information on this guy, but your father never mentioned him again."

"Mario," Steffie repeated, smiling broadly. "Yes, I did adore him."

Charles scowled. "What happened?"

Still smiling, Steffie said, "There was a slight discrepancy in our ages. I'm about twenty years older."

"He's a kid."

"But what a kid. My landlady's son. I was crazy about him." Spending time with a loving, open child like Mario had helped her though a difficult period in her life.

"I see." A slow, easy smile slipped into place. "So you like children."

"Oh, yes, I always have."

"I hope that young man appreciates all he put me through."

"I'm sure he doesn't, but I certainly do. I know what it's like to love someone and have that someone not love you."

Charles considered her words for several moments. "I've always loved you, Stephanie, but I didn't dare let you know. I couldn't trust what we felt for each other then—but I can now."

She avoided his gaze. She had to ask, though she was afraid to. "If that's true, why were you so angry when Dad suggested we get married?"

Charles sighed. "Frustration, I guess. I'd intended to propose the night we went for dinner. I had everything planned, right down to the last detail."

"But why didn't you?"

"I couldn't, not when the past still came between us. You made it clear you didn't want to discuss our misunderstandings. At least not then. So my hands were tied. I hate to admit it, but I was downright nervous—even if you didn't seem to notice."

"I made it one of my wishes," she recalled, and experienced an instant twinge of regret. Her reluctance to discuss the past had cost her a romantic proposal from the man she loved. It was a lesson she'd remember well.

"That still doesn't explain why you were so offended when Dad suggested we marry." His reaction remained a mystery in light of the things he was telling her now.

"A man prefers to propose himself," Charles offered as a simple explanation. "I don't think I could have made my intentions toward you any plainer had I hired a skywriter, and to have first your father and then you..."

"Me?"

"Yesterday I suddenly felt so afraid that you *weren't* lying about why you'd stopped by at the house. To put in the finishing blow, to get me to admit I loved you and then laugh at me..."

"I—I made that part up! You made me so mad—"

"I made you mad?" he cried.

"I know, I know. It's just that I had to say something. I didn't think you'd believe all those ridiculous lies, and then you seemed to and that made everything a thousand times worse. I was just beginning to hope we might have a future together."

"I was, too. That's why it hit me so hard."

"I could never intentionally hurt you, Charles. Not without hurting myself."

His eyes held hers, and everything around Steffie faded into significance. She was on the verge of disclosing all the love in her heart when there was a knock at the kitchen door, followed by her father poking his head inside. "Is it safe yet? You two looked like time bombs about to explode twenty minutes ago."

"It's safe," Charles answered, smiling at Steffie.

"I hope you've got everything worked out because I'm getting tired of waiting. The way I figure it, you should be married by the end of the summer. Your oldest—"

"Dad," Steffie cut in. "I don't think Charles is interested in discussing it right now. Why don't you leave all of that to us?"

"Our oldest?" Charles asked, frowning.

"Child, of course. A girl, followed by a son and then another daughter. Sweethearts, all three of them. The boy will be the spitting image of you, Charles— same dark brown eyes, same facial features."

Charles glanced at Steffie as though he wasn't sure of her father's sanity.

"I think you'd better tell Charles about the dream, Dad."

"You mean you haven't?" He sounded surprised.

"No, I didn't want to frighten the dear man out of marrying into the family."

"What's going on here?" Charles's gaze roved from Steffie to her father and back.

"I'm not sure you're going to believe this," David said, pulling out a chair and settling himself. He grinned, happy as Steffie could ever remember seeing him. "But I got a glimpse of the future. It was a gift from Grace. She wanted to be sure I had a reason to live and so she had me—"

"But isn't Grace—"

"She's in heaven, but then so was I, briefly. It was what they call a near-death experience. You can ask Colby about this if you don't believe me."

"Colby?" Charles repeated.

"I'm not convinced he believes me one hundred percent, but time will prove me right. Look at what's happened with Valerie and Colby, just the way I said it would. And with you two, for that matter. You're going to marry this little girl of mine, aren't you?"

"In a heartbeat," Charles confirmed.

Her father's grin split his face. "That's what I thought. You love him, don't you, Princess?"

Steffie nodded. "More than I thought it was possible to love anyone," she said in a hushed voice.

David smiled knowingly and eased himself out of his chair. "In that case, I'll leave you two to discuss the details of your wedding. I'd like to suggest midsummer, but as I said, I'll leave that up to you." He slipped out of the room.

"Midsummer?" Steffie repeated.

"Sounds good to me. Does that give you enough time?"

She laughed. "Sure, and I'll be able to register for my courses, according to plan—if that's okay with you?'' At his enthusiastic agreement, she added, ''Uh...what do you think about Dad's dream?''

''A boy and two girls, he says.''

Steffie nodded shyly.

''How do *you* feel about that?'' he asked.

''Good, very good. How about you?''

Charles reached for her then, wrapping her in his arms with the strength of a man who'd been too long without love. He buried his face in the gentle curve of her neck and breathed deeply. ''I nearly lost you for the second time.''

''You'd never have lost me, Charles. I've loved you for so long, I don't know how not to love you.'' He'd been a part of her for so many years that she couldn't imagine continuing without him now.

''I love you, Stephanie. Give me a chance to prove it.''

In her eyes, he'd already proved it when he hadn't laughed at her father's dream. She knew what he was thinking, perhaps because she was thinking the same thing herself. They were in love, had already decided to marry, so it didn't matter what her father had predicted after his supposed sojourn in the afterlife. It was the course they'd willingly set for themselves.

He kissed her then, and her heart seemed to overflow with love, just as her eyes overflowed with tears.

''Stephanie,'' Charles whispered, his lips against hers. ''We have a lot of time to make up for.''

''It'll take at least fifty years, won't it?''

''At the very least,'' he murmured, kissing her again with a need that left her breathless.

* * *

David Bloomfield relaxed in his rocker on the front porch, his smile one of utter contentment. It was coming to pass, just as he'd known it would. Just as Grace had told him. First Valerie, and now Steffie. His grin widened.

My heavens, he thought, Norah was in for one wallop of a surprise.

NORAH

To Dorothy Tharp
in appreciation for her many talents

One

This cowboy was too young to die!

Norah Bloomfield stared down at the unconscious face of the man in Orchard Valley Hospital's emergency room. He was suffering from shock, internal injuries and a compound fracture of the right fibula. Yet he was probably the luckiest man she'd ever known. He'd survived.

The team of doctors worked vigorously over him, doing everything humanly possible to keep him alive. Although she was busy performing her own role in this drama, Norah was curious. It wasn't every day a man literally fell out of the sky into their backyard. Whoever he was, he'd been involved in a plane accident. From what she heard when they'd rushed him in, he'd made a gallant effort to land the single-engine Cessna in a wheatfield, but the plane's wing tip had caught the ground, catapulting it into a series of cartwheels. That he'd managed to crawl out of the wreckage was a miracle all its own.

She tightened the blood-pressure cuff around his arm and called out the latest reading. Dr. Adamson, the physician in attendance, briskly instructed her to administer a shot.

Their patient was young, in his early thirties. And handsome in a rugged sort of way. Dark hair, chiseled jaw, stubborn as a mule from the looks of him. His clothes, at least what was left of them, told her he was probably a cowboy. She suspected he rode in the rodeo circuit; successfully, too, if he was flying his own plane.

Her gaze drifted down to his left hand. He wasn't wearing a wedding ring and that eased her mind somewhat. Norah hated the thought of a young wife pacing the floor, anxiously waiting his arrival home. Of course, that didn't necessarily mean he wasn't married. A lot of men didn't wear wedding bands, particularly if they worked with their hands. Too dangerous.

His leg was badly broken, she noted, and once he was stabilized, he'd be sent into surgery. She didn't have a lot of experience with compound fractures, but her guess was that he'd need to be in traction for the next few weeks. A break as complex as this would take months, possibly years, to heal properly.

Norah wasn't scheduled to work tonight, but had been called in unexpectedly. She should have been home, had *planned* to be home, preparing for her oldest sister Valerie's wedding. Half of Orchard Valley would be in attendance—it was widely held to be the event of the year. And five weeks after that, her second sister, Steffie, would be marrying Charles Tomaselli, in a much less formal ceremony.

There was definitely something in the air this summer, Norah mused, with both her sisters getting married so unexpectedly.

Love was what floated in the air, but it had apparently evaded Norah. There wasn't a single man in Orchard Valley who stirred her heart. Not one.

She was thrilled for her sisters, but at the same time she couldn't help feeling a bit envious. If any of the three could be described as "the marrying type," it was Norah. She was by far the most domestic and traditional. Ever since she was a teenager, Norah had assumed she'd be the first of the three sisters to marry, although she was the youngest. Valerie had hardly dated even in college, and Steffie was so impulsive and unpredictable that she'd never stood still long enough to get serious about anyone. Or so it had seemed...

Now both her sisters were marrying. And all this had happened within two short months. Only weeks ago Norah would have been shocked had anyone told her Valerie would become a wife. Her oldest sister was the dedicated career woman, working her way up the corporate ladder for CHIPS, a Texas-based computer software corporation. At least, that was what Valerie *had* been—until she flew home when their father suffered a serious heart attack. Before Norah was entirely aware it had happened, Valerie was head over heels in love with Dr. Colby Winston.

Norah never did understand what had led to their falling in love. Try as she might, she couldn't picture her sister as a wife. Valerie, who was so much like their father, was a dynamic businesswoman. She'd accepted the sales job with CHIPS and in less than four years had moved up into upper management. She was energetic, spirited and strong-willed. If her sister was going to fall in love, Norah couldn't understand how it could be with Dr. Winston. He was just as dedicated to his work, just as headstrong. To Norah's way of thinking, they had little in common except their love for each other. Watching them together had taught Norah a few things about love and commitment. They were both determined to make their marriage work, both willing to make compromises, to change and mediate their differences.

If Valerie was going to marry, Norah had always assumed it should be someone like Rowdy Cassidy, the owner of CHIPS. For months, Valerie's letters had been full of details about the maverick software developer. He'd taken Wall Street by storm with his innovative ideas, and had very soon come to dominate the field. Valerie greatly admired him. But she'd given up her position with CHIPS without so much as a second's regret. There were other jobs, she'd said, but only one Colby Winston. And if she had to choose, as Cassidy had forced her to do, then that choice was clear. But then Norah had never seen anyone more in love—unless it was Steffie.

Her second sister had arrived after a long, difficult trip, to be with their father and almost the same thing had happened. Suddenly, she and Charles Tomaselli, the Orchard Valley *Clarion*'s editor and now its publisher, had clashed. They'd been constantly at odds, but gradually that had changed. Not until much later

did Norah learn that Charles was the reason Steffie
had decided to study in Italy. Steffie had been wildly
in love with him three years earlier. Norah wasn't
entirely sure what had gone wrong back then, but
whatever it was had sent Steffie fleeing. She guessed
there'd been some sort of disagreement between
them, but no one had bothered to explain it to her.
Not that it mattered. What was important, though,
was that Steffie and Charles had managed to patch
things up and admit their true feelings for each other.

In typical Steffie fashion, her sister was planning
a thoroughly untraditional wedding. The exchange of
vows was to take place in the apple orchard, between
the rows of trees with their weight of reddening apples. The reception would be held on the groomed
front lawn; there would be musicians playing cham-
ber music in the background. The wedding cake was
to be a huge chocolate concoction.

So, within a few weeks of each other, her two
sisters would be married. Unlike Valerie, Norah
hadn't recently met a new and wonderful man. And
unlike Steffie, she didn't have a secret love, someone
she'd felt passionate about for years. Unless she
counted Michael York. Norah figured she'd seen
every movie he starred in ten times over. But it
wasn't likely that a dashing actor was going to toss
her over his shoulder and haul her away. A pity,
really.

An hour later, Norah was washing up, preparing
to head home. The cowboy, although listed in critical
condition, had stabilized. He might not feel like it

now, but he was damn lucky to be alive. The surgery on the right fibula would follow, but she wasn't sure exactly when.

Eager to leave the hospital and get home, Norah was on her way out the door when she heard someone mention the cowboy's name.

She stopped abruptly, nearly tripping in her astonishment. "Who did you say he is?" she demanded, turning back to her friends.

"According to the identification he carried, his name is Rowdy Cassidy."

"Rowdy!" Susan Parsons, another nurse, laughed. "It's a perfect name for him, isn't it? He looks rowdy. Personally, I don't want to be around when he wakes up. Two dollars says he's going to have all the charm of an angry yellow jacket."

Rowdy Cassidy. Norah took a deep breath. The man was Valerie's employer. Former employer, she amended. He must have been flying in for the wedding when the accident occurred.

Norah wasn't sure what she could do with the information. Valerie, who was cool as a watermelon on ice when it came to business dealings, was a nervous wreck over this wedding.

Love had taken Valerie Bloomfield by surprise and she hadn't recovered yet. Mentioning Rowdy's accident to her sister now didn't seem right; Valerie had enough on her mind without the additional worry. Yet it didn't seem fair to keep the truth from her, either.

Whom should she tell, then, Norah wondered on

her way to the staff parking lot. Surely someone should know...

It was late, past midnight, when she entered the house. Although there were several lights on, she didn't see anyone around. The wedding was at noon, less than twelve hours away.

Secretly Norah had hoped her father might still be up, but she didn't really expect it. He went to bed early these days and slept late, his body regaining its strength after the physical ordeal of a heart attack and the subsequent life-saving surgery.

"Hi," Steffie said cheerfully. She hurried downstairs, cinching her robe at the waist as she walked. Her long dark hair was damp and fell arrow-straight to the middle of her back. "I wondered what time you'd be home."

Norah stared up at her, frowning in concentration. She'd discuss this with Steffie, see what her sister suggested.

"What happened?" Steffie asked, her voice urgent.

"There was a single-engine-plane crash." Norah hesitated. "Fortunately only one man was aboard."

"Did he survive?"

Norah nodded absently and worried her lower lip. "Is Valerie asleep?"

Steffie sighed. "Who knows? I'd never have believed Valerie would be this nervous before her wedding. Good grief, she's arranged multimillion-dollar business deals."

"Come in the kitchen with me," Norah said,

glancing quickly up the staircase. She didn't want any possibility of Valerie hearing this.

"What is it?" Steffie asked as she followed her into the other room. Valerie's room was directly above, but there was little chance she'd overhear the conversation.

"The man who was involved in the plane accident..."

"Yes," Steffie prodded in a whisper.

"Is Rowdy Cassidy."

Looking stunned, Steffie pulled out a stool at the counter and sank down on it. "You're sure?"

"Positive. Apparently he was flying in for the wedding."

"More likely he intended to stop it," Steffie said sharply.

"Stop it? What do you mean?"

Steffie nodded, her look intense. "Well, you know that when Valerie talked to him about opening a branch on the West Coast, he was in favor of the idea, but he wanted someone else to head it up. He refused to give her the job, unless she could devote twenty-four hours a day to it. In other words, unless she chooses Rowdy Cassidy and her career over Colby and marriage. In fact, she seems to think he can persuade her to do just that."

"What a rotten way to act."

Steffie agreed. "Valerie was furious. She'd hoped to continue working for CHIPS after she's married. Rowdy demanded that she stay in Texas if she wanted to stay with CHIPS. She didn't have any alternative, so she submitted her resignation and announced she was marrying Colby. Apparently Rowdy didn't believe her—still doesn't. He seems to think it was some female ploy to get him to declare his love.''

''I take it Mr. Cassidy doesn't know Valerie very well.'' Her sister was nothing if not direct, Norah mused with a small smile. Valerie would never stoop to orchestrating such a scene, or exploiting a man's feelings for her.

When Valerie first flew home after their father's heart attack, Norah had suspected her sister might have been attracted to her employer. In retrospect, she realized Valerie greatly admired and liked Rowdy, but wasn't in love with him. Her reactions to Colby made that abundantly clear.

''But what makes you think he wanted to stop the wedding?'' Norah asked. If Rowdy did love her sister, he'd certainly waited until the last minute to do something about it.

''He phoned two days ago… I took the call,'' Steffie announced, a guilty expression crossing her face. ''I didn't tell Valerie, but then how could I?''

''Tell her what, exactly?''

''That Rowdy asked her not to do anything…hasty until he'd had a chance to talk to her.''

''Hasty?'' Norah questioned.

''Like go through with the wedding.''

''He had to be joking.''

''I don't think so,'' Steffie said grimly. ''He was dead serious. He claimed he had something important to say to her and that she should put everything on hold until he got here.''

"You didn't tell Valerie?"

"No," Steffie returned, her gaze avoiding Norah's. "I know I should have, but when I told Dad—"

"Dad knows?"

"He didn't seem the least bit surprised, either." Steffie folded her arms around her middle and slowly shook her head. "He just smiled and then he said the most amazing thing."

"When hasn't he?" Norah muttered.

Steffie agreed with a quick smile.

"What was it this time?"

Steffie didn't answer right away. She stared down at the counter for a moment. Finally she glanced up, giving a baffled shrug. "That Rowdy was arriving right on schedule."

Norah found the statement equally puzzling. "Do you think Rowdy might have telephoned earlier and spoken to Dad?"

Once again Steffie shrugged. "Who knows?"

"But Dad seemed to think you shouldn't say anything to Valerie about Rowdy's call?" Norah pressed.

Steffie nodded. "Yeah. He says she's got enough to worry about. I couldn't agree more. As far as I'm concerned, Cassidy's had his chance. He accepted her resignation, which worked out fine since it gave Valerie more time to get everything organized for the wedding. From what she said recently, I think she might start doing some consulting. You know, help companies upgrade their computer systems.''

"That's a great idea,'' Norah murmured. "Valerie's amazing.''

"It isn't the wedding arrangements that have unsettled Val.'' Steffie spoke with the authority of one who knew. "It's being in love.''

"Love,'' Norah repeated wistfully.

"Valerie's never been in love before, that's what threw her. Not the wedding plans or all the organizing or even this job situation.''

"What amazes me the most,'' Norah said, thinking back over the past few weeks, "is how she immediately becomes composed whenever Colby's around.''

"He's her emotional center,'' Steffie said knowingly. "Like Charles is mine. And—''

"Should I say anything to Val about Rowdy Cassidy?'' Norah broke in.

"Sure,'' Steffie told her, "but my advice is to wait until after the ceremony.''

Norah concurred, frowning a little.

"How badly was he injured?'' Steffie asked.

"He's listed in critical condition and is scheduled for surgery on his leg. I think he'll be in traction for some time. He suffered some internal injuries, too, but they don't appear to be as serious as we first assumed.''

"So he'll be pretty well out of it until after the wedding, anyway?''

"Oh, yes. He's not expected to fully regain consciousness until sometime tomorrow afternoon—if then.''

''Then let's leave sleeping dogs lie, shall we?'' Steffie suggested. ''It's not like a visit from Valerie would do him any good—at least, not now.''

''Are you sure we're doing the right thing?'' Norah wasn't nearly as confident as her sister. Valerie had a right to know about her friend's accident.

''No,'' Steffie admitted after a moment. ''I'm not at all sure. But I just can't see upsetting Valerie now, so close to the wedding. Especially when Cassidy isn't likely to know if she goes to see him, anyway.''

Norah didn't know what to think or do. Apparently Rowdy cared enough for her sister to call her, and even to come to Orchard Valley. Perhaps he loved her. If that was the case, though, Rowdy Cassidy's love was too late.

Just before noon the next day, Norah was standing in the vestibule of the church, with the other members of the bride's party. Everyone—except Valerie—was giggling and jittery with nerves. Valerie no longer seemed nervous; now that the day she'd worried over and waited for had finally arrived, she was completely calm. Serene.

But Norah's head was spinning. This wasn't her first wedding by any means. She'd been a bridesmaid three times before. Yet she'd never been more… excited. That was the word for it. Excited and truly happy for these two people she loved so much.

Although she'd never said anything to Valerie and

certainly never to Colby, she'd been a bit sweet on the good doctor herself. Who wouldn't be? He was compassionate and gentle, but he also possessed a rugged appeal. He wasn't one to walk away from a challenge. Loving Valerie had proved as much.

Norah's oldest sister had worked hard on her wedding preparations, and all her careful planning had paid off. The church was lovely. Large bunches of white gardenias decorated the end of each pew. The sanctuary was filled with arrangements of white candles and a profusion of flowers—more gardenias, white and yellow roses, pink apple blossoms.

The bridesmaids' dresses were in different pastels and they carried flowers that complemented their color. Norah's own pale-rose gown was set off by a small bouquet of apple blossoms while Steffie, wearing a soft green gown, carried lemony rosebuds.

The fragrance of the flowers mingled and wafted through the crowded church, carried by a warm breeze that drifted through the open doors.

It was all so beautiful. The flowers, the ceremony, the love between Valerie and Colby as they exchanged their vows. Several times, Norah felt the tears gather in her eyes. She hated being so sentimental, so maudlin, but she couldn't help herself. It was the most touching, most *beautiful*, wedding she'd ever attended.

Valerie was radiant. No other words could describe the kind of beauty that shone from her sister's face as she smiled up at her husband.

The reception, dinner and dance were to follow

immediately afterward at the Orchard Valley Country Club. But first they were subjected to a series of photographs that seemed to take forever. Norah couldn't understand why she felt so impatient, why she seemed to be in such a hurry. It wasn't like her.

After that was finally over, her father took her by the arm as they headed for the limousines, which were lined up outside the church, ready to drive them to the club.

"I heard about Cassidy," he said in a low voice. "How is he?"

"I phoned the hospital this morning," Norah told him. The man had been on her mind most of the night. She hadn't gotten much sleep, which left her with plenty of time to think about Rowdy Cassidy. She'd attributed her restlessness to night-before-the-wedding jitters. She hadn't intended to call the hospital until much later; there was enough to occupy her before the wedding. Valerie had regimented their morning like a drill sergeant, but she'd found a spare moment to make a quick call.

"Carol Franklin was on duty and she told me Rowdy had just come out of surgery."

"And?"

"And he's doing as well as can be expected."

"I thought it might be a good idea if one of us checked up on him later," David Bloomfield said under his breath. "I'll tell Valerie and Colby about the accident myself, after the reception. I'm sure they'll want to see him, too."

"I'll check on him," Norah offered with an eagerness she didn't fully understand.

Her father nodded, and pressed a car key into the palm of her gloved hand. "Steal away when you can. If anyone asks where you are, I'll make up some excuse."

He moved off before Norah could question him. Her father seemed to assume that she'd want to leave the social event of the year, her own sister's wedding, to visit a stranger at the hospital.

And he was right! Without realizing it, she'd been looking for an excuse, a means of doing exactly what her father had suggested. It was the reason she found herself so impatient, so keyed up and restless; she realized that now. Something inside her was calling her back to the hospital. Back to Rowdy Cassidy's bedside.

There was a small break in the wedding festivities between the dinner and the dance. The staff was clearing off the tables and the musicians were tuning up. There should be just enough time for her to leave without anyone's noticing.

Her father caught her eye, and he seemed to be thinking the same thing because he nodded in her direction.

Driving was an exercise in patience with all the layers of taffeta, but Norah managed, although she was sure she made quite a sight.

The hospital was quiet and peaceful when she arrived. If people thought it unusual that she was strolling inside wearing a floor-length rose gown, long white gloves and a broad-brimmed straw hat with a band of ribbon cascading down her back, then they said nothing.

"What room did they put Rowdy Cassidy in?" she asked at the information desk.

"Two fifteen," Janice Wilson told her, after glancing at her computer screen. It was obvious that Janice wanted to ask her a few questions about Valerie and the wedding, but Norah skillfully sidestepped them and hurried down the main hospital corridor.

When she arrived on his floor, she hurried directly into his room. Standing in the darkened doorway, Norah let her eyes adjust to the dim light.

Rowdy's right leg was suspended in the air with a series of levers. His face was turned toward the wall, away from her. Norah walked farther into the room and reached for his medical chart, which was attached to the foot of his bed. She was reading over the notations when she realized intuitively that he was awake. He hadn't made the slightest noise or done anything to indicate he was conscious.

Yet she knew.

Norah moved to the side of his bed, careful not to startle him.

"Hello," she said softly.

His eyes fluttered open.

"Would you like a sip of water?" she asked.

"Please."

She reached for the glass and straw, positioning it at the corner of his mouth. He drank thirstily, and when he finished, raised his eyes to her.

"Am I dead?"

"No," she answered softly, with a reassuring smile. Obviously the medication was continuing to block out the pain, otherwise he'd know exactly how alive he was.

"Should be," he whispered as though speaking demanded a real effort.

"You're a very lucky man, Mr. Cassidy."

He attempted a grin but didn't quite succeed. "Who are you, my fairy godmother?"

"Not quite. I'm Norah Bloomfield, Valerie's sister. And I'm a nurse. I was on call when they brought you in last night."

"Unusual uniform."

Once again Norah found herself smiling. "I was in my sister's wedding this afternoon."

If she hadn't captured his full attention earlier, she did now.

"So Valerie decided to go through with it, after all, did she?"

"Yes."

Silence filled the room.

"Damn fool woman," he muttered after a moment. He turned his head away from her and as he did, Norah noticed that his mouth had tightened with pain. His dark eyes appeared dulled by it.

Norah was left to speculate as to its source, physical or emotional.

Two

"In twenty years I've never worked with a more disagreeable patient," Karen Johnson was saying when Norah walked into the nurses' lounge early Monday morning. "First off, he refuses the painkiller although the doctor ordered it, then he throws a temper tantrum—and his breakfast tray ends up on the other side of the room!"

"I hope you're talking about a patient in pediatrics," Norah said, sitting down next to her friend.

"Nope. Rowdy Cassidy, the guy they brought in from the plane crash. One thing about him, he's certainly earned his name. By the way, he asked for you. At least I think it was you. He said he wanted to talk to the Bloomfield sister who wore fancy dresses. Since we both know Steffie's more likely to wear jeans, and Valerie's on her honeymoon, he must mean you."

Norah smiled to herself, recalling her brief visit with Rowdy the afternoon of Valerie's wedding. So he remembered.

"Don't feel any obligation to go see him," Karen advised. "In my opinion, the man's been catered to once too often. It'd do him a world of good to acquire a little self-restraint.''

From the first, Norah had suspected that Rowdy would be a difficult patient. He was an energetic, decisive man, accustomed to quick action. And he was probably spitting mad about missing Valerie's wedding. He'd been thwarted at every turn, which no doubt added to his deepening frustration.

Although Norah didn't know Valerie's former boss well, she had the distinct impression that he wasn't often foiled. Try as she might, she couldn't help feeling sorry for him. He'd gambled for Valerie's affections and lost. He'd seemed to honestly believe that her sister would have a change of heart and cancel her wedding plans if he came to Orchard Valley.

Norah waited to visit Rowdy until eleven-thirty, when she took her lunch break.

He was lying in bed. His right leg, encased in plaster, was propped at an angle. The blinds were drawn, casting the room into shadow. When he saw her, he levered himself into a sitting position, using a small triangular bar to pull himself upright.

''I heard you wanted to talk to me,'' she said formally, standing just inside the private room.

He didn't say anything for several moments. ''So you were real.''

Norah hid a grin and nodded.

''You *are* a nurse, or is this another costume?''

''I'm a nurse.''

"Valerie went through with the wedding, didn't she?"

Norah raised her eyebrows. "Of course."

His frown darkened.

"What's this I hear about you throwing the breakfast tray?" she asked, stepping farther into the room.

"Who are you, my mother?" he demanded sarcastically.

"No, but when you behave like a child, you can expect to be treated like one." She walked to the window and twisted open the blinds. Sunlight spilled into the room.

Rowdy shielded his eyes. "The thing with the tray was an accident. Now kindly keep those blinds closed," he barked.

"You're in a black enough mood. My advice to you is to lighten up. Literally."

"I didn't ask for your advice."

"Then I'll give it to you without charge. It wouldn't be a bad idea if you took those pain shots, either. You're not afraid of a needle, are you?"

He scowled fiercely. "Close those blinds, dammit. I need my sleep."

"You aren't going to sleep unless you've got something to help you deal with the pain. Taking a painkiller isn't a sign of weakness, you know. It's common sense."

"I don't believe in drugs."

"I wish we'd known that when you were brought into the emergency room," she said with light sarcasm. "Or when you went into surgery, for that matter. It would have made for an interesting operation, don't you think? What would you've suggested we do? Have you bite into a piece of wood?''

"I'm beginning to detect a bit of family resemblance here,'' he muttered. "You don't look anything like Valerie, but you're starting to talk just like her.''

"I'll accept that as a compliment.''

He was clearly growing weaker; levering himself upward must have depleted his strength. Norah was amazed at his ability to move at all.

She neared his bed and rearranged the pillows for him. He slumped back against them and sighed. "Is she happy?''

Norah didn't need Rowdy to explain who he meant by *she*. "I've never seen a more radiant bride,'' she told him quietly. "They've left for a two-week honeymoon. She and Colby stopped by to check on you before they left, but apparently you were still out of it.''

Pain flashed in Rowdy's eyes, and once again Norah was left to wonder if it was from physical discomfort or knowing that he'd truly lost Valerie.

What Rowdy didn't understand, and what Norah couldn't tell him, was that he'd never had a chance with her sister. As far as she was concerned, Valerie's fate had been sealed the minute she met Dr. Colby Winston. Nothing Rowdy said or did from that point forward would have made one iota's difference.

"Where are you going?'' Rowdy revived himself

enough to demand when she started to leave the room.

"I'll be back," she promised.

True to her word, she returned a couple of minutes later with Karen Johnson following her. Karen's right hand was conspicuously hidden behind her back.

"Get her out of here," he said, snarling at Karen.

"Not just yet," Norah countered smoothly.

Karen hesitated, looking to Norah, who nodded.

"What's that?" he roared when Karen brought her arm forward to reveal the needle. She raised it to the light and squeezed gently until a drop of clear liquid appeared at the tip.

"You, Mr. Cassidy, are about to receive an injection," Norah informed him.

"The hell I am."

Norah thought Rowdy's protest could probably be heard from one end of the hospital to the other, but it didn't deter her or Karen from their task. Norah held Rowdy's arm immobile while Karen swiftly administered the pain medication.

Karen fled the room at the first opportunity. Not so Norah, who dragged a chair to his bedside and sat down. Rowdy was furious and made no attempt to hide his displeasure.

Norah checked her watch and calmly waited. His tirade lasted all of three minutes before he slowed down, slurring his words. His dark eyes glared back at her accusingly.

"Have you finished?" she asked politely, when his voice had dwindled to a mere whisper of outrage.

"Not quite. I'll...both...fired...out of... hospital...for this..."

"I'll give you the name of the hospital administrator, if you like," Norah said helpfully. "It's James Bolton."

He muttered under his breath. She could tell that he was fighting off the effects of the medication. His eyes drifted shut and he snapped them open, scowling at her, only to have his lids close again.

"I want you to know I don't appreciate this," he said, surprising her with a rally of strength.

"I know, but it'll help you sleep and that's what you need."

He was growing more tranquil by the moment. "I thought I'd died," he mumbled.

It *was* a miracle he'd survived the plane crash. Norah was thankful he had, for a number of important reasons.

"You're very much alive, Mr. Cassidy."

"An angel came to see me," he told her, his voice fading. "Dressed in pink. So beautiful...almost made me wish I was dead."

"Sleep now," she urged, her heart constricting at his words. He remembered her visit; he'd mentioned it when she first arrived and now, under the influence of the medication, was talking about it again.

She backed away. Although his eyes were closed, he reached out for her. "Don't go," he mumbled. "Stay...a bit longer. Please."

She gave him her hand and was surprised by the vigor of his grip. Touching him had a curious effect on her. He wasn't in pain now, she knew; the tension had left his face. Norah wasn't sure why she felt compelled to gently brush the hair from his forehead. She was rewarded with a drowsy smile.

"An angel," he mumbled once more. Within seconds he was completely asleep. His grip on her hand relaxed, but it was a long time before Norah left his side.

David Bloomfield, Norah's father, was sitting on the front porch of their large colonial home when she arrived home late that afternoon. He still tired easily from his recent surgery and often sat in the warmth of a summer afternoon, gazing out at his apple orchards.

"How's the patient?" he asked, as Norah climbed the porch steps.

"Physically Mr. Cassidy's improving. Unfortunately I can't say the same thing about his disposition."

David chuckled. "I should give that boy a few pointers."

Norah grinned. Her father's own stay at the hospital had been a test of his patience—and the staff's. David hadn't been the most agreeable invalid, especially when he was on the mend. In his eagerness to return home, he'd often been irritable and demanding. Colby had said wryly that David wanted to make sure the hospital staff was just as enthusiastic about his return home as he was himself.

Norah sat on the top step, relaxing for a few

minutes. Her day, much of it spent in the emergency room, had been long and tiring. "Dad," she said carefully, supporting her back against one of the white columns, "what did you mean when you told Steffie that Rowdy Cassidy had arrived right on schedule?"

Her father rocked in his chair for a moment before answering. "I said that?"

Norah grinned. "According to Steffie you did."

He shrugged. "Then I must have."

She removed her nurse's cap and got to her feet. As she entered the house, she could hear the sound of her father's soft chuckle, and wondered what he found so amusing.

Ever since his open-heart surgery, David Bloomfield had been spouting romantic "predictions" regarding Norah's two older sisters. She hoped he wasn't intending to do the same with her.

Valerie and Colby had been the first to fit into his madcap intrigue. Anyone with a nickel's worth of sense could see what was happening between those two. It didn't take a private detective to see they were falling in love. Naturally there were a few problems, but that was to be expected in any relationship.

When their father awoke from his surgery, however, he claimed he'd visited the afterlife and talked with Grace, the girls' mother, who'd died several years earlier from cancer. He claimed he'd looked into the future and knew exactly whom his three daughters would marry. Colby and Valerie inadvertently lent credibility to his "vision." It made perfect

sense to everyone that they'd marry. Certainly no one
at the hospital was surprised when Colby gave Valerie Bloomfield an engagement ring. Their father,
however, had crowed for a week over the happy announcement.

To complicate matters, a short time later, Steffie
and Charles had fallen in love, just as her father had
predicted. That case, too, was perfectly logical. Steffie had been in love with Charles for more than three
years. Charles had felt the same way toward her.

Norah hadn't been privy to that information, but
soon after Steffie arrived home it became apparent
she and Charles were meant to be together. It was
only logical they'd patch up whatever differences existed between them. Especially since their love had
been strong enough to endure a three-year separation.

When Steffie and Charles announced their engagement, David had all but stood up and shouted with
glee. Everything was happening just the way he'd
said it would, after his near-death experience. Talk
about gloating. The man had become impossible ever
since. He'd gone so far as to insist that he knew when
the grandchildren would begin to arrive. Valerie
would be the first, he said; she'd have identical twin
sons nine months and three weeks—to the day—after
marriage.

He said it was just as well that Rowdy had rejected
Valerie as manager of the Pacific Northwest branch,
in light of the fact that she was going to be a mother
of twins so soon.

No one had known what to say to that, although

Valerie had privately assured Steffie and Norah that neither she nor Colby had any intention of starting their family quite so soon.

They'd all decided it was best to let their father think what he wanted. He wasn't hurting anyone, and all his talk about the future seemed to give him pleasure.

Although these proclamations from their father unsettled the Bloomfield sisters, Colby had assured them he'd had other patients who claimed to have experienced near-death encounters. It would all pass in time, he'd said with utter confidence.

Norah couldn't help noticing, however, that her father hadn't said anything to *her* about the man in her life. He'd made some cryptic comment while he was coming out of the anesthesia. He'd smiled up at Norah and mumbled something about six children. Later she realized he was telling her she would someday be the mother of six.

The idea was ludicrous. But he hadn't said a word about it since, which was a relief. She was a medical professional and refused to take his outlandish claims seriously. Neither did she wish to be drawn into discussion concerning them. Besides, anyone who knew the two couples would know they would have married with or without David Bloomfield's dream.

"Rowdy Cassidy's a good man, Norah," her father said from behind her. "Be patient with him."

Pausing, her hand on the screen door, Norah shook her head, trying to force the cowboy, as she still thought of him, from her thoughts. Rowdy was ill-

tempered and arrogant, and she wanted as little to do
with him as possible. Norah had no intention of becoming personally involved with such a spoiled, egocentric man. *"Be patient with him."* Norah scoffed
silently. If anyone needed to learn a little patience,
it was Mr. Rowdy Cassidy.

"Thank goodness you're here," Karen Johnson
said to Norah as she barreled through the double
doors that led to the emergency room. Her face was
red and she was panting slightly, as if she'd run all
the way from the second floor.

"What's wrong?"

"It's Mr. Cassidy again. He wants to talk to you
as soon as possible."

"That's unfortunate, since I'm on duty."

Karen blinked as if she wasn't sure what she
should do next. "I don't think Orchard Valley is
ready for a man like Mr. Cassidy."

"What's he done now?"

"He had a phone installed so he could commu-
nicate with his company in Texas. Some man arrived
late yesterday. I think he's taking up residence.

"Cassidy can barely sit up and already he's conducting business as if he were in some plush office.
I'm not exactly sure how it happened, but we all
seem to be at his beck and call."

"What's he want with me?"

"How am I supposed to know?" Karen snapped.
"It isn't my place to question. My job is to obey."

Norah couldn't keep from laughing. "Karen, he's

only a man. You've dealt with others just like him a hundred times."

Karen grumbled and shook her head. "I've never met anyone like Rowdy Cassidy. Are you coming or not?"

"Not."

Her friend ran a hand through her disheveled hair. "I was afraid you were going to say that. Would you reconsider doing it as a personal favor to me?"

"Karen!"

"I'm serious."

Still Norah hesitated. She wasn't a servant to be summoned by Mr. High-and-Mighty's command. Even if he'd whipped the other members of the hospital staff into shape—the shape of *his* choice—she had no intention of following suit.

"I'll stop in later," she said reluctantly.

"How much later?"

"I'll wait until I'm on break."

Karen's smile revealed her appreciation. "Thanks, Norah, I owe you one for this."

Norah wouldn't have believed it if she hadn't seen it herself. A few days earlier, Karen would've given up her retirement to have Rowdy Cassidy removed from her floor. A mere twenty-four hours later, she was running errands for him like an eager cabin boy wanting to keep his pirate captain content.

"You can leave my lunch tray there," Rowdy instructed the candy striper, pointing to his bedside table.

Norah watched the teenager hesitate as though terrified of crossing the threshold into Rowdy's room. Considering what had happened earlier, Norah didn't blame her.

"Come on, now," Rowdy returned impatiently. "I'm not going to bite you."

"I wouldn't believe him, if I were you," Norah said, taking the tray out of the girl's hands.

Rowdy scowled. "It's about time you got here."

"You're lucky I came at all." She didn't like what was happening. Rowdy had manipulated the staff, bullied them into getting his own way, but such methods wouldn't work with her.

"It's been three days. Where have you been?" he demanded, frowning fiercely.

"I didn't know I was obligated to visit you."

"Obligated no, but you must feel a certain moral responsibility."

She set down the tray, and crossed her arms. "I can't say that I do."

He scowled again. "Where was it you said Valerie and her...husband were honeymooning?"

"I didn't."

"Hawaii, I assume? Carlton probably hasn't got an imaginative bone in his body. Which hotel?"

"Carlton?"

"Whoever Valerie married. I'm right, aren't I? They're in Hawaii. Now kindly tell me the name of the hotel."

"You must be joking, Mr. Cassidy. You don't honestly believe I'd be so foolish as to give you the name of the hotel so you could pester my sister on her honeymoon, do you?''

"Aha! So it *is* Hawaii."

Norah winced.

"I just wanted to send a flower arrangement," he went on, his voice a model of sincerity. "And I thought a bottle of champagne would be in order. I'd like to congratulate them, since I missed their wedding."

"A flower arrangement? Champagne? I'll just bet," Norah muttered under her breath.

Rowdy went still for a moment. "You don't know me very well, do you, Ms. Bloomfield? Or you'd appreciate that I'm not the kind of man to begrudge others their happiness. I was a fool to let Valerie go, but now that she's married Carlton, I—"

"Colby," she interrupted.

"Colby," he repeated, dipping his head slightly. "Well, I'd like to offer them both my most heartfelt congratulations."

Norah rolled her eyes. "I don't have the name of their hotel."

Rowdy's gaze hardened briefly. "Then I have no choice but to wait until the happy couple returns from their honeymoon."

"That's an excellent idea." Norah gripped her hands behind her back; she hadn't been completely honest with Rowdy. "Valerie didn't know about your accident until after the wedding," she told him, not quite meeting his eyes.

Rowdy said nothing for several moments. "I

didn't think she knew," he said, giving the impression that had she been aware of his injuries, she'd never have gone through with the wedding.

"It wouldn't have made any difference," Norah told him, unable to hide her irritation. "Anyway, she had enough on her mind without having to worry about you, so we decided not to tell her until later."

"You kept it from her?" he stormed.

"That's right, we did," she returned calmly.

He was furious; in fact, Norah had never seen a tantrum to equal his. But she ignored his outburst and went about setting up his luncheon tray. She removed the domed cover from the meal, then folded the napkin and laid it across his chest.

When he paused to breathe, Norah asked, "Do you want your lunch now, or would you prefer to wait until you've calmed down?"

Rowdy's mouth snapped shut.

"Is Dr. Silverman aware you've had a phone brought in for business use? Furthermore, is he aware that you're attempting to work out of this room?"

"No. Are you going to tell him?" he asked, eyeing her skeptically.

"I might."

"It doesn't matter. I'm getting out of this hick town as soon as I can arrange it."

"I'm sure the staff will do everything possible to speed up the process. You've made quite a name for yourself in the past few days, Mr. Cassidy."

Before Rowdy could respond, Karen appeared in the doorway, looking frazzled and uncertain. She glanced at Norah, obviously relieved that her friend was close at hand.

"It's time for your injection, Mr. Cassidy," she said.

"I don't want it."

"I'm sure Mr. Cassidy doesn't mean that, Karen," Norah said cheerfully. "He'll be more than happy to take his shot—isn't that right?"

Rowdy glared at her. "Wrong, Ms. Bloomfield."

"Fine, then. I'll hold him for you, Karen, I only hope I don't bump against his leg, since that would be terribly painful. Of course, if he passes out from the agony, it'll make giving him the injection that much simpler."

"If I take the shot I won't be able to answer the phone," Rowdy growled.

"Might I remind you that you're in the hospital to rest, not to conduct your business affairs?"

Norah took one step toward him, staring at his right leg.

"All right, all right," he grumbled, "but I want you to know I'm doing it under protest. You don't play fair—either one of you."

Karen threw Norah a triumphant look. Rowdy turned his head away while she administered the pain medication. In only minutes the medicine began to take effect.

Rowdy's eyes drifted shut.

"Thanks, Norah," Karen whispered.

"What's going on here?" Norah asked. She'd

never known Karen or any of the others to allow a patient to run roughshod over them.

"I wish I knew," Karen muttered. "The only one he's civil to is you. The whole floor's been a madhouse since he arrived. I've never known anyone who can command people the way he does. Even Dr. Silverman seems intimidated."

"Harry?" Norah could hardly believe it.

"I've never looked forward more to a patient's release. The crazy part is that no one's supposed to know he's here. Especially the press. His friend read us the riot act about talking to anyone from the media. They're worried about what'll happen to the stocks."

Norah walked out of Rowdy's room with Karen. Now she understood why the plane crash had received only a brief mention in the news and why Rowdy's name had been omitted. "When will he be able to travel?" she asked.

Karen gave a frustrated shrug. "I don't know, but my guess is it won't be soon. His leg's going to take a long time to heal and the less he moves it now, the better his chances for a complete recovery later. He may end up walking with a cane as it is."

Norah couldn't imagine the proud and mighty Rowdy Cassidy forced to rely on a cane. For his sake, she hoped it wouldn't come to that.

At home that afternoon, Norah was plagued by the thought of a vital man like Rowdy hobbling along with a cane. But she didn't want to think about him.

He wasn't her patient and really, other than the fact that her sister had once worked for him, there was no connection between them.

She'd managed to stay away from him for three days, despite the way she felt herself drawn to his presence. She shook her head, bemused. It amazed her that he'd succeeded in causing so much turmoil. The hospital had become a whirlwind of activity and it all seemed to focus on one man. Rowdy Cassidy.

"Hi," Steffie said, breaking into Norah's thoughts.

Norah, who'd been making a salad for their dinner, realized her hands were idle. Her thoughts were on the hospital eleven miles down the road, instead of her task.

"I didn't know if you'd be back for dinner or not," she said, hoping her voice didn't betray the path her mind had taken.

"I wasn't sure, either," Steffie admitted, automatically heading for the silverware drawer. She counted out cutlery and began to set the kitchen table.

Norah continued with the salad, glancing up now and then to watch Steffie. Her sister looked lovelier than ever and her calm, efficient movements revealed a new contentment. A new self-acceptance, really.

So this was what love did. Her sisters seemed to glow with the love they felt—and the love they received. In both of them, natural beauty was enhanced by happiness.

For most of her life, Norah had been referred to as the most attractive of the three Bloomfield girls. She was blond, blue-eyed, petite. But lately, Norah felt plain and downright dowdy compared to Valerie and Stephanie.

"How's everything at the hospital?" Steffie asked absentmindedly.

"I take it you're asking about Rowdy Cassidy?"

Steffie laughed. "I guess I am. You know, I can't help feeling a bit guilty about not giving Valerie his phone message."

"You weren't the only one."

"You didn't give her his message, either? You mean he called more than once? Oh, dear."

"I didn't talk to him," Norah countered swiftly. "But Dad did." Rowdy had never actually said so, but he'd implied that he had phoned Valerie several times. If Steffie had answered one call and Norah none, that left only their dear, meddling father.

She was about to explain that when the phone rang. Norah reached for the receiver; two minutes later she was so furious that she could barely breathe.

Slamming the phone down, she whirled on her sister. "I don't believe this. Of all the high-handed, arrogant—why, it's outrageous."

Steffie frowned. "Norah, what's wrong?"

Three

"**R**owdy Cassidy has had me transferred out of the emergency room!" Norah shouted, clenching her fists. "The nerve of the man!"

"But why?" Steffie wanted to know.

"So I could be there to wait on him hand and foot like everyone else." Norah stalked angrily to the other side of the kitchen. "I don't believe it! Of all the—"

"Nerve," Steffie supplied.

"Precisely."

"Surely you've got some say in this," Steffie said, as she resumed setting the table. Norah glared at her sister wondering how Steffie could think about dinner at a time like this.

"Apparently I *don't* have a choice in the matter," Norah fumed. "I've been asked to report to Karen Johnson at seven tomorrow morning."

"Oh, dear."

"I'm so furious I could scream."

"What's this yelling all about?" her father asked, strolling into the bright, cheery kitchen.

"It's Rowdy Cassidy again," Steffie explained before Norah had the chance.

David rubbed one hand along his jaw. "I don't think you need to worry—he'll be gone soon enough."

His words were of little comfort to Norah. "Unfortunately, it won't be soon enough to suit me."

Her father chuckled softly and left the kitchen.

Norah arrived on the second floor early the following morning. Karen Johnson was at the nurses' station making entries on a patient's chart when she caught sight of Norah.

"So you heard."

Norah gave her friend a grumpy smile. "I'm not happy about this."

"I didn't imagine you would be, but what else can we do when His Imperial Highness issues a decree?"

"Is he awake?"

Karen nodded. "Apparently he's been up for hours. He's asked to see you as soon as you got here," Karen said, and made a sweeping motion with her arm.

Although Norah was furious with Rowdy, her friend's courtly gesture produced a laugh. "How's he doing?"

"Better physically. Unfortunately, not so well emotionally. Being stuck in a hick-town hospital, as he so graciously describes Orchard Valley General, hasn't exactly improved his disposition. But then, I think he'd find something to complain about in paradise. He wants out, and there isn't a man or woman on this floor who wouldn't grant him his wish if it was possible."

Norah pushed up the sleeves of her white cardigan sweater as she walked into Rowdy's room, prepared to do battle. He smiled boyishly when he saw her, which disarmed and confused her. She hadn't expected him to be in a good mood.

"Morning," he greeted her brightly.

"I want you to know I don't appreciate the fact that you've adjusted my life to suit your own purposes."

"What?" he demanded. "Asking the administrator to assign you to this floor? You were the one who gave me his name, weren't you? Aren't you being a bit selfish?"

"Me? If *I'm* selfish, what does that make you?"

"Lonely. You're the only person I know in this entire town."

"Your acquaintance is with my sister, not me," she forcefully reminded him.

"In this case, it's any port in the storm. I trust you, Norah, though, Lord help me, I'm not sure why. You've already admitted Valerie didn't know about my accident because you didn't tell her until after the wedding. I can only assume you wanted me for yourself."

If he was hoping she'd rise to his bait, he had a long wait coming. She folded her arms and expelled a deep sigh. "I'll be bringing your breakfast in a couple of minutes," she said, turning her back on him.

When she returned a few minutes later, carrying the tray, Rowdy was sitting up in bed. "I need your help," he announced.

"You look perfectly capable of feeding yourself."

"I'm bored out of my mind."

"Do what everyone else does, watch television," she said tartly. Whether he was lonely or not, she refused to pander to his moods. He'd pulled a dirty trick on her and she wasn't going to reward his behavior.

Rowdy glanced up at the blank television screen. "Please don't be annoyed with me, Norah. I'm serious."

"So am I." But she could feel herself weakening. Rowdy could turn on the charm, and when he did, Norah suspected, few would deny him. Karen Johnson, for instance… Norah had no intention of ending up the same way.

"When will you be back?" he asked, grimacing as he examined his meal. The toast was cold. Norah could tell by the way the butter sat hard and flat on top. The eggs were runny and the oatmeal looked like paste. Norah didn't envy him.

"Someone else will be by to pick up your tray in a little while," she answered him.

"You might as well take it now."

"Try and eat something," she suggested sympathetically.

"What? The half-cooked eggs or the lumpy oatmeal? No thanks, I'd rather go without."

"Lunch will be more appetizing," Norah promised.

His brows arched cynically. "Wanna bet?"

Norah left his room, but she came back a few minutes later with two homemade blueberry muffins. Rowdy's eyes lit up when she set them on his breakfast tray. "I can't believe I'm doing this," she muttered.

"Where'd you get those?" As if he feared she'd change her mind, he snatched one off the tray.

"I baked last night and brought them in for the staff for coffee break this morning. Enjoy."

"I intend to." Already he was peeling away the paper. The first muffin disappeared in three bites. "These are wonderful," he said, licking the crumbs from his fingers. "Ever thought about selling the recipe?"

Norah laughed. The recipe had been her mother's and Norah strongly suspected it had originally come from a magazine. "Not lately."

"Well, if you ever do, let me know." He was ready to dig into the second offering. "By the way, Kincade's stopping by this afternoon, so hold off on those damn pain shots, will you?"

"Kincade?"

"My corporate attorney. Being stuck here is frustrating as hell. Kincade and I spoke yesterday and he's hand-carrying some papers that have to be signed, so I'm going to need a clear head. Got that?"

"Yes, Your Highness."

Rowdy frowned, but said nothing.

His phone rang, the sound muted. Norah watched, amazed, as Rowdy ignored the hospital phone on his bedstand and pulled open the drawer, from which he removed a portable telephone. After a few preliminary greetings, he was lost in conversation, unaware she was still in the room.

Norah shrugged, then gathered up the tray and left.

The morning passed quickly and she didn't talk to Rowdy again until near the end of her shift, at three. He was tired and out of sorts. His attorney friend had spent two hours with him, and an exhausted Rowdy had slept fitfully afterward.

"He's much calmer when you're around," Karen commented as they prepared to leave.

Norah didn't believe for a moment that she'd made the slightest difference to Rowdy's behavior. If Karen wanted to thank anyone, it should be Kincade, who'd kept him occupied; at least when he was busy he didn't have time to make everyone else miserable.

On impulse she decided to check on him before she left for home. He was sitting up, listlessly flipping through channels on the television. Apparently nothing appealed to him.

"I didn't know daytime television was in such desperate straits," he muttered when he saw her. He pushed another button and the screen went blank. "I was hoping you'd stop by before you went home."

"How are you feeling?" she asked, trying to gauge his mood. He seemed somewhat revived from the nap.

"Lousy."

Norah was surprised he'd admit it. "Do you want a pain shot?"

He shook his head. "But I wouldn't mind a little distraction. Can you sit down and talk for a few minutes?"

Norah made a show of glancing at her watch, although in reality she hadn't a single reason to hurry home. "I can stay a little while, I guess." She certainly wasn't being gracious about it, but that didn't seem to bother Rowdy.

"Good."

Norah was met with the full force of his smile, and for a moment she basked in its warmth. It was little wonder he inspired such loyalty and confidence in his employees. He definitely had the charisma of true leadership. Valerie had worked with him for nearly four years, dedicating her time and talent to his corporation until she virtually had no life of her own. She'd done it voluntarily, too, inspired by Rowdy's own commitment to CHIPS.

"How'd the meeting with your friend go?" Norah asked conversationally.

He paused as though he'd never considered Kincade his friend. "Fine. Actually, it went very well. We've been able to keep the news of my accident from leaking to the press."

"What would be so terrible about anyone finding out you're in the hospital?" Norah shrugged. "Karen mentioned something about the stocks."

Rowdy cast her an odd look as though he suspected she was teasing. "You honestly don't know?'' He shook his head. ''If the stockholders discovered I was incapacitated, they'd lose confidence in CHIPS and the stock could drop by several points.''

''Would that really be so disastrous?''

''Yes,'' he returned without hesitation. ''If the value declines by even a single point, that's equivalent to losing millions of dollars. Any greater loss and it becomes catastrophic, with a ripple effect that could rock the entire industry.''

Either the man had an elevated sense of his own worth, or he was pessimistic by nature. Though perhaps she was being unnecessarily harsh, Norah mused. She knew next to nothing about business and finance. Nor did she care. She was content to leave the world's financial affairs in the capable hands of people like Rowdy Cassidy and her sister. She stood abruptly and walked toward the door.

''Do you have to go so soon?'' Rowdy asked, disappointment in his dark eyes.

''I'll be right back,'' she promised.

It took her several minutes to find what she was looking for.

Rowdy brightened when she returned. ''What's that?'' he asked, nodding toward the rather battered box she was carrying.

''You do play games, don't you?''

''Often, but I seldom need a board.''

Norah laughed lightly. ''Then I promise you this is right up your alley. It's a game of power, intrigue and skill.'' She set the box on the foot of his bed and slowly, dramatically, lifted the lid. She had Rowdy's full attention now.

"Checkers?" he asked with more than a hint of disbelief.

"Checkers." She drew the bedside table closer, moved some flowers and placed the board on it. Then she pulled up a chair. "You want red or black?"

"Black to match my evil temperament." Rowdy gave an exaggerated leer, twirling an imaginary mustache.

Norah grinned. "I'm not going to argue with you."

They set up the board together. "Generally when I play a game there's something riding on the outcome," he said in a relaxed, offhand manner.

"Like what?" Norah pushed a red checker one space forward.

"Usually the stakes are big. It makes the game more...interesting."

"Are you suggesting we wager something on the outcome of this game?" She'd forgotten how competitive men could be.

"Something small—this time," he said, studying the board.

"Give me an example." It'd been a while since she'd played checkers and she wasn't all that sure of her skills. She'd never taken games, any game, too seriously.

"I don't know..." Rowdy paused, apparently mulling it over. "How about dinner?"

"Dinner? You mean after you're discharged from the hospital?"

"No, I mean tonight."

Norah snickered. "What are you planning to do? Order up a second tray from the kitchen? If that's the case, I'm afraid I'll have to decline the invitation."

"I won't need to order you another dinner tray," he stated calmly, making his first jump and capturing one of her checkers. "I intend to win."

Rowdy did exactly that, and his winning streak continued, even when they decided the wager was two games out of three. After her second loss, Rowdy leaned back against the pillows, folded his arms and threw her a self-satisfied smile. "I'd like rare roast beef, a baked potato with sour cream, green beans, fresh if possible, and three-layer chocolate cake for dessert, preferably with coconut frosting. Homemade would be nice. Do you have a recipe for good chocolate cake?"

Stepping away from his bed, Norah settled her fists on her hips. "Is this your usual diet? Good grief, you're a prime candidate for a heart attack. I'll bet you don't exercise, either."

"Not recently." He looked pointedly at his leg. "Are you going to honor your end of the bargain or not?"

"I'm not sure yet. I'll bring your dinner, but don't hold your breath waiting for rare roast beef."

"I'm a Texan," he challenged. "I was weaned on prime rib."

"Then it's high time you started checking your cholesterol, cowboy. My father recently went through open-heart surgery and it wasn't any picnic. My advice to you is to make a change in your eating habits now."

"All right, all right," Rowdy grumbled. "I'll settle for pizza and to show you just how reasonable I can be, go ahead and order it with those little fish. That's healthy, right?"

"Anchovies? Do you realize how high in sodium anchovies are?"

"There's no satisfying you, is there?" Rowdy chuckled. "If it isn't my cholesterol level you're fussing about, it's sodium count or something. Before you leave, you'll have me on a diet of bread and water, which is basically the only food I've been eating since I got in here, anyway."

Norah found herself laughing again. "I'll see to my dad's dinner and be back later with your pizza," she promised on her way out the door.

"Bring that checkerboard," he told her. "There're a few other wagers I'd like to make."

Norah had a few of her own. If everything went according to her plans, Rowdy would be as docile as a sleepy cat before he left Orchard Valley Hospital.

"You're later than usual," her father commented when Norah walked into the house. "Problems at the hospital?"

"Not really." She wasn't sure how much she should say to him about her time with Rowdy. Her own confusion didn't help. The man was in love with her sister, for heaven's sake! And he annoyed her no end with his tactics. It didn't make sense that she should find herself attracted to him.

"I have to go back to the hospital," she explained on her way upstairs, deciding not to offer any further explanation. She wanted a long bath, a short nap and a change of clothes, in that order.

"Don't worry about dinner," David called up after her. "I can take care of it. Plenty of leftovers in the refrigerator. Besides, I had a big lunch, so I don't have too much of an appetite."

Norah hesitated at the top of the stairs. Her father was right; he was now fully capable of looking after himself. The last thing he needed was her fussing over him. It came as something of a shock to realize that. Then she smiled. It came as a relief, too.

The hospital was quiet when Norah returned a couple of hours later. The head floor nurse smiled when she saw her carrying a boxed pizza. "I wondered what you promised him," LaVern joked. "He's been as good as gold all evening."

Opening the door with a flourish, Norah marched into Rowdy's room, balancing the pizza on the palm of one hand. "Ta da!"

Rowdy reached for the triangular bar dangling above his head and pulled himself upright. "I was beginning to think you were going to renege on our bet."

"A Bloomfield? Never!" She set the pizza box on

the table and wheeled it to his side. "However I must
warn you this pizza is healthy for you."

"Oh, great, you've ordered granola and broccoli
for the toppings."

"Close. Mushroom, green pepper, onion. I had
them put anchovies on your half. Personally I think
you should appreciate my thoughtfulness. I can't
stand those slimy little fish things—they're disgust-
ing."

"Don't worry. I won't force you to eat any."

"Good."

Rowdy helped himself to a napkin and lifted the
first slice from the box. He raised it slowly to his
mouth, then closed his eyes, as if in ecstasy, as he
chewed. "This is excellent, just excellent."

"I demand a rematch," Norah said, dragging her
chair to his bedside. "When we're finished eating.
Winning is a matter of personal pride now."

"Sore loser," he muttered through a mouthful of
pizza.

"What!" Norah felt the annoyance bubble up inside her. Apparently Rowdy noticed it, too, because
he grinned at her. "I was teasing," he assured her.
"Believe me, the last thing I want to do now is bite
the hand that feeds me."

"You ready for another challenge, then?" Norah
asked, eager to clear away the remains of the pizza
and set up the board.

"Any time you want, sweetheart."

Norah didn't think he meant the term as one of

affection and decided to ignore it. At least that was
her intention...

But more than once she found her concentration
drifting away from the game. Before she could stop
herself, she wondered what it would be like to be
Rowdy Cassidy's "sweetheart." He was opinionated
and headstrong, but he could charm the birds out of
the trees, as her mother used to say. He was also a
man who almost always got what he wanted—Valerie Bloomfield being one of the few exceptions. Norah felt oddly deflated, suddenly, as she recalled his
feelings for her sister.

Almost before she realized it, she'd lost two games
in a row. Not until she made a silly mistake that cost
her the second game did she realize they hadn't set
their wager.

"What are you going to want next?" she muttered, irritated with herself for losing so easily. "I
could bring you in another blueberry muffin tomorrow morning."

Rowdy's smile was downright smug.

"How about three games out of five?" she asked
hopefully.

"A deal's a deal."

"Now that's profound," Norah said in a sarcastic
aside. "All right." She spread both hands in a gesture of defeat. "You won. I'm not sure how fair or
square it was, but you won."

"My, my, are you getting testy?"

She couldn't very well admit why she'd been so
distracted. She stared down at the board as she rap-

idly gathered up the checkers. When she'd finished, he reached for her hands, capturing them between his own, drawing her closer to his side. She knew she should protest, or make some effort to pull away from him. But she found it difficult to move, to speak, to do anything but gaze into his eyes.

"I'm going to kiss you, Norah Bloomfield," he announced in a quiet, dispassionate voice. "I want that even more than I wanted the pizza." He gave her hands a tug and she found herself sitting on the edge of the bed. Her heart was pounding hard against her ribs, her breath coming in short, painful bursts.

His mouth settled over hers, his hands in her hair, pressing her close against him. Norah was shocked by the powerful sensuality she experienced. Her eyes closed slowly as excitement overtook common sense.

She didn't doubt for an instant that if she'd given the least protest Rowdy would have released her. His mouth was warm, hard, compelling...

When the kiss ended, she automatically rose to her feet and backed away. She blinked, feeling oddly confused. "Th-that was...unfair," she stammered.

"Unfair? In what way?" he demanded.

"You didn't set the terms of the wager—I wasn't prepared for it!"

"You needed a warning?"

She pressed the tips of her fingers to her lips, at a loss to explain herself. "I'm...not sure. Yes, I think so." She still felt dazed and it made her furious.

"Norah, what's wrong?"

"I don't think playing checkers was such a good

idea, after all,'' she said coldly, recovering as well as she could. Her hands trembled as she hurriedly finished putting away the game. It wasn't until she felt a tear roll down the side of her face that she realized she was crying, and that only served to mortify her further.

"I didn't mean to offend you," Rowdy said, his voice regretful.

"Then why'd you do it? Why couldn't we just be friends? Why does everything have to boil down to…to that?"

"You're making more of this than necessary," he said softly. "I'm sorry if I upset you. That was never my intention, and it won't happen again."

Suddenly Norah wasn't sure she wanted that reassurance. She wasn't sure *what* she wanted; that was the problem. As much as she hated to admit it, she'd enjoyed the kiss.

"We heard from Valerie and Colby," she said abruptly.

He frowned. "Are they having a good time?"

She didn't meet his eyes. "Perfectly wonderful."

"Valerie's going to be bored out of her mind within a month, you know that, don't you?"

Norah shook her head.

"I told her as much when she handed me her resignation." His frown deepened. "She knows it, too."

"Valerie will find something else."

"In Orchard Valley? Don't count on it. Not with her qualifications. What's she going to do? Run the school lunch program?" Rowdy was growing more animated by the minute. "Damn fool woman, letting her emotions dictate her life. I expected better of her."

"My sister made her choice, Mr. Cassidy. If anyone was a fool, it's you."

His mouth tightened at her words and Norah marveled that they could be wrapped in each other's arms one moment and snapping at each other the next.

"She and this Carlton fellow will be very happy, I'm sure," Rowdy said stiffly. He leaned back against the pillows and grimaced in obvious pain.

"It's Colby."

"Whoever," he muttered irritably.

Norah realized it was the discomfort speaking now, and relaxed. "I'll ask LaVern to bring you something for the pain."

"I don't need anything," he growled.

"Perhaps not, but as a favor to me, please take it."

"I don't owe you anything."

Norah was offended at the sharpness of his tone. He glared at her as if he couldn't wait to be rid of her, reminding her once again that it was her sister he was interested in—not her.

"All right," he said curtly. "I'll take the damn shot. Just stop looking at me like I've done something terrible. It was only a kiss! Good Lord, you'd think no one had ever kissed you before."

At his words, Norah understood. That was exactly the way she felt, as if Rowdy Cassidy had been the first man to hold her. The first man to kiss her. It was as if she'd waited all her life for this moment, this man.

Before she could stop herself, she turned and rushed from the room.

Norah dreaded the following morning, since she was again scheduled to report to Rowdy's floor. She avoided seeing him as long as possible—an entire fifteen minutes into her shift.

"Good morning," she greeted him with a bright smile.

"Sounds like you're in better spirits than you were the last time I saw you," he said, watching her closely.

"Having one's ego destroyed in a game of checkers will do that," Norah said with false cheerfulness, carrying his breakfast tray to the bedside table.

"Was it the checkers...or the kiss?"

"It looks like lumpy oatmeal and soft-boiled eggs this morning," she said, ignoring his words.

"Norah." His hand covered hers, preventing her from leaving.

"The checkers," she said dryly. "You flatter yourself if you think a kiss would unsettle me like that. I'm a big girl, Mr. Cassidy."

"Then perhaps we should try again."

"Don't be absurd."

Rowdy's hand tightened over hers. "It isn't as preposterous as you make it sound. You're very sweet,

Norah Bloomfield. A man could grow accustomed to having you around.''

Norah hesitated, not knowing if she should take his words as a compliment or an insult. ''I'm not a plaything for your personal amusement. Now if you'll excuse me, I've got work to do.''

''Will you stop by later?''

''If I have the time.'' Her back was to him; she was eager to make her escape.

''If you bring the checkers game I'll give you another chance to redeem yourself. I might even let you win just so I can give you what *you* want.''

''Ah, but that's where we differ,'' she said as breezily as she could. ''You see, Mr. Cassidy, you don't have anything I want.''

''Ouch,'' he said and as she left the room she glanced over her shoulder to see him clutching at an imaginary wound. She didn't want to laugh, but she couldn't help herself.

Three hours had passed when Karen Johnson sought her out. ''Check on the cowboy, would you, Norah? Something's wrong.''

''Why me?'' Norah protested.

''You're the only one who can go near him without getting your head ripped off.''

''Did he ask for me?''

Karen hesitated. ''Yes, but don't feel complimented. He's throwing out plenty of names, including the governor's and a couple of congressmen. It wouldn't surprise me if they rushed to his side, either.''

Karen hadn't exaggerated. By the time Norah arrived from the far end of the corridor, she could hear Rowdy ranting about something. His words, however, were indistinguishable, which in Norah's opinion was probably for the best.

"Rowdy," she said, standing in the doorway, her hands on her hips. "What's going on in here?"

He glanced up at her, placing his hand on the portable telephone's mouthpiece. "Word leaked out that I was in a plane crash." He sighed heavily. "CHIPS stock has already dropped two points. We're in one hell of a mess here."

Four

"Do you know of a decent secretarial service?" Rowdy demanded as soon as Norah walked in the door the following morning. He might have been sitting behind a mahogany desk preparing to command his empire. His dark eyes were sharp and alert, his jaw tense.

"Uh...I don't think so."

"What I need is a phone book."

Taken aback, Norah twisted around and pointed behind her. "There's one at the end of the hall."

"Get it," he said, then added. "Please."

Still Norah hesitated. "Rowdy, you seem to have forgotten you're in the hospital and not a hotel."

"I wouldn't care if I was in the morgue. I'm not about to watch the business I built up—ten years of blood and sweat—go down the tube because of a stupid broken leg."

"Your leg's far more than—"

"The telephone book," he reminded her crisply.

Norah tossed her hands in the air and retrieved the phone book from the nurses' station.

"This is it?" Rowdy's eyes widened incredulously

when she handed it to him. "I've read short stories longer than this."

"There's always Portland, but to be honest I don't know where I'd find a Portland directory."

"Kincade and Robbins are flying in. They'll be here by noon. I hate to ask Mrs. Emerich to travel, but I may not have any choice. Advise the hospital that I'll be holding a press conference this afternoon." He rubbed the side of his jaw, his look thoughtful. "While you're at it, would you arrange to have a barber drop by sometime this morning? I'm going to need a decent haircut and a shave."

"Rowdy, this is a hospital."

"Not anymore," he told her flatly.

"I don't have time to be running errands for you. In case you've forgotten, you're not the only patient on this floor. I can't allow you to disrupt the entire wing with camera crews and the like."

"The excitement will do them good," he told her, leafing through the Orchard Valley directory. "It'll give your patients something to tell their families during visiting hours."

Norah was beginning to get irritated. "You're not listening to me."

He went on as if she hadn't spoken, his eyes narrowed and resolute. "I'm going to hold a press conference and if I can't do it from here, I'll find someplace I can."

"You can't be moved."

"Don't bet on it, sweetheart."

Norah didn't, not for an instant. Rowdy would

have his way, simply because he made it impossible
to oppose him and win.

Norah left him and reported what he'd told her to
Karen Johnson. Afterward, she was never entirely
sure what happened next. But before the morning
ended, the hospital administrator, James Bolton, had
visited Rowdy's room. Norah had no way of knowing what was discussed, but she learned a little later
that a number of reporters and two camera crews
would be brought into Rowdy's room early that same
afternoon. Just as he'd predicted.

Orchard Valley General Hospital had never seen
anything like it. Charles Tomaselli, Steffie's fiancé,
showed up, and cornered Norah to ask if she could
get him into the press conference.

Norah shrugged. "I'll try." She did and was rewarded with a thumbs-up sign from Charles.

By two that afternoon, the entire ward looked
more like a media carnival than a hospital.

"Did you ever dream it'd come to this?" Karen
asked her, leaning against the counter at the nurses'
station as she viewed the proceedings.

Norah shook her head. She didn't know if Rowdy
had the physical stamina to withstand a lengthy interview. The news conference had been going on for
nearly an hour, with no sign of ending anytime soon.

Reporters were crammed inside his hospital room,
spilling out into the hallway, and jostling one another, cassette recorders held high above their heads.
Cameras flashed.

The patients from the other rooms stood in their

doorways, gawking, trying to find out what they could. Rumors washed like flash floods through the hospital corridors.

At one point Norah heard the president was visiting. Someone else claimed royalty had arrived. Two other people were convinced they'd seen Elvis.

From the corner of her eye, Norah saw Kincade, Rowdy's corporate attorney. He seemed to be searching through the crowd, looking for someone. Intuitively, she realized what was happening. Rowdy had worn himself out.

"Excuse me," Norah said, thinking and acting quickly. Carrying a tray in one hand and a syringe in the other, she edged her way through the reporters and camera crews. The news staff reluctantly parted to make a path for her. She moved into the room, then held up one hand to shade her eyes from the blinding light. It didn't take her an instant to realize Kincade's concerns were well founded. Rowdy was pale and definitely growing weaker, although he struggled to disguise it.

"You'll have to excuse me," she said in her most businesslike voice. "I'm sure this will only take a couple of minutes. It's time for Mr. Cassidy's enema."

The room cleared within seconds.

Rowdy waited until the last reporter had left, then burst out laughing. Kincade and the other man Rowdy had referred to as Robbins were the only two who remained.

"Very clever," Kincade complimented her.

"She isn't worth a damn at checkers, but she's one hell of a nurse," Rowdy said. He lowered himself onto the pillows and closed his eyes in exhaustion. "You'll arrange everything for me, Robbins?" he asked hoarsely.

"Right away," the other man assured him.

Briefly, Nora wondered if Rowdy even knew the first names of his staff members. It was Kincade and Robbins. But then, he'd always referred to his sister as Valerie. He knew *her* first name.

She was about to comment, but she noticed Rowdy was already asleep. Without another word, she ushered the two men out of the room.

"Thanks," Kincade whispered gratefully.

She nodded. It was her job to look out for the welfare of her patients. She hadn't done anything extraordinary. Her means might have been a little unorthodox, but effective.

Robbins was tall and wiry and young, and Kincade was short, stocky and middle-aged. Both men were dressed in identical dark, pin-striped suits—the CHIPS uniforms, Norah thought wryly. She remembered her sister's wearing the female version of that business suit. Though, strangely, Norah couldn't imagine Rowdy in anything but jeans and cowboy boots.

"I understand you're Valerie's sister," Robbins said in a conversational tone.

"That's right." She'd forgotten that the two men had probably worked with Valerie.

"We all miss her."

But not as much as Rowdy does, Norah mused and was surprised by a sharp, fleeting pain at the thought.

"Rowdy's transferring me to Portland to head up the expansion project," Robbins said, eyeing Norah as if she had information to give. "I was hoping that once I got settled, Valerie would consider working with me."

"I don't know," Norah told him. "You'll have to talk to my sister."

Robbins glanced nervously toward Rowdy's room. "Don't say anything to Rowdy. Valerie was by far the more logical choice, but I don't think those two parted on amicable terms. He accepted her resignation and then gave me the assignment that same day. Personally, I'd rather stay in Texas."

It went without saying that Robbins would move simply because Rowdy had asked it of him. Oregon. Alaska. Wherever. Whatever other talents Rowdy possessed, and Norah didn't doubt there were many, he inspired loyalty among his employees.

"Valerie and her husband are on their honeymoon. She should be back from Hawaii sometime this week. You might have the opportunity to tell her all this yourself," Norah said, then turned away.

"Ms.—Bloomfield."

This time it was the corporate attorney who addressed her. "Thanks again," he said.

"No problem. I was happy to be of help."

"This isn't easy for him, you know?" the attorney added. "Rowdy's a physical man and being tied down to his bed, literally, is driving him to distraction. If it wasn't for you, I don't know what he would have done.''

"Wasn't for me?" Norah hadn't done much of anything. She'd provided a little entertainment with the checkers, a little nourishment with the pizza and muffins, and she'd fallen into his schemes, like everyone else in the hospital. But that was it.

"He's mentioned you several times. All of us at CHIPS want you to know we appreciate everything you've done for him."

Norah nodded, accepting his gratitude, but she felt uncomfortably like a fraud. Rowdy must have greatly exaggerated the small things she'd done.

Later that afternoon, just before she was scheduled to be relieved from her shift, the office equipment began to arrive. First came a fax machine, followed by a computer, complete with printer. Then two men carrying a desk with an inverted chair balanced on top passed her in the corridor.

"What's going on *now?*" Karen asked, rubbing her eyes as if she were seeing things.

"I have the feeling," Norah muttered, "that Rowdy Cassidy is about to set up office."

Norah followed the desk and chair to Rowdy's room and stood staring in amazement at the transformation. He'd done exactly what she'd suspected. This wasn't a hospital room any longer, but a communications center. A man from the telephone company was busy installing a multiline phone. Heaven only knew how many extra lines Rowdy had ordered.

Apparently he'd outgrown the portable phone he kept in his drawer.

"I hate to intrude," she muttered sarcastically, "knowing how busy you are and all—but *what* is going on in here?"

"What does it look like?" Rowdy returned curtly. "I'm getting back to work."

"Here?"

"I don't have much choice. Robbins will be in bright and early tomorrow with my secretary. I'll be handling as many of my own affairs as I can."

"I only hope Dr. Silverman and the rest of the hospital staff don't get in your way."

Rowdy didn't hear the sarcasm in her voice, or if he did, he ignored it. Norah sighed.

"Rowdy, this is a hospital. You're here to recover so you can go back to your life. You can't go around conducting business as usual. I'm sorry, I really am, but—"

"Either I conduct my business or there won't be one to go back to," he announced starkly.

"You're exaggerating."

"All four lines are connected and working," the telephone installer said, setting the phone on the bedside table and rolling it within reaching distance.

"Thank you," Rowdy said as the man walked out the door. "Listen, Norah, you're a damn good nurse," he continued, "but you don't know... checkers about managing a corporation. Now loosen up, before I let everyone know what a poor sport you are."

Norah felt the warmth invade her cheeks.

"This all right over here?" one of the men who'd hauled in the desk interrupted.

"Perfect," Rowdy answered, barely glancing in that direction. "Thank you for your trouble."

"No problem." The two men left, closing the door behind them. As soon as he was alone with her, Rowdy reached for Norah's hand. "Have you recovered?" he asked, his eyes holding hers.

"I'm not the one who's sick."

"I meant from the kiss."

His comment intensified the heat in her face. "I— I don't know what you're talking about."

"Yes, you do. You've been thinking about it every minute since." He added in a whisper, "So have I."

"Uh..." What bothered Norah most was how accurate he was. She'd spent a lot of time reflecting on their kiss, despite all her efforts to push it from her mind. She'd dreaded being alone with Rowdy again, fearing he'd know how confused and flustered his touch had left her.

"You're a beautiful woman, Norah." He pressed her palm to his lips. The feel of his tongue against her skin sent hot sensation shooting up her arm.

Norah trembled and closed her eyes. He was drawing her closer to his side and like an obedient lamb she went to him. He reached for her and from somewhere deep inside, she found the strength to resist.

"No...no, Rowdy. I'm Norah, not Valerie. I don't think you've figured out the difference yet." Hurriedly she backed away from him and left the room.

He called for her once, his voice sharp with impatience, but Norah ignored him.

The afternoon was overcast and gloomy; rain threatened. Norah found her father sitting in his favorite chair beside the fireplace in his den, reading.

"I understand there was quite a commotion at the hospital this afternoon," he said, glancing up from Marcia Muller's latest mystery.

"You heard? Already?"

"Charles stopped in and gave Steffie and me a run-down of what happened. Sounds like a three-ring circus."

"It was ridiculous."

Her father chuckled. "I also heard how you broke up the news conference. I always knew you were a clever child, I just don't think I fully appreciated *how* clever."

"Rowdy Cassidy's impossible."

"Oh?" Although the question appeared casual, Norah wasn't fooled. Her father was doing his best to gauge how the relationship was developing between her and Rowdy. The situation with Rowdy was very like his own thirty years earlier, when he'd met Grace, who'd been a nurse, and married her. Theirs had been a hospital romance. Although her father hadn't said much, Norah knew he was hoping history would repeat itself.

In a way it troubled Norah that he hadn't questioned her more about her relationship with Valerie's former employer. She should have been relieved.

He'd barely asked about Rowdy, barely revealed any interest. Nor had he mentioned his near-death dream lately, other than that one cryptic remark about Rowdy's arriving right on schedule. She certainly didn't believe her father's dream—in which he'd supposedly had a conversation, complete with predictions about all three sisters. But it had sustained him and delighted him for so long that she actually found his silence disturbing.

Norah drifted up the stairs to her room. She wished now that she'd allowed Rowdy to kiss her. And yet it angered her that she should be feeling anything—especially when she knew how deeply Rowdy cared for Valerie.

Norah changed out of her uniform and walked slowly down the back stairs that led to the spacious kitchen. Halfway down, she heard Steffie and Charles. They were speaking in low tones, and their words were followed by silences. Lovers exchanging promises.

Not wanting to embarrass them, or herself, Norah made sure they heard her approach. She burst onto the scene with a bright smile to find her sister sitting in Charles's lap. A wooden spoon coated in spaghetti sauce was poised in front of his mouth.

With obvious reluctance, Charles dragged his gaze away from Steffie. "Thanks for getting me into that press conference this afternoon, Norah. I appreciate it."

"No problem." She opened the refrigerator and took out a pitcher of lemonade. Her back to the happy couple, she heard Steffie whisper something, then giggle softly.

"What time's dinner?" Norah asked, refusing to look in their direction. She got a tall glass and added ice before pouring the lemonade.

"Another hour or so."

She couldn't face Steffie and Charles just now. Seeing how happy they were, how much in love, was almost painful. "Do you need any help with dinner?"

"No, thanks," Charles answered for Steffie. "We've got everything under control here."

Norah was sure they had.

It wasn't until she was in her bedroom with the door closed that she realized how tense and rigidly controlled she'd been.

Steffie and Charles's wedding was only a few weeks away, and she was excited and happy for them both. They hadn't wanted the elaborate affair Valerie and Colby had had. It was just as well, since Orchard Valley had yet to recover from the first Bloomfield wedding.

Norah was happy for her sisters. Really happy. They both deserved the love they'd found.

Love.

It had changed Valerie, turned her entire life upside down. Her oldest sister had never been one to reveal her emotions, but from the moment Valerie had accepted Colby's engagement ring, she'd changed. She'd become exuberant, animated. Right before Norah's eyes, love had transformed her sister into someone she barely recognized. Valerie, who'd always been so serious, so business minded, had become giddy with love.

It had the opposite effect on Steffie. Her middle sister had always been the emotional one. No one doubted what Steffie was thinking. She'd never had any qualms about expressing her opinions.

These days Steffie was calm and peaceful. When she was with Charles, she seemed to be a different woman, Norah thought. Her sister had always been in a hurry; there were people to meet, places to go, experiences to live. But no longer. She'd relaxed, slowed down.

Both her sisters were marrying men who balanced them. Men whose personalities complemented and completed theirs.

And then there was Norah.

Expelling her breath, Norah stretched out on her bed and stared at the ceiling. She dated often, but none of the men she was currently seeing affected her the way Colby and Charles had affected her sisters. Still, after watching what had happened to them, she wasn't sure what to expect in her own life. Should she expect her personality to be moderated, too? And in what way? She'd never been as serious as Valerie, or as vivacious as Steffie. She was just plain Norah.

The phone rang, but the first ring was abruptly cut off. A moment later, Steffie came pounding up the stairs, yelling, "Norah! Phone!"

Norah rolled over and reached for the phone on her bedside table. "Hello," she mumbled.

"Do you feel up to a game of checkers?"

"Rowdy?" Her heart quickened at the sound of his voice.

He chuckled. "You mean you've been playing games with other men? I'm shocked."

"I..." She didn't know what to say. Instinct told her to say yes, to agree to another game immediately. But common sense intervened. "No," she told him firmly.

"I promise no more tricks," he said as a means of inducement.

"I'm sorry. I don't think so."

There was a long silence before he spoke again. "I had another reason for calling. I wanted to thank you for everything you did this afternoon."

"It wasn't that much."

"But it helped, and I'm grateful. I've caused quite a ruckus in the orderly world of this hospital, haven't I?"

"Indeed you have," she said with a soft laugh. She had a sneaking suspicion it was the same wherever he went—Orchard Valley, Houston, Texas or New York City.

Rowdy chuckled, too, and then asked her a couple of questions, about the hospital and the town; she answered and asked him a few of her own. The conversation continued in a casual vein.

After what seemed like only minutes, Norah heard Steffie calling her down for dinner. Norah glanced at her watch, amazed to discover she'd been talking to Rowdy for nearly half an hour.

"I have to go."

"Well, thanks again…Norah." He said her name with an odd, breathless catch. "I always seem to be thanking you."

Running down the stairs toward the kitchen, Norah realized she felt completely revived.

It felt as though everyone—her father, Charles and Steffie—turned to stare at her when she walked into the room. "Is something wrong?" she asked, glancing down to be sure her blouse wasn't incorrectly buttoned.

"Not a thing," her father said, reaching for the green salad. "Nope, not a thing." But Norah saw him raise his eyes to Steffie and grin from ear to ear.

Rowdy's room had been transformed into a command post. Men and women were walking briskly in and out from the moment Norah arrived, early the next morning.

She brought Rowdy his breakfast tray and found Robbins sitting behind the desk, working at the computer. A middle-aged woman with her dark hair in a tight chignon sat at a typewriter. No one seemed to notice Norah—least of all Rowdy, who was issuing orders like a general from his headquarters.

"I hope I'm not interrupting anything," Norah said, not bothering to restrain the sarcasm as she set down his breakfast tray.

"Norah." Rowdy's eyes lit up and he laid the file

he was scanning aside. Horn-rimmed reading glasses were perched at the end of his nose; they only made him look more attractive.

"I brought your breakfast."

"I don't suppose you have any more of those blueberry muffins, do you?"

"I might."

"But it's going to cost me, right?"

"Not exactly." She'd read over the notes the night staff had left regarding Rowdy and learned he'd been on the phone all hours of the night. He'd called her, of course, but that had been much earlier in the evening.

She took the thermometer from its slot and stuck it under his tongue.

"I haven't got a fever! Why do you insist on taking my temperature all hours of the day and night?" he fussed when she was through.

She made the notation, and then reached for his wrist. "You were on the phone for nearly eight hours straight."

"Jealous?" He wiggled his eyebrows.

"I might be." She was far more concerned about his apparent lack of concern for his health.

"There were people I needed to talk to, people I had to reassure. By the way, did you see we got coverage on CNN? My plane crash put Orchard Valley on the map."

"I'm sure the mayor is thrilled."

"He offered me the keys to the city."

"Uncle Jack? He didn't!" Norah couldn't believe it.

Rowdy laughed boisterously. "No, he didn't, but he should have."

Norah finished taking his pulse and recorded the information.

"Now do I get those blueberry muffins or are you going to make me beg?"

Norah removed two cellophane-wrapped muffins from her sweater pockets. "Count your blessings, Cassidy. This is the last of the batch. My dad sent them to you with his best wishes."

"Bless him." Rowdy ignored the breakfast tray and unwrapped the muffins instead. "Meet Mrs. Emerich, my secretary. You remember Robbins, don't you?"

Norah smiled at both of Rowdy's employees.

"I know your sister, Valerie," Mrs. Emerich said, "a wonderful young woman. We all miss her dreadfully. Say hello for me, won't you?"

Norah nodded, carefully watching Rowdy. She wondered how he'd react to the mention of her sister's name. He didn't, at least not outwardly.

"Mr. Cassidy will need an hour later this morning," Norah told Robbins and Mrs. Emerich. "Dr. Silverman's scheduled to—"

"What time?" Rowdy demanded.

"The schedule says ten."

"He'll have to change it. I've got an interview with *Time* magazine at ten."

"Rowdy, you can't ask Dr. Silverman to rearrange

his day because you're meeting with a magazine reporter.''

''Why not? He'll understand. *Time*'s flying a reporter all the way from New York. I'm sure he won't mind waiting. He might even want to talk to the guy himself. I'll try to arrange it if I can.''

''Kincade's reporting back to you at eleven,'' Mrs. Emerich reminded Rowdy.

''Damn, that's right. Listen,'' he said, directing his attention back to Norah. ''Maybe it's best if you had Dr. Silverman check with Mrs. Emerich before he does whatever it is he needs to do.''

Norah was too stunned, for a moment, to react. ''Dr. Silverman will be here at ten,'' she said firmly. ''If the reporter from *Time* magazine is here, then he'll need to wait outside the room like everyone else. This is a hospital, Mr. Cassidy. You may have managed to sweet-talk other people around here, but it won't work with me. Is that understood?''

A shocked silence fell after her words. Mrs. Emerich and Robbins both stood with their mouths open, as though they'd never heard anyone speak like this to their boss.

Rowdy's eyes went from dark to darker. ''All right,'' he said finally, his voice sullen and angry.

Norah whirled around and left the room.

The results of Dr. Silverman's examination revealed signs of improvement. If his leg continued to mend, Rowdy could be discharged within two weeks. No one was more relieved than Norah.

The sooner Rowdy left, the better for her. Once he

was gone, Norah felt confident her life would return to normal. Once Rowdy had left Orchard Valley, her heart could forget him.

They'd only kissed once, but it was enough—more than enough. She knew this was a dangerous man. Dangerous to her emotional well-being. More important, he was in love with her sister.

Three days later, on a Monday afternoon, Norah stopped in to find Rowdy resting. The room was silent, which was rare. Norah guessed that Mrs. Emerich and Robbins were out to lunch.

"I've got your medication," she said, spilling two capsules into the palm of his hand and giving him a small paper cup filled with water.

Rowdy swallowed down the pills.

He looked exhausted. It angered Norah that he insisted on working so hard, especially now when he needed to rest. He ran everyone around him ragged, yet he demanded twice as much of himself. She shook off her thoughts as she realized he was speaking to her.

"Did anyone ever tell you how much you look like an angel?" he asked.

"Just you."

He frowned. "You're very beautiful, Norah Bloomfield."

"And you're very tired."

"I must be," he said on the tail end of a yawn. "I wasn't going to say anything until later."

"Say what?" she prompted.

"About your angel face. You don't look a thing like Valerie."

Her sister's name went through her like an icy chill. The sister she loved and admired. The sister she'd always looked up to and idolized. Now, Norah could barely tolerate the sound of her own sister's name.

"Rest," she advised softly.

"Will you be here when I wake up?"

Norah hesitated. The ward was full, and she didn't have time to stay at his bedside, although it was exactly what she wanted to do.

"I'll be back later, when I'm finished with my shift."

"Promise?" His eyelids were drifting down even as he spoke.

"I promise." Impulsively she brushed the hair from his temple, letting her hand linger on his face. He was growing more important to her every moment, which frightened her terribly. She dreaded the day he'd be released, and in the same heartbeat willed it to hurry.

When Robbins and Mrs. Emerich returned half an hour later, Norah suggested they take the rest of the afternoon off. Rowdy would be furious, but she'd deal with him later. He was pushing himself too hard; he needed the rest.

Norah was sitting at his bedside when he awoke. He must have sensed she was there because he moved his head toward her and slowly smiled. "What time is it?"

"Four-thirty."

His eyes widened. "That late? But what about—"

"I gave them the afternoon off."

"Norah," he groaned. "I wish you hadn't. I was expecting several phone calls." He struggled to a half-sitting position and his gaze shot to the telephone. She stood and picked up the plug, dangling it from her fingers.

"You unplugged the phone?"

"As I explained earlier, you needed the rest."

Rowdy's mouth snapped shut and anger leaped into his eyes.

"As I've explained before, this is a hospital, Mr. Cassidy, not Grand Central Station. If the call was that important they'll try again tomorrow."

Rowdy pinched his lips closed. Norah suspected it was to prevent himself from unleashing some blistering invective.

"I do have one small piece of information for you, however," she said matter-of-factly.

Rowdy's eyes met hers, his expression inquiring.

"Valerie and Colby arrived home this afternoon."

Rowdy reached for the bar and sat upright, his face eager. His eyes sharpened the way they did whenever he felt strongly about something—or in this case, someone. "I need to see her right away," he said. "See what you can do to arrange it, would you?"

Five

"Valerie is just home from her honeymoon," Norah felt obliged to remind Rowdy. "You don't really expect me to drag her up here to visit you, do you?"

Rowdy seemed surprised by her question. "Of course I do. Valerie and I have unfinished business."

Norah's stomach tightened into hard knots. She'd been a fool, standing guard over Rowdy all afternoon, protecting him the way she had. Hurrying to his side the moment her shift ended... That had been her first mistake. She was determined not to make a second one. It wasn't Norah he wanted doting over him, it was Valerie.

"Valerie's married, Rowdy. Nothing's going to change that."

Pain flashed into his eyes and there was no mistaking the reason. Now, more than ever, Norah realized what a calamity it would be to risk her heart over a man in love with someone else. Especially when that someone happened to be her own sister.

Suddenly the mist cleared in Norah's mind. Rowdy had had her transferred to his floor, not out of any desire to be near her but to have a source of information about Valerie. Even the kiss, the one she'd treasured, had been nothing but a ploy.

With her heart aching, Norah walked around to the other side of his bed, being careful to avoid the office equipment positioned in every available space.

"I never asked you what you expected to accomplish when you flew into Orchard Valley. I assume you were hoping to do more than celebrate Valerie and Colby's happiness."

"Hell, yes," Rowdy admitted with an abrupt laugh, "I had to be sure Valerie knew what she was doing."

"You *couldn't* have believed Valerie would cancel the wedding!"

"That was something I had to find out. Everyone has their price."

His words stunned Norah. "You really think that, don't you?"

"Why shouldn't I? It works. I didn't want to lose Valerie, but at the same time I wasn't willing to give her what she wanted. So I gambled. She took me at face value, unfortunately, and I lost, but I might not have, except for the plane crash."

Norah shook her head. "What do you mean, you weren't willing to give Valerie what she wanted? What was that?"

"Marriage."

If she'd been shocked before, Norah was completely astounded now. She needed to sit down before her legs gave out and sank, speechless, into the bedside chair. The man was mad. He apparently be-

lieved Valerie had contrived her engagement to
Colby with the intention of prompting Rowdy into a
wedding proposal.

"I'm not the marrying kind, Norah. Valerie must
have known that. I can't say we ever actually talked
about it, but I figure anyone who's worked with me
knows I don't have time for a wife or family. Don't
need 'em."

"I'm sure that's true," Norah said tightly.

Rowdy studied her closely. "Are you upset about
something?"

"No. Yes!" She jumped to her feet. "Let me see
if I understand you correctly. You want me to bring
my sister to you, but as far as I can tell, your reasons
for wanting to see her are entirely self-serving. You
don't care about Valerie and Colby. The only person
you care about is yourself."

He hesitated and his brows knitted together as he
mulled over her words. "I'm not going to tell you
about the nature of my business with your sister, if
that's what you're asking."

"You don't have to," she said coldly, ignoring the
intense pain she felt. "I know everything I need to.
If you want to talk to Valerie, I suggest you draft
someone else to arrange it."

Valerie, tanned and relaxed after her honeymoon,
was potting red geraniums on the sun-washed patio
outside her house—the house she and Colby had
bought near the outskirts of Orchard Valley. Norah
was sipping iced tea, sitting under the shade of a

large umbrella, watching her sister work. The pungent scent of freshly squeezed lemons drifted on the breeze. The afternoon was growing hot and humid, but neither Norah nor Valerie seemed to notice.

"What happened between you and Rowdy Cassidy when you flew back to Texas?" Norah asked.

Valerie paused, her hands deep in the potting soil. "We didn't part on good terms, but I'm afraid it was my fault."

Norah said nothing, but her expression must have revealed her skepticism.

"I'm serious," Valerie insisted.

Norah hesitated before she said, "I was sorry you had to hear about Rowdy's accident on your wedding day. Dad and Steffie and I weren't sure what to do. We didn't tell you right away because you had so much on your mind."

"Don't worry. Dad already talked to me about it. You did the right thing."

Norah's hands closed around the tea glass. She gazed into the distance for a moment, then said in a small voice, "He's in love with you."

With one wrist, Valerie tipped the large straw hat farther back on her head, laughing softly. "Rowdy might think he is, but believe me, Norah, he isn't. However, offering him my letter of resignation didn't help the situation."

She pressed the moist potting soil carefully around a geranium. "I underestimated Rowdy's ego," she explained. "He's a man who doesn't like to lose. He hasn't had much practice at it, and that's the problem. He's so wealthy he can buy anything he wants, and to complicate matters, he can charm a worm right out of an apple when he puts his mind to it."

"I—I know it isn't any of my business," Norah said, feeling as though she was invading her sister's privacy "but what happened when you told him about Colby?"

Valerie straightened, shaking the earth from her hands. "I didn't immediately mention I was engaged, which was a mistake. The first thing I brought up was my feasibility study on expanding CHIPS into the Pacific Northwest. I was eager to show Rowdy all my research. I presented the project in a favorable light, and I convinced him now was the time to do it.

"Before Rowdy knew I was engaged to Colby," Valerie continued, "he committed himself to the project. That thrilled me, of course, because I wanted to be the one to head it up."

"He's very savvy when it comes to business, isn't he? I mean, he's even working from his hospital bed."

"Rowdy's very talented," Valerie agreed. "But he's stubborn and he likes to have his own way."

"I've noticed," Norah said, grinning.

Valerie laughed. "I'll bet you have."

"Anyway, get back to your story."

"Well, I pushed the project, and he gave it the go-ahead—until I told him I wanted to run it myself. Rowdy said he'd rather I stayed in Texas and worked with him. He reached for my hands then and I had the feeling he was about to say something... romantic. I'm only grateful he noticed the engagement ring first. And that was when I told him about Colby.''

Norah's heart went out to Rowdy. "He must have been shocked.''

"He was, and angry, too." Valerie's face tightened at the memory. "He told me he thought I was too smart to let myself fall for that love-and-marriage stuff. He said that marrying Colby would be a disaster for my career." Valerie's gaze skidded self-consciously away from Norah. "I—I don't know if I ever said anything to you about Rowdy, but I was a little sweet on him before I met Colby. When I first got home, just before Dad's surgery, I'd started to believe he might feel the same way toward me.''

"He does.''

Valerie laughed and shook her head. "I hope I'm around to watch what happens when Rowdy actually does fall in love. It's going to knock that poor cowboy for one heck of a wallop.''

"Go on," Norah encouraged.

"Where was I...oh, yes. When Rowdy discovered I was definitely engaged to Colby, he tried to talk me out of it. He even claimed it was his duty as my friend and employer to do whatever he could to keep me from making such a terrible mistake.''

"He doesn't lack impudence, does he?''

"Not in the least," Valerie said with a grin. "He felt that in view of my recent poor judgment, Oregon was the worst place for me to be, so he offered the expansion project to Earl Robbins. In that case, I told him, I didn't have any choice. So I typed up my resignation and handed it to him. He seemed to think I was bluffing. He accepted the resignation, but blithely informed me that I would recognize the error of my ways and come back to CHIPS. I won't, though, not if it means leaving Oregon."

"Did it frighten you to quit like that? You never said. All I can remember is a comment you made about taking an extended vacation until after the honeymoon."

Valerie nodded thoughtfully. "For the first while, I had the wedding plans to keep me occupied, but I soon had that under control. Colby's been wonderfully encouraging, and we've discussed a number of possibilities. I've got my application in with a couple of firms in Portland, but I don't feel a burning need to find a job right away. To be honest, I'm enjoying this time off. It feels good to plant flowers and sit in the sunshine."

"What do you think you'd like to do?" Norah asked.

"Colby and I have discussed the idea of starting a consulting business out of the house. That way I could set my own hours and work when I wanted, which appeals to me. But I'm going to do some research into it before I make any firm decisions. For now I'm content."

"Rowdy wants to see you," Norah said abruptly, her voice unintentionally sharp. "He's been pestering me ever since he heard you and Colby were back.''

Valerie's hands stilled. ''I supposed I should go visit him. It's the least I can do.''

Norah wasn't so sure.

''Did you hear?'' Rowdy asked when Norah saw him next.

''About what?''

''My stock's up two full points, and the price has remained steady all week.''

To Norah's way of thinking, it must be agony to live a life controlled by the Dow Jones Industrial Average, but she didn't comment. ''Congratulations.''

Rowdy watched her closely. ''Are you upset about our last talk?'' He glanced at his two employees and kept his voice low.

''Of course not,'' Norah lied. ''Why should I be? You want to talk to my sister, and that's perfectly understandable. As you reminded me, it isn't any of my business.''

She walked around the end of his bed, removed the chart and made the necessary notations.

''I shouldn't have been so brusque.''

That was only one in a long list of offenses, but Norah didn't bother to say so.

''You haven't been in to see me as often,'' he said next.

''I've been too busy.''

"Even for me?" He used a hurt little-boy tone and Norah couldn't resist smiling.

"You'll be happy to know I saw Valerie yesterday afternoon," she went on, not daring to look up, afraid of what she might read in his eyes. "I explained that you wanted to see her and she said she'd be in sometime in the next few days."

"I hope it's soon because Dr. Silverman's given the go-ahead to get me out of this rigging. I'm scheduled to be released on Friday."

Norah waited a moment, finding it difficult to identify her reactions. She was beginning to know this man, faults and all—and despite everything, she was crazy about him.

Their views often clashed, but that didn't change her feelings. And his employees, at least the ones she'd met, were deeply committed to him. It took a lot more than money to inspire such loyalty.

At the same time, Norah recognized how dangerous it was for her to be around Rowdy much longer. He'd evoked a wide range of emotions: anger, outrage, laughter, pride and others that weren't as simple to define. It would be so easy to fall in love with him.... The mere thought terrified her.

"Aren't you going to say something?" Rowdy asked.

"We'll miss you around here," she said, putting on a false smile. "Good grief, what'll we do for excitement now?"

"You'll think of something," he assured her.

"No doubt, but I don't think Orchard Valley will ever be the same."

"Take a note, Mrs. Emerich," Rowdy insisted, keeping his gaze focused on Norah. "Small Oregon towns are no longer on my agenda. They're a risk to my health."

"I hope you understand that once you're discharged from here, you can't just go back to your regular work schedule," Norah pointed out.

"So I heard," Rowdy said, frowning. "I'm going to be stuck with several months of physical therapy."

"Don't shortchange yourself on that, Rowdy. You're going to need it."

He wasn't too pleased about this additional treatment, Norah knew. Then she sighed; he hadn't even left the hospital and already she was worrying about him. Oh, yes, she was going to miss him.

He must have seen the regret in her eyes because his own grew dark and serious. "Can you come back later?" he asked in a low voice. "Tonight. There's something I need to ask you."

Norah hesitated. "All right," she finally whispered.

"Around seven," he said briskly, "and don't eat dinner."

Norah wasn't sure what to expect that evening. She wore a sleeveless pale pink dress, the shade similar to her bridesmaid's dress. On impulse she'd put on the dangling gold earrings that had belonged to her mother. She wore them only for special occasions....

Her father didn't ask where she was going, but his complacent expression told Norah he knew. "You look absolutely beautiful," he said as she came down the stairs. "You have a wonderful evening, now."

"I'm sure I will." She half expected him to interrogate her, but he didn't even ask one question.

"I won't wait up for you."

"Have a good evening then, Dad."

"I will, sweetheart, I will," he said and then he did the oddest thing. He raised his head, eyes closed, and mumbled something she couldn't hear.

When Norah arrived at the hospital, she discovered that Rowdy had transformed his room into a romantic bower. The window shades were closed, allowing only glimmers of the evening light inside. Candles flickered from a linen-covered table, and half a dozen vases of fresh flowers were strategically placed throughout the room. The office furniture he'd had delivered was pushed as far against the wall as possible. A bottle of white wine was chilling in a silver bucket. Soft, lilting music played in the background. For an instant she wondered if she'd stepped into a dream, a fantasy.

"My goodness." The words escaped on a whisper of awe.

Rowdy wasn't wearing a hospital gown, but had dressed in a black Western shirt with string tie and a pair of jeans slit along one side to accommodate his cast. The effort he'd made touched her deeply.

"I hope you're hungry," he said, with a boyishly pleased grin.

"I'm starved," she assured him, walking over to the bed. The room seemed so private, so cozy, but she didn't hesitate. "What's on the menu?"

"Examine it for yourself. It only got here a minute ago."

Norah lifted the domed lid over the two plates and found crab-and-shrimp-stuffed sole, a wild rice pilaf and fresh broccoli with thin slivers of carrot. Two huge slices of strawberry-covered cheesecake rested next to the wineglasses.

"I had the chef check out the cholesterol count, if you're interested."

"Oh, Rowdy, you amaze me."

"Somehow or another I knew you'd swoon for cheesecake."

Norah laughed, because it was true, and because she was almost giddy with excitement—and happiness.

"Now pick up the gift that's on the edge of the table and open it."

Norah found the small, brightly wrapped box and carried it to his bedside. She raised questioning eyes to his. "What's this?"

"You'll have to open it and see."

Norah frowned. "I didn't do anything to deserve this." She was only one of the medical professionals who'd assisted Rowdy in his recovery.

"Quit arguing with me and open the package," Rowdy instructed. She finally nodded and carefully tore away the paper, uncovering a velvet box with the name of an expensive Portland jeweler etched in a gold flourish across the top.

She glanced at him again, still puzzled.

"Open it," he said again. "I picked it out myself."

Hardly daring to breathe, Norah lifted the lid and discovered a sapphire-and-diamond necklace, exquisite in its simplicity. She released her breath on a soft sigh of appreciation. "Oh, Rowdy...I've never seen anything this lovely."

"Then you like it?"

"Yes, but I could never accept it...."

"Nonsense. Turn around—I want to see it on you." Before she could protest further, he removed the necklace from its plush bed and opened the clasp. He held it with both hands, prepared to place it around her neck.

Norah pivoted slowly around and pressed her hand to the necklace when he positioned it against her throat. She'd never been given something so valuable or so beautiful.

"This is my way of thanking you for everything you did for me, Norah."

"But I—"

"You were my saving grace," he cut in, obviously impatient with her objections. "Arguing with you was the one thing that got me through those early days. You were generous and unselfish, even though I behaved like a spoiled brat. I'm grateful, and I want to express my gratitude."

"Well, then, I accept. And…and I thank you very much." Norah felt tears gather in the corners of her eyes. "Shall we open the wine?" she asked briskly, not wanting Rowdy to know how deeply his generosity had affected her. She lifted the wine bottle from its icy bucket and hesitated. "Are you sure you can cross alcohol with your medication?"

"I have Dr. Silverman's permission. If you don't believe me, you can call him yourself. He left his number with me in case you had any concerns."

Rowdy had thought of everything. Grinning, Norah handed him the bottle and corkscrew and watched as he deftly opened the Chablis. Norah brought over their glasses; he sampled the wine, then filled both goblets.

"We'd better eat before the fish gets cold," he said. Norah returned to the dinner table for his plate. His own place setting was neatly arranged on top of the nightstand.

"Next time we have dinner together, I'll be sitting across the table from you," he promised.

Norah sat down and spread the crisp linen napkin across her lap. In all her years of hospital work, she'd never seen anything like this. Of course, she'd never known anyone like Rowdy Cassidy, either.

"This is fabulous," Norah said after the first bite. She closed her eyes and savored the wonderful blend of seafood, sole and lightly seasoned sauce.

"Save room for dessert."

Norah eyed the huge fresh strawberries on the cheesecake. "No problem there." She felt a bit silly sitting at the table alone and after her second bite, got to her feet and carried her plate to the nightstand. "It'll do me good to stand up and eat," she told him. "I'll have more room for the cheesecake that way."

Rowdy grinned. The room was growing dark as the sun set, a warm, intimate darkness, and the candle flames seemed to dance to the soft music.

It took Norah an instant to realize they'd both stopped eating. Slowly, his eyes holding hers, Rowdy pushed the nightstand away so there was nothing between them. His hands on her waist, he guided her to the bed.

"Sit next to me," he whispered.

She glanced at his leg, needing to gauge the effect her weight would have on the pulleys.

"I'll be fine."

Norah carefully sat on the edge of the bed. Her gaze was level with Rowdy's.

"No wonder I thought you were an angel," he whispered. The husky pitch of his voice thrilled her. "You're so beautiful...."

No man had evoked such emotions in her before. She didn't *want* to feel any of these things, not with a man like Rowdy, but she couldn't stop herself.

He captured her face between his hands and rubbed the side of his thumb across her moist mouth. She sensed a barely restrained urgency in him, and still he didn't kiss her. Excitement raced through her veins.

"Rowdy." His name became a whispered plea.

She wasn't completely sure what she wanted from

him; he seemed to understand better than she did herself. He reached for her and wrapped her unceremoniously in his arms. His mouth claimed hers, and whatever defenses she'd erected against him in the past two weeks, whatever doubts she'd harbored, were banished under the onslaught of his kiss.

Just when Norah thought she might faint with the exhilaration of his touch, Rowdy trailed his mouth across her cheek to the scented hollow of her throat. His tongue made moist, tantalizing forays against her warm skin. She sighed and sagged against him, weak and without will.

"I've wanted to do that from the first time I saw you," he whispered huskily. "When you stood there, in that long pink dress—like an angel." He groaned and shook his head. "I've tried to be patient, tried to wait until I was out of this blasted cast, but I couldn't. Not a moment longer."

Norah buried her hands in his thick, dark hair and spread eager kisses over his face. She'd wanted him, too. Badly. So badly that she'd been afraid to admit it, even to herself.

He kissed her again, a deeper kiss this time. "I thought I'd go crazy these past few weeks," he murmured. "I've thought about nothing except holding you again, kissing you again. You've been so close—and yet so far away from me."

Norah felt warm and weightless in his arms. He kissed her with even greater insistence, and it seemed that she'd never experienced anything this good in her entire life. Tears of joy flooded her eyes as she tipped her head back to grant him easier exploration of her throat. Shivers of excitement danced over her skin and she gave a deep, deep sigh.

"Come to Texas with me." The words were low and urgent. He held her tightly against him as though he never wanted to let her go.

It took a moment for the words to sink past the fog of longing that blurred her thoughts. "Come to Texas with you?" she repeated. Slowly she eased herself from his embrace, her eyes seeking out his. Her heart went wild with expectant hope.

"As my personal nurse."

Norah wasn't sure she'd heard him correctly. His nurse. He wanted her as his nurse. For one soaring moment she'd assumed, she'd hoped, that he wanted her for herself. For always. She'd dreamed he wanted her to— A warm shade of pink blossomed in her cheeks as she realized what a fool she'd been. He'd told her before that he wasn't interested in marriage or family life. If he hadn't been willing to marry Valerie, whom he loved, then he certainly wasn't interested in her. CHIPS was his life, his reason for being. She'd witnessed it herself, the way all his energy, all his emotion, was dedicated to the success of his company.

"I'm going to need someone to look after me," he continued, reaching for her fingers and squeezing lightly, "to make sure I don't do more than I should. Someone who'll bully me into taking care of myself. Will you fly back with me, Norah?" He raised her hand to his lips and kissed her palm. "I need you."

How she'd longed to hear those words from Rowdy, but she'd wanted them to mean something very different.

It didn't take Norah more than a second to decide. "I can't leave Orchard Valley."

His gaze narrowed. "Why not?"

"It's my home. I've lived here all my life. My father's here, my job is here, my family. Everything that's important to me is here."

"You'll be back in a little while. I shouldn't need you for more than...say, a couple of months."

Norah backed away from him but her feet felt as if they'd been weighted down with cement. The little she'd eaten of her dinner rested like a concrete block in the pit of her stomach. Rowdy had arranged everything that evening in an effort to convince her to leave with him. As his nurse. Nothing more.

An overwhelming weariness came over her.

"Reconsider," he pleaded. "I promise you it won't be for long."

Norah shook her head. As far as she was concerned there wasn't anything to reconsider.

His mouth tightened with unconcealed irritation. "I'll make it worth your while. I'll triple whatever the hospital's paying you now."

She didn't doubt it. But financial concerns weren't what held her back. "I'm...pleased that you'd ask me, but it wouldn't work, Rowdy."

"Why the hell not?" he demanded. "I'm going to need someone and I want *you*."

"But I'm not for sale."

"I didn't mean it like that," he flared, running his hand roughly through his hair. Norah could feel the frustration in him. It might have been petty of her, but she felt a fleeting satisfaction. She wanted him to taste her own disappointment.

"I don't know what it is with you Bloomfield women," he grumbled, pushing the nightstand back into place. "There's no pleasing you, is there?" He lowered his voice. "I never met a pair of more headstrong women in my life."

"You'll do just fine without me." She was slowly recovering from the influence of his touch. Valerie was right; Rowdy Cassidy knew how to stack a deck in his favor. Knowing she was attracted to him, he'd attempted to sway her decision with wine and a luscious meal—and kisses.

Rowdy sliced his cheesecake with enough force to crack the plate. "Damn fool woman," he muttered.

Norah couldn't help laughing, despite the dull ache in her heart. "If you want, I'll recommend a reputable agency that provides nurses for private care."

"I don't want anyone but you." He stabbed a strawberry and poised it in front of his mouth. "You still haven't forgiven me for being honest, have you?"

"About what?"

"My feelings toward Valerie. I knew when I told you I'd regret it, and by heaven I was right."

"This doesn't have anything to do with my sister."

"Then why won't you fly back to Texas with me? I've got a private jet coming in. You won't lack for luxury, Norah, and if you're worried about propriety, I'll have Mrs. Emerich move in with us."

"That isn't it."

"I should have guessed you'd be this stubborn. It runs in the family, doesn't it?"

"It most certainly does."

Rowdy leaned over and flipped a switch that turned off the music. "I didn't think this...dinner would work. Mrs. Emerich was the one who suggested it."

Norah walked across the room and opened the blinds. "The evening's too lovely to shut out."

Rowdy folded his arms and muttered something she couldn't hear.

There was a polite knock at the door.

"Come in," Rowdy barked.

The door slowly opened and Valerie Bloomfield Winston stepped inside.

Six

"I'm not interrupting anything, am I?" Valerie asked. She remained on the threshold, oddly hesitant and unsure.

"Of course you're not." Norah recovered enough to speak first. She felt as though she were five years old again, caught with her hand in the cookie jar.

Rowdy merely closed his eyes—in resignation, Norah supposed, at the prospect of facing another Bloomfield. "You might as well come in," he invited ungraciously.

"If you'd rather I stopped by another time..." Valerie suggested, glancing at them doubtfully. "It wouldn't be any problem." Her gaze caught Norah's, who was convinced her cheeks had flamed a fiery red.

"Don't worry," Rowdy muttered, "you weren't interrupting a thing."

"Rowdy asked me to accompany him back to Texas...as his nurse," Norah explained, her tongue stumbling over the words. She gestured weakly toward the elaborately set table and silver wine bucket.

"Ah..." Her sister was smart enough to figure out what had happened.

"Have you decided to take the job?" Valerie asked, looking at Norah.

"No," Norah said emphatically.

Rowdy frowned—again. "I should have known she'd be as stubborn as you. Norah doesn't want the job, even at ten times what she earns here. She wants blood."

"It's time I left," Norah said, reaching for her purse. "I'm sure you two have a lot to talk about."

"Don't go," Valerie countered smoothly. "Fact is, I'd rather you stayed." She lifted the wine bottle from the silver bucket and read the label. Apparently she was impressed, because her eyebrows arched. "I see you didn't spare any expense."

"Are you here to gloat or do you want to talk?" Rowdy demanded irritably.

"He gets feisty," Valerie warned Norah under her breath, "when he can't have his own way."

"Quit talking about me as if I wasn't here." Rowdy snapped. He readjusted himself, using the triangular bar to straighten himself and shift positions. "You and I need to clear the air, Valerie Bloomfield."

"I suspect we do," Valerie agreed. "And the name's Winston now."

Norah knew she should leave, but she felt rooted to the floor. Her eyes strayed from Valerie to Rowdy, wondering how much of his feelings he'd dare reveal to her sister. He'd loved her enough to fly to Orchard Valley, but even now she wasn't completely sure what his intentions had been.

"Despite everything I told you, you went ahead and married Carlton, anyway," he muttered.

"Colby," Valerie and Norah corrected simultaneously.

"Whoever," Rowdy returned irritably. "You married him!" In response, Valerie raised her left hand and wiggled her ring finger.

"You can kiss your career goodbye, but you already know that, don't you?" Rowdy said. "I've seen it happen a thousand times, brilliant careers flushed down the drain and all in the name of love. As far as I'm concerned, it's a bunch of hogwash."

Valerie didn't say anything for a long moment. "At one time, working for you and CHIPS was the most important thing in my life."

"See?" Rowdy shouted, looking at Norah and pointing toward Valerie, "it's happening already! And she's only been married, what? Two weeks."

"Three," Valerie inserted.

"Three weeks and already her mind is warped."

Valerie laughed, and Norah found her amusement somehow reassuring. "Love tends to do that to a person."

"Then heaven help us all." Rowdy crossed his arms over his muscular chest and turned his head to gaze steadfastly out the window. "You were one of the best," he finally said, still not looking directly at the two women. "It's a shame to lose you."

"As I recall, you didn't leave me much choice. You wouldn't give me the job I wanted, and you knew I wouldn't stay in Texas."

He winced and Norah saw a flash of regret in his eyes, a reappearance of the pain she'd noticed whenever Valerie's name was mentioned. Norah experienced a pang of her own, knowing that the man she loved cared so deeply for her sister.

"I...may have acted a bit hastily," Rowdy said with a contriteness he didn't bother to conceal. "Robbins is a good man, don't get me wrong, but he doesn't have the gut instincts you do when it comes to making a go of this expansion project. He took the assignment because I asked him to, but if the truth be known, you were always the person for the job. Not Robbins."

Valerie paced the room in silence; Norah almost demanded her sister say something to ease the tension. Val had told her only a little of the confrontation that had taken place between her and Rowdy, but she knew an apology when she heard one. Valerie's former employer was trying to mend fences.

"What are you saying, Rowdy? That you want me back with CHIPS for the expansion project?"

"That's exactly what I'm saying."

"I'll never be the businesswoman I was, as you've already pointed out. Marriage has ruined me, you know."

Rowdy's face relaxed with the beginnings of a smile. "There might be some hope for you yet. Once you're with CHIPS again, we'll be able to work on your attitude. Of course it'll take time, training and patience, but Robbins and I should be able to whip you into shape."

Valerie didn't say anything. Norah stared at her sister, willing her to answer Rowdy. Willing her to recognize what it had cost his pride to make that offer. If Valerie didn't appreciate how difficult it was for him to admit he'd been wrong, then Norah did. Surely Val understood what he was really saying!

"I'm flattered."

For a moment Rowdy didn't react, then he slammed one hand against the other and swore under his breath. "You're going to turn me down, aren't you? I know that obstinate look of yours. Apparently it runs in the family." He was glaring at Norah as he spoke.

"I'm not committing myself either way just yet. The project will consume every waking minute for months, and I'm not sure that's what I want," Valerie told him honestly.

"You were willing enough to take it on before," Rowdy argued. "What's so different?"

"I'm married. I have responsibilities to someone other than myself. I didn't fully understand what that entailed when I first talked to you, but I know now, and I'm not willing to let CHIPS control my life. Not anymore."

"What do you intend to do? Stay barefoot and pregnant the rest of your life?"

"Rowdy!" Norah chastised, offended that he'd talk to her sister that way. He ignored her, staring combatively at Valerie.

"Colby and I do eventually want children, but I

was toying with the idea of starting my own business.''

"Software?'' His dark eyes became sharp as steel. It went without saying that Valerie could be keen competition if she chose to be.

"No,'' she said with amusement. "Consulting. I'll set my own hours, and I'll train others, so once the business expands—or I do—it won't be unmanageable.'' She grinned at Rowdy. "I'll be able to combine work and a family in whatever way suits me best.''

He nodded. "It makes sense, damn good sense.''

Valerie smiled cheerfully. "That wasn't so hard to admit, now was it?''

"No,'' he agreed. His eyes softened as he studied Valerie. He seemed to have forgotten Norah was in the room. "I was a fool to ever let you leave Texas. We might have had something good between us. Something really good.''

Valerie's gaze met his, and in it Norah read so many things. Her sister greatly admired Rowdy Cassidy, but the respect she held for him could never compare to the love she shared with Colby.

"I know, I know,'' Rowdy said with a weak smile. "It was too little, too late. Well, I want to wish you and Carlton the very best.''

"Colby,'' Valerie and Norah reminded him, and all three burst out laughing.

"You're home earlier than I expected,'' David Bloomfield said when Norah walked in the house an hour later. He was standing in the doorway of his den, dressed in flannel robe and slippers. A magazine lay on the arm of his favorite chair. "I was just going to make myself a cup of hot chocolate. Care to join me?"

"Sure." She trailed her father into the kitchen. "Where's Steffie?"

"She went out to dinner with Charles. I don't think she'll be home for a while."

It didn't seem possible that Steffie and Charles would be married in two weeks' time. They'd decided to have a ceremony next to the apple orchard, with the reception to follow on the huge front lawn. It would be a relaxed affair with plenty of fun, food and laughter.

"Did you enjoy yourself?" David asked in that deceptively casual way of his. Norah knew her father well enough to recognize his interest as more than idle curiosity. He was eager to hear the details. And tonight, Norah was just as eager to talk.

"I had dinner with Rowdy this evening. He had the meal catered." While she was talking, Norah took a saucepan from the cupboard and set it on the stove to heat the milk for their cocoa.

Her father leaned back in his chair, assuming a relaxed pose.

"Dad," Norah said, holding the milk carton in her hand and gazing absently into space. "If you had the opportunity to travel for...a job, would you take it?"

"That depends. Where would I be traveling to?"

"A long way from home—but not too far. Texas,

actually. But it wouldn't be for pleasure—or not exactly. It'd be on the pretense of a job, but not a taxing one." Rowdy might claim he needed her, but Norah knew better. She'd end up twiddling her thumbs ninety percent of the time. Even if she did insist that Rowdy slow down his pace, he wasn't likely to listen to her. As far as she could see, her presence would serve no useful purpose, other than entertainment. Hadn't he said he enjoyed arguing with her?

"Am I to understand Rowdy has asked you to go with him when he leaves Orchard Valley?"

"As his private nurse," Norah explained, pouring milk into the pan. "It'd only be for a few weeks."

"You're not sure what you want, are you? The temptation to go with him is there, but you don't feel good about doing it. Am I right?"

Norah was a little surprised at how easily her father had identified her dilemma, but she merely shrugged in reply.

"You like Rowdy Cassidy, don't you?" her father questioned softly.

Norah added cocoa to the warm milk and stirred briskly. "He's stubborn as a mule, and I swear I've never known anyone more egotistical. His arrogance is beyond explaining and he—"

"But you like him." Her father spoke again, and this time his words were a statement and not a question.

Norah's hand stilled. "I think there must be something wrong with me, Dad. Rowdy's in love with

Valerie—he might as well have come right out and said it.''

"You're sure about that?"

Norah wasn't sure of anything. Not now. For one thing, it just didn't make sense that Rowdy could hold her and kiss her the way he had if he was really in love with her sister.

"Valerie came to see him...while I was there. He asked her to come and work for him again.'' She turned back to the stove and resumed stirring. Her feelings about what had taken place between Rowdy and her sister hadn't sorted themselves out in her mind yet. What did his offer to Valerie really mean? Was he so desperate to have her back in his life that he was willing to ignore her marriage to Colby? A flashing pain cut through her at the thought.

"Are you sure you're not mistaking regret for love?" her father asked gently. "Rowdy and Valerie had worked together a heck of a long time. Her engagement came as a shock to him. My feeling about their last confrontation—when Val flew to Houston—was that they both said things they later regretted.''

"Valerie didn't turn down his offer, but she did ask for time to think it over. She refused to make a commitment either way." Norah poured the steaming cocoa into mugs and carried them to the table. "But you know, I think that was exactly what Rowdy expected from her. He was angry at first, but I had the impression it was more for show than anything.''

David chuckled, then sipped his hot chocolate.

"My guess is that being thwarted by two of my girls in one evening came as something of a shock to the boy."

Norah paused. "How'd you know I turned him down?"

David shrugged. "I just do. I'm not exactly sure why, but I knew you had. Are you having second thoughts now?"

"And third. Earlier I was so sure I'd made the right decision—and now I'm not."

Knowing that Rowdy would be out of her life in a matter of days had given her pause. His reaction was apparently the same. He didn't need a private nurse, and even if she'd accepted his generous offer, she wouldn't serve any useful purpose. She'd be there to provide entertainment... Norah gave a deep, heartfelt sigh.

Her father pointed at the sapphire-and-diamond necklace. "Is that new?" he asked.

Norah's hand went to her throat and she nodded. "Rowdy gave it to me—as a bribe I suspect. I suppose I should return it to him. Actually, I'd forgotten I had it on. It's beautiful, isn't it?"

"Very. If you want my advice about the necklace, keep it. Rowdy never intended it as a bribe. He's truly grateful for everything you've done." He swallowed down the last of his chocolate and stood.

"How can you be so certain?" Norah wanted to know.

Her father hesitated, frowning slightly. "I just am." With that, he turned and walked away.

* * *

When Norah arrived at the hospital late the following morning, Rowdy's bed was empty.

She walked into the room and for a moment was too stunned to move. After spending a restless night weighing the pros and cons of his offer, she felt she had to talk to him again, even if it meant visiting the hospital on her day off.

"Looking for someone?" Rowdy asked from behind her.

She whirled around to discover him sitting in a wheelchair, his leg extended and supported. "When did this happen?"

"Only a few minutes ago. Damn, but it feels good to be out of that bed."

Norah laughed and knew immediately what she wanted to do. "I imagine it does. Stay here a minute. I'll be right back, I promise." She checked in at the nurses' station, scanned Rowdy's chart and quickly returned to his room.

"What are you doing now?" he asked when she stepped behind the wheelchair and began to push him down the hallway. "Hey, where are we going? Not so fast," he muttered. "I'm getting dizzy... Besides, I want a chance to take in the view. All I've seen for weeks are the four same walls."

"Just be patient," Norah said, enjoying herself. Finding his bed empty had sent her into a tailspin. But once she'd realized what she should do, she'd experienced an overwhelming sense of relief. She was almost giddy with it.

"Are you kidnapping me?" he joked, when she

backed him into the elevator. "It sounds a bit kinky, but I could go for that."

"Hush now," she said, smiling at a visiting priest who shared the elevator with them.

"I always knew you were crazy about me," Rowdy continued. "But I never realized how much."

"Rowdy!" She rolled her eyes, then looked in the priest's direction. "You'll have to excuse him, Father, he's just spent the past few weeks tied to a bed."

"So I see." The priest glanced toward Rowdy's right leg.

"There were...other complications," Norah said with an exaggerated sigh.

"Poor fellow. I'll be saying a prayer for you, young man."

"Thank you, Father," Rowdy said so seriously that it was all Norah could do not to break into giggles.

The morning was gorgeous. The sun was shining, but the earth remained fresh with dew and the scent of blooming flowers drifted past on a warm breeze. Robins, goldfinches and bluebirds flitted about, chirping exuberantly.

Following a paved pathway, Norah pushed the wheelchair to a small knoll of rosebushes that overlooked the town. Orchard Valley lay spread out like an intricate quilt below them. Norah stepped forward to watch Rowdy's face when he saw her home.

For a long moment he said nothing. "It's a peaceful sort of place, isn't it?"

"Yes," she said quietly. "People still care about one another here." She sat on a stone bench and breathed in the fresh morning air.

"Is this the reason you won't come with me?" Rowdy asked, gazing out over the town. "Because you don't want to leave Orchard Valley?"

"No," she answered honestly. "You're the reason."

"Me?" He wore a puzzled, hurt look. "It's the necklace, isn't it? You assume because I gave you a gift that I was asking you to be more than my nurse."

"No," she told him quickly. "That didn't even cross my mind. It's so many other things." She sighed and leaned back, resting her hands on the sun-warmed bench. "I've never been more impressed by anyone than by you, Rowdy Cassidy. Your business judgment, your decisiveness, your sheer nerve. Your kindness, too. Just when I'm convinced you're the most egotistical, vain man I've ever known, you do something wonderful that completely baffles me."

"Like what?"

"Like offering my sister her job back."

"I'd behaved like a fool with Valerie. We both knew it, and it was up to me to make amends. I suppose you think it's because I'm carrying a torch for her." He paused as if he were trying to decipher her expression. "But I swear that isn't the case. If you must know, I felt cheated when Valerie returned to Houston engaged. I'd missed her like hell for all those weeks, and I was looking forward to having her back. Next thing I know, she announces she's going to marry some doctor.'' He shook his head. ''I'll tell you, it felt like a slap in the face when I heard about Colby.''

A weight seemed to lift from Norah's shoulders. Impulsively, she leaned forward just enough to brush her lips against his cheek.

Perplexed, Rowdy raised his hand to his jaw. ''What was that for?''

''A reward for getting Colby's name right.'' She smiled in relief. Rowdy's resentment toward Valerie's husband was gone and, however reluctantly, he'd accepted both the situation and the man. She also had a glimmer of insight into his feelings: his pride had taken a severe battering. Rowdy was used to being in control, and suddenly—with Valerie—he wasn't. ''Sorry,'' she said, ''I didn't mean to interrupt you.''

''Don't be so hasty.'' He folded his arms, relaxing in the warm sun. ''What will you do if I say Colby's name three times in rapid succession?''

Norah smiled. ''I don't know. I might go completely wild.''

Rowdy laughed outright, then grew serious. ''Damn, but I'm going to miss you.''

Norah lowered her eyes as the dread filled her. ''I'm going to miss you, too,'' she whispered.

He reached for her hands, covering them with his own. ''Come with me, Norah,'' he asked her again. ''I'll work out something with the hospital. I'll buy the whole damn building if I have to, but I want you by my side.''

The temptation was so strong that Norah briefly closed her eyes against the almost physical pull she experienced. "I...can't."

"Why?" he demanded, clearly exasperated. "I don't understand it. You want to come, I know you do, and I want you with me. Is that so difficult to understand?"

Norah pressed her hands against the sides of his face. He was so dear to her. When she said goodbye to him, she was sure a small part of her would die.

"Answer me," he pleaded.

Norah felt the emotion building in her, felt tears crowd into her eyes. "You need to understand something about me, Rowdy. Right now, you know me as a competent nurse, as Valerie's little sister, but you don't really *know* me. I have lots of friends and I like to go out, but basically I'm a homebody. Oh, I enjoy traveling now and again, but home is where my heart is. I love to bake and knit. Every year I plant a huge vegetable garden.''

His expression revealed how mystified he was.

"I'm nothing like Valerie. She's so talented in ways I'm not.''

"Do you think I've got the two of you confused in my mind?"

"No," she answered softly. "I just don't want you to think of me as her replacement.''

His eyes widened and he slowly shook his head. "No, Norah, I swear to you that isn't the case.''

"You don't need a nurse. You'll do fine if you use a bit of common sense. Once the cast is off, you'll require physical therapy for a while, but I won't be able to help you with that. I'm not trained for it."

"I like being with you," he said defensively. "Is that so wrong?"

"No."

"Then what exactly is the problem?"

"You don't know the kind of person I am...."

"That's what I'd like to find out," he argued, "if you'd give me half a chance and quit being so damn stubborn."

"I'm traditional and old-fashioned," she said, ignoring his outburst, "and...you're not. I'm the kind of woman who enjoys sitting by the fireplace and knitting at night. I'm not an adventurer, a risk-taker, like Valerie. I love my own familiar little world. And...and someday I want to marry and raise a family."

"I wanted to hire you as a nurse," Rowdy growled. "Next thing I know, you're talking about marriage and babies. It's enough to give a man heart failure. You're right. Forget I ever suggested the idea."

Norah hadn't explained herself well. She feared it sounded as though she was looking for a marriage proposal, and she wasn't. Refusing his job offer was simply a form of self-protection. Because it would be so easy to lose her heart to Rowdy Cassidy and she couldn't allow that to happen.

By his own admission, he wasn't the marrying kind, despite what he'd felt for Valerie. Nothing in Rowdy's life, not a wife, not children, would ever be more important to him than CHIPS.

Rowdy was due to be discharged from the hospital early the following morning. Norah had been on duty since 7:00 a.m.; at exactly nine, the flowers started arriving. Huge bouquets of roses and orchids, enough for every staff member on the second floor. Rowdy had ordered them to show his appreciation for the excellent care he'd received. The gesture touched Norah's heart, reminding her how thoughtful and generous he could be.

She'd braced herself for this day. Within a few hours, the infamous Rowdy Cassidy would be released from the hospital. He'd be out of Orchard Valley and out of her life.

Arrangements had been made for a limousine to pick him up at the hospital's side entrance, to avoid the ever-curious press.

Karen Johnson had asked Norah if she wanted to be the one to wheel him out, and she'd agreed. From the hospital the limousine would drive Rowdy into Portland, where he was scheduled to hold a short news conference before boarding a Lear jet for Texas.

His stay at Orchard Valley Hospital would soon be behind him. CHIPS and the world he knew best were waiting for him. Instinctively, Norah understood that once he left Orchard Valley he'd never return.

An hour later she was wheeling an empty chair down the corridor to his room when she saw her father. She was so surprised that she went stock-still.

"Dad, what are you doing here?"

"Can't a man come visiting without being drilled with questions?"

"Of course, but I didn't know any of your friends were here."

"They aren't. I've come to talk to that rascal Cassidy."

"Rowdy?"

"Got any other rascal cowboys I don't know about?"

"No...it's just that he's about to be discharged." She couldn't imagine what her father planned to say. In fact, the whole family seemed to be taking a new interest in Rowdy. Karen had mentioned that Colby had stopped in to see him the day before. Apparently the two men had hit it off and could be heard laughing. Rowdy hadn't mentioned the meeting to Norah, but then she hadn't had much of a chance to talk to him.

"Rowdy's driver will wait," her father said confidently. "I promise I won't keep him long."

"But, Dad..."

"Give us ten minutes, will you? And make sure we're not disturbed."

Norah's heart started to race. "You'd better tell me what you intend to say to him."

Her father abruptly stopped walking and placed a gentle hand on her shoulder. "I'm not going to say anything about my dream, if that's what's worrying you. It's likely to scare him so bad we'll never see hide nor hair of him again."

"Dad!"

"It wouldn't be a good idea, Norah. The minute he heard about those six youngsters, he'd be out of here so fast it'd make your head spin."

Rowdy, nothing. *Her* head was spinning a mile a minute. "Then why do you want to see him?"

"That, my darling Norah, is between me and the cowboy."

Norah possessed her mother's calm nature. She wasn't easily flustered, but her father had managed to do it in a matter of seconds. She paced outside Rowdy's door, wishing desperately that the walls weren't so thick and she could listen in on their conversation.

In less than the predicted ten minutes, which felt more like a lifetime, her father reappeared, grinning from ear to ear. Norah stopped cold when he sauntered out of the room.

"He's a decent fellow, isn't he?"

Norah was too numb to do anything more than nod.

With a roguish wink, her father walked away.

It took her a moment to compose herself. When she hurried into Rowdy's room, he was sitting on the bed, fully dressed, his Stetson beside him.

"Your father was just here."

"I know," she said, doing her best to act casually. "Did he have anything important to say?"

Rowdy didn't answer right away, then he nodded. "Yeah, he did." But he didn't elaborate, and Norah was left with a long list of unanswered questions.

Robbins arrived to say the limousine was waiting. Norah brought in the wheelchair and adjusted Rowdy's leg in the most comfortable position. She took her time, until she realized she was only delaying the inevitable. Sooner or later she'd have to wheel him outside.

Mrs. Emerich was already sitting inside the limousine. The driver was waiting to assist Rowdy, and Robbins, too, seemed eager to do what he could. But Rowdy dismissed their offers. "In a minute," he told them.

With the help of his crutches he maneuvered his way out of the wheelchair and stood upright. It was the first time Norah had seen him standing and she was amazed at what a large man he was. She came barely to his shoulders.

"Well, angel face," he said softly, his gaze holding hers, "this is goodbye."

She nodded, but found she couldn't speak for the lump in her throat.

"I wish I could say it's been fun."

Norah laughed. "You'll be your normal self again before you know it."

"I expect I will," he agreed. He reached out and very gently touched her face. "Take care, you hear?" Then he turned away.

Seven

Rowdy Cassidy was a fool, Norah decided as he drove away without so much as a backward glance. The least he could have done was kiss her goodbye. The least he could have done was give her one last memory...

Norah straightened, more determined than ever to put the man out of her mind. And out of her heart.

She'd start immediately, she decided, marching back to the hospital with every intention of calling Ray Folsom, of the X-ray department. He'd asked her out to dinner a week or so earlier, but she'd been busy with Rowdy and had declined. Norah stopped at the receptionist's desk, planning to leave a message for Ray. Janice Wilson, who was on duty, glanced up expectantly when Norah approached.

"Anything I can do for you?" Janice asked.

Sighing, Norah placed both hands on the counter and opened her mouth to speak. Then she shook her head. She wasn't ready to date anyone.

Unless, of course, it was Rowdy Cassidy.

A week passed, and Norah swore it was the longest seven days of her life. Fortunately, the preparations for Steffie's wedding helped fill the void left by Rowdy's absence. There was some task to occupy almost every evening and for that, at least, Norah was grateful.

She noticed how closely her family watched her, and she did her best to seem cheerful and unconcerned. It went without saying that Rowdy wouldn't call. He'd laid his best offer on the table and she'd turned him down. It was over; he'd made that clear.

"Have you heard from Rowdy?" Valerie asked while the three of them sat around the kitchen table assembling wedding favors. They filled plastic champagne glasses with foil-covered Belgian chocolates and wrapped each one in pastel-colored netting, then tied a silk apple blossom to the stem with pink ribbon.

"No," Norah said, resenting the question. She struggled to keep the disappointment out of her voice. "And I don't expect I will." It was on the tip of her tongue to ask her sister the same question, but she didn't. She assumed Valerie hadn't made a decision yet.

"Knowing Rowdy, he's probably waiting for you to get in touch with him," Valerie suggested.

"Me?" Norah asked, surprised by the suggestion "Whatever for?"

"To tell him you've changed your mind and want to come and work for him. I should know—it's the same game he played with me."

Norah bristled. Her sister was baiting her, questioning her resolve, and that angered Norah. "He knows better," she said stiffly, "and so do you!"

Valerie grinned, apparently pleased. "He's well-known for his ability to play a waiting game."

"There's no point in trying that with me." Norah twisted the netting around the plastic glass with unnecessary vigor and handed it to Steffie, who attached the ribbon.

"Men don't seem to learn things like that as quickly as women," Steffie mused. "Rowdy Cassidy has a few things to figure out."

Norah didn't respond to her comment, and the discussion soon returned to more general topics.

The idea of calling Rowdy had never occurred to Norah. But suddenly it made sense that, as his nurse, she should inquire about his progress. Valerie had placed the idea in her mind, and now Norah began to consider it seriously.

"I wonder how Rowdy's doing," she said conversationally to her father that same evening. She would have thought he'd be the first to suggest she ask Rowdy about his recovery, but he hadn't.

"We would've heard something if he wasn't doing well, don't you think?" he answered grumpily. "The way those newspeople reported every little detail of his life, you can bet it'd be on national television if he suffered the least little setback."

So much for that. "Ray Folsom called this morning. I—I'm going to dinner with him tomorrow evening," she told her father. Dredging up some enthusiasm for the date was going to require an effort. But after a week of moping around the house, pretending she didn't miss Rowdy, Norah was determined to enjoy herself.

Ray had seemed surprised when Norah accepted the invitation. Despite her previous refusal, she'd decided, not entirely on impulse, to go out with him. He was exactly what she needed, she told herself. Even Valerie approved when she learned that Norah was going out.

"It'll do you a world of good," Valerie assured her.

But when the time came for Ray to pick her up, Norah was no longer so sure of that. He brought her flowers and she found this thoughtfulness endearing but wished he hadn't. She instantly felt guilty; although she'd agreed to dinner with him, her mind was on Rowdy Cassidy, and that seemed unfair to Ray, who was gentle and considerate.

"Oh, Ray," she said, holding the small bouquet of pink carnations to her nose to breathe in their light scent. "How lovely."

He gave her a pleased smile. "I've been hoping we could get together, Norah."

She smiled back, biting her lip. Again she wondered if she'd made the right decision.

The phone rang while she was looking for a vase. Steffie caught it on the second ring and poked her head into the kitchen where Norah was busy chatting with Ray and arranging the flowers.

"It's for you. Do you want me to take a message?"

"Ah..." She glanced at Ray, who was leaning against the counter.

"Go ahead," Ray said, checking his watch. "We've got plenty of time."

Norah picked up the kitchen extension. "Hello," she said distractedly.

"Hello yourself, angel face."

Norah nearly slumped to her knees, she was so shocked. "Rowdy." She was grateful her back was to Ray. The color had drained from her face, and she felt weak and shaky.

"Have you missed me?"

"I—I've been busy."

"Me too, but that hasn't kept me from thinking about you."

Norah didn't dare admit he'd been on her mind from the moment he was discharged from the hospital. Not with Ray standing only a few feet from her. It wasn't in her to be so heartless.

"Listen, angel face," Rowdy continued when she said nothing. "I'm in Portland."

"You are?" Her heart pounded with glad excitement. He was less than sixty miles away.

"I'm working out some of the details on the expansion project with Robbins—I should be done in an hour or two. I was thinking I'd send a car for you now and by the time you arrive I'll be finished and we could have dinner."

"Oh, Rowdy."

"It'll be good to see you again. Damn it, I've missed you, and I'm hoping you feel the same way."

Norah felt like crying; Rowdy's timing couldn't have been worse. "I can't," she told him. "I'm sorry, but I can't."

"Why not?" he demanded impatiently. "Are you working?"

"I've already got other plans."

"Break them," he said with his usual confidence. "I probably won't be in the area again soon."

"I can't do that."

"Why the hell not?"

"I'm going to dinner with a friend and we're due to leave any minute."

A pause followed her announcement. "Male or female?"

"Male."

Norah could almost feel his anger vibrating through the wire. Rowdy seemed to think she should be willing to drop everything the moment he called her. He obviously assumed she'd spent the past week longing for him. True, she had, but she was determined to put those feelings behind her and to get on with her life. The man was impossible, she fumed. He must have known he was going to be in the area; it would have been a simple matter to arrange their meeting in advance. Instead he'd waited until the very last minute. As far as Norah was concerned, if he was angry at having his plans thwarted, he had no one to blame but himself.

She might have told him that if Ray hadn't been there.

"I see," Rowdy said after a long silence. "Enjoy yourself, then."

"I'm sure I will."

"Goodbye, Norah." Before she could say another word, the line was disconnected.

She closed her eyes, needing a moment to compose herself. When she turned around, she discovered Ray involved in conversation with Steffie. Her sister's eyes sought hers. "That was Rowdy," she said, hoping Steffie realized she would have appreciated some warning before she'd picked up the phone.

"I wasn't sure," Steffie admitted wryly, "but I thought it might have been. Next time I'll know."

"Are you ready?" Ray asked. He seemed unaware that anything was troubling her.

Norah nodded.

It surprised her how much she enjoyed her dinner with Ray. He was genuinely charming and Norah couldn't help responding to his carefree mood.

"You're in love with that cowboy, aren't you?" Ray asked suddenly as he drove her home. When she didn't respond immediately, he added, "I understand, you know."

"I...don't know what I feel anymore," Norah admitted in a troubled voice.

"Love's like that sometimes," Ray said quietly. "I like you, Norah, and I was hoping there'd be a chance for us. But—" he shrugged and reached for her hand "—everything will work out in the end," he said, squeezing her fingers gently. "It generally does. If you need proof of that, look at what's happened to your sisters over the past few months."

Norah didn't know what to say. Ray was a wonderful man, considerate and gracious, and he'd make some woman very happy one day. But not her.

Still holding her hand, he walked her to the porch. He kissed her cheek, then whispered, "I wish it was me you were so crazy about."

"I've been rotten company, haven't I?" Norah asked guiltily.

He smiled, shaking his head. "Not at all. I just hope that cowpoke realizes how lucky he is."

Norah sincerely doubted it. "Thank you for dinner, Ray. I had a wonderful time."

He kissed her once more on the cheek. "Good luck with your cowboy."

She opened the door and waited while Ray walked down the porch steps and got into his car. She waved goodbye, staring down the driveway until he was out of sight before she stepped into the house.

Steffie was waiting in the entry. "Thank goodness you're back!" she burst out urgently.

"Is it Dad? Did he—"

"Rowdy Cassidy's here," her sister broke in, nodding toward the den.

"Here? Now?"

"Dad's kept him occupied," Steffie informed her, "but he's been here the better part of an hour and getting more restless by the minute."

Norah's heart was hammering wildly. She forced

herself to calm down before walking into the den, even managing a smile.

Her eyes immediately went to Rowdy, who stood, leaning heavily on his crutches, gazing out the window that overlooked the front porch. It was obvious that he'd witnessed Ray's kiss. It was equally obvious that he wasn't pleased. He looked tall and lean and so damnably handsome that it was all Norah could do to stop herself from rushing into his arms.

"Rowdy," she said huskily. "This is…an unexpected surprise."

Her father got to his feet and winked at her. "I'll bring both of you a cup of coffee," he told them and conveniently exited the room, leaving Norah alone with Rowdy.

Using his crutches, Rowdy levered himself around to face her, his right leg thrust out in front of him. "I trust you had an enjoyable dinner," he said stiffly.

"Very," she returned, clasping her hands together.

"I'm glad to hear it." Although he sounded anything but glad. He was frowning as he studied her, and Norah felt uncomfortable under his close scrutiny.

"Please sit down," she invited, gesturing toward the chair. "I didn't know you planned to stop by."

"Would it have mattered?"

Norah winced at the undisguised anger she heard in his voice. "I hope Dad kept you entertained," she said, avoiding his question.

"He did." Rowdy sank into her father's chair and Norah sat across from him, on the ottoman.

"Is there anything I can do for you?" she asked.

He nodded slowly. "You offered to give me the name of a reputable agency," he said gruffly. "I'm still in the market for a private nurse. I assumed I could do without one. You seemed so sure I'd be just fine on my own." The last words came as an accusation.

"And you're not?"

"No," he told her angrily. "I'm having one hell of a time adjusting to these damn crutches."

"It'll get easier with practice. A nurse can't do that for you, Rowdy. You'll have to learn to walk with them yourself."

He muttered something she couldn't distinguish, which was just as well, judging by the disgruntled look he wore.

"I'll get the name and number of the agency for you," she told him.

"Fine."

She left the room and discovered Steffie and her father standing just outside the door. They looked startled, then glanced at her guiltily. Norah glared at them both, knowing they'd blatantly listened in on her conversation with Rowdy.

Steffie cast her an apologetic smile, then hurried up the stairs; her father chuckled with wry amusement and wandered toward the kitchen, mumbling something about coffee.

Rowdy was massaging his right thigh when Norah returned with a slip of paper. "Your leg still aches?" she asked.

"It hurts like hell," he said in a blatant effort to gain her sympathy.

"Are you taking the medication as prescribed?" She handed him the paper.

"I forget," he answered brusquely. "That's another reason I need a good nurse."

"Nurse or nursemaid?" she inquired sweetly.

"Nurse," Rowdy muttered.

Norah knew exactly what Rowdy Cassidy was doing, and she wanted it understood right now that she refused to be manipulated. If he wanted something, he'd have to ask for it in plain English.

"You honestly think this agency will have what I need?" he asked, eyeing her closely.

"I'm sure of it."

"I prefer someone young," he said, then added, "and blond, if possible. Oh, and pretty."

Norah nearly laughed out loud. Since she hadn't immediately volunteered for the position, he was hoping to make her jealous. "You might be wiser to request someone competent, Rowdy."

For a long moment he said nothing. "It's been one week," he told her, his eyes steadily holding hers. "Seven days."

"It seems longer, doesn't it?" she asked softly, looking away, not wanting him to see how miserable and lonely she'd been and how hard she'd worked at pretending otherwise.

"Much longer," he admitted grudgingly. "Damn, but I didn't expect to miss you this much." He glared at her, and it took Norah a second to realize he was waiting for her to change her mind, to accept the position.

"I've missed you, too," Norah told him, weakening. He'd played on her sympathies and that hadn't worked. But her heart was vulnerable, and he knew it.

"Ever been to Texas this time of year?" he asked, clambering to his feet. Using the crutches with surprising deftness, he worked his way closer to her until mere inches separated them. Until there was only a single step between them. One small step, and she could walk directly into his arms.

Norah didn't know where she found the strength to stand still, to resist him.

"Have you?" he asked again.

Norah shook her head.

"It's the most beautiful place on earth."

"As beautiful as Orchard Valley?"

Rowdy chuckled. "You'll have to make that judgment for yourself." He was waiting. Waiting for her to come to him, to swallow her pride and sacrifice her own needs to his.

Norah knew exactly what would happen if she took that step, if she agreed to leave with Rowdy. She'd fall so deeply in love with him that she'd give up her own hopes and plans, her own pleasures—all the things that made her Norah. She'd be unable to refuse him anything. Already she was halfway there.

He'd made it perfectly clear that he had no intention of marrying. Nor was he interested in raising a family. Rowdy had admitted that even if Valerie had broken off her engagement to Colby, he wouldn't have married her.

And if he hadn't been willing to marry her sister, he wouldn't want her, either. For that matter, Norah wasn't sure she'd agree if he *did* propose. When she married, she wanted a husband, a man who'd be a constant part of her life, a man who shared her need for a settled existence, with a home and a family. Not a man like Rowdy...

Norah was too sensible and pragmatic not to recognize they'd face these issues sooner or later, even if he hadn't raised them now. And when it did happen, she wanted to be sure he knew where she stood. Because she'd be so head over heels in love with him that she couldn't think clearly.

"If the agency here isn't able to find you a nurse..."

"Yes?" he asked eagerly.

"I'm sure there are several in Texas with excellent reputations. I could ask around for you."

His face tightened. "Lord, you're stubborn."

"It runs in the family. I'm surprised you didn't butt heads with Valerie more often."

"I'm not," he muttered, moving awkwardly away from her. "We were both working toward the same goals. You and I are working at cross purposes." He limped toward the phone and called for his car. "You want something I'm not willing to give you."

"What's that?" she asked.

His eyes darkened. "You want my pride."

He was wrong, but no amount of arguing was going to convince him of that and Norah hadn't the strength to try.

"It was good seeing you again, Norah," he said unemotionally.

"You too, Rowdy."

"If you go out with Ralph again—"

"Ray," she corrected.

"Of course, Ray. I must have forgotten."

"There's no need to be sarcastic."

"You're right," he said in a tone so cool that it seemed to frost the air between them. "In any event, I wish you the very best. I'm sure the two of you have a lot in common."

Norah said nothing.

"I came the minute I heard." Valerie's concerned voice drifted into the kitchen from the front entry the following morning. "What did he say to her?" she demanded of Steffie.

"I'm not entirely sure. It seems he wanted her to reconsider and go to Texas with him as his nurse."

"Norah turned him down, didn't she?"

"She must have."

Her sisters appeared in the kitchen, both wearing compassionate expressions.

"I understand Rowdy stopped by last night," Valerie said gently, as though she considered Norah emotionally fragile.

"He was here, all right," she muttered, continuing to stir the batter for oatmeal-and-raisin muffins. Baking had always been a means of escape for her. Some women shopped when they felt depressed; some read or slept or went to exercise classes. Norah baked.

"And?"

"And he left."

"Do you think he'll come here again?"

Clutching the bowl against her stomach, Norah whipped the batter vigorously. "Who knows?" But she hadn't expected to hear anything from him after his discharge; his visit had come as a complete surprise. However, Norah wasn't fool enough to believe it would happen again. Rejection was difficult for any man and harder for Rowdy than most, since he'd become so accustomed to getting his own way.

He'd come to her twice, and she'd turned down his offer both times. He wasn't likely to try again.

"Rowdy's been spoiled rotten," Valerie warned her.

"Isn't every man?" Norah returned calmly.

Valerie and Steffie exchanged a glance. "She'll be just fine," Steffie murmured and, smiling, Valerie agreed.

Norah wished she felt as confident.

Rowdy's name wasn't mentioned again until the following evening. Norah's father was watching the news when he excitedly called for her. "Come quick," he shouted.

Norah raced in from the kitchen to discover her father pointing toward the television. "Rowdy's on the local news."

She sank into a chair and braced herself for the sight of him. The Portland news anchor reported the expansion of the Texas-based software company

CHIPS, which would soon be building in the area. He went on to comment that the final papers had been signed and that the owner of CHIPS, Rowdy Cassidy, was currently in town. The ground-breaking ceremony was due to take place in two weeks.

The camera switched from the anchor to a clip of Rowdy. Norah didn't focus on him, but on the statuesque blond woman in a nurse's uniform who stood behind him.

Her stomach felt as if someone had kicked her.

Young and blond, just the way he'd said. And pretty...

"Norah?" Her father's voice broke into her thoughts. "Are you all right?"

"Fine, Dad," she answered cheerfully. "Why shouldn't I be?"

The phone rang shortly afterward. Her father answered; apparently it was Valerie. Norah wandered back to the kitchen to finish preparing the evening meal. She went determinedly about the task, refusing to allow emotion to take control of her.

She'd made her decision.

Rowdy had made his.

"Oh, Steffie," Norah said breathlessly, gazing at her sister. "You're so beautiful."

Steffie had chosen not to wear a traditional wedding gown, but a tea-length cream-colored lace dress with a dropped waist. A garland of fresh baby's breath and rosebuds was woven into her glossy dark hair.

Norah couldn't stop staring at the transformation

she saw in her sister. Steffie looked not only beautiful but supremely happy; she glowed with serenity and a calm, sure joy.

"Everyone's outside and waiting," Valerie announced when she walked into the bedroom. She stopped abruptly when she saw Steffie.

"Oh, Steffie," she breathed, the tears welled in her eyes. "Mom would be so proud."

"I feel just as if she were here," Steffie whispered, reaching for her wedding bouquet. "I thought I was going to miss her so much today and the most amazing thing has happened. It's as if she's been standing right beside me. I don't think I've ever felt her presence more."

"I felt the same way the day Colby and I were married," Valerie confessed. "Her love is here," she added simply.

Norah had felt it, too, although she hadn't been able to put it into words.

"Dad's waiting," Valerie told them.

Emotion swirled through Norah. She was truly happy for her sister and Charles, but her heart ached. Never had she felt more alone, set apart from those she loved. Valerie had Colby and Steffie had Charles, but there was no one for her.

She walked down the stairs with her two older sisters and paused at the top of the porch steps.

White linen-covered tables dotted the sweeping expanse of the front lawn, its grass a cool, luscious green. White wrought-iron chairs were scattered about. A number of long tables groaned with an opulent display of food. The three-tiered wedding cake sat on a table of its own, protected by a small, flower-draped canopy.

The actual ceremony was to take place next to the apple orchard. The trees were heavy with fruit, and a warm summer breeze drifted through the rows, rustling the leaves. Soft music floated toward Norah and she realized the time had come for her to lead the small procession.

The side yard was filled with friends and family. Norah led the others down the center aisle to the flower-decked archway; Valerie followed and took her place beside her sister.

Steffie came next, escorted by their father. Every eye was on the bride, and Norah gazed proudly at her beautiful sister.

The loneliness she'd felt earlier unexpectedly left her. She sensed her mother's presence again, a sensation so strong that Norah was tempted to turn around, to see if Grace were actually there, perhaps standing behind her. The pain she'd experienced was replaced by a certainty that one day she, too, would discover the love her sisters had each found that summer.

Steffie paused before Pastor Wallen, who'd married Valerie and Colby a short five weeks earlier. She gently kissed her father's cheek and turned, smiling, to Charles.

Norah had never seen Charles look more dashing. She noticed the private smile he exchanged with his bride, the tenderness of his expression. Their love for each other was almost tangible.

Norah stood beside Valerie. Her own dress was

the pink one she'd worn to Valerie's wedding. Val's was pale lavender. A sprig of baby's breath and silk apple blossoms was tucked at Norah's ear, and Valerie wore a pearl comb that had been their mother's. Steffie handed her bridal bouquet, of white rosebuds and pale silk apple blossoms, to Norah to hold during the ceremony.

Minutes later, Stephanie Bloomfield had pledged her love to Charles Tomaselli, and Pastor Wallen had pronounced them husband and wife.

A happy cheer rose from their guests, and Steffie and Charles fled laughing from a hail of birdseed.

Norah smiled after the happy couple, then frowned. An irregular, beating sound could be heard in the distance. She glanced about, wondering at its source.

It took her a few moments to realize a helicopter was approaching.

Everyone stopped and gaped in wonder as the aircraft slowly descended from the sky, landing on the driveway. Norah looked at her father, who moved forward.

Norah did, too, her heart pounding as hard and as loud as the whirling blades.

The door opened and two crutches appeared before Rowdy Cassidy levered himself out. He scanned the crowd until he found Norah. Then he grinned.

"I'm not interrupting anything, am I?" he asked.

Eight

"Are you *interrupting* anything?" Norah repeated, laughing incredulously. "This is Steffie and Charles's wedding!"

Using the crutches, Rowdy swung his legs forward, then stopped abruptly. "*Another* wedding?"

Norah laughed again, so happy to see him that it didn't matter that they'd parted on such bad terms only a week earlier. She hurried to his side, threw her arms around his neck and hugged him.

She felt his sigh and knew he was no less delighted to be with her. The crowd started to disperse as the newlywed couple reappeared to lead the way across the lawn to the reception area.

"If I'd known there was a wedding taking place I would have avoided this place like the plague," Rowdy muttered.

"Why are you so set against marriage?" Norah asked, glancing up at him.

"Look what happened to me the last time I showed up for one of your family weddings." He moved his right leg forward for her to examine the cast, which reached halfway up his thigh.

"Good to see you again, Rowdy," Colby said, his

arm tucked securely around Valerie's waist. The two men exchanged quick handshakes. David stepped forward to welcome him, too, chuckling about Rowdy's propensity for making grand entrances.

"When it comes to your daughters, I certainly seem to have a bad sense of timing," Rowdy told her father.

"Not in the least," David Bloomfield assured him, his gaze lighting on Norah. "In fact, it couldn't be better. Isn't that right, Norah?"

Laughing, she nodded, eager to agree. Not long before, she'd been feeling lonely and despairing; now Rowdy's dramatic arrival was like an unexpected gift.

The others drifted back to the wedding party, leaving Norah and Rowdy alone for the first time.

"How long can you stay?" Norah asked. It went without saying that their time together would be limited.

"A few hours. The ground-breaking ceremony for CHIPS Northwest is scheduled to take place later this afternoon."

Norah led him to a chair and helped him sit down. As he laid the crutches on the grass beside him, she glanced about. "Where is she?" she asked, referring to his blond nurse.

Rowdy didn't pretend not to know what she was talking about. He frowned and muttered something unpleasant under his breath.

"Pardon? I didn't quite hear that," she said sweetly.

"That's because it wasn't meant for you to hear. If I tell you, you'll gloat."

"No, I won't," she promised, doing her best to swallow a laugh.

"All right," Rowdy muttered, "since you insist on knowing. She didn't work out."

"And why's that? You were so sure you needed a nurse."

"I do…that is, I did need one. Unfortunately the nurse I hired was a daughter of Attila the Hun. The problem with you blondes is that you're deceptive-looking. You *look* like you'd be all sweetness and light."

"But we are."

Rowdy said nothing, but the grimace he sent her caused her to laugh outright.

"I still need a nurse," Rowdy argued, "but I only want you. Since you're being so blasted stubborn, I'm forced to make do on my own."

In a silent-film gesture, Norah pressed the back of her hand against her forehead and expelled a beleaguered sigh. "Life is tough, Rowdy."

He waved his index finger under her nose. "I knew you'd gloat."

"I'm sorry," she told him between giggles. "I really am, but I couldn't help myself."

Rowdy reached for her hands, gripping them in his own. "You're a sight for tired eyes, Norah. I've missed you more than—"

"What you miss is getting your own way," she interrupted tartly.

Rowdy grinned. "Tell me, have you gone out with Ralph lately?"

"It's Ray, and no, I haven't."

Rowdy hesitated. "I don't have the right to ask you not to date anyone else."

"No, you don't," Norah agreed.

"Nevertheless..." Rowdy's scowl deepened. "I don't mind admitting I was concerned about that guy."

"Why?" Anyone looking at her would know in an instant how deeply she cared for Rowdy. Ray was a friend, nothing more. She hadn't intended to make Rowdy jealous.

"I guess I'm more selfish than I realized," he said grudgingly. "I want you for myself."

Norah made a conscious effort to change the subject. There was no point in pursuing this; it was too painful and she knew nothing was going to change.

"Are you hungry?" she asked, noting that the guests were helping themselves to the large array of hors d'oeuvres and other dishes prepared by the caterers.

"Starved," Rowdy answered, but when she stood to get him a plate, he caught her hand. "It isn't food I need." His dark eyes held hers and Norah could feel herself moving toward him.

"Not here," she murmured, stopping herself.

"Where, then? Norah, I need to hold you so damn much. It's been driving me crazy from the moment I left the hospital."

"Rowdy, this is my sister's wedding."

"Surely you're allowed a few minutes alone."

"Yes, but..."

"Norah," he said decisively, "we need to talk."

"It isn't talking that interests you, Rowdy Cassidy, and we both know it."

"Ah, but what interests *you?*"

Norah sighed. "You already know," she admitted in a low voice.

Rowdy glanced around them, reached for the crutches and got to his feet. "Lead the way."

"Rowdy...I'm not sure about this."

"We'll pretend we're getting something to eat and before anyone notices we'll casually slip away. A few minutes, Norah, that's all I'm asking."

She hadn't the heart to refuse him—or herself. Their time together was so brief, and she needed him. She needed him more than she'd ever needed anyone, she thought.

If there were people who noticed how Norah and Rowdy eased themselves away from the festive crowd assembled on the front lawn, they didn't say. She steered Rowdy toward the side yard, near the orchard, where the ceremony had taken place. It was quiet and peaceful there. A light breeze wafted through the fruit trees.

Knowing it was more comfortable for Rowdy to sit rather than stand, she guided him to the first row of chairs in front of the archway.

"I certainly hope you're not hinting at something here," he muttered, nodding toward the tall flower-filled baskets. He carefully lowered himself into the chair, and Norah sat down next to him. Rowdy's arm settled over her shoulders. She rested her head on his chest and, sighing, closed her eyes.

She'd dreamed of moments like this. Moments of peace, without all the tension between them.

He stroked her hair and sighed, too. "I've never known a woman quite like you." His lips grazed her temple. "I've never known a woman who played checkers quite as poorly, either."

They both laughed, and Norah leaned her head back to look into his face. The laughter fled from his eyes. Instinctively, Norah moistened her lips in preparation for his kiss.

Rowdy didn't disappoint her. He lowered his mouth to hers in a kiss that was both gentle and undemanding.

Norah had never experienced anything sweeter. "Oh, Rowdy," she whispered with a soft moan of pleasure, her eyes closed. "I've missed you."

His mouth returned to hers, and this time, the kiss was long and hard. Norah was flooded with a need so powerful that she twisted around in her chair to entwine her arms around his neck. When they broke apart they were breathless.

"Come with me this afternoon," he pleaded.

The offer was so tempting that it was all Norah could do to refuse. "I want to, but I can't leave my family. Not on Steffie's wedding day."

Rowdy tensed and she realized he was dealing with his own disappointment. "I understand. I don't like it, but I understand."

"Tell me again," she whispered, glancing up at him, "how dreadful the blond nurse was."

"Were you jealous?"

"Insanely."

"Enough to change your mind?" he asked hopefully.

She shook her head. "I'm amazed at how well you've adapted to the crutches, though. You're doing splendidly without me."

His eyes grew serious. "That's where you're wrong, Norah." He kissed her again with an unleashed need that left her clinging and dizzy.

They wandered back to the wedding party a little later. Norah brought them both plates piled high with fresh fruit and a variety of hors d'oeuvres—bacon-wrapped scallops, tiny quiches, skewered shrimp. They fed each other tidbits, shared a glass of champagne and talked and laughed for what seemed like minutes but was in reality hours.

The helicopter arrived just after Steffie and Charles had cut the wedding cake. Norah watched the aircraft approach, feeling a sense of dread, knowing it would take Rowdy away from her.

She forced herself to smile. He'd been with her for several wonderful hours, the most uninterrupted time they'd had together in weeks.

Deep in her heart, she realized it would always be like this with Rowdy. A few minutes here, an hour there, squeezed in between appointments, stolen from schedules.

She stood alone on the lawn, the guests for the

reception behind her, as the helicopter lifted toward the sky. She waved, her hand high above her head, until she was certain Rowdy couldn't see her any longer.

He hadn't told her when he'd see her again, but Norah knew it would be soon. It had to be. Neither of them could bear being apart like that again.

Valerie hurried to her side. "Are you going to be all right?"

Norah offered her sister a brave smile. "I'll be fine."

"You're sure?"

Eyes blurry with tears, she nodded.

Rowdy phoned her the next three nights, and they talked for nearly an hour each time. They spoke of nonsensical trifles, of daily details and of important things, too. She told him about Steffie and Charles's romance and why the newlyweds were honeymooning in Italy. Rowdy told her about his family, or rather lack of one—how his parents were killed when he was young and he'd been raised in a series of foster homes.

He always called late in the evening, and with the time difference it was well past midnight in Texas when they ended their conversations. He didn't need to tell Norah that he was missing an hour's sleep in order to talk to her. She knew it.

"I'm leaving for San Francisco first thing in the morning to meet with a group of important stockholders," he told her on Tuesday night. "The meetings will probably run late. I doubt I'll get a chance to call you."

"I understand." And she truly did. CHIPS would always come first for Rowdy, because it was the family he'd never had, the security he'd grown up without. She understood his obsession with the business now, and the needs that drove him.

"It isn't what I want, Norah."

"I know." She wasn't angry, not in the least. "It's all right, Rowdy." She was trying to resign herself to the fact that it would always come to this. His company would remain the emotional center of his life. "When will you get home?"

"Saturday afternoon at the earliest."

"I'm working this weekend," she said, more because she needed to keep talking than because she felt he'd be interested in the information. "I had to trade with a friend of mine in order to have the weekend off for Steffie's wedding. We work on a rotating schedule at the hospital. It changes every four weeks so we can spend as much time with our families as possible."

"Why do you work?" He wasn't being facetious or sarcastic; his curiosity was genuine. It wasn't financially necessary for her to hold down a job, but she loved nursing and she *needed* to work, to occupy her time in a productive, responsible and fulfilling way. She expected Rowdy to empathize with those feelings.

"My mother was a nurse. Did you know that?"

"I must have, because it doesn't come as any surprise."

Norah smiled into the telephone receiver. "From the time I was a little girl, I knew I'd go into the medical profession."

"Did your mother work outside the home?"

"No, she quit soon after she and Dad married, when she was pregnant with Valerie."

"Did she miss the hospital?"

"I'm sure she did, but once we were a bit older she used her medical skills in other ways. When the migrant workers came to pick apples at our orchard and a couple of neighboring ones, Mom organized a health clinic for them—until she became too ill to do it any longer. Then she and Dad set up a fund, so the workers and their families could afford to go to the clinic at Orchard Valley." Norah swallowed hard. "She was a special woman, Rowdy. I wish you'd known her."

"I wish I had, too, but I already guessed she was someone unusual. She raised you, didn't she?"

That was about as romantic as Rowdy ever got with her. Norah didn't expect flowery words from him, certainly nothing more than a careless term of affection. Like "angel face"...

"It'd be a whole lot more convenient for us if you worked regular hours like everyone else," Rowdy said after a moment. "Some days you're on duty, some days you're not. Half the time you end up staying later than you're scheduled. I'm surprised you don't burn out with those long hours."

"Me work long hours?" she challenged with a short laugh. "Ha! You do the same thing. Even more so. It's a wonder *you* didn't burn out years ago."

"That's different."

"It is not," she insisted, "and we both know that. Only you're too proud to admit it." She paused thoughtfully. "Rowdy," she said, "I do agree that there's a difference. My life isn't dictated by my job the way yours is."

"What's so unusual about my dedication to CHIPS?" Rowdy countered sharply. "Don't forget I started the company. CHIPS is more than a job. No one's hiring me to work eighteen hours a day—I do it by choice."

Norah didn't need to be reminded of the truth of his words. With a small inward sigh, she changed the topic, asking questions instead about the San Francisco meetings.

When she'd finished the call with Rowdy, Norah wandered downstairs. Without consciously realizing where she'd been headed, she found herself standing in the doorway of her father's den.

"Would you like a cup of hot chocolate?" she asked. The offer was an excuse to talk, and she suspected her father would recognize it as such.

He did. Automatically setting aside his book, he glanced up at her. "Sure. Would you like some help?"

Before she had a chance to answer, he stood and followed her into the kitchen. While she took out the saucepan, her father retrieved the milk from the refrigerator. Norah was gratified to see how much more energetic he'd become lately; his recovery really had been nothing short of miraculous, she decided.

"How's Rowdy?" he asked almost as if he'd known exactly what she wanted to discuss.

"Good," she answered, hoping to appear nonchalant. "He's taking a business trip to San Francisco in the morning. I asked him how often he's been there, and he told me he's visited the Bay area a dozen or more times in the past half year."

"As I recall, Valerie took several trips there with him."

"I remember that," Norah said, "but did you know that in spite of all those times Rowdy's visited San Francisco, he's never been down to Fisherman's Wharf or walked through Chinatown or taken a cruise around the Bay. When I pressed him, he admitted he's never seen anything more than the airport and the inside of a hotel meeting room."

"Rowdy Cassidy's a busy man."

"Don't you understand?" Norah cried, surprised by the intensity of her emotion. "He's working himself to death, and for what? Some software company that will pass on to a distant relative he hasn't seen in twenty years. A relative who'll probably just sell his share of the stock. To strangers!"

"It bothers you that Rowdy doesn't have any heirs?" her father asked as he brought down two earthenware mugs.

"What bothers me," she returned heatedly, "is that he's working himself to death for no real reason.

He's a candidate for a heart attack—the same way you were. He's got atrocious eating habits, doesn't exercise and works too hard.''

David nodded and grinned. "You know what it sounds like to me?" he asked, and not waiting for a reply added, "Rowdy Cassidy needs a wife. Don't you agree?"

As hard as she tried to concentrate on her own duties, Norah couldn't keep her mind off Rowdy. He'd already told her he wouldn't be able to phone her, since his meetings with several important stockholders would last until all hours of the night. For reasons she didn't understand, Norah was restless all afternoon.

When she arrived home she found her father weeding the garden she'd planted earlier that summer. He straightened, grinning, and waved when he saw her.

"Looks like we've got enough lettuce here for a decent salad."

Norah squatted down in the freshly weeded row and picked a handful of radishes. "We can add a few of these, as well."

It was good to see her father soaking up the sunshine, looking healthy and relaxed. He was working part-time, managing the orchard, which kept him occupied without overtaxing him.

"Before I forget," her father said, "an envelope was delivered for you this afternoon. I think it's from Rowdy."

Norah didn't linger outside a moment longer. She

couldn't imagine what Rowdy had sent her, but she wasn't waiting to find out. When they'd spoken the night before, he hadn't mentioned anything.

The envelope was propped against a vase of roses left over from Steffie's wedding. Norah's name was inked with a lavish hand across the front. Eagerly tearing it open, she discovered a first-class airline ticket to Houston.

Norah stared at it for a moment before she slowly replaced it in the envelope, which she set back on the end table. Apparently Rowdy had forgotten she was scheduled to work that weekend.

The phone rang, and when she answered it she heard Rowdy's voice. "Norah," he said, "I'm glad I caught you. Listen, I've only got a couple of minutes between meetings. I wanted to be sure the ticket was delivered. This is crazy. I'm supposed to be here negotiating an important deal, but all I can think about is how long it's going to be before I can see you again. Trust me, this is not the way to run a company."

"I can't fly to Houston this weekend, Rowdy," she said without preamble. "You already know that."

"Why not?"

"I'm working, remember?"

"Forgot." He swore under his breath. "Can't you get a replacement?"

"Not easily. Weekends are precious to us all, and even more so to those who are married and have families."

He didn't hesitate for an instant. "Tell whoever will work in your place that I'll pay them ten times what they normally make in a weekend. I need to see you, Norah."

"I won't do that."

She could feel his anger. "Why not?"

"I can talk until I'm blue in the face and you still won't understand. Just take my word for it, your plan won't work."

"You mean to say there isn't a single nurse in Orchard Valley who wouldn't leap at the chance to earn ten times her normal salary just for working your shift?"

Norah could see that nothing useful would result from her arguing. "That's what I'm saying."

"I don't believe it."

Norah sighed. "You're entitled to believe anything you wish, but I know the people I work with. It may come as a shock to you, but family is more important than money."

"Damn it," Rowdy said angrily. "Why do you make it so difficult?"

"Rowdy, I can't live my life to suit yours. I'm sorry, I really am, but I have a commitment to my job and to my peers. I can't rush off to Texas because you happen to want me there. Nor will I allow our relationship to become nothing more than a few hours snatched between meetings and at airports."

"You seem to be taking a good deal for granted," he said stiffly.

"How's that?"

"Who told you we had a relationship?"

Norah breathed in sharply at the pain his words inflicted. "Certainly not you," she answered calmly, belying the turmoil she felt. "You're right, of course," she said when he didn't respond. "I—I guess I'd put more stock in our friendship than you intended. I apologize, Rowdy, for taking our—*my*— feelings for granted—"

"Norah," he interrupted. "I didn't mean that."

She could hear a conversation going on behind Rowdy, but she couldn't make out the details.

"Norah, I've got to go. Everyone's waiting on me."

"I know...I'm sorry about this weekend, Rowdy, but it can't be helped. Please understand."

"I'm trying, Norah. Heaven help me, I'm trying. If I get a chance later, I'll give you a call."

"All right." She didn't want their conversation to end on a negative note, but knew it was impossible for him to talk longer.

"Rowdy," she called, her heart pounding. "I... love you."

Her words were met with the drone of a disconnected line. He hadn't heard her, and even if he had, would it have made any difference?

Norah showed up for work Saturday morning, her thoughts bleak. She'd been reassigned to the emergency room, but her heart was in a plane somewhere over California on its way to Houston, Texas.

Refusing Rowdy's offer to spend the weekend

with him, had been one of the most difficult things she'd ever done. And yet she'd had no choice.

Her relationship with Rowdy—and she *did* believe they had a relationship, his harsh words to the contrary—had made it over several hurdles. They were only beginning to understand and appreciate each other. Despite the present and future problems, Norah felt a new and still shaky confidence, a sense of optimism.

She hadn't heard from Rowdy, other than the one harried phone call, since he'd left Texas. She remembered his saying that he'd be back in Houston sometime Saturday afternoon. Norah was scheduled to leave the hospital at three and hoped to hear from Rowdy shortly after she arrived home.

He hadn't said he'd phone, but she hoped—Norah pulled herself up short. She was doing it already. Although she'd promised herself she'd never allow a man to rule her life, she'd willingly surrendered her heart—and her freedom—to Rowdy Cassidy. There wasn't a single reason to hurry home, she reminded herself. If Rowdy phoned while she was out, she'd return his call later.

Satisfied that she'd put her thinking back on track, she went about her duties. A little after eleven, the new intern, Dr. Fullbright, came into the emergency room to tell her she had a visitor in the waiting room. Thinking it must be Valerie, who sometimes dropped by to visit Colby, Norah thought nothing of the summons.

When she saw that it was Rowdy, she stopped

cold. He was exhausted, she noted. His eyes were sunken and his features pale, but it didn't matter to Norah. Never had she been more thrilled to see anyone.

"Rowdy?" she whispered, walking into his arms. One crutch fell to the floor as he held her against him. Norah drank in the sensation of solid warmth and felt an unexpected urge to weep. He was pushing himself too hard, putting in too many hours.

Repeatedly she'd refused his offer to become his private nurse, and for the first time she wondered if she'd made a mistake. Obviously he did need someone.

She knew from what Robbins had said that Rowdy hadn't hired a replacement for Valerie, convinced he'd be able to persuade her sister to return to CHIPS. Norah didn't know if that was still the case, but she assumed he was continuing to carry both loads himself.

"What are you doing here?" she asked.

"If you wouldn't come to me, I figured I'd have to come to you." His hand tangled in her hair as he spoke. "Have you had lunch yet?"

"No. I'll check and see if I can go now. We're not too busy, but I'll need to stay on the hospital grounds."

Rowdy nodded. "Can we go someplace private?"

If there was any such place in the hospital, Norah had yet to find it. "The cafeteria shouldn't be very crowded."

Rowdy didn't look wildly enthusiastic at her suggestion, but he agreed.

Norah led the way to the elevator, smiling at the two other nurses already inside, and regretted that she and Rowdy couldn't be alone. If they'd had at least the brief elevator ride to themselves, she might have found the courage to repeat what she'd confessed at the end of their last telephone conversation.

Norah was right; the cafeteria wasn't crowded and they were afforded some privacy in the farthest corner. Once Rowdy was comfortably seated, his crutches leaning against the wall, he caught her hand, effectively preventing her from moving to the opposite side of the table. "Sit beside me, Norah."

Something in his voice, in the way he was looking at her, told Norah this wasn't an ordinary conversation. When he'd asked for someplace private she'd assumed it was because he wanted to kiss her.

"Yes?" she asked, taking the seat.

Rowdy glanced around, apparently checking for eavesdroppers. "All right," he said with a heavy sigh. "You win."

"I win?" she repeated, frowning.

"I knew from the first what you wanted."

"You did?"

"It's what every woman wants. A gold ring on her left hand. I told you earlier, and I meant it, I'm not the marrying kind. I don't have time for a wife and a family."

Norah was utterly confused, but she said nothing.

"I couldn't sleep last night," he muttered, "until

I figured out your game plan. Even when I had, it didn't make any difference. I love you so damn much I can't even think clearly anymore.''

Norah remained bewildered, not knowing what to think or say. She'd tried to tell him she loved him, but he hadn't heard her in his rush to get back to his meetings.

"I love you, too, Rowdy," she told him now, her voice soft.

His eyes gentled. "That helps. Not much, but...it helps."

Norah shook her head in confusion. "I'm afraid I've missed something here. What are you trying to say?"

His mouth dropped. "You mean you honestly don't know?"

Norah shook her head again.

"I'm asking you to marry me. I'm not happy about it, but as far as I can see it's the only way."

Nine

"**Y**ou're not happy about asking me to marry you," Norah echoed, too stunned to know what she was feeling.

"I told you before that I had no intention of ever marrying."

"Then what are you doing proposing to me?" she demanded. "Did you think I was so desperate for a husband I'd leap at your offer?" The numbness was gradually wearing away, and she was furious.

Norah had always been the Bloomfield with the cool head and the even temper. But her much-practiced calm was no match for this situation. Only a man like Rowdy Cassidy would have the nerve to insult a woman and propose marriage to her in the same breath.

"You're not desperate. It's just that—"

"That's not what I heard," she interrupted. "According to this oh-so-romantic proposal, you're declaring me the winner of some great prize, which I suppose is you. Well, I've got news for you, Rowdy Cassidy. I wasn't even aware I'd entered the contest!"

Rowdy clenched his jaw in an unmistakable effort

to hold on to his own temper. "I don't believe that. You have me so tied up in knots, I don't know which way is which anymore. It wasn't enough that you turned down the job, but you had to torment me by dating other men!"

"One date! How was I supposed to know you'd want to see me the one and only night I'd made other arrangements? I'm not a mind reader, you know. Was I supposed to be so flattered, so—so *overwhelmed* by your summons that I'd cancel my evening with Ray?"

"Yes!" he shouted.

"I refused to do that then, and I refuse to do it now. I *will not* spend my life waiting for an opening in your absolutely ridiculous schedule."

Rowdy's hand sliced the air between them. "All right, fine. Let's just drop this thing with Ralph."

"Ray!" she shouted, attracting attention from those around her.

Both were silent for several embarrassed moments.

Finally, Rowdy exhaled sharply and said. "Shall we try this again?" He studied her through half-closed eyes before proceeding. "I'll admit there were better ways of asking you to be my wife. The only excuse I have is thirty hours with no sleep."

Norah mellowed somewhat. "Thirty hours?"

Rowdy nodded. "It didn't help that I was looking forward to your being there when I returned home. You might recall that you turned me down on that, as well."

"It's not as though I didn't want to be with you,"

she assured him. "But you knew I was scheduled to work this weekend...I'd told you so myself, remember?"

"What's more important," he said through gritted teeth, "your job or me?"

"We keep rehashing the same thing," she said, throwing her hands in the air. "You want me to be at your beck and call. You're suggesting I should spend my life in limbo, waiting for you to find time for me."

"That's not what I mean at all," he said in a dangerously quiet voice. "But if you cared about me half as much as I care about you, you'd be willing to make a few minor adjustments."

"You want far more than *minor* adjustments. You want absolute control and I refuse to give you that."

"You're not even willing to compromise," he said bitterly. "With you, it's all or nothing." He looked away from her, glaring.

"Rowdy, I am willing to compromise. All I'm asking for is a little advance warning, so I know what to expect. Do you realize everything we've done has been on the spur of the moment? Nothing has ever been planned."

He nodded, a bit sheepishly. "That's not typical for me, you know. Falling in love with you has shot my concentration, not to mention my organizational abilities, all to hell."

"Oh, Rowdy." He could be so sweet and funny when he wanted. But he acted as if loving her was some kind of...weakness. He didn't see love as something that gave you strength, the way Norah did.

"Norah," he said, his voice softening. His hand reached for hers and his gaze was level with her own. "I love you. Will you do me the honor of becoming my wife?"

The tears that filled her eyes and her throat made speaking impossible. All because she loved him so much.... Norah blinked and realized there was no help for it. She grabbed a napkin from the shiny chrome dispenser in the middle of the table and blew her nose.

"I didn't have time to buy a ring," he told her, "but I figure you'd rather pick one out yourself. Go to any jeweler you want and have them send me the bill. Buy a nice big diamond—money's no problem. All I'm concerned about is making you happy."

Norah froze and closed her eyes at the unexpected stab of pain. Rowdy just didn't realize. No woman wanted to pick out her wedding ring alone, but she doubted Rowdy would understand that.

"I never meant to fall in love with you," she said softly, when she could speak.

"I didn't mean to fall for you, either," he admitted gruffly. "Hell, I didn't even know what love was. I liked Valerie and I missed her when she was here with you and Steffie during your father's surgery, but—" he shrugged "—love had nothing to do with it."

"What do you mean?"

"I thought I loved Valerie. I know how angry I

got when I learned she was marrying Colby Winston. The fact is, I did everything I could to get her to change her mind. My ego took something of a beating, thanks to your sister.''

Norah grinned at the memory. Rowdy wasn't accustomed to losing, and it had sorely injured his pride to have Valerie defy him.

''What I realized,'' he continued, ''was that even if Valerie had broken off the engagement, I wouldn't have offered to marry her.'' Norah had already known that but made no comment. Rowdy sought out her gaze. ''I was never in love with your sister. I might have thought I was at one time, but I know what love is now.''

''You do?''

Rowdy nodded. ''I'm not the marrying sort—fact is, I never thought I'd ever want a wife, but damn it all, Norah, you've got me so confused I'd be willing to do just about anything to make matters right between us. I'm offering you what I never would your sister or any other woman. If nothing else, that should tell you how serious I am.''

Tears ran unabashed down her cheeks.

''Say you'll marry me, Norah,'' he coaxed.

Norah reached for another napkin and dabbed at her cheeks. ''I...felt so lonely when Valerie and Steffie fell in love. It was as if the whole world had someone, but me.''

''Not anymore, Norah. We have each other.''

''Do we?'' she asked softly. Rowdy was making

this so difficult. "You'll have me, but who will I have? Who will be there for me?"

His eyes revealed how perplexed he was. "I will, of course."

"How can you possibly ask me to be your wife when you already have one?"

"That's ridiculous," Rowdy returned impatiently. "I've never been married in my life. You're the only woman I've loved in more than thirty years. I don't know where you heard anything so outlandish, but it isn't true."

"It isn't a woman I'm talking about, Rowdy, it's CHIPS."

He shook his head and frowned at her. "I don't understand."

"You and I don't mean the same thing when we say love. To you CHIPS is everything. It's the one thing you really love—your family, your wife, your children. Your emotional security."

"You don't know what you're saying!"

"But I do! I've seen it happen over and over again. From the moment you were admitted to the hospital. Karen and I had to practically set up roadblocks in order to give you time to convalesce. Your corporate attorney was waiting outside the hospital door practically the instant he learned about your accident. You even had a phone installed with—I've forgotten how many lines. Remembering what a panic you went into the day word leaked out that you'd been involved in a plane crash?"

"I'm not likely to forget it. Stock in CHIPS dropped two points."

"You acted as if the world was coming to an end."

"You would, too, if you had a hundred million dollars at stake," he argued.

"Don't you understand?" she pleaded. "You don't have *time* in your life for anything or anyone else. Not me, not a family. No one."

Rowdy tensed. "What do you want from me, Norah? Blood?"

"In a manner of speaking, I guess I do. You can't go on the way you have been, working so many hours, not taking care of yourself. Eventually you'll collapse. As far as I can see, you're a prime candidate for a heart attack a few years down the road. I know you've got a management team, because Valerie was part of it, but you don't let them manage— you do it all yourself."

"I'm a candidate for a heart attack? Hell, you're just full of warmth and cheer, aren't you?"

"It's important that I explain my feelings. I don't mean to sound so pessimistic, but I'm worried about you."

"I wouldn't be too concerned if I were you," he muttered sarcastically. "I've got an excellent life insurance policy, and since you're so worried, I'll make sure you're listed as the beneficiary. Revise my will, too."

"Oh, Rowdy, for heaven's sake. I don't want your money, I want *you*."

He shrugged in apparent unconcern. "You wanted to be realistic? I'm only complying with your forecast of gloom and doom. And if I'm such a poor health risk, you'd best marry me now. The sooner the better, since my time's so limited."

"How can you joke about something like this?"

"You're the one who brought it up."

He was purposely misunderstanding everything she was trying to say. "What's important in life isn't things; it's people and relationships. It's the two of us building a life together, raising our family, making time for each other."

"Family," he repeated as if he'd never heard the word before. Sighing, he sagged against the back of the chair. "I should have known you'd want children. All right, we'll work around that. I'll agree to a child, but we stop with one, boy or girl. Agreed?"

Norah was too dumbstruck to respond.

Rowdy glanced at his watch, scowling. As usual, he was on a tight schedule, Norah thought wryly. He needed an answer and he needed it now. The luxury of his presence would always be limited, even to her.

Norah felt as though the whole world was crashing down around her. It was going to break her heart to refuse him, and what made it all the more painful was that she doubted Rowdy would ever really understand. He'd view her as irrational, demanding, sentimental.

"I've never wanted anything more in the world," she said, trying desperately to keep the emotion from her voice. She leaned toward him and pressed her hand to his face, then gently kissed his lips.

Rowdy seemed surprised by the small display of tenderness. "I'll make the arrangements with a jeweler," he said, preparing to leave. He reached for his crutches.

"Rowdy," she said quietly.

He must have heard a telltale inflection in her voice, because he turned back to her. She watched, amazed, as he read the look in her eyes.

The air between them went still and heavy. "You're turning me down, aren't you?"

She slowly exhaled, closing her eyes, and nodded.

Rowdy threw his Stetson down on the table in disgust. "Damn it all!" he shouted. "I should have known you were going to do this."

She sniffled and said, "Despite what you're thinking, this isn't easy for me."

"The hell it isn't." He stood and in his rush to leave, dropped one of his crutches, which frustrated him even more. Before he could prevent it, the second slammed to the floor and he slumped back down in the chair.

"I want a *husband*. It takes more than a few words said before a preacher to make a marriage."

"But you aren't going to marry me, so there's no need to belabor the point, is there?" He managed to pick up one crutch, and with it was able to retrieve the second. He obviously wanted to get away from her as quickly as possible, moving awkwardly through the cafeteria. She followed close behind.

"You got what you wanted—what you were after in the first place. You worked everything out well in advance, didn't you?"

"Worked out what?" A sick feeling attacked Norah's stomach.

He paused to look at her, his expression cynically admiring. "I have to hand it to you, Norah Bloomfield, you're quite the actress. Am I right in guessing that you worked all this out beforehand so I'd make a fool of myself proposing and you'd have the pleasure of turning me down?"

"Rowdy, that isn't true." Shocked, she trailed him out of the cafeteria. "It's just that I'd never be content with the leftover pieces of your life, with a few minutes shaved here and there."

"Then it's best to know that now, isn't it?"

"Yes, but—"

"You're fighting a losing battle, sweetheart. I suggest you drop it. CHIPS made me what I am today, and I'm not about to give up my company so you can lead me around by a ring through the nose." He forcefully jammed his thumb against the button to summon the elevator.

"I don't want you to give up CHIPS," she protested, but he cut her off.

"Why is it we're discussing all *your* wants? Frankly, they're overwhelming." He held himself stiffly away from her, leaning heavily on his crutches and staring at the floor numbers above the door.

When the elevator arrived, Norah stepped back and allowed Rowdy to enter. With some difficulty he did so, then turned around to face her. If he was surprised she hadn't followed him inside, he didn't reveal it.

"Goodbye, Rowdy."

"It *is* goodbye, Norah. Don't worry about me. I plan on having a damn good life without you."

The elevator doors glided shut, and she slowly pressed her hand over her mouth to hold in a cry of pain. Deliberately, she removed her hand, as if she were throwing him a farewell kiss.

"How is she?"

Valerie's voice drifted through the cubicle door. Norah could have answered for herself. She'd been emotionally devastated, but she was much better now.

Although Norah had returned to the emergency room, she wasn't in any condition to work. Not knowing what to do, her supervisor had called Colby, who was on duty.

Colby had tried to listen, but hadn't been able to understand her, she was crying so hard. Her incoherent attempts to explain had merely frustrated him. Apparently he'd phoned Valerie, and she'd rushed to the hospital.

"She should go home, but I don't think she's in any shape to drive," Norah heard Dr. Adamson tell her sister.

Everyone was making it seem far worse than it was, Norah thought grumpily. Okay, so she was a bit weepy when she returned from lunch. And it was true that she hadn't been able to speak too clearly, which made her cry even more with frustration. But everything was under control now—well, almost everything.

"Norah?" Valerie knocked softly on the door of the emergency-room cubicle, before letting herself in.

"Hi," Norah said, raising her right hand limply. "I'm doing much better than Dr. Adamson would have you believe."

"Colby's the one who's so concerned. He's never seen you like this."

"I don't think I have, either," she said, making an effort to smile. A pile of crumpled tissues lay on the gurney beside her. "I'm sorry everyone was worried about me, but really I'm fine. Or at least I will be in a little while."

"Do you want to tell me what happened?"

Norah shrugged and reached for a fresh tissue, clenching it tightly in her fist. "There's not that much to tell. Rowdy dropped in unexpectedly and asked me to marry him. I...didn't feel I had any option but to refuse."

Valerie looked as if she suddenly needed to sit down. "Let me see if I understand you correctly. Rowdy—Rowdy *Cassidy*—actually proposed?"

Norah nodded.

"He asked you to *marry* him?" Valerie asked incredulously.

Again Norah nodded. "I don't know why—he

doesn't have time for me in his life. He...he wanted me to pick out my own engagement ring.''

"I don't understand," Valerie said, frowning. "I thought you were in love with him."

"I am, and I'm sure he loves me—as much as Rowdy's capable of loving anyone."

It was as though Valerie hadn't heard her as she started pacing the tiny cubicle. "Every single person who saw you and Rowdy at Steffie's wedding was convinced your engagement would be next."

"He's already married—to CHIPS," Norah whispered sadly.

"So?"

"Don't *you* understand?" Norah cried, disappointed in her sister. She'd expected sympathy from Valerie, not censure.

"I guess I don't," Valerie admitted reluctantly. "What do you expect him to do—resign from the company, give up everything he's worked so hard to achieve all these years?"

"No...of course not." Norah felt shaken. All along she'd assumed she was right, but Valerie was forcing her to question her own actions.

"Now isn't the time to worry about it," Valerie said soothingly. "Dr. Adamson asked me to drive you home. You're much too upset to work."

"But what if—"

"Don't worry, Colby said he'd cover for you."

Norah didn't even get a chance to finish. She'd started to say *What if Rowdy calls and I'm not here?* But he wouldn't phone. Norah would have staked her career on it. He was much too angry—he'd told her their goodbye was final.

Someone must have called her father, because David was standing at the front door waiting when Valerie pulled into the driveway in front of the house. He poured Norah a stiff drink, told her to sip it slowly and then advised her to nap.

Norah did so without argument. She must have been more exhausted than she realized; she didn't awaken until late the following morning.

Valerie was speaking to her father when Norah walked down the back staircase into the kitchen. They abruptly stopped talking when she appeared. It didn't take a genius to figure out what they were discussing.

"Well," Norah said casually, "what did you two decide?"

"About what?" her father questioned.

"Me. And Rowdy."

"There isn't anything for me to decide," David said, exchanging a knowing smile with Valerie. "You've got a good head on your shoulders. You know what's best for yourself."

Norah wished she shared her father's confidence. Rejecting Rowdy's marriage proposal was the right thing to do—wasn't it? Good grief, he didn't even have half an hour to look for an engagement ring with her! Their marriage would be a continual battle of wills. She could fight another woman for his affections, but she was defenseless against a company he'd built from the ground up, a company that was his whole life. She had no choice but to make a stand now or be miserable later.

Ten days passed, and Norah lived with a constant sense of expectation. But she wasn't sure what she was waiting for. Rowdy had made it plain that she wouldn't be hearing from him again.

Her father, too, seemed smitten with a feeling of hopefulness. More times than she could count, Norah saw him sitting on the porch, his gaze focused in the distance as if he was waiting for someone to come barreling down the long driveway.

"He isn't coming, Dad," Norah said one evening after dinner. She brought him a cup of coffee and sat down on the front step near him.

"You're not talking about Rowdy, are you?"

"Yes, Dad, that's exactly who I'm talking about."

"I don't expect he'll come. He's got too much pride for that. Can't say as I blame him. Poor fellow's head over heels in love, and by heaven, he doesn't know what to do about it. I feel sorry for the poor chap."

"He was furious with me. He might have loved me at one point, but he doesn't now." She was certain that Rowdy had completely blotted her from his mind.

"Isn't he scheduled to be out of his cast soon?"

Norah had to stop and think. She tasted the coffee, hoping its warmth would chase away the chill she felt whenever she thought about Rowdy. Her life felt so lonely, so cold without him.

"If I remember right, he should have had the cast removed on Monday." She didn't envy his physical therapist. Rowdy Cassidy was going to be a cantankerous and difficult patient.

As they were talking, Norah noticed a thin trail of dust rising from the driveway. Her father saw it, too, and Norah watched him relax, as though a long-awaited visitor had finally arrived. But Norah didn't recognize the car—or the driver.

Not until Earl Robbins climbed out of the car did Norah remember who he was. Rowdy's employee. The one who was heading up CHIPS Northwest.

"Hello again, Norah," he greeted her, closing his door and walking toward the porch.

"Hello," she said, trying to disguise her puzzlement. She introduced her father, and as she did so, tried to imagine what had brought Robbins to see her. A sense of panic filled her when she realized something must be wrong with Rowdy.

"Is Rowdy all right?" she asked, hoping he didn't hear the near-hysteria in her voice. "I mean, he's not ill, is he?"

Robbins glanced toward David and shook his head. "I'm here because of Rowdy, but I don't want you to worry. To the best of my knowledge, he's in fine health."

"Take the young man into my den," her father instructed. "I'll see about getting some iced tea, unless you'd prefer coffee or something stronger."

"Iced tea would be fine," Robbins said with a grateful smile.

Norah directed him into her father's den and closed the door, leaning against it with her hands behind her as she tried to compose herself.

"Valerie suggested I come and talk to you," he explained, pacing as he spoke. "To be honest, I'm not sure I'm doing the right thing. I do know that Rowdy wouldn't approve of my being here. He'd have my job if he knew I was within fifty miles of this place."

If Earl Robbins didn't feel the need to sit down, Norah did. She sank onto the ottoman and clenched her hands together in her lap. "How is he?" she asked, hungry for news of him.

Robbins ceased pacing. "Physically I'd say he's on the mend. The cast is off, and he's walking with the help of a cane. He's more mobile than he was, which helps—but not much."

"You didn't come here to tell me how well his leg is mending, did you?"

Robbins grinned wryly. "No, I didn't." He walked over to her father's desk and turned around to face her. "It isn't any of my business what went on between you and Rowdy. In fact, I'd rather not know.

"I realize he's in love with you. Both Kincade and I saw it happening. We sort of enjoyed watching the transformation. I'm no expert when it comes to love. Hell, I'm not married myself. But it seemed to me that you felt just as strongly about Rowdy."

"I do," Norah admitted. "Oh, I do."

"From the minute Rowdy was discharged from the hospital, all he did was think about you. He drove the staff crazy. It's a miracle that group of stockholders didn't walk out on him in San Francisco. Mrs. Emerich told me he bolted upright in the middle of the conference, as if he didn't know where he was, then he sat down and mumbled something no one heard."

"He was probably worried about what was happening to his stock," Norah said.

"I don't think so. My guess, and that of everyone else who's close to him, is that it was you he was thinking about in San Francisco. The same way he has ever since you two met."

"He isn't thinking about me any longer," Norah said, swallowing the hurt.

"Don't kid yourself. I'm not here for my health, Norah, and if Rowdy ever found out, he'd have my hide, as well as my job. He's miserable."

"I suppose he's making everyone else miserable, too."

"No, and that's what's got us worried. I've never known Rowdy to be so...nice. He's keeping his unhappiness to himself. He's polite, cordial, thoughtful. No one knows what to make of it."

"I—I'm sure it'll pass."

"Perhaps," Robbins agreed, "but I can't help thinking it might not. No one's ever seen Rowdy like this. We don't know what to do to help him. You've got your family, but Rowdy doesn't have anyone."

"He's got CHIPS," she said stiffly, not meeting the man's direct gaze.

A knock sounded on the door then, and her father brought a glass of iced tea to Robbins. He glanced from him to Norah and back again, then edged out the door.

"Thank you." Robbins took a sip of tea and set the glass aside. "I came because Valerie seemed to think it was important for you to know what was happening to Rowdy. She wants you to understand how very much he misses you…how lonely and lost he is. That's all. Now I won't take up any more of your time."

"Thank you for telling me." Although Norah knew Valerie had encouraged him to come, she remained grateful. Earl Robbins had given her a lot to think about.

He nodded. "Listen, if it wouldn't be too much to ask, I'd appreciate if you didn't say anything to Rowdy about my stopping in."

"Of course," Norah agreed.

Robbins looked significantly relieved.

It took Norah only about two minutes to decide what she needed to do with the information Robbins had given her, and two days to make the arrangements.

She kissed her father on the cheek late Thursday afternoon, picked up her suitcase and headed down the porch steps to Valerie's car. Her sister was waiting to drive her to the airport.

"You call, you hear?" her father shouted after her.

"Of course I will," Norah promised. "Although he just might throw me out on my ear."

David chuckled. "That isn't likely. That man needs you—the same way I needed your mother. Be gentle with him. The poor devil doesn't have a clue what's about to happen."

Norah found his parting words a bit odd. She didn't have a clue herself as to what was going to happen. All she could do was hope for the best.

Early Friday morning, Norah arrived at CHIPS dressed in her best suit. The seventeen-floor headquarters was an amazing piece of architecture, designed in smoky black glass and glistening steel.

The first thing she realized was how far from Orchard Valley she'd come, but that didn't deter her from her purpose. Armed with Valerie's directions and an elevator code, Norah entered the top floor that housed Rowdy's office.

"Ms. Bloomfield," Rowdy's secretary said softly when she saw Norah. The middle-aged woman slowly stood up and beamed her a wide smile.

"Hello, Mrs. Emerich," Norah said uncertainly. She was having a difficult time taking everything in. She'd had no idea CHIPS was so big.

"Oh, my heavens, I'm so glad you're here." Rowdy's secretary hurried from behind the desk and hugged Norah enthusiastically. "It was what we've all been praying would happen—your coming, that is. Rowdy isn't in the office just yet...I never know when he's going to show up these days. Would you like to wait for him?"

Norah nodded and followed Mrs. Emerich into Rowdy's private office.

"I'll get you some coffee," the older woman said, hands fluttering in her eagerness. "Sit down, anywhere you like. Just make yourself right at home." She turned to leave. "Oh, Norah, I'm so glad you've come..."

Perhaps it was a bit presumptuous of her, but Norah chose Rowdy's chair. She sat in the plush black leather and whirled around to face the window, with its dramatic view of Houston.

Hearing someone step inside the room, she turned around and smiled, expecting to see the secretary. Only it wasn't Mrs. Emerich who'd entered the room, it was Rowdy Cassidy himself. And he didn't look pleased.

"Just what the hell do you think you're doing in my office?" he demanded.

Ten

"Rowdy." Norah couldn't take her eyes off him. It was the first time she'd seen him stand without his crutches. He looked tall and proud—and unyielding. It didn't matter; Norah had never loved him more than she did at that moment.

"What are you doing here?" he demanded a second time.

"I—I came to talk. Sit down, please."

He leveled the full force of his scowl at her. "You're in my chair."

"Oh...sorry." She leaped up as though propelled by a spring and hurried around to the other side of the desk.

"Unfortunately, you made an error in assuming I wished to speak to you," he informed her coldly once he was seated. "As it happens, I have several appointments this morning."

Just then Mrs. Emerich appeared, carrying two steaming coffee mugs, which she set down on the desk. "Good morning, Mr. Cassidy," she said cheerfully. Winking at Norah, she continued, "Mr. Deavon called and canceled his nine o'clock appointment."

Rowdy glared at her as if he didn't believe her. "Call Kincade and have him here by nine."

"I'm sorry, sir, but Mr. Kincade phoned in sick."

"Murphy, then!"

"Mr. Murphy's out, as well," she informed him, then glanced at Norah and winked again. With that, she was out the door, closing it quietly behind her.

"Damn fool woman," Rowdy muttered. "All right," he growled, "you wanted to talk. So talk." He looked at his wristwatch. "I'll give you exactly five minutes."

Norah made herself comfortable in the leather chair across from him and deposited her large purse in her lap. The zipper made a hissing sound as she opened it. She rummaged through, then gave up and leaned forward to sip her coffee, noticing that Rowdy hadn't touched his.

"I thought you wanted to talk," Rowdy reminded her impatiently.

"I do, but I brought a list with me and I want to go over it with you."

"A list?"

She nodded absently, sorting through a variety of objects in her purse. "There are several important issues I feel we have to discuss." She still couldn't seem to locate what she needed and ended up setting her billfold and a paperback novel on the edge of his desk. She could feel Rowdy's disapproval, but was determined not to let him distract her. "Here it is," she said triumphantly, taking the folded slip of paper from the bottom of her oversized bag.

After returning everything to her purse, she zipped it shut. "Now," she began in a businesslike voice, "the first thing has to do with the engagement ring."

Rowdy's face tightened. "You can skip that one."

"Why?" She looked up from her list.

"Because there won't be one."

"All right," she said with a meaningful sigh. "I'll go on to item number two. The vice president. You've got an excellent management team, but as I said earlier, you take on far more than necessary yourself, so I'm suggesting you appoint a vice president you could work closely with over the next few years."

"Vice president of what?"

"CHIPS," she returned shortly. "What else? The way I figure it, you're going to need two, and possibly three. Valerie said she'd recommend Bill Somerset, John Murphy and/or Earl Robbins. All three are familiar with the operation of CHIPS and excellent managers. Valerie also seemed to think it would be a good move because you're probably going to lose Somerset if you don't promote him."

"In a pig's eye," Rowdy argued. "Bill's completely happy working for me."

"Perhaps now, but he'll be wooed away by some other company that'll trust him with added responsibilities. A vice presidency is a natural progression for him."

"What makes you so confident of all this?"

"I'm not," she readily admitted, "but Valerie obviously knows a lot more about it than I do. These are her recommendations.''

''I gathered as much.''

She moved her fingernail down the list. ''Another thing. We'll need to make some kind of compromise on the issue of traveling.''

''Traveling?'' he repeated.

''I'm not sure how much is justified or necessary, but I'd appreciate having it held down to a minimum. I imagine I'll be able to go with you on some trips. It would be ideal if we could combine business with pleasure. Maybe two or three times a year—depending, of course, on our schedules.''

Rowdy's response was a humorless laugh. ''You must be joking. I take that many trips in a month.''

''Exactly. That's far too much. The children won't even know they have a father if you're gone that often.''

''Children?'' he exploded.

''That's point number seven, but since you mention it, I'll address the subject now. I'd like more than one child. I enjoy children, Rowdy, and I'm looking forward to being a mother. Now, I agree that six may be out of line, but—''

''Six.'' He leaned forward, arms rigid and hands clutching the edge of his desk.

''I know, I know,'' she said with a sigh. ''My dad seems to have that number fixed in his mind. But don't worry, I was thinking four would be quite adequate. It'd be nice if we had two boys and two girls, but it really doesn't matter.''

Rowdy eyed her as if she'd gone completely berserk.

"Item number three," Norah went on without a pause. "You probably won't ever work less than forty hours a week and more likely it'll be fifty. Valerie told me there were times you didn't even bother to go home—you just slept at the office. However, I feel that would be detrimental to your health and to our relationship. If I'm going to marry you and move to Houston, I'd appreciate if you made an effort to come home every night. I do realize you're needed here and I can live with whatever hours you deem necessary, provided the house is within easy commuting distance."

"Anything else?"

"Oh, yes, there are several smaller items. Things any couple needs to go over before marriage."

Rowdy made a show of glancing at his watch. "You might want to hurry since you've got approximately two minutes left."

"Only two minutes?"

He nodded, his look stern and unwavering.

"All right," she said, folding the slip of paper in her hand. "I won't waste any more of your time with compromises."

"Fine."

"I'll talk about the most important reason for my coming here. I made a mistake when I rejected your marriage proposal, Rowdy. You caught me off guard—I wasn't expecting it. You were right, all I could think of was what I wanted, not what you were looking for in our relationship. So I've given you my list of possible compromises to think over."

"One minute left."

Norah stood, forgetting that her purse was in her lap. It fell unceremoniously to the floor. She stooped down to pick it up and straightened awkwardly. "Could we meet and talk again soon? Then I'll listen to whatever you have to say. Actually, I'd be interested in knowing why you want to marry me when you've always been so dead set against marriage."

"Which is the question I've been asking myself for the past two weeks. It's unfortunate that you don't understand business practices, Norah."

"I don't even pretend to."

"And that explains your coming. You see, the offer was made and you rejected it."

"Yes, but as I told you, I acted in haste. I should have thought things through before I—"

"Apparently you don't understand," he said without emotion. "I've withdrawn my offer."

She blinked, and a feeling of dread attacked her heart. "But—"

"It's too late, Norah. Two weeks too late."

A numbness took hold of her limbs and she forced herself to exhale slowly. "I see... I'm sorry. I assumed, erroneously it seems, that your proposal was genuine."

"At the time it was."

"No, Rowdy, it couldn't have been. Love isn't a business transaction, something to be offered and retracted at will. It's a *feeling* and it's a commitment. That doesn't disappear overnight.''

"I'm not an impulsive man, Norah...generally," he added with some reluctance. "But I was when I proposed to you. Actually you did us both a favor by rejecting my offer.''

Norah was too stunned to respond for a moment. "You don't mean that?"

Rowdy said nothing, and since there didn't seem to be anything more for her to say either, she turned away from him, barely aware of where she was going.

"Goodbye, Norah.''

She didn't answer him and walked blindly out of his office. She paused and closed her eyes for a moment to compose herself before proceeding.

Mrs. Emerich's voice drifted toward her. "My, that didn't take long, did it?''

"Not at all," Norah returned cordially, smiling at the older woman. She stood, as though paralyzed, in the outer office. She'd made such a fool of herself coming to Rowdy like this!

"Are you all right?"

It took a moment for the secretary's question to sink into her consciousness. "Ah...oh, yes, I'm fine. Thank you for asking." She glanced toward the closed door that led to Rowdy's office. "Take care of him for me, will you, Mrs. Emerich? He doesn't eat right and he works far too many hours. He—he needs someone.''

"I've been telling him that myself for the past five years, but he doesn't listen."

"He's too stubborn for his own good," Norah agreed with a weak smile.

"Won't *you* be here? I was so hoping you two could patch up your differences."

Norah slowly, sadly, shook her head. "I'm afraid I...waited too long."

Mrs. Emerich's eyes revealed her dismay. "Oh dear, and I was sure everything would work out between you."

"So was I," Norah whispered and headed toward the elevator.

The hotel where she was booked was a short distance from CHIPS's headquarters. Norah almost wished she'd walked, but with traffic so heavy and huge semitrucks roaring up and down the streets it didn't seem prudent, so she opted for a taxi.

The first person she called when she arrived back at the hotel was Valerie. When she told her sister what had happened, Valerie exploded.

"The man's a fool!" her oldest sister insisted. "He's pulling the same thing with you that he tried with me. Obviously he didn't learn anything the first time. Fine, we'll just have to teach him all over again."

"He didn't try to bribe me, Valerie, nor did he issue any threats."

"How could he? You're holding all the cards."

Norah didn't understand her sister, and frankly she

felt so defeated and miserable that it didn't matter. "I've already changed my flight plans. I'll be home this afternoon."

"No, you won't," Valerie told her forcefully. "That's exactly what Rowdy expects you to do. He doesn't mean a word of it, you know."

"That's not the impression he gave me."

"Wait and see," Valerie assured her. "My advice to you is stay exactly where you are. Take in the sights, do a little shopping, relax, vacation. The last place Rowdy will ever think of looking for you is in his own backyard."

"But, Valerie—"

"Promise me," Valerie demanded. "Not a peep out of you. I can't get over this," she fumed. "That man's certainly a slow learner! Don't you worry, though, we're going to educate him once and for all."

"He isn't going to call me."

"I'm betting you'll hear from him in twenty-four hours. Thirty, tops."

"All right," Norah agreed reluctantly, although from the look on his face, Norah couldn't imagine hearing from Rowdy in thirty *days*, let alone thirty hours.

"Trust me, Norah. I know how Rowdy Cassidy operates. The only way he can deal with emotions is by treating everything like a tricky negotiation. A business deal."

"I did what we discussed. I approached him as

though it was a business deal, and I went through my list.''

''Good. That he can understand.''

''But it didn't do any good.''

''It will, it will. Now stay right where you are, and I'll let you know as soon as we hear from the great and mighty Rowdy Cassidy.''

Norah wasn't sure she was up to playing hide and seek, but she trusted her sister and readily accepted Valerie's advice. Really, she had no other option if she intended to work out her relationship with Rowdy.

For two days she lazed around the hotel pool in the morning, shopped in the afternoon, and visited museums and art galleries. In the evenings she dressed for dinner and dined alone at the hotel. She'd never felt lonelier.

On the morning of the third day, her phone rang. Norah was still in bed, although it was almost noon. She'd stayed awake most of the night worrying, certain that she should have arranged a flight back to Orchard Valley. Hanging around a hotel room like this was crazy.

''He's here,'' Valerie whispered when Norah answered the phone. ''Dad's talking to him now, and he's doing a masterful job of keeping a straight face. He's pretending he doesn't know where you are.''

Norah scrambled into an upright position. ''You mean Rowdy's there…in Orchard Valley…right this minute?''

"Exactly. None too happy, either, by the looks of him."

"Aren't you going to tell him I'm in Houston?"

"I might. Then again I might not."

"Valerie Winston, that's cruel. Put Rowdy on the phone right now. I insist. Do you hear me?"

"I'll make it up to him," Valerie promised with a delighted chuckle. "Colby and I've talked it over and I've decided to accept Rowdy's offer to head up CHIPS Northwest. Hold on a minute, and I'll get him for you."

A minute had never lasted longer. Although she strained to hear what was happening in the background, Norah could only catch bits and pieces of the conversation. The next instant Rowdy was on the line.

"Norah?"

"Hello, Rowdy. I—"

"Valerie says you're in Houston. Is that true?"

"Yes."

He cursed under his breath. "No doubt Valerie put you up to this. If I wasn't so grateful she's agreed to take on the Northwest assignment, I'd have her hide for this." Norah could hear her sister saying something in the background and Rowdy saying something in return.

"Listen, I'm on my way back to Houston. Will you meet me at the airport?"

"Of course. I love you, Rowdy. I kept thinking of all the things I should have said to you and didn't. It wasn't until I got back to the hotel that I realized

I hadn't said the most important thing of all, and that was how much I love you."

"I love you, too. You are going to marry me, aren't you?"

"Oh, yes."

"Bring your list with you. There're a couple of points we need to discuss. Oh, before I forget, Bill Somerset's my new vice president."

"Oh, Rowdy, I do love you!"

"You know," he said with a heavy sigh, "I could get used to hearing you say that. Fact is, I could even get accustomed to being a husband—and father."

"I'll be waiting at the airport for you when you land," Norah promised eagerly.

She met his plane four hours later. Rowdy was the first one to disembark and he walked out of the jetway and directly to Norah. They just stood there for an instant, staring at each other, before he sighed and pulled her into his embrace.

"Damn fool woman," he muttered, then he kissed her hungrily.

"Who, me or Valerie?" she asked, wrapping her arms around his neck. He'd lifted her clear off the floor, leaving her feet dangling.

"Both of you."

"Love isn't a business deal, Rowdy. It's you and me settling our differences. I don't ever want to go through this again."

"You?" he cried, and buried his face in her neck. "I don't think my heart could bear it." He laughed shakily. "Until I met you, Norah Bloomfield, I didn't even know I had a heart."

Gradually he lowered her back to the floor. His eyes, so loving and intense, continued to hold hers. "I thought I'd go crazy the past couple of days," he admitted. "So did everyone around me. Mrs. Emerich was so furious with me that she threatened to resign."

"She really is a dear."

Rowdy chuckled. "Maybe, but I advise you not to make her angry."

Norah laughed softly and slipped her arm around his waist. "What changed your mind?"

Rowdy kissed the top of her head. "Something you said a long time back."

"Something I said?"

He nodded and kissed her cheek. "About what's really important in life. You said love and fulfillment came from people and relationships. I was sitting at my desk last night, and I realized I was working myself to death for no good reason. I was filling up all the emptiness I've felt in my life with business. What I really wanted was you. I wanted you to lecture me about my cholesterol count. I wanted you to argue with me about what we're going to name our children and where we're going to spend our vacations. I wanted you to kiss me."

"Oh, Rowdy." Tears filled her eyes until his precious face blurred before her.

"Damn, but I'm crazy about you." He drew her

into his arms again. "Let's start with the kissing part," he whispered.

Norah smiled through her tears. "That's one thing I won't argue about."

Epilogue

"Oh, Rowdy, I'm so anxious to see my family," Norah breathed as she settled into the airplane beside her husband. She didn't know if she'd ever grow accustomed to flying in the small jet Rowdy kept for personal use, but it was a definite convenience since the Lear could land at the tiny Orchard Valley airport.

"I don't know why Valerie had to plan a big reunion three weeks before your due date," Rowdy returned, glancing anxiously at Norah's swollen abdomen. A toddler slept in his arms, head resting on Rowdy's broad shoulder. Rowdy lovingly held his hand against his son's back.

"Don't fuss. She planned this get-together a year ago, before we knew about the baby."

"I still don't think you should be traveling."

Norah smiled reassuringly at her husband. "We couldn't be in finer company. If the baby does decide to arrive early, Colby will be there to help with the delivery. Besides, Jeff arrived a week late."

"There's nothing to say this baby might come early," Rowdy argued. "Anyway, Colby's a heart surgeon."

"He knows everything there is to know about babies," Norah countered, smiling softly to herself. She never would have believed Rowdy would fret so much over her pregnancies. He was fiercely protective when it came to Norah and their family.

For the first time since they entered the aircraft, Rowdy grinned. "Colby certainly *should* know about babies. Even now, it's difficult for me to picture Valerie as the mother of twins."

"Valerie amazes me," Norah said, with a genuine sigh of admiration. Her eldest sister continued to head CHIPS Northwest, cared for both her sons and accomplished more in one day than Norah thought about doing in a week. Her family and CHIPS both thrived.

Rowdy's eyes softened as they met Norah's. "*You* amaze me."

"I do?"

If there'd been any surprises in her marriage, they had come from the changes she'd seen in Rowdy. No wife could ask for a more attentive husband. He'd learned to delegate duties, and CHIPS was now served by four vice presidents. He'd promoted Valerie almost immediately after she'd agreed to accept the Northwest position.

The most incredible thing had happened as Rowdy gradually released the tight control he held over every aspect of his company. CHIPS prospered. The stock had nearly doubled in the two and a half years since Norah and Rowdy's marriage.

"I have so much to thank you for," Rowdy said,

tucking his arm around her shoulder and drawing her closer to him. He rested his free hand on her stomach and Norah watched his eyes widen as he felt their child kick against his palm.

"The baby moved!"

Norah laughed. "Yes, I know."

Rowdy's grin broadened. "The closer the time comes for this one to be born, the more excited I get." He kissed Jeff's blond head. "It surprises me how anyone so little could take up so much of my heart," he said solemnly.

"You're a wonderful father," Norah whispered. "And you know what else?" she asked, nestling against him. "You're a wonderful husband, too."

"You make that very easy, angel face." He settled his arm around her shoulders and Norah felt him kiss the top of her head. He rested his chin there. "I was thinking the other day that if we have a girl, we should name her Grace—after your mother."

Norah smiled softly to herself. "I'm so happy you said that."

"Does your father think baby number two will be a boy or a girl?"

Norah sighed. "Just because he was right about Valerie and Colby having twin boys, and Steffie and Charles having a little girl, that doesn't mean what he predicted for us would come true. Having six kids is probably excessive—even for us!"

Norah felt Rowdy go still. She raised her head to look into her husband's dark eyes. "You're thinking about those children again, aren't you?" she said quietly, referring to the recent, tragic death of one of his employees, who'd left two orphaned children.

Rowdy nodded. "I know what it's like to lose your mother and father. I hate the thought of those two spending the rest of their lives being shuffled from foster home to foster home the same way I was."

"You have a soft heart, Rowdy Cassidy. I have a distinct feeling we're going to end up with six children, after all."

"Would you mind?"

"I wouldn't mind in the least," she assured him.

The drone of the airplane quickly put Norah to sleep. When she awoke, it was nearly time for them to land. Steffie and Charles had volunteered to pick them up at the tiny Orchard Valley airport and drive them to the house.

Norah stepped off the plane first and was greeted with a hug from Steffie. Marriage hadn't changed her. Steffie was as graceful as a ballerina and so beautiful that it took Norah a moment to stop looking at her.

"It's so good to see you," Steffie squealed. Charles was holding a squirming toddler against his hip. "Hello, Amy," Norah said, holding out her arms to her ten-month-old niece. "Do you remember your Auntie Norah?"

"She might," Steffie teased, "but I don't think she's so sure about the tummy."

"She's far more interested in reacquainting herself with Jeff," Charles suggested as the two cousins eyed each other.

"How's Dad?" Norah asked as they walked toward the car.

"Never better," Charles answered. "He's so excited about this family get-together that he can hardly stand it. I swear he must have been up before the crack of dawn this morning. Wait until you see the spread he's arranged. The front yard is all ready for the barbecue."

"Dad's turned into a professional Grandpa," Steffie put in. "He's wonderful with Amy and the boys. I never thought I'd see Dad down on his hands and knees giving horsey rides. Trust me, it's a sight to behold."

Norah grinned. It seemed impossible that a few short years ago she'd been convinced they would lose him. He'd lost the will to live and given up the struggle to regain his health.

They talked at least once a week on the phone, and sometimes more often. Her father loved to fill her in on the Orchard Valley news. Since Charles was the local newspaper's publisher and editor, David had an inside track on the town's affairs. It seemed something was always going on. Their weekly calls had helped Norah those first weeks, when she'd missed home so much....

David Bloomfield was standing on the front porch, waiting for his family to arrive. When Rowdy helped Norah out of the car, he saw the gruff cowboy watching her tenderly as he carried their young son. Charles and Steffie and little Amy appeared next. David saw the gentle communication between his second daughter and her husband, saw how proud Steffie was of him and how deeply they loved their child.

Valerie and Colby, who'd been occupied playing with their identical twin sons on the swing set, waved and shouted a cheer of welcome. The two boys took off running toward the parked car, laughing, their eyes shining with joy. Hand in hand, Valerie and Colby followed them. The children's peals of laughter rippled through the early afternoon air, and David grinned. His heart swelled at the sight of his three daughters and their families. Valerie and Colby with the twins, Steffie and Charles with their little girl, and Norah with her son and another one due within the month.

"It's just the way you said it would be," David said hoarsely, looking to the heavens. "More than I ever dreamed it would be." He wiped a stray tear from his eye and whispered, "Thank you, Grace."

Let DEBBIE MACOMBER take you into the HEART OF TEXAS.

Let her take you back to...

PROMISE, TEXAS

Dear Reader,

In Promise, Texas, people know that family, home, community are the things that really count. They know that love gives meaning to every single day of their lives.

Some of the people in Promise are from old ranching families—like the Westons and the Pattersons, who first came to the hill country more than a century ago. And there are newcomers like Annie Applegate, who agrees to marry a widowed veterinarian for the sake of his children...and discovers that this marriage can lead to a great deal more.

MDM502A

DEBBIE MACOMBER